SANINE

SANINE

MIKHAIL ARTZIBASHEV

Translated by
PERCY PINKERSON

WILDSIDE PRESS

PREFACE

Michael Petrovich Artzibashev, who was born in 1878, is one of the foremost writers of the inter-revolutionary period of modern Russian literature. That period covers the years between the revolution of 1905 and the Bolshevist revolution of 1917, and it coincides with a definite literary epoch, that which separates the contemporary writers of Soviet Russia from Chekhov. When Chekhov died, in 1904, his work was recognized as marking the culminating point of the second phase of Russian realism, which succeeded the great age of Turgenev, Dostoevsky and Tolstoy. Around him were lesser men, Gorky, Sologub, and Kuprin, just as the older novelists brought into their orbit Garshin, Korolenko, and Potapenko, but Chekhov alone belongs to the main tradition. He was the last of the line of Pushkin, Gogol, Turgenev, Dostoevsky and Tolstoy.

Artzibashev is the product of an age of transition, when not only the hopes of the revolution of 1905 were dying, but the shifting tendencies of Chekhov's successors showed that he was to have no succession. It is significant that while the names of most of the important writers from Pushkin to Chekhov are familiar through translation to English-speaking readers, there are curious lacunæ in our subsequent knowledge. We have seen something of Alexander Blok, but nothing of Andrey Bely. Bunin's *The Gentleman from*

San Francisco seems only to have deflected attention from his other work. As for Kuzmin, Chirikov, Remizov, Zamiatin, and Alexey Tolstoy, although some of them have recently been translated, they are scarcely more than names in this country. They are no more familiar than some of the writers of the Soviet revolutionary period, Iury Libedinsky and Boris Pilniak, for example, to mention two representatives of the latest phase of Russian literature.

Of the authors who made their reputations prior to the Soviet revolution, Gorky, Artzibashev, and Andreyev are those best known in English to the general public. Gorky, of course, had several volumes to his credit before the death of Chekhov, but the two others are essentially writers of the transition. Artzibashev has stated that his first story, *Pasha Tumanov,* which is included in the volume *Tales of the Revolution,* was written in 1901. It had been accepted for publication by "one of the most distinguished Russian reviews, but it was not allowed to appear," he says, "because the censorship at that time categorically forbade any statements to be made which did not show life in the schools in a pleasing light. Thus it was impossible for the story to be made public at the right time, and it did not appear until some years later in book form. That has been the fate moreover of many of my things."

It so happens, *Sanine* met with a similar fate, for it was written in 1903, but did not appear until 1907, after the author had attracted attention with *The Death of Ivan Lande,* which was published in 1904, and appears in English in the collection of stories entitled *The Millionaire.* This story shows the influence of Kuprin and Gorky, rather than that

of Chekhov, whose death thus coincided with the beginning
of Artzibashev's career. The latter, in turn, coincided with
the outbreak of the revolution, and in that event Artzibashev
was to find not only the inspiration for the tales which he
named after it, but also the basis of his enormous popularity.
"Society," to quote his own account, "rushed to literature,
which in quantity, if not in quality, had received a new im-
petus. The editors of the monthly review who had refused
my *Sanine* remembered it and were the first to publish it.
It evoked almost unprecedented discussions, like those at
the time of Turgenev's *Fathers and Children.*"

Some critics, chiefly Russian, have asserted that the book
owed its success to a passing vogue for radicalism spiced
with sex, but in Germany, where it was seized by the Ba-
varian authorities, Ludwig Ganghofer declared in court
that "in the history of Russian literature *Sanine* will take the
place it deserves beside the masterpieces of Gogol, Turgenev,
Dostoevsky, and Goncharov." Without joining the hostile
critics, it is fair to say that Artzibashev is at least entitled to
rank with the author of *Oblomov* and *The Precipice*. His
own answer to the attacks upon him has been to point out
the date when the book was written. "This fact," he writes,
"is wilfully suppressed by the Russian critics; moreover they
try to persuade the public that *Sanine* is an outcome of the
reaction of the year 1907, and that I have followed the fashionable tendency of contemporary Russian literature. In
reality, however, the novel had been read by the editors of
two reviews and by many celebrated authors as early as 1903
. . . I owe it to the censorship and the timidity of publish-
ers that it was not brought out at the time . . . In this way

Sanine made its appearance five years too late. This was very much against it: at the time of its appearance literature had been flooded by streams of pornographic and even homosexual works, and my novel was liable to be judged by these."

In justice to Artzibashev the curious may test the soundness of his contention by comparing the much denounced *Sanine* with some of the books by his contemporaries, which doubtless excited less adverse comment because their authors were not favored by translations into every European language. The year before *Sanine* appeared Michael Kuzmin's *Wings* exalted the pleasures of homosexual love, and *The Castle of Cards* carried the argument a step further. In 1909 Anastasia Verbitzkaya introduced Manya, "a Sanine in petticoats," in a novel, with many sequels, called *The Key to Happiness*. Anatol Kamensky was likewise prompted to emulate Schnitzler's *Reigen* in *Four,* the story of four women, one a school-girl, who give themselves to the same man at the end of a twenty-four hour journey. His supreme achievement, however, was *Leda,* in which the heroine never received her friends unless she was attired only in a pair of gilt slippers. This was not only her pleasure but her duty, for she protested against a social order which "thrust the lovely human body into linen sacks and made it the object of vulgar curiosity." Kamensky dramatized this charming fancy, but, it appears, no producer was found until a more enlightened régime permitted it in 1917.

Despite Artzibashev's denial that this novel "was written in the despair which seized the Intelligentsia of Russia after the last abortive revolution," the words I have quoted were

used in the preface to the first edition of the English translation, which was published just before the World War.
Then Mr. Gilbert Cannan's preoccupation was to read into
the book a social purpose, a lesson of the type which, in those
days, it seemed imperative to demand from an author whose
ideas were unconventional. In this case Artzibashev was
credited with advocating the right of women to have children without the bond of marriage. So much water has
flowed under the bridges of Western civilization since 1914
that it would be idle nowadays either to affect horror at this
frank analysis of sex in society or to ask Michael Artzibashev
what is his message. *Nous avons changé tout cela,* it appears.

Individualism is the platitude of literature to-day, as the
service of man was the platitude of the advanced literature
which flourished before the war. Freedom for the sexes and
the right to discuss all problems and aspects of human life
are now the accepted privilege of writers who have gone beyond the once startling frankness of *Sanine.* Now the facts
are stated, their causes and effects are indicated, and we are
expected, as persons of adult mind, to draw our own con-
clusions. Consequently, we do not ask the modern writer
to justify his method by the worthiness of his aim or the
soundness of the moral he would inculcate. Even the physical details which aroused tremors either of delight or of indignation twenty years ago are no longer noticeable.
Amongst other things, we have become more familiar with
the body, so that a fashionably undressed woman in 1925
would have seemed as shocking in 1905 as Kamensky's
Leda might—possibly—seem to-day.

Our time, in other words, is one of rapid emancipation,

which has induced in us a mood and a point of view comparable to those of the inter-revolutionary period in Russia, in so far as we are between an old order that is dead, or dying, and a new order which has not yet taken shape. Then, at least, the illusion was possible that ideas governed men's destinies, that by theories changes could be effected. Hence in *Sanine* an insistence upon the abstract rights of the individual which will seem a little heavy-handed to a generation which has seen how much more powerful life itself is than theory. Artzibashev himself saw that; but he could not rid his characters of the ideology which was an inseparable part of the atmosphere of the time. He once said that the revolution of 1905 had distracted him from his real purpose, "the preaching of anarchial individualism," and he expressly claimed that *Sanine* was "neither a novel of ethics nor a libel on the younger generation," but "an apology for individualism." In this view most readers nowadays will have no difficulty in concurring, and in this judgment upon his own work Artzibashev establishes contact with some of the most vital forces in our contemporary fiction.

ERNEST BOYD

CHAPTER I

THAT important period in his life when character is influenced and formed by its first contact with the world and with men, was not spent by Vladimir Sanine at home with his parents. There had been none to guard or guide him; and his soul developed in perfect freedom and independence, just as a tree in the field.

He had been away from home for many years, and, when he returned, his mother and his sister Lida scarcely recognized him. His features, voice, and manner had changed but little, yet something strange and new and riper in his whole personality gave a light to his countenance and endowed it with an altered expression. It was in the evening that he came home, entering the room as quietly as if he had only left it five minutes before. As he stood there, tall, fair, and broad-shouldered, his calm face with its slightly mocking expression at the corners of the mouth showed not a sign of fatigue or of emotion, and the boisterous greeting of his mother and sister subsided of itself.

While he was eating, and drinking tea, his sister, sitting opposite, gazed steadfastly at him. She was in love with him, as most romantic girls usually are with their absent brother. Lida had always imagined Vladimir to be an extraordinary person, as strange as any to be found in books. She pictured his life as one of tragic conflict, sad and lonely as that of some great, uncomprehended soul.

"Why do you look at me like that?" asked Sanine, smiling.

This quiet smile and searching glance formed his usual expression, but, strange to say, they did not please Lida. To her, they seemed self-complacent, revealing nought of spiritual suffering and strife. She looked away and was silent. Then, mechanically, she kept turning over the pages of a book.

When the meal was at an end, Sanine's mother patted his head affectionately, and said:

"Now, tell us all about your life, and what you did there."

"What I did?" said Sanine, laughing. "Well, I ate, and drank, and slept; and sometimes I worked; and sometimes I did nothing!"

It seemed at first as if he were unwilling to speak of himself, but when his mother questioned him about this or that, he appeared pleased to narrate his experiences. Yet, for some reason or other, one felt that he was wholly indifferent as to the impression produced by his tales. His manner, kindly and courteous though it was, in no way suggested that intimacy which only exists among members of a family. Such kindliness and courtesy seemed to come naturally from him as the light from a lamp which shines with equal radiance on all objects.

They went out to the garden terrace and sat down on the steps. Lida sat on a lower one, listening in silence to her brother. At her heart she felt an icy chill. Her subtle feminine instinct told her that her brother was not what she had imagined him to be. In his presence she felt shy and embarrassed, as if he were a stranger. It was now evening; faint

shadows encircled them. Sanine lit a cigarette and the delicate odour of tobacco mingled with the fragrance of the
garden. He told them how life had tossed him hither and
thither; how he had often been hungry and a vagrant; how
he had taken part in political struggles, and how, when
weary, he had renounced these.

Lida sat motionless, listening attentively, and looking as
quaint and pretty as any charming girl would look in summer twilight.

The more he told her, the more she became convinced that
this life which she had painted for herself in such glowing
colours was really most simple and commonplace. There
was something strange in it as well. What was it? That she
could not define. At any rate, from her brother's account, it
seemed to her very simple, tedious and boring. Apparently
he had lived just anywhere, and had done just anything; at
work one day, and idle the next; it was also plain that he
liked drinking, and knew a good deal about women. But life
such as this had nothing dark or sinister about it; in no way
did it resemble the life she imagined her brother had led. He
had no ideas to live for; he hated no one; and for no one had
he suffered. At some of his disclosures she was positively
annoyed, especially when he told her that once, being very
hard up, he was obliged to mend his torn trousers himself.

"Why, do you know how to sew?" she asked involuntarily,
in a tone of surprise and contempt. She thought it paltry;
unmanly, in fact.

"I did not know at first, but I soon had to learn," replied
Sanine, who smilingly guessed what his sister thought.

The girl carelessly shrugged her shoulders, and remained

silent, gazing at the garden. It seemed to her as if, dreaming
of sunshine, she awoke beneath a grey, cold sky.

Her mother, too, felt depressed. It pained her to think that
her son did not occupy the position to which, socially, he was
entitled. She began by telling him that things could not go
on like this, and that he must be more sensible in future. At
first she spoke warily, but when she saw that he paid scarcely
any attention to her remarks, she grew angry, and obstinately
insisted, as stupid old women do, thinking her son was trying
to tease her. Sanine was neither surprised nor annoyed: he
hardly seemed to understand what she said, but looked amiably indifferent, and was silent.

Yet at the question, "How do you propose to live?" he answered, smiling, "Oh! somehow or other."

His calm, firm voice and open glance made one feel that
those words, which meant nothing to his mother, had for him
a deep and precise significance.

Maria Ivanovna sighed, and after a pause said anxiously:

"Well, after all, it's your affair. You're no longer a child.
You ought to walk round the garden. It's looking so pretty
now."

"Yes, of course! Come along, Lida; come and show me the
garden," said Sanine to his sister, "I have quite forgotten
what it looks like."

Roused from her reverie, Lida sighed and got up. Side by
side they walked down the path leading to the green depths
of the dusky garden.

The Sanines' house was in the main street of the town, and,
the town being small, their garden extended as far as the
river, beyond which were fields. The house was an old man-

sion, with rickety pillars on either side and a broad terrace. The large gloomy garden had run to waste; it looked like some dull green cloud that had descended to earth. At night it seemed haunted. It was as if some sad spirit were wandering through the tangled thicket, or restlessly pacing the dusky floors of the old edifice. On the first floor there was an entire suite of empty rooms dismal with faded carpets and dingy curtains. Through the garden there was but one narrow path or alley, strewn with dead branches and crushed frogs. What modest, tranquil life there was appeared to be centered in one corner. There, close to the house, yellow sand and gravel gleamed, and there, beside neat flower-beds bright with blossom, stood the green table on which in summer-time tea or lunch was set. This little corner, touched by the breath of simple peaceful life, was in sharp contrast to the huge, deserted mansion, doomed to inevitable decay.

When the house behind them had disappeared from view and the silent, motionless trees, like thoughtful witnesses, surrounded them, Sanine suddenly put his arm round Lida's waist and said in a strange tone, half fierce, half tender:

"You've become quite a beauty! The first man you love will be a happy fellow."

The touch of his arm with its muscles like iron sent a fiery thrill through Lida's soft, supple frame. Bashful and trembling, she drew away from him as if at the approach of some unseen beast of prey.

They had now reached the river's edge. There was a moist, damp odour from the reeds that swayed pensively in the stream. On the other side, fields lay dim in twilight beneath the vast sky where shone the first pale stars.

Stepping aside, Sanine seized a withered branch, broke it in two, and flung the pieces into the stream where swiftly circles appeared on its surface and swiftly vanished. As if to hail Sanine as their comrade, the reeds bent their heads.

CHAPTER II

IT was about six o'clock. The sun still shone brightly, but in the garden there were already faint green shadows. The air was full of light and warmth and peace. Maria Ivanovna was making jam, and under the green linden-tree there was a strong smell of boiling sugar and raspberries. Sanine had been busy at the flower-beds all the morning, trying to revive some of the flowers that suffered most from the dust and heat.

"You had better pull up the weeds first," suggested his mother, as from time to time she watched him through the blue, quivering steam. "Tell Grounjka, and she'll do it for you."

Sanine looked up, hot and smiling. "Why?" said he, as he tossed back his hair that clung to his brow. "Let them grow as much as they like. I am fond of everything green."

"You're a funny fellow!" said his mother, as she shrugged her shoulders, good-humouredly. For some reason or other, his answer had pleased her.

"It is you yourselves that are funny," said Sanine, in a tone of conviction. He then went into the house to wash his hands, and, coming back, sat down at his ease in a wicker arm-chair near the table. He felt happy, and in a good temper. The verdure, the sunlight and the blue sky filled him with a keener sense of the joy of life. Large towns with their bustle and din were to him detestable. Around him were sunlight

7

and freedom; the future gave him no anxiety; for he was disposed to accept from life whatever it could offer him. Sanine shut his eyes tight, and stretched himself; the tension of his sound, strong muscles gave him pleasurable thrills.

A gentle breeze was blowing. The whole garden seemed to sigh. Here and there, sparrows chattered noisily about their intensely important but incomprehensible little lives, and Mill, the fox-terrier, with ears erect and red tongue lolling out, lay in the long grass, listening. The leaves whispered softly; their round shadows quivered on the smooth gravel path.

Maria Ivanovna was vexed at her son's calmness. She was fond of him, just as she was fond of all her children, and for that very reason she longed to rouse him, to wound his self-respect, if only to force him to heed her words and accept her view of life. Like an ant in the sand, she had employed every moment of a long existence in building up the frail structure of her domestic well-being. It was a long, bare, monotonous edifice, like a barrack or a hospital, built with countless little bricks that to her, as an incompetent architect, constituted the graces of life, though in fact they were petty worries that kept her in a perpetual state of irritation or of anxiety.

"Do you suppose things will go on like this, later on?" she said, with lips compressed, and feigning intense interest in the boiling jam.

"What do you mean by 'later on'?" asked Sanine, and then sneezed.

Maria Ivanovna thought that he had sneezed on purpose to annoy her, and, absurd though such a notion was, looked cross.

"How nice it is to be here with you!" said Sanine, dreamily.

"Yes, it's not so bad," she answered drily. She was secretly pleased at her son's praise of the house and garden that to her were as lifelong kinsfolk.

Sanine looked at her, and then said, thoughtfully:

"If you didn't bother me with all sorts of silly things, it would be nicer still."

The bland tone in which these words were spoken seemed at variance with their meaning, so that Maria Ivanovna did not know whether to be vexed or amused.

"To look at you, and then to think that, as a child, you were always rather odd," said she, sadly, "and now——"

"And now?" exclaimed Sanine, gleefully, as if he expected to hear something specially pleasant and interesting.

"Now you are more crazy than ever!" said Maria Ivanovna sharply, shaking her spoon.

"Well, all the better!" said Sanine, laughing. After a pause, he added, "Ah! here's Novikoff!"

Out of the house came a tall, fair, good-looking man. His red silk shirt, fitting tight to his well-proportioned frame, looked brilliant in the sun; his pale blue eyes had a lazy, good-natured expression.

"There you go! Always quarrelling!" said he, in a languid, friendly tone. "And in Heaven's name, what about?"

"Well, the fact is, mother thinks that a Grecian nose would suit me better, while I am quite satisfied with the one that I have got."

Sanine looked down his nose and, laughing, grasped the

other's big, soft hand.

"So, I should say!" exclaimed Maria Ivanovna, pettishly.

Novikoff laughed merrily; and from the green thicket came a gentle echo in reply, as if some one yonder heartily shared his mirth.

"Aha! I know what it is! Worrying about your future."

"What, you, too?" exclaimed Sanine, in comic alarm.

"It just serves you right."

"Ah!" cried Sanine. "If it's a case of two to one, I had better clear out."

"No, it is I that will soon have to clear out," said Maria Ivanovna with sudden irritation at which she herself was vexed. Hastily removing her saucepan of jam, she hurried into the house, without looking back. The terrier jumped up, and with ears erect watched her go. Then it rubbed its nose with its front paw, gave another questioning glance at the house and ran off into the garden.

"Have you got any cigarettes?" asked Sanine, delighted at his mother's departure.

Novikoff with a lazy movement of his large body produced a cigarette-case.

"You ought not to tease her so," said he, in a voice of gentle reproof. "She's an old lady."

"How have I teased her?"

"Well, you see——"

"What do you mean by 'well, you see'? It is she who is always after me. I have never asked anything of anybody, and therefore people ought to leave me alone."

Both remained silent.

"Well, how goes it, doctor?" asked Sanine, as he watched

the tobacco-smoke rising in fantastic curves above his head.

Novikoff, who was thinking of something else, did not answer at once.

"Badly."

"In what way?"

"Oh, in every way. Everything is so dull and this little town bores me to death. There's nothing to do."

"Nothing to do? Why, it was you that complained of not having time to breathe!"

"That is not what I mean. One can't be always seeing patients, seeing patients. There is another life besides that."

"And who prevents you from living that other life?"

"That is rather a complicated question."

"In what way is it complicated? You are a young, good-looking, healthy man; what more do you want?"

"In my opinion that is not enough," replied Novikoff, with mild irony.

"Really!" laughed Sanine. "Well, I think it is a very great deal."

"But not enough for me," said Novikoff, laughing in his turn. It was plain that Sanine's remark about his health and good looks had pleased him, and yet it had made him feel shy as a girl.

"There's one thing that you want," said Sanine, pensively.

"And what is that?"

"A just conception of life. The monotony of your existence oppresses you; and yet, if some one advised you to give it all up, and go straight away into the wide world, you would be afraid to do so."

"And as what should I go? As a beggar? H—m!"

"Yes, as a beggar, even! When I look at you, I think: there is a man who in order to give the Russian Empire a constitution would let himself be shut up in Schlusselburg * for the rest of his life, losing all his rights, and his liberty as well. After all, what is a constitution to him? But when it is a question of altering his own tedious mode of life, and of going elsewhere to find new interests, he at once asks, 'how should I get a living? Strong and healthy as I am, should I not come to grief if I had not got my fixed salary, and consequently cream in my tea, my silk shirts, stand-up collars, and all the rest of it?' It's funny, upon my word it is!"

"I cannot see anything funny in it at all. In the first case, it is the question of a cause, an idea, whereas in the other—"

"Well?"

"Oh! I don't know how to express myself!" And Novikoff snapped his fingers.

"There now!" said Sanine, interrupting. "That's how you always evade the point. I shall never believe that the longing for a constitution is stronger in you than the longing to make the most of your own life."

"That is just a question. Possibly it is."

Sanine waved his hand, irritably.

"Oh! don't, please! If somebody were to cut off your finger, you would feel it more than if it were some other Russian's finger. That is a fact, eh?"

"Or a cynicism," said Novikoff, meaning to be sarcastic when he was merely foolish.

"Possibly. But, all the same, it is the truth. And now

---

* A fortress for political prisoners.

though in Russia and in many other States there is no constitution, nor the slightest sign of one, it is your own unsatis-
factory life that worries you, not the absence of a constitution.
And if you say it isn't, then you're telling a lie. What is
more," added Sanine, with a merry twinkle in his eyes, "you
are worried not about your life, but because Lida has not yet
fallen in love with you. Now, isn't that so?"

"What utter nonsense you're talking!" cried Novikoff,
turning as red as his silk shirt. So confused was he, that tears
rose to his calm, kindly eyes.

"How is it nonsense, when besides Lida you can see nothing else in the whole world? The wish to possess her is written in large letters on your brow."

Novikoff winced perceptibly and began to walk rapidly
up and down the path. If anyone but Lida's brother had
spoken to him in this way it would have pained him deeply,
but to hear such words from Sanine's mouth amazed him;
in fact at first he scarcely understood them.

"Look here," he muttered, "either you are posing, or
else——"

"Or else—what?" asked Sanine, smiling.

Novikoff looked aside, shrugged his shoulders, and was
silent. The other inference led him to regard Sanine as an
immoral, bad man. But he could not tell him this, for, ever
since their college days, he had always felt sincere affection
for him, and it seemed to Novikoff impossible that he should
have chosen a wicked man as his friend. The effect on his
mind was at once bewildering and unpleasant. The allusion
to Lida pained him, but, as the goddess whom he adored, he
could not feel angry with Sanine for speaking of her. It

pleased him, and yet he felt hurt, as if a burning hand had seized his heart and had gently pressed it.

Sanine was silent, and smiled good-humouredly.

After a pause he said:

"Well, finish your statement; I am in no hurry!"

Novikoff kept walking up and down the path, as before. He was evidently hurt. At this moment the terrier came running back excitedly and rubbed against Sanine's knees, as if wishful to let everyone know how pleased he was.

"Good dog!" said Sanine, patting him.

Novikoff strove to avoid continuing the discussion, being afraid that Sanine might return to the subject which for him personally was the most interesting in the whole world. Anything that did not concern Lida seemed futile to him—dull.

"And—where is Lidia Petrovna?" he asked mechanically, albeit loth to utter the question that was uppermost in his mind.

"Lida? Where should she be? Walking with officers on the boulevard, where all our young ladies are to be found at this time of day."

A look of jealousy darkened his face, as Novikoff asked:

"How can a girl so clever and cultivated as she waste her time with such empty-headed fools?"

"Oh! my friend," exclaimed Sanine, smiling, "Lida is handsome, and young, and healthy, just as you are; more so, in fact, because she has that which you lack—keen desire for everything. She wants to know everything, to experience everything—why, here she comes! You've only got to look at her to understand that. Isn't she pretty?"

Lida was shorter and much handsomer than her brother.

Sweetness combined with supple strength gave to her whole personality charm and distinction. There was a haughty look in her dark eyes, and her voice, of which she was proud, sounded rich and musical. She walked slowly down the steps, moving with the lithe grace of a thoroughbred, while adroitly holding up her long grey dress. Behind her, clinking their spurs, came two good-looking young officers in tightly-fitting riding-breeches and shining top-boots.

"Who is pretty? Is it I?" asked Lida, as she filled the whole garden with the charm of her voice, her beauty and her youth. She gave Novikoff her hand, with a side-glance at her brother, about whose attitude she did not feel quite clear, never knowing whether he was joking or in earnest. Grasping her hand tightly, Novikoff grew very red, but his emotions were unnoticed by Lida, used as she was to his reverent, bashful glance that never troubled her.

"Good evening, Vladimir Petrovitch," said the elder, handsomer and fairer of the two officers, rigid, erect as a spirited stallion, while his spurs clinked noisily.

Sanine knew him to be Sarudine, a captain of cavalry, one of Lida's most persistent admirers. The other was Lieutenant Tanaroff, who regarded Sarudine as the ideal soldier, and strove to copy everything he did. He was taciturn, somewhat clumsy, and not so good-looking as Sarudine. Tanaroff rattled his spurs in his turn, but said nothing.

"Yes, you!" replied Sanine to his sister, gravely.

"Why, of course I am pretty. You should have said indescribably pretty!" And, laughing gaily, Lida sank into a chair, glancing again at Sanine. Raising her arms and thus emphasizing the curves of her shapely bosom, she proceeded to remove her hat, but, in so doing, let a long hat-pin fall on the gravel, and her veil and hair became disarranged.

"Andrei Pavlovitch, do please help me!" she plaintively cried to the taciturn lieutenant.

"Yes, she's a beauty!" murmured Sanine, thinking aloud, and never taking his eyes off her. Once more Lida glanced shyly at her brother.

"We're all of us beautiful here," said she.

"What's that? Beautiful? Ha! Ha!" laughed Sarudine, showing his white, shining teeth. "We are at best but the modest frame that serves to heighten the dazzling splendour of your beauty."

"I say, what eloquence, to be sure!" exclaimed Sanine, in surprise. There was a slight shade of irony in his tone.

"Lidia Petrovna would make anybody eloquent," said Tanaroff the silent, as he tried to help Lida to take off her hat, and in so doing ruffled her hair. She pretended to be vexed, laughing all the while.

"What?" drawled Sanine. "Are you eloquent too?"

"Oh! let them be!" whispered Novikoff, hypocritically, though secretly pleased.

Lida frowned at Sanine, to whom her dark eyes plainly said:

"Don't imagine that I cannot see what these people are. I intend to please myself. I am not a fool any more than you are, and I know what I am about."

Sanine smiled at her.

At last the hat was removed, and Tanaroff solemnly placed it on the table.

"Look! Look what you've done to me, Andrei Pavlovitch!" cried Lida half peevishly, half coquettishly. "You've got my hair into such a tangle! Now I shall have to go indoors."

"I'm so awfully sorry!" stammered Tanaroff, in confusion.

Lida rose, gathered up her skirts, and ran indoors laughing, followed by the glances of all the men. When she had gone they seemed to breathe more freely, without that nervous sense of restraint which men usually experience in the presence of a pretty young woman. Sarudine lighted a cigarette which he smoked with evident gusto. One felt, when he spoke, that he habitually took the lead in a conversation, and that what he thought was something quite different from what he said.

"I have just been persuading Lidia Petrovna to study singing seriously. With such a voice, her career is assured."

"A fine career, upon my word!" sullenly rejoined Novikoff, looking aside.

"What is wrong with it?" asked Sarudine, in genuine amazement, removing the cigarette from his lips.

"Why, what's an actress? Nothing else but a harlot!" replied Novikoff, with sudden heat. Jealousy tortured him; the thought that the young woman whose body he loved could appear before other men in an alluring dress that would exhibit her charms in order to provoke their passions.

"Surely it is going too far to say that," replied Sarudine, raising his eyebrows.

Novikoff's glance was full of hatred. He regarded Sarudine as one of those men who meant to rob him of his beloved; moreover, his good looks annoyed him.

"No, not in the least too far," he retorted. "To appear half nude on the stage and in some voluptuous scene exhibit one's personal charms to those who in an hour or so take their leave as they would of some courtesan after paying the usual fee! A charming career indeed!"

"My friend," said Sanine, "every woman in the first instance likes to be admired for her personal charms."

Novikoff shrugged his shoulders irritably.

"What a silly, coarse statement!" said he.

"At any rate, coarse or not, it's the truth," replied Sanine. "Lida would be most effective on the stage, and I should like to see her there."

Although in the others this speech roused a certain instinctive curiosity, they all felt ill at ease. Sarudine, who thought himself more intelligent and tactful than the rest, deemed it his duty to dispel this vague feeling of embarrassment.

"Well, what do you think the young lady ought to do? Get married? Pursue a course of study, or let her talent be lost? That would be a crime against nature that had endowed her with its fairest gift."

"Oh!" exclaimed Sanine, with undisguised sarcasm, "till now the idea of such a crime had never entered my head."

Novikoff laughed maliciously, but replied politely enough to Sarudine.

"Why a crime? A good mother or a female doctor is worth a thousand times more than an actress."

"Not at all!" said Tanaroff, indignantly.

"Don't you find this sort of talk rather boring?" asked Sanine.

Sarudine's rejoinder was lost in a fit of coughing. They

all of them really thought such a discussion tedious and unnecessary; and yet they all felt somewhat offended. An unpleasant silence reigned.

Lida and Maria Ivanovna appeared on the veranda. Lida
had heard her brother's last words, but did not know to what
they referred.

"You seem to have soon become bored!" cried she, laughing. "Let us go down to the river. It is charming there,
now."

As she passed in front of the men, her shapely figure swayed
slightly, and there was a look of dark mystery in her eyes
that seemed to say something, to promise something.

"Go for a walk till supper-time," said Maria Ivanovna.

"Delighted," exclaimed Sarudine. His spurs clinked, as
he offered Lida his arm.

"I hope that I may be allowed to come too," said Novikoff,
meaning to be satirical, though his face wore a tearful expression.

"Who is there to prevent you?" replied Lida, smiling at
him over her shoulder.

"Yes, you go, too," exclaimed Sanine. "I would come with
you if she were not so thoroughly convinced that I am her
brother."

Lida winced somewhat, and glanced swiftly at Sanine, as
she laughed, a short, nervous laugh.

Maria Ivanovna was obviously displeased.

"Why do you talk in that stupid way?" she bluntly exclaimed. "I suppose you think it is original?"

"I really never thought about it at all," was Sanine's rejoinder.

Maria Ivanovna looked at him in amazement. She had never been able to understand her son; she never could tell when he was joking or in earnest, nor what he thought or felt, when other comprehensible persons felt and thought much as she did herself. According to her idea, a man was always bound to speak and feel and act exactly as other men of his social and intellectual status were wont to speak and feel and act. She was also of opinion that people were not simply men with their natural characteristics and peculiarities, but that they must be all cast in one common mould. Her own environment encouraged and confirmed this belief. Education, she thought, tended to divide men into two groups, the intelligent and the unintelligent. The latter might retain their individuality, which drew upon them the contempt of others. The former were divided into groups, and their convictions did not correspond with their personal qualities, but with their respective positions. Thus, every student was a revolutionary, every official was bourgeois, every artist a free thinker, and every officer an exaggerated stickler for rank. If, however, it chanced that a student was a Conservative, or an officer an Anarchist, this must be regarded as most extraordinary, and even, unpleasant. As for Sanine, according to his origin and education he ought to have been something quite different from what he was; and Maria Ivanovna felt as Lida, Novikoff and all who came into contact with him felt, that he had disappointed expectation. With a mother's instinct she quickly saw the impression that her son made on those about him; and it pained her.

Sanine was aware of this. He would fain have reassured

her, but was at a loss how to begin. At first he thought of
professing sentiments that were false, so that she might be
pacified; however, he only laughed, and, rising, went indoors. There, for a while, he lay on his bed, thinking. It
seemed as if men wished to turn the whole world into a sort
of military cloister, with one set of rules for all, framed with
a view to destroy all individuality, or else to make this submit to one vague, archaic power of some kind. He was even
led to reflect upon Christianity and its fate, but this bored
him to such an extent that he fell asleep, and did not wake
until evening had turned to night.

Maria Ivanovna watched him go, and she, too, sighing
deeply, became immersed in thought. Sarudine, so she said
to herself, was obviously paying court to Lida, and she hoped
that his intentions were serious.

"Lida's already twenty, and Sarudine seems to be quite a
nice sort of young man. They say he'll get his squadron this
year. Of course, he's heavily in debt— But oh! why did I
have that horrid dream? I know it's absurd, yet somehow
I can't get it out of my head!"

This dream was one that she had dreamed on the same day
that Sarudine had first entered the house. She thought that
she saw Lida, dressed all in white, walking in a green
meadow bright with flowers.

Maria Ivanovna sank into an easy chair, leaning her head
on her hand, as old women do, and she gazed at the darkening sky. Thoughts gloomy and tormenting gave her no
respite, and there was an indefinable something which
caused her to feel anxious and afraid.

CHAPTER III

It was already quite dark when the others returned from their walk. Their clear, merry voices rang out through the soft dusk that veiled the garden. Lida ran, flushed and laughing, to her mother. She brought with her cool scents from the river that blended delightfully with the fragrance of her own sweet youth and beauty which the companionship of sympathetic admirers heightened and enhanced.

"Supper, mamma, let's have supper!" she cried playfully dragging her mother along. "Meanwhile Victor Sergejevitsch is going to sing something to us."

Maria Ivanovna, as she went out to get supper ready, thought to herself that Fate could surely have nothing but happiness in store for so beautiful and charming a girl as her darling Lida.

Sarudine and Tanaroff went to the piano in the drawing-room, while Lida reclined lazily in the rocking-chair on the veranda. Novikoff, mute, walked up and down on the creaking boards of the veranda floor, furtively glancing at Lida's face, at her firm, full bosom, at her little feet shod in yellow shoes, and her dainty ankles. But she took no heed of him nor of his glances, so enthralled was she by the might and magic of a first passion. She shut her eyes, and smiled at her thoughts.

In Novikoff's soul there was the old strife; he loved Lida,

yet he could not be sure of her feelings towards himself. At times she loved him, so he thought; and again, there were times when she did not. If he thought "yes," how easy and pleasant it seemed for this young, pure, supple body to surrender itself to him. If he thought "no," such an idea was foul and detestable; he was angry at his own lust, deeming himself vile, and unworthy of Lida.

At last he determined to be guided by chance.

"If I step on the last board with my right foot, then I've got to propose; and if with the left, then——"

He dared not even think of what would happen in that case.

He trod on the last board with his left foot. It threw him into a cold sweat; but he instantly reassured himself.

"Pshaw! What nonsense! I'm like some old woman! Now then; one, two, three—at three I'll go straight up to her, and speak. Yes, but what am I going to say? No matter! Here goes! One, two, three! No, three times over! One, two, three! One, two——"

His brain seemed on fire, his mouth grew parched, his heart beat so violently that his knees shook.

"Don't stamp like that!" exclaimed Lida, opening her eyes. "One can't hear anything."

Only then was Novikoff aware that Sarudine was singing. The young officer had chosen that old romance.

> I loved you once! Can you forget?
> Love in my heart is burning yet.

He did not sing badly, but after the style of untrained singers who seek to give expression by exaggerated tone-colour. Novikoff found nothing to please him in such a performance.

"What is that? One of his own compositions?" asked he, with unusual bitterness.

"No! Don't disturb us, please, but sit down!" said Lida, sharply. "And if you don't like music, go and look at the moon!"

Just then the moon, large, round and red, was rising above the black tree-tops. Its soft evasive light touched the stone steps, and Lida's dress, and her pensive, smiling face. In the garden the shadows had grown deeper; they were now sombre and profound as those of the forest.

Novikoff sighed, and then blurted out:

"I prefer you to the moon"—thinking to himself, "That's an idiotic remark!"

Lida burst out laughing.

"What a lumpish compliment!" she exclaimed.

"I don't know how to pay compliments," was Novikoff's sullen rejoinder.

"Very well, then, sit still and listen," said Lida, shrugging her shoulders, pettishly.

> But you no longer care, I know,
> Why should I grieve you with my woe?

The tones of the piano rang out with silvery clearness through the green, humid garden. The moonlight became more and more intense and the shadows harder. Crossing the grass, Sanine sat down under a linden-tree and was about to light a cigarette. Then he suddenly stopped and remained motionless, as if spell-bound by the evening calm that the

sounds of the piano and of this youthfully sentimental voice
in no way disturbed, but rather served to make more complete.

"Lida Petrovna!" cried Novikoff hurriedly, as if this particular moment must never be lost.

"Well?" asked Lida mechanically, as she looked at the
garden and the moon above it and the dark boughs that
stood out sharply against its silver disc.

"I have long waited—that is—I have been anxious to say
something to you," Novikoff stammered out.

Sanine turned his head round to listen.

"What about?" asked Lida, absently.

Sarudine had finished his song and after a pause began to
sing again. He thought that he had a voice of extraordinary
beauty, and he much liked to hear it.

Novikoff felt himself growing red, and then pale. It was
as if he were going to faint.

"I—look here—Lidia Petrovna—will you be my wife?"

As he stammered out these words he felt all the while that
he ought to have said something very different and that his
own emotions should have been different also. Before he
had got the words out he was certain that the answer would
be "no"; and at the same time he had an impression that
something utterly silly and ridiculous was about to occur.

Lida asked mechanically. "Whose wife?" Then suddenly, she blushed deeply, and rose, as if intending to speak.
But she said nothing and turned aside in confusion. The
moonlight fell full on her features.

"I—love you!" stammered Novikoff.

For him, the moon no longer shone; the evening air

seemed stifling, the earth, he thought, would open beneath his feet.

"I don't know how to make speeches—but—no matter, I love you very much!"

("Why, very much?" he thought to himself, "as if I were alluding to ice-cream.")

Lida played nervously with a little leaf that had fluttered down into her hands. What she had just heard embarrassed her, being both unexpected and futile; besides, it created a novel feeling of disagreeable restraint between herself and Novikoff, whom from her childhood she had always looked upon as a relative, and whom she liked.

"I really don't know what to say! I had never thought about it."

Novikoff felt a dull pain at his heart, as if it would stop beating. Very pale, he rose and seized his cap.

"Good-bye," he said, not hearing the sound of his own voice. His quivering lips were twisted into a meaningless smile.

"Are you going? Good-bye!" said Lida, laughing nervously and proffering her hand.

Novikoff grasped it hastily, and without putting on his cap strode out across the grass, into the garden. In the shade he stood still and gripped his head with both hands.

"My God! I am doomed to such luck as this! Shoot myself? No, that's all nonsense! Shoot myself, eh?"

Wild, incoherent thoughts flashed through his brain. He felt that he was the most wretched and humiliated and ridiculous of mortals.

Sanine at first wished to call out to him, but checking the

impulse, he merely smiled. To him it was grotesque that
Novikoff should tear his hair and almost weep because a
woman whose body he desired would not surrender herself
to him. At the same time he was rather glad that his pretty
sister did not care for Novikoff.

For some moments Lida remained motionless in the same
place, and Sanine's curious gaze was riveted on her white
silhouette in the moonlight. Sarudine now came from the
lighted drawing-room on to the veranda. Sanine distinctly
heard the faint jingling of his spurs. In the drawing-room
Tanaroff was playing an old-fashioned, mournful waltz
whose languorous cadences floated on the air? Approaching Lida, Sarudine gently and deftly placed his arm round
her waist. Sanine could perceive that both figures became merged into one that swayed in the misty light.

"Why so pensive?" murmured Sarudine, with shining
eyes, as his lips touched Lida's dainty little ear. Lida was at
once joyful and afraid. Now, as on all occasions when Sarudine embraced her, she felt a strange thrill. She knew that in
intelligence and culture he was her inferior, and that she
could never be dominated by him; yet at the same time she
was aware of something delightful and alarming in letting
herself be touched by this strong, comely young man. She
seemed to be gazing down into a mysterious, unfathomable
abyss, and thinking, "I could hurl myself in, if I chose."

"We shall be seen," she murmured half audibly.

Though not encouraging his embrace, she yet did not
shrink from it; such passive surrender excited him the
more.

"One word, just one!" whispered Sarudine, as he crushed

her closer to him, his veins throbbing with desire; "will you come?"

Lida trembled. It was not the first time that he had asked her this question, and each time she had felt strange tremors that deprived her of her will.

"Why?" she asked in a low voice, as she gazed dreamily at the moon.

"Why? That I may have you near me, and see you, and talk to you. Oh! like this, it's torture! Yes, Lida, you're torturing me! Now, will you come?"

So saying, he strained her to him, passionately. His touch, as that of glowing iron, sent a thrill through her limbs; it seemed as if she were enveloped in a mist, languorous, dreamy, oppressive. Her lithe, supple frame grew rigid and then swayed towards him, trembling with pleasure and yet with fear. Around her all things had undergone a curious sudden change. The moon was a moon no longer; it seemed close, close to the trellis-work of the veranda, as if it hung just above the luminous lawn. The garden was not the one that she knew, but another garden, sombre, mysterious, that, suddenly approaching, closed round her. Her brain reeled. She drew back, and with strange languor, freed herself from Sarudine's embrace.

"Yes," she murmured with difficulty. Her lips were white and parched.

With faltering steps she re-entered the house, conscious of something terrible yet alluring that inevitably drew her to the brink of an abyss.

"Nonsense!" she reflected. "It's not that at all. I am only joking. It just interests me, and it amuses me, too."

Thus did she seek to persuade herself, as she stood facing the darkened mirror in her room, wherein she only saw herself *en silhouette* against the glass door of the brightly lighted dining-room. Slowly she raised both arms above her head, and lazily stretched herself, watching meanwhile the sensuous movements of her supple body.

Left to himself, Sarudine stood erect and shook his shapely limbs. His eyes were half closed, and, as he smiled, his teeth shone beneath his fair moustache. He was accustomed to have luck, and on this occasion he foresaw even greater enjoyment in the near future. He imagined Lida in all her voluptuous beauty at the very moment of surrender. The passion of such a picture caused him physical pain.

At first, when he paid court to her, and after that, when she had allowed him to embrace her and kiss her, Lida had always made him feel somewhat afraid. While he caressed her, there was something strange, unintelligible in her dark eyes, as though she secretly despised him. She seemed to him so clever, so absolutely unlike other women to whom he had always felt himself obviously superior, and so proud, that for a kiss he looked to receive a box on the ear. The thought of possessing her was almost disquieting. At times he believed that she was just playing with him and his position appeared simply foolish and absurd. But to-day, after this promise, uttered hesitatingly, in faltering tones such as he had heard other women use, he felt suddenly certain of his power and that victory was near. He knew that things would be just as he had desired them to be. And to this sense of voluptuous expectancy was added a touch of spite; this proud, pure, cultured girl should surrender to him, as all

the others had surrendered; he would use her at his pleasure,
as he had used the rest. Scenes libidinous and debasing rose
up before him. Lida nude, with hair dishevelled and inscrutable eyes, became the central figure in a turbulent orgy
of cruelty and lust. Suddenly he distinctly saw her lying
on the ground; he heard the swish of the whip; he observed
a blood-red stripe on the soft, nude, submissive body. His
temples throbbed, he staggered backwards, sparks danced
before his eyes. The thought of it all became physically intolerable. His hands shook as he lit a cigarette; again his
strong limbs twitched convulsively, and he went indoors.
Sanine, who had heard nothing yet who had seen and com-
prehended all, followed him, roused almost to a feeling of
jealousy.

"Brutes like that are always lucky," he thought to himself. "What the devil does it all mean? Lida and he?"

At supper, Maria Ivanovna seemed in a bad temper. Tanaroff as usual said nothing. He thought what a fine thing it
would be if he were Sarudine, and had such a sweetheart as
Lida to love him. He would have loved her in quite a different way, though. Sarudine did not know how to appreciate his good fortune. Lida was pale and silent, looking
at no one. Sarudine was gay, and on the alert, like a wild
beast that scents its prey. Sanine yawned as usual, ate, drank
a good deal of brandy and apparently seemed longing to go
to sleep. But when supper was over, he declared his intention of walking home with Sarudine. It was near mid-
night, and the moon shone high overhead. Almost in
silence the two walked towards the officers' quarters. All
the way Sanine kept looking furtively at Sarudine, won-

dering if he should, or should not, strike him in the face.

"Hm! Yes!" he suddenly began, as they got close to the house, "there are all sorts of blackguards in this world!"

"What do you mean by that?" asked Sarudine, raising his eyebrows.

"That is so; speaking generally. Blackguards are the most fascinating people."

"You don't say so?" exclaimed Sarudine, smiling.

"Of course they are. There's nothing so boring in all the world as your so-called honest man. What is an honest man? With the programme of honesty and virtue everybody has long been familiar; and so it contains nothing that is new. Such antiquated rubbish robs a man of all individuality, and his life is lived within the narrow, tedious limits of virtue. Thou shalt not steal, nor lie, nor cheat, nor commit adultery. The funny thing is, that all that is born in one! Everybody steals, and lies, and cheats and commits adultery as much as he can."

"Not everybody," protested Sarudine loftily.

"Yes, yes; everybody! You have only got to examine a man's life in order to get at his sins. Treachery, for instance. Thus, after rendering to Cæsar the things that are Cæsar's, when we go quietly to bed, or sit down to table, we commit acts of treachery."

"What's that you say?" cried Sarudine, half angrily.

"Of course we do. We pay taxes; we serve our time in the army, yes; but that means that we harm millions by warfare and injustice, both of which we abhor. We go calmly to our beds, when we should hasten to rescue those who in that very moment are perishing for us and for our ideas. We eat more than we actually want, and leave others to starve, when, as virtuous folk, our whole lives should be devoted to their welfare. So it goes on. It's plain enough. Now a black-guard, a real, genuine blackguard is quite another matter. To begin with he is a perfectly sincere, natural fellow."

"Natural?"

"Of course he is. He does only what a man naturally does. He sees something that does not belong to him, some-thing that he likes—and, he takes it. He sees a pretty woman who won't give herself to him, so he manages to get her, either by force or by craft. And that is perfectly natural, the desire and the instinct for self-gratification being one of the few traits that distinguish a man from a beast. The more animal an animal is, the less it understands of en-joyment, the less able it is to procure this. It only cares to satisfy its needs. We are all agreed that man was not created in order to suffer, and that suffering is not the ideal of human endeavour."

"Quite so," said Sarudine.

"Very well, then, enjoyment is the aim of human life. Paradise is the synonym for absolute enjoyment, and we all of us, more or less, dream of an earthly paradise. This legend of paradise is by no means an absurdity, but a sym-bol, a dream."

"Yes," continued Sanine, after a pause, "Nature never meant men to be abstinent, and the sincerest men are those who do not conceal their desires, that is to say, those who socially count as blackguards, fellows such as—you, for in-stance."

Sarudine started back in amazement.

"Yes, you," continued Sanine, affecting not to notice this, "You're the best fellow in the world, or, at any rate, you think you are. Come now, tell me, have you ever met a better?"

"Yes, lots of them," replied Sarudine, with some hesitation. He had not the least idea what Sanine meant, nor if he ought to appear amused or annoyed.

"Well, name them, please," said Sanine.

Sarudine shrugged his shoulders, doubtfully.

"There, you see!" exclaimed Sanine gaily. "You yourself are the best of good fellows, and so am I; yet we both of us would not object to stealing, or telling lies or committing adultery—least of all to committing adultery."

"How original!" muttered Sarudine, as he again shrugged his shoulders.

"Do you think so?" asked the other, with a slight shade of annoyance in his tone. "Well, I don't! Yes, blackguards, as I said, are the most sincere and interesting people imaginable, for they have no conception of the bounds of human baseness. I always feel particularly pleased to shake hands with a blackguard."

He immediately grasped Sarudine's hand and shook it vigorously as he looked him full in the face. Then he frowned, and muttered curtly, "Good-bye, good-night," and left him.

For a few moments Sarudine stood perfectly still and watched him depart. He did not know how to take such speeches as these of Sanine; he became at once bewildered and uneasy. Then he thought of Lida, and smiled. Sanine was her brother, and what he had said was really right after all. He began to feel a sort of brotherly attachment for him.

"An amusing fellow, by Gad!" he thought, complacently, as if Sanine in a way belonged to him, also. Then he opened the gate, and went across the moonlit courtyard to his quarters.

On reaching home, Sanine undressed and got into bed, where he tried to read "Thus spake Zarathustra" which he had found among Lida's books. But the first few pages were enough to irritate him. Such inflated imagery left him unmoved. He spat, flung the volume aside, and soon fell fast asleep.

CHAPTER IV

COLONEL Nicolai Yegorovitch Svarogitsch, who lived in the little town, awaited the arrival of his son, a student at the Moscow Polytechnic.

The latter was under the surveillance of the police and had been expelled from Moscow as a suspected person. It was thought that he was in league with revolutionists. Yourii Svarogitsch had already written to his parents informing them of his arrest, his six months' imprisonment, and his expulsion from the capital, so that they were prepared for his return. Though Nicolai Yegorovitch looked upon the whole thing as a piece of boyish folly, he was really much grieved, for he was very fond of his son, whom he received with open arms, avoiding any allusion to this painful subject. For two whole days Yourii had travelled third-class, and owing to the bad air, the stench, and the cries of children, he got no sleep at all. He was utterly exhausted, and had no sooner greeted his father and his sister Ludmilla (who was always called Lialia) than he lay down on her bed, and fell asleep.

He did not wake until evening, when the sun was near the horizon, and its slanting rays, falling through the panes, threw rosy squares upon the wall. In the next room there was a clatter of spoons and glasses; he could hear Lialia's merry laugh, and also a man's voice both pleasant and re-

35

fined which he did not know. At first it seemed to him as
if he were still in the railway-carriage and heard the noise
of the train, the rattle of the window-panes and the voices
of travellers in the next compartment. But he quickly remembered where he was, and sat bolt upright on the bed.
"Yes, here I am," he yawned, as, frowning, he thrust his
fingers through his thick, stubborn black hair.

It then occurred to him that he need never have come
home. He had been allowed to choose where he would stay.
Why, then, did he return to his parents? That he could not
explain. He believed, or wished to believe, that he had
fixed upon the most likely place that had occurred to him.
But this was not the case at all. Yourii had never had to
work for a living; his father kept him supplied with funds,
and the prospect of being alone and without means among
strangers seemed terrible to him. He was ashamed of such
a feeling, and loth to admit it to himself. Now, however,
he thought that he had made a mistake. His parents could
never understand the whole story, nor form any opinion regarding it; that was quite plain. Then again, the material
question would arise, the many useless years that he had
cost his father—it all made a mutually cordial, straightforward understanding impossible. Moreover, in this little
town, which he had not seen for two years, he would find it
dreadfully dull. He looked upon all the inhabitants of petty
provincial towns as narrow-minded folk, incapable of being
interested in, or even of understanding those philosophical
and political questions which for him were the only really
important things of life.

Yourii got up, and, opening the window, leaned out.

Along the wall of the house there was a little flower-garden bright with flowers, red, yellow, blue, lilac and white. It was like a kaleidoscope. Behind it lay the large dusky garden that, as all gardens in this town, stretched down to the river, which glimmered like dull glass between the stems of the trees. It was a calm, clear evening. Yourii felt a vague sense of depression. He had lived too long in large towns built of stone, and though he liked to fancy that he was fond of nature, she really gave him nothing, neither solace, nor peace, nor joy, and only roused in him a vague, dreamy, morbid longing.

"Aha! You're up at last! it was about time," said Lialia, as she entered the room.

Oppressed as he was by the sense of his uncertain position and by the melancholy of the dying day, Yourii felt almost vexed by his sister's gaiety and by her merry voice.

"What are you so pleased about?" he asked abruptly.

"Well, I never!" cried Lialia, wide-eyed, while she laughed again, just as if her brother's question had reminded her of something particularly amusing.

"Imagine your asking me why I am so pleased? You see, I am never bored. I have no time for that sort of thing."

Then, in a graver tone, and evidently proud of her last remark, she added:

"We live in such interesting times that it would really be a sin to feel bored. I have got the workmen to teach, and then the library takes up a lot of my time. While you were away, we started a popular library, and it is going very well indeed."

At any other time this would have interested Yourii, but

now something made him indifferent. Lialia looked very serious, waiting, as a child might wait, for her brother's praise. At last he managed to murmur:

"Oh! really!"

"With all that to do, can you expect me to be bored?" said Lialia contentedly.

"Well, anyhow, everything bores me," replied Yourii involuntarily. She pretended to be hurt.

"That's very nice of you, I am sure. You've hardly been two hours in the house, and asleep most of the time, yet you are bored already!"

"It is not my fault, but my misfortune," replied Yourii, in a slightly arrogant tone. He thought it showed superior intelligence to be bored rather than amused.

"Your misfortune, indeed!" cried Lialia, mockingly. "Ha! Ha!" She pretended to slap him. "Ha! Ha!"

Yourii did not perceive that he had already recovered his good humour. Lialia's merry voice and her joy of living had speedily banished his depression which he had imagined to be very real and deep. Lialia did not believe in his melancholy, and therefore his remarks caused her no concern.

Yourii looked at her, and said with a smile:

"I am never merry."

At this Lialia laughed, as though he had said something vastly droll.

"Very well, Knight of the Rueful Countenance, if you aren't you aren't. Never mind, come with me, and I will introduce you to a charming young man. Come!"

So saying she took her brother's hand, and laughingly led

him along.

"Stop! Who is this charming young man?"

"My fiancé," cried Lialia, as, joyful and confused, she twisted sharply round so that her gown was puffed out. Yourii knew already, from his father's and sister's letters, that a young doctor recently established in the town had been paying court to Lialia, but he was not aware that their engagement was a *fait accompli*.

"You don't say so?" said he, in amazement. It seemed to him so strange that pretty, fresh-looking little Lialia, almost a child, should already have a lover, and should soon become a bride—a wife. It touched him to a vague sense of pity for his sister. Yourii put his arm around Lialia's waist and went with her into the dining-room where in the lamplight shone the large, highly polished samovar. At the table, by the side of Nicolai Yegorovitch sat a well-built young man, not Russian in type, with bronzed features and keen bright eyes.

He rose in simple, friendly fashion to meet Yourii.

"Introduce me."

"Anatole Pavlovitch Riasantzeff!" cried Lialia, with a gesture of comic solemnity.

"Who craves your friendship and indulgence," added Riasantzeff, joking in his turn.

With a sincere wish to become friends, the two shook hands. For a moment it seemed as if they would embrace, but they refrained, merely exchanging frank, amicable glances.

"So this is her brother, is it?" thought Riasantzeff, in surprise, for he had imagined that a brother of Lialia, short, fair, and merry, would be short, fair and merry too. Yourii, on the contrary, was tall, thin and dark, though as good-looking as Lialia, and with the same regular features.

And, as Yourii looked at Riasantzeff, he thought to himself: "So this is the man who in my little sister Lialia, as fresh and fair as a spring morning, loves the woman; loves her just as I myself have loved women." Somehow, it hurt him to look at Lialia and Riasantzeff, as if he feared that they would read his thoughts.

The two men felt that they had much that was important to say to each other. Yourii would have liked to ask:

"Do you love Lialia? Really and truly? It would be sad, and indeed shameful, if you were to betray her; she's so pure, so innocent!"

And Riasantzeff would have liked to answer:

"Yes, I love your sister deeply; who could do anything else but love her? Look how pure and sweet, and charming she is; how fond she is of me; and what a pretty dimple she's got!"

But instead of all this, Yourii said nothing, and Riasantzeff asked:

"Have you been expelled for long?"

"For five years," was Yourii's answer.

At these words Nicolai Yegorovitch, who was pacing up and down the room, stopped for a moment and then, recollecting himself, he continued his walk with the regular, precise steps of an old soldier. As yet he was ignorant of the details of his son's exile, and this unexpected news came as a shock.

"What the devil does it all mean?" he muttered to himself.

Lialia understood this movement of her father's. She was afraid of scenes, and tried to change the conversation.

"How foolish of me," she thought, "not to have remembered to tell Anatole!"

But Riasantzeff did not know the real facts, and, replying to Lialia's invitation to have some tea, he again began to question Yourii.

"And what do you think of doing now?"

Nicolai Yegorovitch frowned, and said nothing. Yourii at once knew what his father's silence meant; and before he had reflected upon the consequences of such an answer he replied defiantly and with irritation,

"Nothing for the moment."

"How do you mean—nothing?" asked Nicolai Yegorovitch, stopping short. He had not raised his voice, but its tone clearly conveyed a hidden reproach. "How can you say such a thing? As if I were obliged always to have you round my neck! How can you forget that I am old, and that it is high time that you earned your own living? I say nothing. Live as you like! But can't you yourself understand?" The tone implied all this. And the more it made Yourii feel that his father was right in thinking as he did, the more he took offence.

"Yes, nothing! What do you expect me to do?" he asked provocatively.

Nicolai Yegorovitch was about to make a cutting retort, but said nothing, merely shrugging his shoulders and with measured tread resuming his march from one corner of the room to the other. He was too well-bred to wrangle with his

son on the very day of his arrival. Yourii watched him with
flashing eyes, being hardly able to control himself and ready
on the slightest chance to open the quarrel. Lialia was almost in tears. She glanced imploringly from her brother
to her father. Riasantzeff at last understood the situation,
and he felt so sorry for Lialia, that, clumsily enough, he
turned the talk into another channel.

Slowly, tediously, the evening passed. Yourii would not
admit that he was blameworthy, for he did not agree with
his father that politics were no part of his business. He considered that his father was incapable of understanding the
simplest things, being old and void of intelligence. Unconsciously he blamed him for his old age and his antiquated
ideas: they enraged him. The topics touched upon by
Riasantzeff did not interest him. He scarcely listened, but
steadily watched his father with black, glittering eyes.
Just at supper-time came Novikoff, Ivanoff and Semenoff.

Semenoff was a consumptive student who for some
months past had lived in the town, where he gave lessons.
He was thin, ugly, and looked very delicate. Upon his face,
which was prematurely aged, lay the fleeting shadow of
approaching death. Ivanoff was a schoolmaster, a long-
haired, broad-shouldered, ungainly man. They had been
walking on the boulevard, and hearing of Yourii's arrival
had come to salute him. With their coming things grew
more cheerful. There was laughter and joking, and at
supper much was drunk. Ivanoff distinguished himself in
this respect. During the few days that followed his unfortunate proposal to Lida, Novikoff had become somewhat
calmer. That Lida had refused him might have been ac-

cidental, he thought; it was his fault, indeed, as he ought to have prepared her for such an avowal. Nevertheless it was painful to him to visit the Sanines. Therefore he endeavoured to meet Lida elsewhere, either in the street, or at the house of a mutual friend. She, for her part, pitied him, and, in a way, blamed herself which caused her to treat him with exaggerated cordiality, so that Novikoff once more began to hope.

"What do you say to this?" he asked, just as they were all going. "Let's arrange a picnic at the convent, shall we?"

The convent, situated on a hill at no great distance from the town, was a favourite place for excursions. It was near the river, and the road leading to it was good.

Devoted as she was to every kind of amusement such as bathing, rowing and walks in the woods, Lialia welcomed the idea with enthusiasm.

"Yes, of course! Of course! But when is it to be?"

"Well, why not to-morrow?" said Novikoff.

"Who else shall we ask?" asked Riasantzeff, equally pleased at the prospect of a day's outing. In the woods he would be able to hold Lialia in his arms, to kiss her, and feel that the sweet body he coveted was near.

"Let us see. We are six. Suppose we ask Schafroff?"

"Who is he?" inquired Yourii.

"Oh! he's a young student."

"Very well; and Ludmilla Nicolaijevna will invite Karsavina and Olga Ivanovna."

"Who are they?" asked Yourii once more.

Lialia laughed. "You will see!" she said, kissing the tips of her fingers and looking very mysterious.

"Aha!" said Yourii, smiling. "Well, we shall see what we shall see!"

After some hesitation, Novikoff with an air of indifference, remarked:

"We might ask the Sanines too."

"Oh! we *must* have Lida," cried Lialia, not because she particularly liked the girl, but because she knew of Novikoff's passion, and wished to please him. She was so happy herself in her own love, that she wanted all those about her to be happy also.

"Then we shall have to invite the officers, too," observed Ivanoff, maliciously.

"What does that matter? Let us do so. The more the merrier!"

They all stood at the front door, in the moonlight.

"What a lovely night!" exclaimed Lialia, as unconsciously she drew closer to her lover. She did not wish him to go yet. Riasantzeff with his elbow pressed her warm, round arm.

"Yes, it's a wonderful night!" he replied, giving to these simple words a meaning that they two alone could seize.

"Oh! you, and your night!" muttered Ivanoff in his deep bass. "I'm sleepy, so good-night, sirs!"

And he slouched off, along the street, swinging his arms like the sails of a windmill.

Novikoff and Semenoff went next, and Riasantzeff was a long while saying good-bye to Lialia, pretending to talk about the picnic.

"Now, we must all go to bye-bye," said Lialia, laughingly, when he had taken his leave. Then she sighed, being loth to leave the moonlight, the soft night air, and all for which

her youth and beauty longed. Yourii remembered that his
father had not yet retired to rest, and feared that, if they met,
a painful and useless discussion would be inevitable.

"No!" he replied, his eyes fixed on the faint blue mist
about the river. "No! I don't want to go to sleep. I shall
go out for a while."

"As you like," said Lialia, in her sweet, gentle voice.
Stretching herself, she half closed her eyes like a cat, smiled
at the moonlight, and went in. For a few minutes Yourii
stood there, watching the dark shadows of the houses and
the trees; then he went in the same direction that Semenoff
had taken.

The latter had not gone far, walking slowly and stooping
as he coughed. His black shadow followed him along the
moonlit road. Yourii soon overtook him and at once noticed
how changed he was. During supper Semenoff had joked
and laughed more perhaps than anyone else, but now he
walked along, gloomy and self-absorbed, and in his hollow
cough there was something hopeless and threatening like
the disease from which he suffered.

"Ah! it's you!" he said, somewhat peevishly, as Yourii
thought.

"I wasn't sleepy. I'll walk back with you, if you like."

"Yes, do!" replied Semenoff, carelessly.

"Aren't you cold?" asked Yourii, merely because this distressing cough made him nervous.

"I am always cold," replied Semenoff irritably.

Yourii felt pained, as if he had purposely touched a sore
point.

"Is it a long while since you left the University?" he asked.

Semenoff did not immediately reply.

"A long while," he said, at last.

Yourii then spoke of the feeling that actually existed among the students and of what they considered most important and essential. He began simply and impassively, but by degrees let himself go, expressing himself with fervour and point.

Semenoff said nothing, and listened.

Then Yourii deplored the lack of revolutionary spirit among the masses. It was plain that he felt this deeply.

"Did you read Bebel's last speech?" he asked.

"Yes, I did," replied Semenoff.

"Well, what do you say?"

Semenoff irritably flourished his stick, which had a crooked handle. His shadow similarly waved a long black arm which made Yourii think of the black wings of some infuriated bird of prey.

"What do I say?" he blurted out. "I say that I am going to die."

And again he waved his stick and again the sinister shadow imitated his gesture. This time Semenoff also noticed it.

"Do you see?" said he bitterly. "There, behind me, stands Death, watching my every movement. What's Bebel to me? Just a babbler, who babbles about this. And then some other fool will babble about that. It is all the same to me! If I don't die to-day, I shall die to-morrow."

Yourii made no answer. He felt confused and hurt.

"You, for instance," continued Semenoff, "you think that it's very important, all this that goes on at the University, and what Bebel says. But what I think is that, if you knew for certain, as I do, that you were going to die you would not care in the least what Bebel or Nietzsche or Tolstoi or anybody else said."

Semenoff was silent.

The moon still shone brightly, and ever the black shadow followed in their wake.

"My constitution's done for!" said Semenoff suddenly in quite a different voice, thin and querulous. "If you knew how I dread dying . . . Especially on such a bright, soft night as this," he continued plaintively, turning to Yourii his ugly haggard face and glittering eyes. "Everything lives, and I must die. To you that sounds a hackneyed phrase, I feel certain. 'And I must die.' But it is not from a novel, not taken from a work written with 'artistic truth of presentment.' I really *am* going to die, and to me the words do not seem hackneyed. One day you will not think that they are, either. I am dying, dying, and all is over."

Semenoff coughed again.

"I often think that before long I shall be in utter darkness, buried in the cold earth, my nose fallen in, and my hands rotting, and here in the world all will be just as it is now, while I walk along alive. And you'll be living, and breathing this air, and enjoying this moonlight, and you'll go past my grave where I lie, hideous and corrupted. What do you suppose I care for Bebel, or Tolstoi or a million other gibbering apes?" These last words he uttered with sudden fury. Yourii was too depressed to reply.

"Well, good-night!" said Semenoff faintly. "I must go in."

Yourii shook hands with him, feeling deep pity for him,

hollow-chested, round-shouldered, and with the crooked
stick hanging from a button of his overcoat. He would have
liked to say something consoling that might encourage hope,
but he felt that this was impossible.

"Good-bye!" he said, sighing.

Semenoff raised his cap and opened the gate. The sound
of his footsteps and of his cough grew fainter, and then all
was still. Yourii turned homewards. All that only one short
half-hour ago had seemed to him bright and fair and calm—
the moonlight, the starry heaven, the poplar-trees touched
with silvery splendour, the mysterious shadows—all were
now dead, and cold and terrible as some vast, tremendous
tomb.

On reaching home, he went softly to his room and opened
the window looking on to the garden. For the first time in
his life he reflected that all that had engrossed him, and for
which he had shown such zeal and unselfishness, was really
not the right, the important thing. If, so he thought, some
day, like Semenoff, he were about to die, he would feel no
burning regret that men had not been made happier by his
efforts, nor grief that his life-long ideals remained unreal-
ized. The only grief would be that he must die, must lose
sight, and sense, and hearing, before having had time to taste
all the joys that life could yield.

He was ashamed of such a thought, and, putting it aside,
sought for an explanation.

"Life is conflict."

"Yes, but conflict for whom, if not for one's self, for one's
own place in the sun?"

Thus spake a voice within. Yourii affected not to hear it

and strove to think of something else. But his mind reverted to this thought without ceasing; it tormented him even to bitter tears.

CHAPTER V

WHEN Lida Sanine received Lialia's invitation, she showed it to her brother. She thought that he would refuse; in fact, she hoped as much. She felt that on the moonlit river she would again be drawn to Sarudine, and would again experience that sensation at once delicious and disquieting. At the same time she was ashamed that her brother should know that it was Sarudine, of all people, whom he cordially despised.

But Sanine at once accepted with pleasure.

The day was an ideal one; bright sunlight and a cloudless sky.

"No doubt there will be some nice girls there, whose acquaintance you may care to make," said Lida mechanically.

"Ah! that's good!" said Sanine. "The weather is lovely, too; so let's go!"

At the time appointed, Sarudine and Tanaroff drove up in the large *lineika* belonging to their squadron with two big regimental horses.

"Lidia Petrovna, we are waiting for you," cried Sarudine, looking extremely smart in white, and heavily scented.

Lida in a light gauzy dress with a collar and waist-band of rose-coloured velvet ran down the steps and held out both her hands to Sarudine. For a moment he grasped them tightly, as he glanced admiringly at her person.

"Let us go, let us go," she exclaimed, in excitement and confusion, for she knew the meaning of that glance.

Very soon the *lineika* was swiftly rolling along the little-used road across the steppes. The tall stems of the grass bent beneath the wheels; the fresh breeze as it lightly touched the hair, made the grasses wave on either side. Outside the town they overtook another carriage containing Lialia, Yourii, Riasantzeff, Novikoff, Ivanoff, and Semenoff. They were cramped and uncomfortable, yet all were merry and in high spirits. Only Yourii, after last night's talk, was puzzled by Semenoff's behaviour. He could not understand how the latter could laugh and joke like the others. After all that he had told him, such mirth seemed strange. "Was it all put on?" he thought, as he furtively glanced at Semenoff. He shrank from such an explanation. From both carriages there was a lively interchange of wit and raillery. Novikoff jumped down and ran races through the grass with Lida. Apparently there was a tacit understanding between them to appear to be the best of friends, for they kept merrily teasing each other all the time.

They now approached the hill on whose summit stood the convent with its glittering cupolas and white stone walls. The hill was covered by woods, and the curled tips of the oak-trees looked like wool. There were oak-trees also on the islands at the foot of it, where the broad, calm river flowed.

Leaving the road, the horses trotted over the moist, rich turf in which the carriage-wheels made deep ruts. There was a pleasant odour of earth and of green leaves.

At the appointed place, a meadow, seated on the grass were a young student and two girls wearing the dress of Little Russia. Being the first to arrive, they were busily preparing tea and light refreshments.

When the carriage stopped, the horses snorted and whisked away flies with their tails. Everybody jumped down, enlivened and refreshed by the drive and the sweet country air. Lialia bestowed resounding kisses upon the two girls who were making tea, and introduced them to her brother and to Sanine, whom they regarded with shy curiosity. Lida suddenly remembered that the two men did not know each other. "Allow me," she said to Yourii, "to introduce to you my brother Vladimir." Sanine smiled and grasped Yourii's hand, but the latter scarcely noticed him. Sanine found everybody interesting and liked making new acquaintances. Yourii considered that very few people in this world were interesting, and always felt disinclined to meet strangers. Ivanoff knew Sanine slightly and liked what he had heard about him. He was the first to go up to him and begin talking, while Semenoff ceremoniously shook hands with him.

"Now we can all enjoy ourselves after these tiresome formalities," cried Lialia.

At first a certain stiffness prevailed, for many of the party were complete strangers to each other. But as they began to eat, when the men had had several liqueurs, and the ladies wine, such constraint gave way to mirth. They drank freely, and there was much laughter and joking. Some ran races and others clambered up the hill-side. All around was so calm and bright and the green woods so fair, that nothing sad or sinister could cast its shadow on their souls.

"If everybody were to jump about and run like this," said Riasantzeff, flushed and breathless, "nine-tenths of the world's diseases would not exist."

"Nor the vices either," added Lialia.

"Well, as regards vice there will always be plenty of that," observed Ivanoff, and although no one thought such a remark either witty or wise, it provoked hearty laughter.

As they were having tea, it was the sunset hour. The river gleamed like gold, and through the trees fell the slanting rays of warm red light.

"Now for the boat!" cried Lida, as, holding up her skirts, she ran down to the river-bank. "Who'll get there first?"

Some ran after her, while others followed at a more leisurely pace, and amid much laughter they all got into a large painted boat.

"Let her go!" cried Lida, in a merry voice of command. The boat slid away from the shore leaving behind it two broad stripes on the water that disappeared in ripples at the river's edge.

"Yourii Nicolaijevitch, why are you so silent?" asked Lida.

Yourii smiled. "I've got nothing to say."

"Impossible!" she answered, with a pretty pout, throwing back her head as if she knew that all men thought her irresistible.

"Yourii doesn't like talking nonsense," said Semenoff. "He requires . . ."

"A serious subject, is that it?" exclaimed Lida, interrupting.

"Look! there is a serious subject!" said Sarudine, pointing to the shore.

Where the bank was steep, between the gnarled roots of a rugged oak one could see a narrow aperture, dark and mysterious, which was partially hidden by weeds and grasses.

"What is that?" asked Schafroff, who was unfamiliar

with this part of the country.

"A cavern," replied Ivanoff.

"What sort of a cavern?"

"The devil only knows! They say that once it was a coiners' den. As usual they were all caught. Rather hard lines, wasn't it?" said Ivanoff.

"Perhaps you'd like to start a business of that sort yourself and manufacture sham twenty-copeck pieces?" asked Novikoff.

"Copecks? Not I! Roubles, my friend, roubles!"

"Hm!" muttered Sarudine, shrugging his shoulders. He did not like Ivanoff, whose jokes to him were unintelligible.

"Yes, they were all caught, and the cave was filled up; it gradually collapsed, and no one ever goes into it now. As a child I often used to creep in there. It is a most interesting place."

"Interesting? I should rather think so!" exclaimed Lida.

"Victor Sergejevitsch, suppose you go in? You're one of the brave ones."

"Why?" asked Sarudine, somewhat perplexed.

"I'll go!" exclaimed Yourii, blushing to think that the others would accuse him of showing off.

"It's a wonderful place!" said Ivanoff by way of encouragement.

"Aren't you going too?" asked Novikoff.

"No, I'd rather stop here!"

At this they all laughed.

The boat drew near the bank and a wave of cold air from the cavern passed over their heads.

"For heaven's sake, Yourii, don't do such a silly thing!"

said Lialia, trying to dissuade her brother. "It really is silly of you!"

"Silly? Of course it is." Yourii, smiling, assented. "Semenoff, just give me that candle, will you?"

"Where shall I find it?"

"There is one behind you, in the hamper."

Semenoff coolly produced the candle.

"Are you really going?" asked a tall girl, magnificently proportioned. Lialia called her Sina, her surname being Karsavina.

"Of course I am. Why not?" replied Yourii, striving to show utter indifference. He recollected having done this when engaged in some of his political adventures. The thought for some reason or other was not an agreeable one.

The entrance to the cavern was damp and dark. "Brrr!" exclaimed Sanine, as he looked in. To him it seemed absurd that Yourii should explore a disagreeable, dangerous place simply because others watched him doing it. Yourii, as self-conscious as ever, lighted the candle, thinking inwardly, "I am making myself rather ridiculous, am I not?" But so far from seeming ridiculous, he won admiration, especially from the ladies, who were in an agreeable state of curiosity. bordering on alarm. He waited till the candle burnt more brightly and then, laughing to avoid being laughed at, disappeared in the darkness. The light seemed to have vanished, also. They all suddenly felt concern for his safety and intense, curiosity as to what would happen.

"Look out for wolves!" cried Riasantzeff.

"It's all right. I've got a revolver!" came the answer. It sounded faint and weird.

Yourii advanced slowly and with caution. The sides of the cavern were low, uneven, and damp as the walls of a large cellar. The ground was so irregular that twice Yourii just missed falling into a hole. He thought it would be best to turn back, or to sit down and wait a while so that he could say that he had gone a good way in.

Suddenly he heard the sound of footsteps behind him slipping on the wet clay, and some one breathing hard. He held the light aloft.

"Sinaida Karsavina!" he exclaimed in amazement.

"Her very self!" replied Sina gaily, as she caught up her dress and jumped lightly over a hole. Yourii was glad that she, this merry, handsome girl, had come, and he greeted her with laughing eyes.

"Let us go on," said Sina shyly.

Yourii obediently advanced. No thoughts of danger troubled him now, and he was specially careful to light the way for his companion. He perceived several exits, but all were blocked. In one corner lay a few rotten planks, that looked like the remains of some old coffin.

"Not very interesting, eh?" said Yourii, unconsciously lowering his voice. The mass of earth oppressed him.

"Oh, yes it is!" whispered Sina, and as she looked round her wide eyes gleamed in the candle-light. She was nervous, and instinctively kept close to Yourii for protection. This Yourii noticed. He felt a strange sympathy for his fair, frail companion.

"It is like being buried alive," she continued. "We might scream, but nobody would hear us."

"Of course not," laughed Yourii.

Then a sudden thought caused his brain to reel. This beautiful girl, so fresh, so desirable, was at his mercy. No one could see or hear them. . . . To Yourii such a thought seemed unutterably base. He quickly banished it, and said:

"Suppose we try?"

His voice trembled. Could Sina have read his thoughts?

"Try what?" she asked.

"Suppose I fire?" said Yourii, producing his revolver.

"Will the earth fall in on us?"

"I don't know," he replied, though he felt certain that nothing would happen. "Are you afraid?"

"Oh no! Fire away!" said Sina, as she retreated a step or so. Holding out the revolver, he fired. There was a flash, and a dense cloud of smoke enveloped them, as the echo of the report slowly died away.

"There! That's all," said Yourii.

"Let us go back."

They retraced their steps, but as Sina walked out in front of Yourii the sight of her round, firm hips again brought sensuous thoughts to his mind that he found it hard to ignore.

"I say, Sina Karsavina!" His voice faltered. "I am going to ask you an interesting psychological question. How was it that you did not feel afraid to come here with me? You said yourself that if we screamed no one would hear us. . . . You don't know me in the least!"

Sina blushed in the darkness and was silent. At last she murmured: "Because I thought that you were to be trusted."

"And suppose that you had been mistaken?"

"Then, I should . . . have drowned myself," said Sina almost inaudibly.

The words filled Yourii with pity. His passion subsided, and he felt suddenly solaced.

"What a good little girl!" he thought, sincerely touched by such frank, simple modesty.

Proud of her reply, and gratified by his silent approval, Sina smiled at him, as they returned to the entrance of the cavern. Meanwhile she kept wondering why his question had not seemed offensive or shameful to her, but on the contrary, quite agreeable.

CHAPTER VI

AFTER waiting a while at the entrance, and making sundry jokes at the expense of Sina and Yourii, the others wandered along the river-bank. The men lit cigarettes and threw the matches into the water, watching them make large circles on the surface of the stream. Lida, with arms a-kimbo, tripped along, singing softly as she went, and her pretty little feet in dainty yellow shoes now and again executed an impromptu dance. Lialia picked flowers, which she flung at Riasant-zeff, caressing him with her eyes.

"What do you say to a drink?" Ivanoff asked Sanine.

"Splendid idea!" replied the other.

Getting into the boat, they uncorked several bottles of beer and proceeded to drink.

"Shocking intemperance!" cried Lialia, pelting them with tufts of grass.

"First-rate stuff!" said Ivanoff, smacking his lips.

Sanine laughed.

"I have often wondered why people are so dead against alcohol," he said jestingly. "In my opinion only a drunken man lives his life as it ought to be lived."

"That is, like a brute!" replied Novikoff from the bank.

"Very likely," said Sanine, "but at any rate a drunken man only does just that which he wants to do. If he has a mind to sing, he sings; if he wants to dance, he dances; and is not ashamed to be merry and jolly."

"And he fights too, sometimes," remarked Riasantzeff.

"Yes, so he does. That is, when men don't understand how to drink."

"And do you like fighting when you are drunk?" asked Novikoff.

"No," replied Sanine, "I'd rather fight when I am sober, but when I'm drunk I'm the most good-natured person imaginable, for I have forgotten so much that is mean and vile."

"Everybody is not like that," said Riasantzeff.

"I'm sorry for them, that's all," replied Sanine. "Besides, what others are like does not interest me in the least."

"One can hardly say that," observed Novikoff.

"Why not, if it is the truth?"

"A fine truth, indeed!" exclaimed Lialia, shaking her head.

"The finest I know, anyhow," replied Ivanoff for Sanine.

Lida, who had been singing loudly, suddenly stopped, looking vexed.

"They don't seem in any hurry," she said.

"Why should they hurry?" replied Ivanoff. "It is a great mistake to do anything in a hurry."

"And Sina, I suppose she is the heroine *sans peur et sans reproche?*" said Lida ironically.

Tanaroff's thoughts were too much for him at this juncture. He burst out laughing, and then looked thoroughly sheepish. Lida, her hands on her hips and swaying gracefully to and fro, turned to look at him.

"I dare say they are enjoying themselves," she observed with a shrug of the shoulders.

"Hark!" said Riasantzeff, as the sound of firing reached them.

"That was a shot," exclaimed Schafroff.

"What's the meaning of it?" cried Lialia, as she nervously clung to her lover's arm.

"Don't be frightened! If it is a wolf, at this time of year they are tame, and would never attack two people." Thus Riasantzeff sought to reassure her, while secretly annoyed at Yourii's childish freak.

"Tomfoolery!" growled Schafroff, who was equally vexed.

"They are coming, they are coming! Don't worry!" said Lida contemptuously.

A sound of footsteps could now be heard, and soon Sina and Yourii emerged from the darkness.

Yourii blew out the light and smiled uneasily, as he was not sure of his reception. He was covered with yellow clay, and Sina's shoulders bore traces of this, for she had rubbed against the side of the cavern.

"Well?" asked Semenoff languidly.

"It was quite interesting in there," said Yourii half apologetically. "Only the passage does not lead very far. It has been filled up. We saw some rotten planks lying about."

"Did you hear us fire?" asked Sina, and her eyes sparkled.

"My friends," shouted Ivanoff, interrupting, "we have drunk all the beer, and our souls are abundantly refreshed. Let us be going."

By the time that the boat reached a broader part of the stream the moon had already risen. It was a strangely calm, clear evening. Above and below, in the heaven as in the river, the golden stars gleamed. It was, as if the boat was suspended between two fathomless spaces. The dark woods at the edge of the stream had a look of mystery. A nightin-

gale sang, and all listened in silence, not believing it to be a
bird, but rather some joyous dreamer in the gloom. Removing her large straw hat, Sina Karsavina now began to sing
a Russian popular air, sweet and sad like all Russian songs.
Her voice, a high soprano, though not powerful, was sympathetic in quality.

Ivanoff muttered, "That's sweet!" and Sanine exclaimed
"Charming!" When she had finished they all clapped their
hands and the sound was echoed strangely in the dark woods
on either side.

"Sing something else, Sinotschka!" cried Lialia; "or, better
still, recite one of your own poems."

"So you're a poetess, too?" asked Ivanoff. "How many
gifts does the good God bestow upon his creatures!"

"Is that a bad thing?" asked Sina in confusion.

"No, it's a very good thing," replied Sanine.

"If a girl's got youth and good looks, what does she want
with poetry, I should like to know?" observed Ivanoff.

"Never mind! Recite something, Sinotschka, do!" cried
Lialia, amorous and tender.

Sina smiled, and looked away self-consciously before she
began to recite in her clear, musical voice the following lines:

> Oh! love, my own true love,
> To thee I'll never tell it,
> Never to thee I'll tell my burning love!
> But I will close those amorous eyes,
> And they shall guard my secret well.
> Only by days of yearning is it known.
> The calm blue nights, the golden stars,
> The dreaming woods that whisper in the night,

These, yes, they know it, but are dumb;
They will not show the mystery of my great love.

Once more there was great enthusiasm, and they all loudly applauded Sina, not because her little poem was a good one, but because it was expressive of their mood, and because they were all longing for love and love's delicious sorrow.

"O Night, O Day! O lustrous eyes of Sina, I pray you tell me that it is I, the happy man!" cried Ivanoff ecstatically in a deep bass voice which startled them all.

"Well, I can assure you that it is not you," replied Semenoff.

"Ah! woe is me!" wailed Ivanoff; and everybody laughed.

"Are my verses bad?" Sina asked Yourii.

He did not think that they had much originality, for they reminded him of hundreds of similar effusions. But Sina was so pretty and looked at him with those dark eyes of hers in such a pleading way that he gravely replied:

"I thought them quite charming and melodious."

Sina smiled, surprised that such praise could please her so much.

"Ah! you don't know my Sinotschka yet!" said Lialia, "she is all that is beautiful and melodious."

"You don't say so!" exclaimed Ivanoff.

"Yes, indeed I do!" persisted Lialia. "Her voice is beautiful and melodious, and so are her poems; she herself is a beauty; her name, even, is beautiful and melodious."

"Oh! my goodness! What more can you say than that!" cried Ivanoff. "But I am quite of your opinion."

At all these compliments Sina blushed with pleasure and

confusion.

"It is time to go home," said Lida abruptly. She did not like to hear Sina praised, for she considered herself far prettier, cleverer, and more interesting.

"Are you going to sing something?" asked Sanine.

"No," she replied, "I am not in voice."

"It really is time to be going," observed Riasantzeff, for he remembered that early next morning he must be in the dissecting-room of the hospital. All the others wished that they could have stayed for a while. On their homeward way they were silent, feeling tired and contented. As before, though unseen, the tall stems of the grasses bent beneath the carriage-wheels, and the dust soon settled on the white road again. The bare grey fields looked vast and limitless in the faint light of the moon.

CHAPTER VII

THREE days afterwards, late in the evening, Lida came home sad, tired, and heavy-hearted. On reaching her room, she stood still, with hands clasped, and stared at the floor. She suddenly realized, to her horror, that in her relations with Sarudine she had gone too far. For the first time since that strange moment of irreparable weakness she perceived what a humiliating hold this empty-headed officer had over her, inferior as he was to herself in every way. She must now come if he called; she could no longer trifle with him as she liked, submitting to his kisses or laughingly resisting them. Now, like a slave, she must endure and obey.

How this had come about she could not comprehend. As always, she had ruled him, had borne with his amorous attentions; all had been as agreeable, amusing, and exciting, as heretofore. Then came a moment when her whole frame seemed on fire and her brain clouded as by a mist, annihilating all except the one mad desire to plunge into the abyss. It was as if the earth gave way beneath her feet; she lost control of her limbs, conscious only of two magnetic eyes that gazed boldly into hers. Her whole being was thrilled and shaken with passion; she became the sacrifice of overwhelming lust; and yet she longed once more that such passionate experiences might be repeated. At the very thought of it all Lida trembled; she raised her shoulders and hid her

65

face in her hands. With faltering steps she crossed the room and opened the window. For a long while she gazed at the moon that hung just above the garden, and in distant foliage a nightingale sang. Grief oppressed her. She felt strangely agitated by a sense of remorse and of wounded pride to think that she had ruined her life for a silly, shallow man, and that her false step had been foolish, base, and, indeed, accidental. The future seemed threatening; but she sought to dissipate her fears by obstinate bravado.

"Well, I did it, and there's an end of it!" she said to herself, frowning and striving to find some sort of grim satisfaction from this hackneyed phrase. "What nonsense it all is! I wanted to do it and I did it; and I felt so happy—oh, so happy! It would have been silly not to enjoy myself when the moment came. I must not think of it; it can't be helped, now."

She languidly withdrew from the window and began to undress, letting her clothes slip from her on to the floor. "After all, one only lives once," she thought, shivering at the touch of the cool night air on her bare shoulders and arms. "What should I have gained by waiting till I was lawfully married? And of what good would that have been to me? It's all the same thing! What is there to worry about?"

All at once it seemed to her that in this hazard she had got all that was best and most interesting; and that now, free as a bird, an eventful life of happiness and pleasure lay before her.

"I'll love if I will; if I don't, then I won't!" sang Lida softly to herself, thinking meanwhile that her voice was a much better one than Sina Karsavina's. "Oh! it's all nonsense! If I like, I'll give myself to the devil!" Thus she made sudden answer to her thoughts, holding her bare arms above her head so that her bosom shook.

"Aren't you asleep yet, Lida?" said Sanine's voice outside the window.

Lida started back in alarm, and then, with a smile, flung a shawl round her shoulders as she approached the window.

"What a fright you gave me!" she said.

Sanine came nearer and leant with both elbows on the window-sill. His eyes shone, and he smiled.

"There was no need for that!" he muttered playfully.

Lida looked round.

"Without a shawl you looked much nicer," he said in a low voice, impressively.

Lida looked at him in amazement, and instinctively drew the shawl tighter round her.

Sanine laughed. In confusion, she also leant upon the window-sill, and now she felt his breath on her cheek.

"What a beauty you are!" he said.

Lida glanced swiftly at him, fearful of what she thought she could read in his face. With her whole body she felt that her brother's eyes were fixed upon her, and she turned away in horror. It was so terrible, so loathsome, that her heart seemed frozen. Every man looked at her just like that, and she liked it, but for her brother to do so was incredible, impossible. Recovering herself, she said smiling:

"Yes, I know."

Sanine calmly watched her. The shawl and her chemise had slipped when she leant on the window-sill, and partly disclosed her tender bosom, white in the moonlight.

"Men always build up a Wall of China between themselves and happiness," he said in a low, trembling voice. Lida was terrified.

"How do you mean?" she asked faintly, her eyes still fixed on the garden for fear of encountering his. To her it seemed that something was going to happen of which one hardly dared to think. Yet she had no doubt as to what it was. It was awful, hideous, and yet interesting. Her brain was on fire; she could scarcely see, as with horror and yet with curiosity she felt hot breath against her cheek that stirred her hair and sent shivers through her frame.

"Why, like this!" replied Sanine, and his voice faltered.

As if by an electric shock, Lida started backwards and, without knowing what she did, leant over the table and blew out the light.

"It is bed-time," she said, and shut the window.

The light having been extinguished, it seemed less dark out of doors, and Sanine's figure was clearly discernible, his features appearing bluish in the moonlight. He stood in the long, dew-drenched grass and smiled.

Lida left the window and sat down mechanically on her bed. She trembled in every limb, unable to collect her thoughts, and the sound of Sanine's footsteps on the grass outside set her heart beating violently.

"Am I going mad?" she asked herself in disgust. "How awful! A chance phrase like that to put such thoughts into my head! Is this erotomania? Am I really so bad, so depraved? I must have sunk very low to think of such a thing!"

Burying her face in the pillows, she wept bitterly.

"Why am I weeping?" she thought, not knowing the reason for such tears, but feeling miserable, humiliated, and unhappy. She wept because she had yielded herself to Sarudine, because she was no longer a proud, pure maiden, and because of that insulting, horrible look in her brother's eyes. Formerly he would never have looked at her like that. It was, so she thought, because she had fallen.

But the bitterest, most harassing thought of all was that she had now become a woman, and that as long as she was young, strong, and good-looking her best powers must be at the service of men and devoted to their gratification, while the greater enjoyment she procured for them and for herself the more would they despise her.

"Why should they? Who gave them this right? Am I not free just as much as they are?" she asked herself, as she gazed into the dreary darkness of her room. "Shall I never get to know another, better life?"

Her whole youthful physique imperiously told her that she had a right to take from life all that was interesting, pleasurable and necessary to her; and that she had a right to do whatever she chose with her strong, beautiful body that belonged to her alone. But this idea was lost in a tangle of confused and conflicting thoughts.

CHAPTER VIII

For some time past Yourii Svarogitsch had been working at painting, of which he was fond, and to which he devoted all his spare time. It had once been his dream to become an artist, but want of money, in the first place, and also his political activity prevented this, so that now he painted occasionally, as a pastime, without any special end in view.

For this reason, indeed, and because he had no training, art gave him no pleasant satisfactions; it was a source of chagrin and of disenchantment. Whenever his work did not prove successful, he became irritable and depressed; if, on the other hand, it came out well, he fell into a sort of gloomy reverie, conscious of the futility of his efforts that brought him neither happiness nor success. Yourii had taken a great fancy to Sina Karsavina. He liked tall, well-formed young women with fine voices and romantic eyes. He thought her beauty and purity of soul were what attracted him, though really it was because she was handsome and desirable. However, he tried to persuade himself that, for him, her charm was a spiritual, not a physical one, this being, as he thought, a nobler, finer definition, though it was precisely this maidenly purity and innocence of hers which fired his blood and aroused desire. Ever since the evening when he first met her, he had felt a vague yet vehement longing to sully her innocence, a longing indeed that the presence of any handsome woman provoked.

And now that his thoughts were set on a comely girl, blithe, wholesome, and full of the joy of life, Yourii had an idea that he would paint "Life." As most new ideas were wont to do, this one stirred him to enthusiasm, and on this occasion he believed that he would bring his task to a successful end.

Having prepared a huge canvas, he set to work with feverish haste, as if he dreaded delay. When he first touched the canvas with colour, producing a harmonious and pleasing effect, he felt a thrill of delight, and the picture that was to be stood clearly before him with all its details. As, however, the work progressed, so technical difficulties became more numerous, and with these Yourii felt unable to cope. All that in his imagination seemed luminous and beautiful and strong, became thin and feeble on the canvas. Details no longer fascinated him, but were annoying and depressing. In fact, he ignored them and began to paint in a broad, slap-dash style. Thus, instead of a clear, powerful portrayal of life, the picture became ever more plain of a tawdry, slovenly female. There was nothing original or charming about such a dull stereotyped piece of work, so he thought; a veritable imitation of a Moukh drawing, banal in idea as in execution; and, as usual, Yourii became sad and gloomy.

Had it not for some reason or other seemed shameful to weep, he would have wept, hiding his face in the pillow, and sobbing aloud. He longed to complain to some one about something, but not about his own incompetence. Instead of this he gazed ruefully at the picture thinking that life generally was tedious and sad and feeble, containing nothing of

interest to him, personally. It horrified him to look forward
to living, as he would have to do, for many years in this little town.

"Why, it is simply death!" thought Yourii, as his brow
grew cold as ice. Then he felt a desire to paint "Death."
Seizing a knife he angrily began to scrape off his picture of
"Life." It vexed him that that which he had wrought with
such enthusiasm should disappear with such difficulty. The
colour did not come off easily; the knife slipped twice and cut
the canvas. Then he found that chalk would make no mark
on the oil paint. This greatly troubled him. With a brush
he commenced to sketch in his subject in ochre, and then
painted slowly, carelessly, in a spiritless, dejected way. His
present work, however, did not lose, but gained by such
slipshod methods and by the dull, heavy colour scheme.
The original idea of "Death" soon disappeared of itself; and
so Yourii proceeded to depict "Old Age" as a lean hag tot-
tering along a rough road in the dusk. The sun had sunk,
and against the livid sky sombre crosses were seen *en silhouette.* Beneath the weight of a heavy black coffin the woman's
bony shoulders were bent, and her expression was mournful
and despairing, as with one foot she touched the brink of an
open grave. It was a picture appalling in its misery and
gloom. At lunch-time they sent for Yourii, but he did not
go, and continued working. Later on, Novikoff came to
tell him something, but he neither listened nor replied.
Novikoff sighed, and sat down on the sofa. He liked to be
quiet and think matters over. He only came to see Yourii,
because, at home, by himself, he was sad and worried. Lida's
refusal still distressed him, and he could not be sure if he

felt grieved or humiliated. As a straightforward, indolent fellow, he had so far heard nothing of the local gossip concerning Lida and Sarudine. He was not jealous, but only sorrowful that the dream which brought happiness so near to him had fled.

Novikoff thought that his life was a failure, but it never occurred to him to end it, since to live on was futile. On the contrary, now that his life had become a torture to him, he considered that it was his duty to devote it to others, putting his own happiness aside. Without being able to account for it, he had a vague desire to throw up everything and go to St. Petersburg where he could renew his connection with "the party" and rush headlong to death. This was a fine, lofty thought, so he believed, and the knowledge that it was his lessened his grief, and even gladdened him. He became grand in his own eyes, crowned as with a shining aureole, and his sadly reproachful attitude towards Lida almost moved him to tears.

Then he suddenly felt bored. Yourii went on painting, and gave him no attention whatever. Novikoff got up lazily and approached the picture. It was still unfinished, and for that reason produced the effect of a somewhat powerful sketch. Yourii had got as far as he could go. Novikoff thought it was wonderful, as with open mouth he gazed in childish admiration at the artist.

"Well?" said Yourii, stepping backwards.

Personally, he thought it the most interesting picture that he had ever seen, though certainly it had defects both obvious and considerable. Why he was of this opinion he could not tell, but if Novikoff had thought the picture a bad one, he would have felt thoroughly hurt and annoyed. However, Novikoff murmured ecstatically,

"Ve ... ry fine indeed!"

Yourii felt as if he were a genius despising his own work. He sighed and flung down his brush which stained the edge of the couch, and he moved away without looking at the picture.

"Ah! my friend!" he exclaimed. He was on the point of confessing to himself and to Novikoff the doubt which destroyed his pleasure in succeeding, as he felt that he could never do anything with what was now a promising sketch. However, after a moment of reflection he merely said:

"All that is of no use at all."

Novikoff thought that this was pose on his friend's part, and mindful of his own bitter disappointment he inwardly observed:

"That's true."

Then after a while he asked:

"How do you mean that it is of no use?"

To this question Yourii could give no exact answer, and he remained silent. Novikoff examined the picture once more, and then lay down on the sofa.

"I read your article in the *Krai*," he said. "It was pretty hot."

"The deuce take it!" replied Yourii, angrily, yet unable to account for his anger, as he remembered Semenoff's words. "What good will it do? It won't stop executions and robberies and violence; they will go on just as before. Articles won't help matters. For what purpose, pray? To be read by two or three idiots! Much good that is! After all, what busi-

ness is it of mine? And why dash one's brains out against
a wall?"

Passing before his eyes, Yourii seemed to see the early
years of his political activity; the secret meetings, propa-
ganda, risks and reverses, his own enthusiasm and the profound apathy of those whom he was so eager to save. He
walked up and down the room, gesticulating.

"Then, it is not worth while doing anything," drawled
Novikoff, and, thinking of Sanine, he added,

"Egoists, that's all you are!"

"No, it's not!" replied Yourii vehemently, influenced by
his memories of the past and by the dusk that gave a grey
look to all things in the room.

"If one speaks of Humanity, of what good are all our
efforts in the cause of constitutions or of revolutions if one
cannot even approximately estimate what humanity really
requires? Perhaps in this liberty of which we dream lie the
germs of future degeneracy, and man, having realized his
ideal, will go back, walking once more on all fours? Thus,
all would have to be recommenced. And if I care for nothing but myself, what then? What do I gain by it? The most
I could do would be to get fame by my talents and achieve-
ments, intoxicated by the respect of my inferiors, that is to
say by the respect of those whom I do not esteem and whose
veneration ought to be valueless to me. And then? To go
on living, living until the grave—nothing after that! And the
crown of laurels would fit my skull so closely, that I should
soon find it irksome!"

"Always about himself!" muttered Novikoff, mockingly.

Yourii did not hear him, being morbidly pleased with

his own eloquence. There was a beautiful gloom about his utterances, so he thought; they seemed to ennoble him, to heighten his sense of self-respect.

"At the worst, I should become a genius misjudged, a ridiculous dreamer, a theme for humorous tales, a foolish individual, of no use to anybody!"

"Aha!" cried Novikoff, as he rose from the couch. "Of no use to anybody. You admit that yourself, then?"

"How absurd you are!" exclaimed Yourii. "Do you really think that I don't know for what to live and in what to believe? Possibly I should gladly submit to crucifixion if I believed that my death could save the world. But I don't believe this; and whatever I did would never alter the course of history; moreover, my help would be so slight, so insignificant, that the world would not have suffered a jot if I had never existed. Yet, for the sake of such infinitesimal help, I am obliged to live, and suffer, and sorrowfully wait for death."

Yourii did not perceive that he was now talking of something quite different, replying, not to Novikoff, but to his own strange, depressing thoughts. Suddenly he remembered Semenoff, and stopped short. A cold shiver ran down his spine.

"The fact is, I dread the inevitable," he said in a low tone, as he looked stolidly at the darkening window. "It is natural, I know, and that I can do nothing to avoid it, but yet it is awful—hideous!"

Novikoff, though inwardly horrified at the truth of such a statement, replied:

"Death is a necessary physiological phenomenon."

"What a fool!" thought Yourii, as he irritably exclaimed:

"Good gracious me! What does it matter if our death is necessary to anyone else or not?"

"How about your crucifixion?"

"That is a different thing," replied Yourii, with some hesitation.

"You are contradicting yourself," observed Novikoff in a slightly patronizing tone.

This greatly annoyed Yourii. Thrusting his fingers through his unkempt black hair, he vehemently retorted:

"I never contradict myself. It stands to reason that if, of my own free will, I choose to die——"

"It's all the same," continued Novikoff obdurately, in the same tone. "All of you want fireworks, applause, and the rest of it. It's nothing else but egoism!"

"What if it is? That won't alter matters."

The discussion became confused. Yourii felt that he had not meant to say that, but the thread escaped him which a moment before had seemed so clear and tense. He paced up and down the room, endeavouring to overcome his vexation, as he said to himself:

"Sometimes one is not in the humour. At other times one can speak as clearly as if the words were set before one's eyes. Sometimes I seem to be tongue-tied, and I express myself clumsily. Yes, that often happens."

They were both silent. Yourii at last stopped by the window and took up his cap.

"Let us go for a stroll," he said.

"All right," Novikoff readily assented, secretly hoping, while joyful yet distressed, that he might meet Lida Sanine.

CHAPTER IX

THEY walked up and down the boulevard once or twice, meeting no one they knew, and they listened to the band which was playing as usual in the garden. It was a very poor performance; the music being harsh and discordant, but at a distance it sounded languorous and sad. They only met men and women joking and laughing, whose noisy merriment seemed at variance with the mournful music and the dreary evening. It irritated Yourii. At the end of the boulevard Sanine joined them, greeting them effusively. Yourii did not like him, so conversation was scarcely brisk. Sanine kept on laughing at everybody he saw. Later on·they met Ivanoff, and Sanine went off with him.

"Where are you going?" asked Novikoff.

"To treat my friend," replied Ivanoff, producing a bottle of vodka which he showed to them in triumph.

Sanine laughed.

To Yourii this vodka and laughter seemed singularly coarse and vulgar. He turned away in disgust. Sanine observed this, but said nothing.

"God, I thank Thee, that I am not as other men," exclaimed Ivanoff mockingly.

Yourii reddened. "A stale joke like that into the bargain!" he thought, as, shrugging his shoulders contemptuously, he walked away.

"Novikoff, guileless Pharisee, come along with us!" cried Ivanoff.

"What for?"

"To have a drink."

Novikoff glanced round him ruefully, but Lida was not to be seen.

"Lida is at home, doing penance for her sins!" laughed Sanine.

"What nonsense!" exclaimed Novikoff testily. "I've got to see a patient . . ."

"Who is quite able to die without your help," said Ivanoff. "For that matter, we can polish off the vodka without your help, either."

"Suppose I get drunk?" thought Novikoff. "All right! I'll come," he said.

As they went away, Yourii could hear at a distance Ivanoff's gruff bass voice and Sanine's careless, merry laugh. He walked once more along the boulevard. Girlish voices called to him through the dusk. Sina Karsavina and the schoolmistress Dubova were sitting on a bench. It was now getting dark, and their figures were hardly discernible. They wore dark dresses, were without hats, and carried books in their hands. Yourii hastened to join them.

"Where have you been?" he asked.

"At the library," replied Sina.

Without speaking, her companion moved to make room for Yourii who would have preferred to sit next to Sina, but, being shy, he took a seat beside the ugly school-teacher, Dubova.

"Why do you look so utterly miserable?" asked Dubova,

pursing up her thin, dry lips, as was her wont.

"What makes you think that I am miserable? On the contrary I am in excellent spirits. Somewhat bored, perhaps."

"Ah! that's because you've nothing to do," said Dubova.

"Have you so much to do, then?"

"At any rate, I have not the time to weep."

"I am not weeping, am I?"

"Well," said Dubova, teasing him, "you're in the sulks."

"My life," replied Yourii, "has caused me to forget what laughing is."

This was said in such a bitter tone that there was a sudden silence.

"A friend of mine told me that my life is most instructive," said Yourii after a pause, though no one had ever made such a statement to him.

"In what way?" asked Sina cautiously.

"As an example of how not to live."

"Oh! do tell us all about it. Perhaps we might profit by the lesson," said Dubova.

Yourii considered that his life was an absolute failure, and that he himself was the most luckless and wretched of men. In such a belief there lay a certain mournful solace, and it was pleasant to him to complain about his own life and mankind in general. To men he never spoke of such things, feeling instinctively that they would not believe him, but to women, especially if they were young and pretty, he was ever ready to talk at length about himself. He was good-looking, and talked well, so women always felt for him affectionate pity. On this occasion also, if jocular at the outset, Yourii relapsed into his usual tone; discoursing at great length about his own life. From his own description he appeared to be a man of extraordinary powers, cramped and crushed by the force of circumstances, misunderstood by his party, and one who by unlucky chance and human folly was doomed to be just a mere student in exile instead of a leader of the people! Like all extremely self-satisfied persons Yourii entirely failed to perceive that all this in no way proved his extraordinary powers, and that men of genius were surrounded by just such associates, and hampered by just such misfortunes. It seemed to him that he alone was the victim of an inexorable destiny. As he talked well and with great vivacity and point, what he said sounded true enough, so that girls believed him, pitied him, and sympathized with him in his misfortunes. The band was still playing its sad, discordant tunes, the evening was gloomy and depressing, and they all three felt in a melancholy mood. When Yourii ceased talking, Dubova, meditating on her own dull, monotonous existence and vanishing youth without joy or love, asked him in a low voice,

"Tell me, Yourii, has the thought of suicide never crossed your mind?"

"Why do you ask me that?"

"Oh! well, I don't know . . ."

They said no more.

"You are on the committee, aren't you?" asked Sina eagerly.

"Yes," replied Yourii curtly, as if unwilling to admit the fact, but in reality pleased to do so, because he thought that to this charming girl he would appear weirdly interesting. He then walked back with them to their house, and on the way they laughed and talked much. All depression had vanished.

"How nice he is!" said Sina, when Yourii had gone.

Dubova shook her finger threateningly:

"Mind that you don't fall in love with him."

"What an idea!" laughed Sina, though secretly afraid.

Yourii reached home in a brighter, more hopeful mood. He went to look at the picture that he had begun. It produced no impression upon him, and he lay down contentedly to sleep. That night in dreams he had visions of fair women, radiant and alluring.

CHAPTER X

On the following evening Yourii went to the same spot where he had met Sina Karsavina and her companion. Throughout the day he had thought with pleasure of his talk with them on the previous evening, and he hoped to meet them again, discuss the same subjects, and perceive the same look of sympathy and tenderness in Sina's gentle eyes.

It was a calm evening. The air was warm, and a slight dust floated above the streets. Except for one or two passers-by, the boulevard was absolutely deserted. Yourii walked slowly along, his eyes fixed on the ground.

"How boring!" he thought. "What am I to do?"

Suddenly Schafroff, the student, walking briskly, and swinging his arm, approached him with a friendly smile on his face.

"Why are you dawdling along like this, eh?" he asked, stopping short, and giving Yourii a big, strong hand.

"Oh! I am bored to death, and there's nothing to do. Where are you going?" asked Yourii, in a languid, patronizing tone. He always spoke thus to Schafroff, because, as a former member of the revolutionary committee he looked upon the lad as just an amateur revolutionist. Schafroff smiled as one thoroughly pleased with himself.

"We have got a lecture to-day," he said, pointing to a packet of thin pamphlets in coloured wrappers. Yourii mechanically took one, and, opening it, read the long dry preface to a popular Socialistic address, once well known to him, but which he had quite forgotten.

"Where is the lecture to be given?" he asked with the same slightly contemptuous smile as he handed back the pamphlet.

"At the school," replied Schafroff, mentioning the one at which Sina Karsavina and Dubova were teachers. Yourii remembered that Lialia had once told him about these lectures, but he had paid no attention.

"May I come with you?" he asked.

"Why, of course!" replied Schafroff, eager to assent to this proposal. He looked upon Yourii as a real agitator, and, over-estimating his political abilities, felt a reverence for him that bordered on affection.

"I am greatly interested in such matters." Yourii felt it necessary to say this, being all the while glad that he had now got an engagement for the evening, and that he would see Sina again.

"Why, yes, of course," said Schafroff.

"Then, let us go."

They walked quickly along the boulevard and crossed the bridge, from each side of which came humid airs, and they soon reached the school where people had already assembled.

In the large, dark room with its rows of benches and desks the white cloth used for the magic lantern was dimly visible, and there were sounds of suppressed laughter. At the window, through which could be seen the dark green boughs of trees in twilight, stood Lialia and Dubova. They gleefully greeted Yourii.

"I am so glad that you have come!" said Lialia.

Dubova shook him vigorously by the hand.

"Why don't you begin?" asked Yourii, as he furtively glanced round, hoping to see Sina.

"So Sinaida Pavlovna doesn't attend these lectures?" he observed with evident disappointment.

At that moment a lucifer-match flashed close to the lecturer's desk on the platform, illuminating Sina's features. The light shone upon her pretty fresh face; she was smiling gaily.

"Don't I attend these lectures?" she exclaimed, as, bending down to Yourii, she held out her hand. He gladly grasped it without speaking, and leaning lightly on him she sprang from the platform. He felt her sweet, wholesome breath close to his face.

"It is time to begin," said Schafroff, who came in from the adjoining room.

The school attendant with heavy tread walked round the room, lighting one by one the large lamps which soon shed a bright light. Schafroff opened the door leading to the passage, and said in a loud voice: "This way, please!"

Shyly at first, and then in noisy haste, the people entered the lecture-room. Yourii scrutinized them closely; his keen interest as a propagandist was roused. There were old folk, young men, and children. No one sat in the front row; but, later on, it was filled by several ladies whom Yourii did not know; by the fat school-inspector; and by masters and mistresses of the elementary school for boys and girls. The rest of the room was full of men in caftans and long coats, soldiers, peasants, women, and a great many children in coloured shirts and frocks.

Yourii sat beside Sina at a desk and listened while Schafroff read, calmly, but badly, a paper on universal suffrage. He had a hard, monotonous voice and everything he read sounded like a column of statistics. Yet everybody listened attentively with the exception of the intellectual people in the front row, who soon grew restless and began whispering to each other. This annoyed Yourii, and he felt sorry that Schafroff should read so badly. The latter was obviously tired, so Yourii said to Sina:

"Suppose I finish reading it for him? What do you say?"

Sina shot a kindly glance at him from beneath her drooping eyelashes.

"Oh! yes, do read! I wish you would."

"Do you think it will matter?" he whispered, smiling at her as if she were his accomplice.

"Matter? Not in the least. Everybody will be delighted."

During a pause, she suggested this to Schafroff, who being tired and aware how badly he had read, accepted with pleasure.

"Of course! By all means!" he exclaimed, as usual, giving up his place to Yourii.

Yourii was fond of reading, and read excellently. Without looking at anyone, he walked to the desk on the platform and began in a loud, well modulated voice. Twice he looked down at Sina, and each time he encountered her bright, expressive glance. He smiled at her in pleasure and confusion, and then, turning to his book, began to read louder and with greater emphasis. To him it seemed as if he were doing a most excellent and interesting thing. When he had finished there was some applause in the front seats. Yourii bowed gravely, and as he left the platform he smiled at Sina as much as to say, "I did that for your sake." There was some murmuring, and a noise of chairs being pushed back as the listeners rose to go. Yourii was introduced to two ladies who complimented him on his performance. Then the lamps were put out and the room became dark.

"Thank you very much," said Schafroff as he warmly shook Yourii's hand. "I wish that we always had some one to read to us like that."

Lecturing was his business, and so he felt obliged to Yourii as if the latter had done him a personal service, although he thanked him in the name of the people. Schafroff laid stress on the word "people." "So little is done here for the people," he said, as if he were telling Yourii a great secret, "and if anything *is* done, it is in a half-hearted, careless way. It is most extraordinary. To amuse a parcel of bored gentlefolk dozens of first-rate actors, singers and lecturers are engaged, but for the people a lecturer like myself is quite good enough." Schafroff smiled at his own bland irony. "Everybody's quite satisfied. What more do they want?"

"That is quite true," said Dubova. "Whole columns in the newspapers are devoted to actors and their wonderful performances; it is positively revolting; whereas here . . ."

"Yet what a good work we're doing!" said Schafroff, with conviction, as he gathered his pamphlets together.

"Sancta Simplicitas!" ejaculated Yourii inwardly.

Sina's presence, however, and his own success inclined him to be tolerant. Indeed Schafroff's utter ingenuousness almost touched him.

"Where shall we go now?" asked Dubova, as they came out into the street.

Outside it was not nearly so dark as in the lecture-room, and in the sky a few stars shone.

"Schafroff and I are going to the Ratoffs'," said Dubova. "Will you take Sina home?"

"With pleasure," said Yourii.

Sina lodged with Dubova in a small house that stood in a large, barren-looking garden. All the way thither she and Yourii talked of the lecture and its impression upon them, so that Yourii felt more and more convinced that he had done a good and great thing. As they reached the house, Sina said:

"Won't you come in for a moment?" Yourii gladly accepted. She opened the gate, and they crossed a little grass-grown courtyard beyond which lay the garden.

"Go into the garden, will you?" said Sina, laughing. "I would ask you to come indoors, but I am afraid things are rather untidy, as I have been out ever since the morning."

She went in, and Yourii sauntered towards the green, fragrant garden. He did not go far, but stopped to look round with intense curiosity at the dark windows of the house, as if something were happening there, something strangely beautiful and mysterious. Sina appeared in the doorway. Yourii hardly recognized her. She had changed her black dress, and now wore the costume of Little Russia, a thin bodice cut low, with short sleeves and a blue skirt.

"Here I am!" she said, smiling.

"So I see!" replied Yourii with a certain mysterious emphasis that she alone could appreciate.

She smiled once more, and looked sideways, as they walked along the garden-path between long grasses, and branches of lilac. The trees were small ones, most of them being cherry-trees, whose young leaves had an odour of resinous gum. Behind the garden there was a meadow where wild flowers bloomed amid the long grass.

"Let us sit down here," said Sina.

They sat down by the fence that was falling to pieces, and looked across the meadow at the dying sunset. Yourii caught hold of a slender lilac-branch, from which fell a shower of dew.

"Shall I sing something to you?" asked Sina.

"Oh! yes, do!" replied Yourii.

As on the evening of the picnic, Sina breathed deeply, and her comely bust was clearly defined beneath the thin bodice, as she began to sing, "Oh, beauteous Star of Love." Pure and passionate, her notes floated out on the evening air. Yourii remained motionless, gazing at her, with bated breath. She felt that his eyes were upon her, and, closing her own, she sang on with greater sweetness and fervour. There was silence everywhere, as if all things were listening; Yourii thought of the mysterious hush of woodlands in spring when a nightingale sings.

As Sina ceased on a clear, high note, the silence seemed yet more intense. The sunset light had faded; the sky grew dark and more vast. The leaves and the grass quivered imperceptibly; across the meadow and through the garden there passed a soft, perfumed breeze; faint as a sigh. Sina's eyes, shining in the gloom, turned to Yourii.

"Why so silent?" she asked.

"It is almost too delightful here!" he murmured, and again he grasped a dewy branch of lilac.

"Yes, it is very beautiful," replied Sina dreamily.

"In fact it is beautiful to be alive," she added.

A thought, vague and disquieting, crossed Yourii's mind, but it vanished without taking any clear shape. Some one loudly whistled twice on the other side of the meadow, and then came silence, as before.

"Do you like Schafroff?" asked Sina suddenly, being inwardly amused at so apparently inept a question.

Yourii felt a momentary pang of jealousy but with a slight effort he replied gravely: "He's a good fellow."

"How devoted he is to his work."

Yourii was silent.

A faint grey mist rose from the meadow and the grass grew paler in the dew.

"It is getting damp," said Sina, shivering slightly.

Yourii unconsciously looked at her round, soft shoulders, feeling instantly confused, and she, aware of his glance, became confused also, although it was pleasant to her.

"Let us go."

Regretfully they returned along the narrow garden-path, each brushing lightly against the other at times as they walked. All around seemed dark and deserted, and Yourii fancied that now the garden's own life was about to begin, a life mysterious and to all unknown. Yonder, amid the trees and across the dew-laden grass strange shadows soon would steel, as the dusk deepened, and voices whispered in green, silent places. This he said to Sina, and her dark eyes wistfully peered into the gloom. If, so Yourii thought, she were suddenly to fling all her clothing aside, and rush all white and nude and joyous over the dewy grass towards the dim thicket, this would not be in the least strange, but beautiful and natural; nor would it disturb the life of the green, dark garden, but would make this more complete. This, too, he had a wish to tell her, but he dared not do so, and spoke instead of the people and of lectures. But their conversation flagged, and then ceased, as if they were only wasting words. Thus they reached the gateway in silence, smiling to themselves, brushing the dew from the branches with their shoulders. Everything seemed as calm and happy and pensive as they were themselves. As before, the courtyard was dark and solitary, but the outer gate was open, and a sound of hasty footsteps in the house could be heard, and of the opening and shutting of drawers.

"Olga has come back," said Sina.

"Oh! Sina, is that you?" asked Dubova from within, and the tone of her voice suggested some sinister occurrence. Pale and agitated, she appeared in the doorway.

"Where were you? I have been looking for you. Semenoff is dying!" she said breathlessly.

"What!" exclaimed Sina, horror-struck.

"Yes, he is dying. He broke a blood-vessel. Anatole Pavlovitch says that he's done for. They have taken him to the hospital. It was dreadfully sudden. There we were, at the Ratoffs' having tea, and he was so merry, arguing with Novikoff about something or other. Then he suddenly began to cough, stood up, and staggered, and the blood spurted out, on the table-cloth, and into a little saucer of jam ... all black, and clotted. . . ."

"Does he know it himself?" asked Yourii with a grim interest. He instantly remembered the moonlight night, the sombre shadow, and the weak, broken voice, saying, "You will be alive, and you'll pass my grave, and stop, whilst I ..."

"Yes, he seems to know," replied Dubova, with a nervous movement of the hands. "He looked at us all, and asked 'What is it?' And then he shook from head to foot and said, 'Already!' . . . Oh! isn't it awful?"

"It's too shocking!"

All were silent.

It was now quite dark, yet, though the sky was clear, to them it seemed suddenly to have grown gloomy and sad.

"Death is a horrible thing!" said Yourii, turning pale.

Dubova sighed, and gazed into vacancy. Sina's chin trembled, and she smiled helplessly. She could not feel so shocked as the others; young as she was, and full of life, she could not fix her thoughts on death. To her it was incredible, inconceivable that on a beautiful summer evening, radiantly pleasant such as this, some one should have to suffer and to die. It was natural, of course, but, for some reason or other, to her it seemed wrong. She was ashamed to have such a feeling, and strove to suppress it, endeavouring to appear sympathetic, an effort which made her distress seem greater than that of her companions.

"Oh! poor fellow! ... is he really ... ?"

Sina wanted to ask: "Is he really going to die very soon?" but the words stuck in her throat, and she plied Dubova with fatuous and incoherent questions.

"Anatole Pavlovitch says that he will die to-night or to-morrow morning," replied Dubova, in a dull voice.

"Shall we go to him?" whispered Sina. "Or do you think that we had better not? I don't know."

This was the question uppermost in the minds of them all. Should they go and see Semenoff die? Was it a right or wrong thing to do? They all wanted to go, and yet were fearful of what they should see. Yourii shrugged his shoulders.

"Let us go," he said. "Very likely they won't admit us, and perhaps, too——"

"Perhaps he might wish to see some one," added Dubova, as if relieved.

"Come on! We'll go!" said Sina with decision.

"Schafroff and Novikoff are there," added Dubova, as if to justify herself.

Sina ran indoors to fetch her hat and coat, and then they went sadly through the town to the large, grey, three-storied building, the hospital where Semenoff lay dying.

The long, vaulted passages were dark, and smelt strongly of iodoform and carbolic. As they passed the section for the insane, they heard a strident, angry voice, but no one was visible. They felt scared, and anxiously hastened towards a dark little window. An old, grey-haired peasant, with a long white beard and wearing a large apron, came clattering along the passage in his heavy top-boots to meet them.

"Who is it you wish to see?" he asked, stopping short.

"A student has been brought here—Semenoff—to-day!" stammered Dubova.

"No. 6, please, upstairs," said the attendant, and passed on. They could hear him spit noisily on the flooring and

then wipe it with his foot. Upstairs it was brighter and
cleaner; and the ceiling was not vaulted. A door with "Doctors' Room" inscribed on it stood ajar. A lamp was burning
in this room, where a jingling of bottles and glasses could be
heard. Yourii looked inside, and called out. The jingling
ceased, and Riasantzeff appeared, looking fresh and hearty,
as usual.

"Ah!" he exclaimed in a cheery voice, being evidently accustomed to events such as that which saddened his visitors.
"I am on duty to-day. How do you do, ladies?" Yet, frowning suddenly, he added with grave significance: "He seems
to be still unconscious. Let us go to him. Novikoff and the
others are there."

As they walked in single file along the clean, bare passage,
past big white doors with black numbers on them, Riasantzeff said:

"A priest has been sent for. It's astonishing how quickly
the end came. I was amazed. But latterly he caught cold,
you know, and that was what did it. Here we are."

Riasantzeff opened a white door and went in, the others
following in awkward fashion as they pushed against each
other on the threshold.

The room was clean and spacious. Four of the six beds
in it were empty, each one having its coarse grey coverlet
folded neatly, and strangely suggestive of a coffin. On the
fifth bed sat a little wizened old man in a dressing-gown,
who glanced timidly at the newcomers; and on the sixth bed
beneath a similar coarse coverlet, lay Semenoff. At his side,
in a bent posture, sat Novikoff, while Ivanoff and Schafroff
stood by the window. To all of them it seemed odd and

painful to shake hands in the presence of the dying man, yet not to do so seemed equally embarrassing, as though by such omission they hinted that death was near. Some greeted each other, and some refrained, while all stood still gazing with grim curiosity at Semenoff.

He breathed slowly and with difficulty. How different he looked from the Semenoff they knew! Indeed, he hardly seemed to be alive. Though his features and his limbs were the same, they now appeared strangely rigid and dreadful to behold. That which naturally gave life and movement to the bodies of other human beings no longer seemed to exist in his. Something horrible was being swiftly, secretly accomplished within his motionless frame, an important work that could not be postponed. All that remained to him of life was, as it were, concentrated upon this work, observing it with keen, inexplicable interest.

The lamp hanging from the ceiling shone clearly upon the dying man's lifeless visage. All standing there gazed upon it, holding their breath as if fearing to disturb something infinitely solemn; and in such silence the laboured, sibilant breathing of the patient sounded terribly distinct.

The door opened, and with short, senile steps a fat little priest entered, accompanied by his psalm-singer, a dark, gaunt man. With these came Sanine. The priest, coughing slightly, bowed to the doctors and to all present, who acknowledged his greeting with excessive politeness, and then remained perfectly silent as before. Without noticing anybody, Sanine took up his position by the window, eyeing Semenoff and the others with great curiosity as he sought to discern what the patient and those about him actually felt and thought. Semenoff remained motionless, breathing just as before.

"He is unconscious, is he?" asked the priest gently, without addressing anyone in particular.

"Yes," replied Novikoff, hastily.

Sanine murmured something unintelligible. The priest looked questioningly at him, but, as Sanine remained silent, he turned away, smoothed his hair back, donned his stole and in high-pitched, unctuous tones began to chant the prayers for the dying.

The psalm-singer had a bass voice, hoarse and disagreeable, so that the vocal contrast was a painfully discordant one as the sound of this chanting rose to the lofty ceiling. No sooner had it commenced than the eyes of all were fixed in terror upon the dying man. Novikoff, standing nearest to him, thought that Semenoff's eyelids moved slightly, as if the sightless eyeballs had turned in the direction of the chanting. To the others, however, Semenoff appeared as strangely motionless as before.

At the first notes Sina began to cry, gently but persistently, letting the tears course down her youthful, pretty face. All the others looked at her, and Dubova in her turn began to weep. To the men's eyes tears also rose, which by clenching their teeth they strove to keep back. Every time the chanting grew louder, the girls wept more freely. Sanine frowned, and shrugged his shoulders irritably, thinking how intolerable to Semenoff, if he heard it, such wailing must be when to healthy normal men it was so utterly depressing.

"Not so loud!" he said to the priest irritably.

The latter amiably bent forward to hear this remark, and,

when he understood it, he frowned and only sang louder. His companion glared at Sanine and the others looked at him as well, in fear and astonishment, as if he had said something offensive. Sanine showed his annoyance by a gesture, but said nothing.

When the chanting ceased, and the priest had wrapped up the crucifix in his stole, the suspense was more painful than ever. Semenoff lay there as rigid, as motionless as before. Suddenly the same thought, dreadful but irresistible, came into the minds of all. If only it could all end quickly! If only Semenoff would die! In fear and shame they sought to suppress this wish, exchanging timid glances.

"If only this were over!" said Sanine in an undertone. "Ghastly, isn't it?"

"Yes!" replied Ivanoff.

They spoke almost in whispers, and it was plain that Semenoff could not hear them, but yet all the others looked shocked.

Schafroff was about to say something, but at that moment, a new sound, indescribably plaintive, echoed through the room, sending a shiver through all.

"Ee—ee—ee!" moaned Semenoff.

And, as if he had got that mode of expression which he wanted, he continued to give out this long-drawn note, only interrupted by his laboured, hoarse breathing.

At first the others could not conceive what had happened to him, but soon Sina and Dubova and Novikoff began to weep. Slowly and solemnly the priest resumed his chanting. His fat good-tempered face showed evident sympathy and emotion. A few minutes passed. Suddenly Semenoff ceased moaning.

"It is all over," murmured the priest.

Then slowly, and with much effort, Semenoff moved his tightly-glued lips, and his face became contracted as if by a smile. The onlookers heard his hollow, weird voice that, issuing from the depth of his chest, sounded as if it came through a coffin-lid.

"Silly old fool!" he said, looking hard at the priest. His whole body trembled, his eyes rolled madly in their sockets, and he stretched himself at full length.

They had all heard these words, but no one moved; and for a moment the sorrowful expression vanished from the priest's fat, moist face. He looked about him anxiously, but encountered no one's glance. Only Sanine smiled.

Semenoff again moved his lips, yet no sound escaped from them, while one side drooped of his thin, fair moustache. Once more he stretched his limbs, and became longer and more terrible. There was no sound, nor the slightest movement whatever. Nobody wept now. The approach of death had been more grievous, more appalling than its actual advent; and it seemed strange that so harrowing a scene should have ended so simply and swiftly. For a few moments they stood beside the bed and looked at the dead, peaked features, as if they expected something else to happen. Wishful to rouse within themselves a sense of horror and pity, they watched Novikoff intently as he closed the dead man's eyes and crossed his hands on his breast. Then they went out quietly and cautiously. In the passages lamps were now lighted, and all seemed so familiar and simple that everyone breathed more freely. The priest went first tripping along with short steps. Desiring to say a few words of consolation to the young people, he sighed, and then began softly:

"Dear, dear! It is very sad. Such a young man, too. Alas! it is plain that he died unrepentant. But God is merciful, you know——"

"Yes, yes, of course," replied Schafroff, who walked next to him and wished to be polite.

"Does his family know?" asked the priest.

"I really can't tell you," said Schafroff.

They all looked at each other in astonishment, as it seemed odd and not altogether decent to be unable to say who Semenoff's people were.

"His sister is at the high school, I believe," observed Sina.

"Ah! I see! Well, good-bye!" said the priest, slightly raising his hat with plump fingers.

"Good-bye!" they replied in unison.

On reaching the street, they sighed, as if relieved.

"Where shall we go now?" asked Schafroff.

After brief hesitation, they all took leave of each other, and went their different ways.

CHAPTER XI

WHEN Semenoff saw the blood, and felt the awful void around him and within him; when they lifted him up, carried him away and laid him down, and did all for him that throughout his life he had been in the habit of doing, then he knew that he was going to die, and wondered why he felt not the least fear of death.

Dubova had spoken of his terror because she herself was terrified, assuming that, if the healthy dreaded death, the dying must dread it far more. His pallor and his wild look, the result of loss of blood and weakness, she took to be an expression of fear. But, in reality this was not so. At all times, and especially since he knew that he had got consumption, Semenoff had dreaded death. At the outset of his malady, he was in a state of abject terror, much as that of a condemned man for whom hope of a reprieve there was none. It almost seemed to him as if from that moment the world no longer existed; all in it that formerly he found fair, and pleasant, and gay had vanished. All around him was dying, dying, and every moment, every second, might bring about something fearful, unendurable, hideous as a black, yawning abyss. It was as an abyss, huge, fathomless, and sombre as night, that Semenoff imagined death. Wherever he went, whatever he did, this black gulf was ever before him; in its impenetrable gloom all sounds, all colours, all emotions were lost. Such a state of mind was appalling, yet it did not last long; and, as the days went by, as Semenoff approached death, the more remote and vague and incomprehensible did it seem to him.

Everything around him, sounds, colours, and emotions, now once more regained their former value for him. The sun shone as brightly as ever; folk went about their business as usual, and Semenoff himself had important things, as also trivial ones, to do. Just as before, he rose in the morning, washed with scrupulous care, and ate his midday meal, finding food pleasant or unpleasant to his taste. As before, the sun and the moon were a joy to him, and rain or damp an annoyance; as before, he played billiards in the evening with Novikoff and others; as before, he read books, some being interesting, and some both foolish and dull. That all things remained unchanged was irritating, even painful to him at first. Nature, his environment, and he himself, all were the same; and he strove to alter this by compelling people to be interested in him and in his death, to comprehend his appalling position, to realize that all was at an end. When, however, he told his acquaintances of this, he perceived that he ought not to have done so. They appeared astonished at first, and then sceptical, professing to doubt the accuracy of the doctor's diagnosis. Finally, they endeavoured to banish the unpleasant impression by abruptly changing the subject, and Semenoff found himself talking with them about all sorts of things, but never about death.

Then he sought to live in seclusion, to become absorbed in himself, and in solitude to suffer, having full, steadfast consciousness of his impending doom. Yet, as in his life and his daily surroundings, all remained the same as formerly, it seemed absurd to imagine that it could be otherwise, or that he, Semenoff, would no longer exist as at the present. The thought of death, which at first had made so deep a wound, grew less poignant; the soul oppressed found freedom. Moments of complete forgetfulness became more and more frequent, and life once again lay before him, rich in colour, in movement, in sound.

It was only at night-time, when alone, that he was haunted by the sense of a black abyss. After he had put out the lamp, something devoid of form or features rose up slowly above him in the gloom, and whispered, "Sh . . . sh . . . sh!" without ceasing, while to this whispering another voice, as from within him, made hideous answer. Then he felt that he was gradually becoming part of this murmuring and this abysmal chaos. His life in it seemed as a faint, flickering flame that might at any moment fade for ever. Then he decided to keep a lamp burning in his room throughout the night. In the light, the strange whispering ceased, the darkness vanished; nor had he the impression of being poised above a yawning abyss, because light made him conscious of a thousand trivial and ordinary details in his life; the chairs, the light, the inkstand, his own feet, an unfinished letter, an *ikon,* with its lamp that he had never lighted, boots that he had forgotten to put outside the door, and many other every-day things that surrounded him.

Yet, even then, he could hear whisperings that came from the corners of the room which the light of the lamp did not reach, and again the black gulf yawned to receive him. He was afraid to look into the darkness, or even to think of it, for then, in a moment, dreadful gloom surrounded him, veiling the lamp, hiding the world as with a cold, dense mist from his view. It was this that tortured, that appalled him. He felt as if he must cry like a child, or beat his head against the wall. But as the days went past, and Semenoff drew nearer to death, he grew more used to such impressions. They only became stronger and more awful if by a word or a gesture, by the sight of a funeral or of a graveyard, he was reminded that he, too, must die. Anxious to avoid such warnings, he never went into any street that led to the cemetery, nor ever slept on his back with hands folded across his breast.

He had two lives, as it were; his former life, ample and obvious, which could not give a thought to death, but ignored it, being concerned about its own affairs, while hoping to live on for ever, cost what it might; and another life, mysterious, indefinite, obscure, that, as a worm in an apple, secretly gnawed at the core of his former life, poisoning it, making it insufferable.

It was owing to this double life that Semenoff, when at last he found himself face to face with death and knew that his end was nigh, felt scarcely any fear. "Already?" That is all he asked, in order to know exactly what to expect.

When in the faces of those around him he read the answer to his question, he merely wondered that the end should seem so simple, so natural, like that of some heavy task, which had overtaxed his powers. At the same time, by a new and strange inner consciousness he perceived that it could not be otherwise, and that death was the normal result of his enfeebled vitality. He only felt sorry that he would never see anything again. As they took him in a *droschky* to the hospital, he gazed about him with wide-opened eyes, striving to note everything at a glance, grieved that he could not firmly fix in his memory every little detail of this world with its ample sky, its human beings, its verdure, and its distant blue horizons. Equally dear, in fact, unspeakably precious to him, were all the little things that he had never noticed, as well as those which he had always found full of beauty and importance; the heaven, dark and vast, with its golden stars; the driver's gaunt back, in its shabby smock; Novikoff's troubled countenance; the dusty road; houses with their lighted windows; the dark trees that silently stayed behind; the jolting wheels; the soft evening breeze—all that he could see, and hear, and feel.

Later on, in the hospital, his eyes wandered swiftly round the large room, watching every movement, every figure intently until prevented by physical pain which produced a sense of utter isolation. His perceptions were now concentrated in his chest, the source of all his suffering. Gradually, very gradually, he began to drift away from life. When now he saw something, it seemed to him strange and meaningless. The last fight between life and death had begun; it filled his whole being; it created a new world, strange and lonely, a world of terror, agony and despairing conflict. Now and again there were more lucid moments; the pain ceased; his breathing was deeper and calmer, and through the white veil sounds and shapes became more or less plain. But all seemed faint and futile, as if they came from afar. He heard sounds plainly, and then again they were inaudible: the figures moved noiselessly as those in a cinematograph; familiar faces appeared strange and he could not recollect them.

On the adjoining bed a man with a quaint, clean-shaven face was reading aloud, but why he read, or to whom he read, Semenoff never troubled to think. He distinctly heard that the parliamentary elections had been postponed, and that an attempt had been made to assassinate a Grand Duke, but the words were empty and meaningless; like bubbles, they burst and vanished, leaving no trace. The man's lips moved, his teeth gleamed, his round eyes rolled, the paper rustled, and the lamp shone from the ceiling round which large, black, fierce-looking flies revolved. In Semenoff's brain something seemed to flame upwards, illuminating all that surrounded him. He was suddenly conscious that all was now of no account to him, and that all the work and business in the world could not add one single hour to his life; but that he must die. Once more he sank down into the waves of black mist; again the silent conflict began between two terrible and secret forces, the one convulsively striving to destroy the other.

The second time that Semenoff regained consciousness was when he heard weeping and chanting. This seemed to him utterly unnecessary, having no sort of relation to all that was going on within him. For a moment, however, it lighted up the flame in his brain, and Semenoff clearly perceived the mock-mournful face of a man who was absolutely uninteresting to him. That was the last sign of life. What followed was for those living wholly beyond the pale of their thought or comprehension.

CHAPTER XII

"COME to my place, and we will hold a memorial service for the departed," said Ivanoff to Sanine. The latter nodded his acceptance. On the way, they bought vodka and *hors d'œuvres,* and overtook Yourii Svarogitsch, who was walking slowly along the boulevard, looking much depressed.

Semenoff's death had made a confused and painful impression upon him which he found it necessary, yet almost impossible, to analyse.

"After all, it is simple enough!" said Yourii to himself, endeavouring to draw a straight, short line in his mind. "Man never existed before he was born; that does not seem to be terrible nor incomprehensible. Man's existence ends when he dies. That is equally simple and easy to comprehend. Death, the complete stoppage of the machine that creates vital force, is perfectly comprehensible; there is nothing terrible about it. There was once a boy named Youra who went to college and fought with his comrades, who amused himself by chopping off the heads of thistles and lived his own special and interesting life in his own special way. This Youra died, and in his place quite another man walks and thinks, the student, Yourii Svarogitsch. If they were to meet, Youra would not understand Yourii, and might even hate him as a possible tutor ready to cause him no end of annoyance. Therefore, between them there is a gulf, and

therefore, if the boy Youra is dead, I am dead myself, though
till now I never noticed it. That is how it is. Quite natural
and simple, after all! If one reflects, what do we lose by dying? Life, at any rate, contains more sadness than happiness.
True it has its pleasures and it is hard to lose them, but
death rids us of so many ills, that in the end we gain by it.
That's simple, and not so terrible, is it?" said Yourii, aloud,
with a sigh of relief, but suddenly he started, as another
thought seemed to sting him. "No, a whole world, full of
life and extraordinarily complicated, suddenly transformed
into nothing? No, that is not the transformation of the
boy Youra into Yourii Svarogitsch! That is absurd and revolting, and therefore terrible and incomprehensible!"

With all his might Yourii strove to form a conception of
this state which no man finds it possible to support, yet which
every man supports, just as Semenoff had done.

"He did not die of fear, either," thought Yourii, smiling
at the strangeness of such a reflection. "No, he was laughing at us all, with our priest, and our chanting, and tears.
How was it that Semenoff could laugh, knowing that in a few
moments all would be at an end? Was he a hero? No; it
was not a question of heroism. Then death is not as terrible
as I thought."

While he was musing thus Ivanoff suddenly hailed him
in a loud voice.

"Ah! it's you! Where are you going?" asked Yourii, shuddering.

"To say a mass for our departed friend," replied Ivanoff,
with brutal jocularity. "You had better come with us.
What's the good of being always alone?"

Feeling sad and dispirited, Yourii did not find Sanine and Ivanoff as distasteful to him as usual.

"Very well, I will," he replied, but suddenly recollecting his superiority, he thought to himself, "what have I really in common with such fellows? Am I to drink their vodka, and talk commonplaces?"

He was on the point of turning back, but he felt such an utter horror of solitude that he went along with them. Ivanoff and Sanine proffered no remarks, and thus in silence they reached the former's lodging. It was already quite dark. At the door, the figure of a man could be dimly seen. He had a thick stick with a crooked handle.

"Oh! it's Uncle Peter Ilitsch!" exclaimed Ivanoff gleefully.

"Yes! that's he!" replied the figure, in a deep, resonant voice. Yourii remembered that Ivanoff's uncle was an old, drunken chorister. He had a grey moustache like one of the soldiers at the time of Nicholas the First, and his shabby black coat had a most unpleasant smell.

"Boum! Boum!" His voice seemed to come out of a barrel, when Ivanoff introduced him to Yourii, who awkwardly shook hands with him, hardly knowing what to say to such a person. He recollected, however, that for him all men should be equal, so he politely gave precedence to the old singer as they went in.

Ivanoff's lodging was more like an old lumber-room than a place for human habitation, being very dusty and untidy. But when his host had lighted the lamp, Yourii perceived that the walls were covered with engravings of pictures by Vasnetzoff, and that what had seemed rubbish were books piled up in heaps. He still felt somewhat ill at ease, and, to hide this, he began to examine the engravings attentively.

"Do you like Vasnetzoff?" asked Ivanoff as, without waiting for an answer, he left the room to fetch a plate. Sanine told Peter Ilitsch that Semenoff was dead. "God rest his soul!" droned the latter. "Ah! well, it's all over for him now."

Yourii glanced wistfully at him, and felt a sudden sympathy for the old man.

Ivanoff now brought in bread, salted cucumbers, and glasses, which he placed on the table that was covered with a newspaper. Then, with a swift, scarcely perceptible movement, he uncorked the bottle, not a drop of its contents being spilt.

"Very neat!" exclaimed Ilitsch approvingly.

"You can tell in a minute if a man knows what he's about," said Ivanoff, with a self-complacent air, as he filled the glasses with the greenish liquid.

"Now, gentlemen," said he, raising his voice as he took up his glass. "To the repose of the departed, &c.!"

With that they began to eat, and more vodka was consumed. They talked little, and drank the more. Soon the atmosphere of the little room grew hot and oppressive. Peter Ilitsch lighted a cigarette, and the air was filled with the bluish fumes of bad tobacco. The drink and the smoke and the heat made Yourii feel dizzy. Again he thought of Semenoff.

"There's something dreadful about death," he said.

"Why?" asked Peter Ilitsch. "Death? Ho! ho!! It's absolutely necessary. Death! Suppose one went on living for ever? Ho! ho!! You mustn't talk like that! Eternal life, indeed! What would eternal life be, eh?"

Yourii tried at once to imagine what living for ever would be like. He saw an endless grey stripe that stretched aimlessly away into space, as though swept onward from one wave to another. All conception of colour, sound and emotion was blurred and dimmed, being merged and fused in one grey turbid stream that flowed on placidly, eternally. This was not life, but everlasting death. The thought of it horrified him.

"Yes, of course," he murmured.

"It appears to have made a great impression upon you," said Ivanoff.

"Upon whom does it not make an impression?" asked Yourii. Ivanoff shook his head vaguely, and began to tell Ilitsch about Semenoff's last moments. It was now insufferably close in the room. Yourii watched Ivanoff, as his red lips sipped the vodka that shone in the lamplight. Everything seemed to be going round and round.

"A—a—a—a—a!" whispered a voice in his ear, a strange small voice.

"No! death is an awful thing!" he said again, without noticing that he was replying to the mysterious voice.

"You're over-nervous about it," observed Ivanoff contemptuously.

"Aren't you?" said Yourii.

"I? N—no! Certainly, I don't want to die, as there's not much fun in it, and living is far jollier. But, if one has to die, I should like it to be quickly, without any fuss or nonsense."

"You have not tried yet!" laughed Sanine.

"No; that's quite true!" replied the other.

"Ah! well," continued Yourii, "one has heard all that before. Say what you will, death is death, horrible in itself, and sufficient to rob a man of all pleasure in life who thinks of such a violent and inevitable end to it. What is the meaning of life?"

"It has no meaning," cried Ivanoff irritably.

"No, that is impossible," replied Yourii, "everything is too wisely and carefully arranged, and——"

"In my opinion," said Sanine, "there's nothing good anywhere."

"How can you say that? What about Nature?"

"Nature! Ha, ha!" Sanine laughed feebly, and waved his hand in derision. "It is customary, I know, to say that Nature is perfect. The truth is, that Nature is just as defective as mankind. Without any great effort of imagination any of us could present a world a hundred times better than this one. Why should we not have perpetual warmth and light, and a garden ever verdant and ever gay? As to the meaning of life, of course it has a meaning of some sort, because the aim implies the march of things; without an aim all would be chaos. But this aim lies outside the pale of our existence, in the very basis of the universe. That is certain. We cannot be the origin nor the end of the universe. Our rôle is a passive and auxiliary one. By the mere fact of living we fulfil our mission. Our life is necessary; thus our death is necessary also."

"For what?"

"How should I know?" replied Sanine, "and, besides, what do I care? My life means my sensations, pleasant or unpleasant; what is outside those limits; well, to the deuce with it all! Whatever hypothesis we may like to invent, it will always remain an hypothesis upon which it would be folly to construct life. Let him who likes worry about it; as for me, I mean to live!"

"Let us all have a drink on the strength of it!" suggested Ivanoff.

"But you believe in God, don't you?" said Ilitsch, looking at Sanine with bleared eyes. "Nowadays nobody believes in anything—not even in that which is easy of belief."

Sanine laughed. "Yes, I believe in God. As a child I did that, and there's no need to dispute or to affirm any reasons for doing so. It's the most profitable thing, really, for if there is a God, I offer Him sincere faith, and, if there isn't, well, all the better for me."

"But on belief or on unbelief all life is based?" said Yourii.

Sanine shook his head and smiled complacently.

"No, my life is not based on such things," he said.

"On what, then?" asked Yourii, languidly. "A—a—a! I mustn't drink any more," he thought to himself, as he drew his hand across his cold, moist brow. If Sanine made any reply he did not hear it. His head was in a whirl, and for a moment he felt quite overcome.

"I believe that God exists," continued Sanine, "though I am not certain, absolutely certain. But whether He does or not, I do not know Him, nor can I tell what He requires of me. How could I possibly know this, even though I professed the most ardent faith in Him? God is God, and, not being human, cannot be judged by human standards. His created world around us contains all; good and evil, life and death, beauty and ugliness—everything, in fact, and thus all sense and all exact definition are lost to us, for His sense is not human, nor His ideas of good and evil human, either. Our conception of God must always be an idolatrous one, and we shall always give to our fetish the physiognomy and the garb suitable to the climatic conditions of the country in which we live. Absurd, isn't it."

"Yes, you're right," grunted Ivanoff, "quite right!"

"Then, what is the good of living?" asked Yourii, as he pushed back his glass in disgust, "or of dying, either?"

"One thing I know," replied Sanine, "and that is, that I don't want my life to be a miserable one. Thus, before all things, one must satisfy one's natural desires. Desire is everything. When a man's desires cease, his life ceases, too, and if he kills his desires, then he kills himself."

"But his desires may be evil?"

"Possibly."

"Well, what then?"

"Then . . . they must just be evil," replied Sanine blandly, as he looked Yourii full in the face with his clear, blue eyes.

Ivanoff raised his eyebrows incredulously and said nothing. Yourii was silent also. For some reason or other he felt embarrassed by those clear, blue eyes, though he tried to keep looking at them.

For a few moments there was complete silence, so that one could plainly hear a night-moth desperately beating against the window-pane. Peter Ilitsch shook his head mournfully, and his drink-besotted visage drooped towards the stained, dirty newspaper. Sanine smiled again. This perpetual smile irritated and yet fascinated Yourii.

"What clear eyes he has!" thought he.

Suddenly Sanine rose, opened the window, and let out the moth. A wave of cool, pleasant air, as from soft wings, swept through the room.

"Yes," said Ivanoff, in answer to his own thoughts, "there are no two men alike, so, on the strength of that, let's have another drink."

"No," said Yourii, shaking his head, "I won't have any more."

"Eh—why not?"

"I never drink much."

The vodka and the heat had made his head ache. He longed to get out into the fresh air.

"I must be going," he said, getting up.

"Where? Come on, have another drink!"

"No really, I ought to——" stammered Yourii, looking for his cap.

"Well, good-bye!"

As Yourii shut the door he heard Sanine saying to Ilitsch: "Of course you're not like children; they can't distinguish good from bad; they are simple and natural; and that is why they——" Then the door was closed, and all was still.

High in the heavens shone the moon, and the cool night-air touched Yourii's brow. All seemed beautiful and romantic, and as he walked through the quiet moonlit streets the thought to him was dreadful that in some dark, silent chamber Semenoff lay on a table, yellow and stiff. Yet, somehow, Yourii could not recall those grievous thoughts that had recently oppressed him, and had shrouded the whole world in gloom. His mood was now one of tranquil sadness, and he felt impelled to gaze at the moon. As he crossed a white deserted square he suddenly thought of Sanine.

"What sort of man is that?" he asked himself.

Annoyed to think that there was a man whom he, Yourii, could not instantly define, he felt a certain malicious pleasure in disparaging him.

"A phrase-maker, that's all he is! Formerly the fellow posed as a pessimist, disgusted with life and bent upon airing impossible views of his own; now, he's trifling with animalism."

From Sanine Yourii's thoughts reverted to himself. He came to the conclusion that he trifled with nothing but that his thoughts, his sufferings, his whole personality, were original, and quite different from those of other men.

This was most agreeable; yet something seemed to be missing. Once more he thought of Semenoff. It was grievous to know that he should never set eyes upon him again, and though he had never felt any affection for Semenoff, he now had become near and dear to him. Tears rose to his eyes. He pictured the dead student lying in the grave, a mass of corruption, and he remembered these words of his:

"You'll be living, and breathing this air, and enjoying this moonlight, and you'll go past my grave where I lie."

"Here, under my feet, lie human beings, too," thought Yourii, looking down at the dust. "I am trampling on brains, and hearts, and human eyes! Oh! . . . And I shall die, too, and others will walk over me, thinking just as I think now. Ah! before it is too late, one must live, one must live! Yes; but live in the right way, so that not a moment of one's life be lost. Yet how is one to do that?"

The market-place lay white and bare in the moonlight. All was silent in the town.

> Never more shall singer's lute
> Tidings of him tell.

Yourii hummed this softly to himself. Then he said, aloud: "How tedious, sad, and dreadful it all is!" as if complaining to some one. The sound of his own voice alarmed him, and he turned round to see if he had been overheard. "I am drunk," he thought.

Silent and serene, the night looked down.

CHAPTER XIII

WHILE Sina Karsavina and Dubova were absent on a visit, Yourii's life seemed uneventful and monotonous. His father was engaged, either at the club or with household matters, and Lialia and Riasantzeff found the presence of a third person embarrassing, so that Yourii avoided their society. It thus became his habit to go to bed early and not to rise till the midday meal. All day long, when in his room, or in the garden, he brooded over matters, waiting for a supreme access of energy that should spur him on to do some great work.

This "great work" each day assumed a different form. Now it was a picture, or, again, it was a series of articles that should show the world what a huge mistake the social democrats had made in not giving Yourii a leading rôle in their party. Or else it was an article in favour of adherence to the people and of strenuous co-operation with it—a very broad, imposing treatment of the subject. Each day, however, as it passed, brought nothing but boredom. Once or twice Novikoff and Schafroff came to see him. Yourii also attended lectures and paid visits, yet all this seemed to him empty and aimless. It was not what he sought or fancied that he sought.

One day he went to see Riasantzeff. The doctor had large, airy rooms filled with all such things as an athletic, healthy man needs for his amusement; Indian clubs, dumb-bells, rapiers, fishing-rods, nets, tobacco-pipes, and much else that savoured of wholesome, manly reaction.

Riasantzeff received him with frank cordiality, chatted pleasantly, offered him cigarettes, and finally asked him to go out shooting with him.

"I have not got a gun," said Yourii.

"Have one of mine. I have got five," replied Riasantzeff. To him, Yourii was the brother of Lialia, and he was anxious to be as kind to him as possible. He therefore insisted upon Yourii's acceptance of one of his guns, eagerly displaying them all, taking them to pieces, and explaining their make. He even fired at a target in the yard, so that at last Yourii laughingly accepted a gun and some cartridges, much to Riasantzeff's pleasure.

"That's first-rate!" he said, "I had meant to get some duck-shooting to-morrow, so we'll go together, shall we?"

"I should like it very much," replied Yourii.

When he got home he spent nearly two hours examining his gun, fingering the lock, and taking aim at the lamp. He then carefully greased his old shooting-boots.

On the following day, towards evening, Riasantzeff, fresh, hearty as ever, drove up in a *droschky* with a smart bay to fetch Yourii.

"Are you ready?" he called out to him through the open window.

Yourii, who had already donned cartridge-belt and game bag, and carried his gun, came out, looking somewhat over-weighted and ill at ease.

"I'm ready, I'm ready," he said.

Riasantzeff, who was lightly and comfortably clad, seemed somewhat astonished at Yourii's accoutrements.

"You'll find those things too heavy," he said smiling. "Take them all off and put them here. You needn't wear them till we get there." He helped Yourii to divest himself of his shooting-kit and placed them underneath the seat. Then they drove away at a good pace. The day was drawing to a close, but it was still warm and dusty. The *droschky* swayed from side to side so that Yourii had to hold tightly to the seat. Riasantzeff talked and laughed the whole time, and Yourii was compelled to join in his merriment. When they got out into the fields where the stiff meadow-grass brushed against their feet it was cooler, and there was no dust.

On reaching a broad level field Riasantzeff pulled up the sweating horse and, placing his hand to his mouth, shouted in a clear, ringing voice, "Kousma—a . . . Kousma—a—a!"

At the extreme end of the field, like silhouettes, a row of little men could be descried who, at the sound of Riasant-zeff's voice, looked eagerly in his direction.

One of the men then came across the field, walking carefully between the furrows. As he approached, Yourii saw that he was a burly, grey-haired peasant with a long beard and sinewy arms.

He came up to them slowly, and said, with a smile, "You know how to shout, Anatole Pavlovitch!"

"Good day, Kousma; how are you? Can I leave the horse with you?"

"Yes, certainly you can," said the peasant in a calm, friendly voice, as he caught hold of the horse's bridle.

"Come for a little shooting, eh? And who is that?" he asked, with a kindly glance at Yourii.

"It is Nicolai Yegorovitch's son," replied Riasantzeff.

"Ah, yes! I see that he is just like Ludmilla Nicolaijevna! Yes, yes!"

Yourii was pleased to find that this genial old peasant knew his sister and spoke of her in such a simple, friendly way.

"Now, then, let us go!" said Riasantzeff, in his cheery voice, as he walked first, after getting his gun and game-bag.

"May you have luck!" cried Kousma, and then they could hear him coaxing the horse as he led it away to his hut.

They had to walk nearly a verst before they reached the marsh. The sun had almost set, and the soil, covered with lush grasses and reeds, felt moist beneath their feet. It looked darker, and had a damp smell, while in places water shimmered. Riasantzeff had ceased smoking, and stood with legs wide apart, looking suddenly grave as if he had to begin an important and responsible task. Yourii kept to the right, trying to find a dry comfortable place. In front of them lay the water which, reflecting the clear evening sky, looked pure and deep. The other bank, like a black stripe, could be discerned in the distance.

Almost immediately, in twos and threes, ducks rose and flew slowly over the water, starting up suddenly out of the rushes, and then passing over the sportsmen's heads, a row of silhouettes against the saffron sky. Riasantzeff had the first shot, and with success. A wounded duck tumbled sideways into the water, beating down the rushes with its wings.

"I hit it!" exclaimed Riasantzeff, as he gaily laughed

aloud.

"He's really a good sort of fellow," thought Yourii, whose turn it was to shoot. He brought down his bird also, but it fell at such a distance that he could not find it, though he scratched his hands and waded knee-deep through the water. This disappointment only made him more keen; it was fine fun, so he thought.

Amid the clear, cool air from the river the gun-smoke had a strangely pleasant smell, and, in the darkening landscape, the merry shots flashed out with charming effect. The wounded wild fowl, as they fell, described graceful curves against the pale green sky where now the first faint stars gleamed. Yourii felt unusually energetic and gay. It was as if he had never taken part in anything so interesting or exhilarating. The birds rose more rarely now, and the deepening dusk made it more difficult to take aim.

"Hullo there! We must get home!" shouted Riasantzeff, from a distance.

Yourii felt sorry to go, but in accordance with his companion's suggestion he advanced to meet him, stumbling over rushes and splashing through the water which in the dusk was not distinguishable from dry soil. As they met, their eyes flashed, and they were both breathless.

"Well," asked Riasantzeff, "did you have any luck?"

"I should say so," replied Yourii, displaying his well-filled bag.

"Ah! you're a better shot than I am," said Riasantzeff pleasantly.

Yourii was delighted by such praise, although he always professed to care nothing for physical strength or skill. "I don't know about better," he observed carelessly. "It was just luck."

By the time they reached the hut it was quite dark. The melon-field was immersed in gloom, and only the foremost rows of melons shimmered white in the firelight, casting long shadows. The horse stood, snorting, beside the hut, where a bright little fire of dried steppe-grass burnt and crackled. They could hear men talking and women laughing, and one voice, mellow and cheery in tone, seemed familiar to Yourii.

"Why, it's Sanine," said Riasantzeff, in astonishment. "How did he get here?"

They approached the fire. Grey-bearded Kousma, seated beside it, looked up, and nodded to welcome them.

"Any luck?" he asked, in his deep bass voice, through a drooping moustache.

"Just a bit," replied Riasantzeff.

Sanine, sitting on a huge pumpkin, also raised his head and smiled at them.

"How is it that you are here?" asked Riasantzeff.

"Oh! Kousma Prokorovitch and I are old friends," explained Sanine, smiling the more.

Kousma laughed, showing the yellow stumps of his decayed teeth as he slapped Sanine's knee good-naturedly with his rough hand.

"Yes, yes," he said. "Sit down here, Anatole Pavlovitch, and taste this melon. And you, my young master, what is your name?"

"Yourii Nicolaijevitch," replied Yourii, pleasantly.

He felt somewhat embarrassed, but he at once took a lik-

ing to this gentle old peasant with his friendly speech, half
Russian, half dialect.

"Yourii Nicolaijevitch! Aha! We must make each other's
acquaintance, eh? Sit you down, Yourii Nicolaijevitch."

Yourii and Riasantzeff sat down by the fire on two big
pumpkins.

"Now then, show us what you have shot," said Kousma.

A heap of dead birds fell out of the game-bags, and the
ground was dabbled with their blood. In the flickering firelight they had a weird, unpleasant look. The blood was almost black, and the claws seemed to move. Kousma took up
a duck, and felt beneath its wings.

"That's a fat one," he said approvingly. "You might spare
me a brace, Anatole Pavlovitch. What will you do with such
a lot?"

"Have them all!" exclaimed Yourii, blushing.

"Why all? Come, come, you're too generous," laughed
the old man. "I'll just have a brace, to show that there's no
ill-feeling."

Other peasants and their wives now approached the fire,
but, dazzled by the blaze, Yourii could not plainly distinguish
them. First one and then another face swiftly emerged from
the gloom, and then vanished. Sanine, frowning, regarded
the dead birds, and, turning away, suddenly rose. The sight
of these beautiful creatures lying there in blood and dust,
with broken wings, was distasteful to him.

Yourii watched everything with great interest as he
greedily ate large, luscious slices of a ripe melon which
Kousma cut off with his pocket-knife that had a yellow bone
handle.

"Eat, Yourii Nicolaijevitch; this melon's good," he said. "I know your little sister, Ludmilla Nicolaijevna, and your father, too. Eat, and enjoy it."

Everything pleased Yourii; the smell of the peasants, an odour as of newly-baked bread and sheepskins; the bright blaze of the fire; the gigantic pumpkin upon which he sat; and the glimpse of Kousma's face when he looked down-wards, for when the old man raised his head it was hidden in the gloom and only his eyes gleamed. Overhead there was darkness now, which made the lighted place seem pleasant and comfortable. Looking upwards, Yourii could at first see nothing, and then suddenly the calm, spacious heaven appeared and the distant stars.

He felt, however, somewhat embarrassed, not knowing what to say to these peasants. The others, Kousma, Sanine, and Riasantzeff, chatted frankly and simply to them about this or that, never troubling to choose some special theme for talk.

"Well, how's the land?" he asked, when there was a short pause in the conversation, though he felt that the question sounded forced and out of place.

Kousma looked up, and answered:

"We must wait, just wait a while, and see." Then he began talking about the melon-fields and other personal matters, Yourii feeling only more and more embarrassed, although he rather liked listening to it all.

Footsteps were heard approaching. A little red dog with a curly white tail appeared in the light, sniffing at Yourii and Riasantzeff, and rubbing itself against Sanine's knees, who patted its rough coat. It was followed by a little, old

man with a sparse beard and small bright eyes. He carried
a rusty single-barrelled gun.

"It is grandfather, our guardian," said Kousma. The old
man sat down on the ground, deposited his weapon, and
looked hard at Yourii and Riasantzeff.

"Been out shooting; yes, yes!" he mumbled, showing his
shrivelled, discoloured gums. "He! He! Kousma, it's time
to boil the potatoes! He! He!"

Riasantzeff picked up the old fellow's flint-lock, and
laughingly showed it to Yourii. It was a rusty old barrel-
loader, very heavy, with wire wound round it.

"I say," said he, "what sort of a gun do you call this?
Aren't you afraid to shoot with it?"

"He! He! I nearly shot myself with it once! Stepan
Schapka, he told me that one could shoot without ... caps?
He! He! ... without caps! He said that if there were any
sulphur left in the gun one could fire without a cap. So I put
the loaded rifle on my knee like this, and fired it off at full
cock with my finger, like this, see? Then bang! it went off!
Nearly killed myself! He! He! Loaded the rifle, and bang!!
Nearly killed myself!"

They all laughed, and there were tears of mirth in Yourii's
eyes, so absurd did the little man seem with his tufted grey
beard and his sunken jaws.

The old fellow laughed, too, till his little eyes watered.
"Very nearly killed myself! He! He!"

In the darkness, and beyond the circle of light, one could
hear laughter, and the voices of girls whom shyness had kept
at a distance. A few feet away from the fire, and in quite a
different place from where Yourii imagined him to be

seated, Sanine struck a match. In the reddish flare of it Yourii saw his calm, friendly eyes, and beside him a young face whose soft eyes beneath their dark brows looked up at Sanine with simple joy.

Riasantzeff, as he winked to Kousma, said:

"Grandfather, hadn't you better keep an eye on your granddaughter, eh?"

"What's the good!" replied Kousma, with a careless gesture. "Youth is youth."

"He! He!" laughed the old man in his turn, as with his fingers he plucked a red-hot coal from the fire.

Sanine's laugh was heard in the darkness. The girls may have felt ashamed, for they had moved away, and their voices were scarcely audible.

"It is time to go," said Riasantzeff, as he got up. "Thank you, Kousma."

"Not at all," replied the other, as with his sleeve he brushed away the black melon-pips that had stuck to his grey beard. He shook hands with both of them, and Yourii again felt a certain repugnance to the touch of his rough, bony hand. As they retreated from the fire, the gloom seemed less intense. Above were the cold, glittering stars and the vast dome of heaven, serenely fair. The group by the fire, the horses, and the pile of melons all became blacker against the light.

Yourii tripped over a pumpkin and nearly fell.

"Look out!" said Sanine. "Good-bye!"

"Good-bye!" replied Yourii, looking round at the other's tall, dark form, leaning against which he fancied that he saw another, the graceful figure of a woman. Yourii's heart beat faster. He suddenly thought of Sina Karsavina, and envied Sanine.

Once more the wheels of the *droschky* rattled, and once again the good old horse snorted as it ran.

The fire faded in the distance, as did the sound of voices and laughter. Stillness reigned. Yourii slowly looked upwards to the sky with its jewelled web of stars. As they reached the outskirts of the town, lights flashed here and there, and dogs barked. Riasantzeff said to Yourii:

"Old Kousma's a philosopher, eh?"

Seated behind, Yourii looked at Riasantzeff's neck, and roused from his own melancholy thoughts, endeavoured to understand what he said.

"Oh! . . . Yes!" he replied hesitatingly.

"I didn't know that Sanine was such a gay dog," laughed Riasantzeff.

Yourii was not dreaming now, and he recalled the momentary vision of Sanine and that pretty girlish face illumined by the light of a match. Again he felt jealous, yet suddenly it occurred to him that Sanine's treatment of the girl was base and contemptible.

"No, I had no idea of it, either," said Yourii, with a touch of irony that was lost upon Riasantzeff, who whipped up the horse and, after a while, remarked:

"Pretty girl, wasn't she? I know her. She's the old fellow's grandchild."

Yourii was silent. His contemplative mood was in a moment dispelled, and he now felt convinced that Sanine was a coarse, bad man.

Riasantzeff shrugged his shoulders, and at last blurted out:

"Deuce take it! Such a night, eh? It seems to have got hold of me, too. I say, suppose we drive back, and——"

Yourii did not at first understand what he meant.

"There are some fine girls there, you know. What do you say? Shall we go back?" continued Riasantzeff, sniggering.

Yourii blushed deeply. A thrill of animal lust shot through his frame, and enticing pictures rose up before his heated imagination. Yet, controlling himself, he answered, in a dry voice:

"No; it is time that we were at home." Then he added, maliciously: "Lialia is waiting for us."

Riasantzeff collapsed.

"Oh, yes, of course; yes, we ought to be back by now!" he hastily muttered.

Yourii ground his teeth, and, glaring at the driver's broad back in its white jacket, remarked aggressively:

"I have no particular liking for adventures of that sort."

"No, no; I understand. Ha! Ha!" replied Riasantzeff, laughing in a faint half-hearted way. After that he was silent.

"Damn it! How stupid of me!" he thought.

They drove home without uttering another word, and to each the way seemed endless.

"You will come in, won't you?" asked Yourii, without looking up.

"Er . . . No! I have got to see a patient. Besides it is rather late," replied Riasantzeff hesitatingly.

Yourii got out of the *droschky*, not caring to take the gun or the game. Everything that belonged to Riasantzeff he now seemed to loathe. The latter called out to him.

"I say, you've left your gun!"

Yourii turned round, took this and the bag with an air of disgust. After shaking hands awkwardly with Riasantzeff, he entered the house. The latter drove on slowly for a short distance and then turned sharply into a side-street. The rattle of wheels on the road could now be heard in another direction. Yourii listened to it, furious, yet secretly jealous. "A bad lot!" he muttered, feeling sorry for his sister.

CHAPTER XIV

HAVING carried the things indoors, Yourii, for want of something else to do, went down the steps leading to the garden. It was dark as the grave, and the sky with its vast company of gleaming stars enhanced the weird effect. There, on one of the steps, sat Lialia; her little grey form was scarcely perceptible in the gloom.

"Is that you, Yourii?" she asked.

"Yes, it is," he replied, as he sat down beside her. Dreamily she leant her head on his shoulder, and the fragrance of her fresh, sweet girlhood touched his senses.

"Did you have good sport?" said Lialia. Then after a pause, she added softly, "and where is Anatole Pavlovitch? I heard you drive up."

"Your Anatole Pavlovitch is a dirty beast!" is what Yourii, feeling suddenly incensed, would have liked to say. However, he answered carelessly:

"I really don't know. He had to see a patient."

"A patient," repeated Lialia mechanically. She said no more but gazed at the stars.

She was not vexed that Riasantzeff had not come. On the contrary, she wished to be alone, so that, undisturbed by his presence, she might give herself to delicious meditation. To her, the sentiment that filled her youthful being was strange and sweet and tender. It was the consciousness of a climax, desired, inevitable, and yet disturbing, which should close the page of her past life and commence that of her new one. So new, indeed, that Lialia was to become an entirely different being.

To Yourii it was strange that his merry, laughing sister should have become so quiet and pensive. Depressed and irritable himself, everything—Lialia, the dark garden, the distant starlit sky—seemed to him sad and cold. He did not perceive that this dreamy mood concealed not sorrow, but the very essence and fulness of life. In the wide heaven surged forces immeasurable and unknown; the dim garden drew forth vital sap from the earth; and in Lialia's heart there was a joy so full, so complete, that she feared lest any movement, any impression should break the spell. Radiant as the starry heaven, mysterious as the dark garden, harmonies of love and yearning vibrated within her soul.

"Tell me, Lialia, do you love Anatole Pavlovitch very much?" asked Yourii, gently, as if he feared to rouse her.

"How can you ask?" she thought, but, recollecting herself, she nestled closer to her brother, grateful to him for not speaking of anything else but of her life's one interest—the man she adored.

"Yes, very much," she replied, so softly that Yourii guessed rather than heard what she said, striving to restrain her tears of joy. Yet Yourii thought that he could detect a certain note of sadness in her voice, and his pity for her, as his hatred of Riasantzeff, increased.

"Why?" he asked, feeling amazed at such a question.

Lialia looked up in astonishment, and laughed gently.

"You silly boy! Why, indeed! Because . . . Well, have

you never been in love yourself? He's so good, so honest and upright . . ."

"So good-looking and strong," she would have added, but she only blushed and said nothing.

"Do you know him well?" asked Yourii.

"I ought not to have asked that," he thought, inwardly vexed, "for, of course, she thinks that he is the best man in the whole world."

"Anatole tells me everything," replied Lialia timidly, yet triumphantly.

Yourii smiled, and, aware now that there was no going back, retorted, "Are you quite sure?"

"Of course I am; why should I not be?" Lialia's voice trembled.

"Oh! nothing. I merely asked," said Yourii, somewhat confused.

Lialia was silent. He could not guess what was passing through her mind.

"Perhaps you know something about him?" she said suddenly. There was a suggestion of pain in her voice, which puzzled Yourii.

"Oh! no," he said, "not at all. What should I know about Anatole Pavlovitch?"

"But you would not have spoken like that, otherwise," persisted Lialia.

"All that I meant was—well," Yourii stopped short, feeling half ashamed, "well, we men, generally speaking, are all thoroughly depraved, all of us."

Lialia was silent for a while, and then burst out laughing.

"Oh! yes, I know that!" she exclaimed.

Her laughter to him seemed quite out of place.

"You can't take matters so lightly," he replied petulantly, "nor can you be expected to know everything that goes on. You have no idea of all the vile things of life; you are too young, too pure."

"Oh! indeed!" said Lialia, laughing, and flattered. Then in a more serious tone she continued: "Do you suppose that I have not thought of such things? Indeed, I have; and it has always pained and grieved me that we women should care so much for our reputation and our chastity, being afraid to take a step lest we—well, lest we should fall, while men almost look upon it as an heroic deed to seduce a girl. That is all horribly unjust, isn't it?"

"Yes," replied Yourii, bitterly, finding a certain pleasure in lashing his own sins, though conscious that he, Yourii, was absolutely different from other men. "Yes; that is one of the most monstrously unjust things in the world. Ask any one of us if he would like to marry" (he was going to say "a whore," but substituted) "a *cocotte*, and he will always tell you 'No.' But in what respect is a man really any better than a *cocotte*? She sells herself at least for money, to earn a living, whereas a man simply gives rein to his lust in wanton and shameless fashion."

Lialia was silent.

A bat darted backwards and forwards beneath the balcony, unseen, struck the wall repeatedly with its wings and then, with faint fluttering, vanished. Yourii listened to all these strange noises of the night, and then he continued speaking with increasing bitterness. The very sound of his voice drew him on.

"The worst of it is that not only do they all know this, and tacitly agree that it must be so, but they enact complete tragi-comedies, allowing themselves to become betrothed, and then lying to God and man. It is always the purest and most innocent girls, too," (he was thinking jealously of Sina Karsavina) "who become the prey of the vilest debauchees, tainted physically and morally. Semenoff once said to me, 'the purer the woman, the filthier the man who possesses her,' and he was right."

"Is that true?" asked Lialia, in a strange tone.

"Yes, most assuredly it is." Yourii smiled bitterly.

"I know nothing—nothing about it," faltered Lialia, with tears in her voice.

"What?" cried Yourii, for he had not heard her remark.

"Surely Tolia is not like the rest? It's impossible."

She had never spoken of him by his pet name to Yourii before. Then, all at once, she began to weep.

Touched by her distress, Yourii seized her hand.

"Lialia! Lialitschka! What's the matter? I didn't mean to— Come, come, my dear little Lialia, don't cry!" he stammered, as he pulled her hands away from her face and kissed her little wet fingers.

"No! It's true! I know it is!" she sobbed.

Although she had said that she had thought about this, it was in fact pure imagination on her part, for of Riasantzeff's intimate life she had never yet formed the slightest conception. Of course she knew that she was not his first love, and she understood what that meant, though the impression upon her mind had been a vague and never a permanent one.

She felt that she loved him, and that he loved her. This was the essential thing; all else for her was of no importance whatever. Yet now that her brother had spoken thus, in a tone of censure and contempt, she seemed to stand on the verge of a precipice; that of which they talked was horrible, and indeed irreparable; her happiness was at an end; of her love for Riasantzeff there could be no thought now.

Almost in tears himself, Yourii sought to comfort her, as he kissed her and stroked her hair. Yet still she wept, bitterly, hopelessly.

"Oh! dear! Oh! dear!" she sobbed, just like a child.

There, in the dusk, she seemed so helpless, so pitiful, that Yourii felt unspeakably grieved. Pale and confused, he ran into the house, striking his head against the door, and brought her a glass of water, half of which he spilt on the ground and over his hands.

"Oh! don't cry, Lialitschka! You mustn't cry like that! What is the matter! Perhaps Anatole Pavlovitch is better than the rest, Lialia!" he repeated in despair. Lialia, still sobbing, shook violently, and her teeth rattled against the rim of the glass.

"What is the matter, miss?" asked the maid-servant in alarm, as she appeared in the doorway. Lialia rose, and, leaning against the balustrade, went trembling and in tears towards her room.

"My dear little mistress, tell me, what is it? Shall I call the master, Yourii Nicolaijevitch?"

Nicolai Yegorovitch at that moment came out of his study, walking in slow, measured fashion. He stopped short in the doorway, amazed at the sight of Lialia.

"What has happened?"

"Oh! nothing! A mere trifle!" replied Yourii, with a forced laugh. "We were talking about Riasantzeff. It's all nonsense!"

Nicolai Yegorovitch looked hard at him and suddenly his face wore a look of extreme displeasure.

"What the devil have you been saying?" he exclaimed as, shrugging his shoulders, he turned abruptly on his heel and withdrew.

Yourii flushed angrily, and would have made some insolent reply, but a sudden sense of shame caused him to remain silent. Feeling irritated with his father, and grieved for Lialia, while despising himself, he went down the steps into the garden. A little frog, croaking beneath his feet burst like an acorn. He slipped, and with a cry of disgust sprang aside. Mechanically he wiped his foot for a long while on the wet grass, feeling a cold shiver down his back.

He frowned. Disgust mental and physical made him think that all things were revolting and abominable. He groped his way to a seat, and sat there, staring vacantly at the garden, seeing only broad black patches amid the general gloom. Sad, dismal thoughts drifted through his brain.

He looked across to where in the dark grass that poor little frog was dying, or perhaps, after terrible agony, lay dead. A whole world had, as it were, been destroyed; an individual and independent life had come to a hideous end, yet utterly unnoticed and unheard.

And then, by ways inscrutable, Yourii was led to the strange, disquieting thought that all which went to make up a life, the secret instincts of loving or of hating that involuntarily caused him to accept one thing and to reject another; his intuitive sense regarding good or bad; that all this was merely as a faint mist, in which his personality alone was shrouded. By the world in its huge, vast entirety all his profoundest and most agonizing experiences were as utterly and completely ignored as the death-agony of this little frog. In imagining that his sufferings and his emotions were of interest to others, he had expressly and senselessly woven a complicated net between himself and the universe. The moment of death sufficed to destroy this net, and to leave him, devoid of pity or pardon, utterly alone.

Once more his thoughts reverted to Semenoff and to the indifference shown by the deceased student towards all lofty ideals which so profoundly interested him, Yourii, and millions of his kind. This brought him to think of the simple joy of living, the charm of beautiful women, of moonlight, of nightingales, a theme upon which he had mournfully reflected on the day following his last sad talk with Semenoff.

At that time he had not understood why Semenoff attached importance to futile things such as boating or the comely shape of a girl, while deliberately refusing to be interested in the loftiest and most profound conceptions. Now, however, Yourii perceived that it could not have been otherwise for it was these trivial things that constituted life, the real life, full of sensations, emotions, enjoyments; and that all these lofty conceptions were but empty thoughts, vain verbiage, powerless to influence in the slightest the great mystery of life and death. Important, complete though these might be, other words, other thoughts no less weighty and important must follow in the future.

At this conclusion, evolved unexpectedly from his thoughts concerning good and evil, Yourii seemed utterly nonplussed. It was as though a great void lay before him, and, for a moment, his brain felt free and clear, as one in a dream feels able to float through space just whither he will. It alarmed him. With all his might he strove to collect his habitual conceptions of life, and then the alarming sensation disappeared. All became gloomy and confused as before.

Yourii came near to admitting that life was the realization of freedom, and consequently that it was natural for a man to live for enjoyment. Thus Riasantzeff's point of view, though inferior, was yet a perfectly logical one in striving to satisfy his sexual needs as much as possible, they being the most urgent. But then he had to admit that the conceptions of debauchery and of purity were merely as withered leaves that cover fresh grown grass, and that girls romantic and chaste as Lialia or Sina Karsavina, had the right to plunge into the stream of sensual enjoyment. Such an idea shocked him as being both frivolous and nasty, and he endeavoured to drive it from his brain and heart with his usual vehement, stern phrases.

"Well, yes," he thought, gazing upwards at the starry sky, "life is emotion, but men are not unreasoning beasts. They must master their passions; their desires must be set upon what is good. Yet, is there a God beyond the stars?"

As he suddenly asked himself this, a confused, painful sense of awe seemed to crush him to the ground. Persistently he gazed at a brilliant star in the tail of the Great Bear and recollected how Kousma the peasant in the melon-field had called this majestic constellation a "wheel-barrow." He felt annoyed, in a way, that such an irrelevant thought should have crossed his mind. He gazed at the black garden in sharp contrast to the shining sky, pondering, meditating.

"If the world were deprived of feminine purity and grace, that are as the first sweet flowers of spring, what would remain sacred to mankind?"

As he thought thus, he pictured to himself a company of lovely maidens, fair as spring flowers, seated in sunlight on green meadows beneath blossoming boughs. Their youthful breasts, delicately moulded shoulders, and supple limbs moved mysteriously before his eyes, provoking exquisitely voluptuous thrills. As if dazed, he passed his hand across his brow.

"My nerves are overwrought; I must get to bed," thought he. With sensuous visions such as these before his eyes, depressed and ill at ease, Yourii went hurriedly indoors. When in bed, after vain efforts to sleep, his thoughts reverted to Lialia and Riasantzeff.

"Why am I so indignant because Lialia is not Riasantzeff's only love?"

To this question he could find no reply. Suddenly the image of Sina Karsavina rose up before him, soothing his heated senses. Yet, though he strove to suppress his feelings, it became ever clearer to him why he wanted her to be just as she was, untouched and pure.

"Yes, but I love her," thought Yourii, for the first time, and it was this idea that banished all others, even bringing tears to his eyes. But in another moment he was asking himself with a bitter smile, "Why, then, did I make love to other women, before her! True, I did not know of her existence, yet neither did Riasantzeff know of Lialia. At that time we both thought that the woman whom we desired to possess was the real, the sole, the indispensable one. We were wrong then; perhaps we are wrong now. It comes to this, that we must either remain perpetually chaste, or else enjoy absolute sexual liberty, allowing women, of course, to do the same. Now, after all, Riasantzeff is not to blame for having loved other women before Lialia, but because he still carries on with several; and that is not what I do."

The thought made Yourii feel very proud and pure, but only for a moment, for he suddenly recollected his seductive vision of sweet, supple girls in sunlight. He was utterly overwhelmed. His mind became a chaos of conflicting thoughts.

Finding it uncomfortable to lie on his right side, he awkwardly turned over on his left. "The fact is," he thought, "not one of all the women I have known could ever satisfy me for the whole of my life. Thus, what I have called true love is impossible, not to be realized; and to dream of such a thing is sheer folly."

Feeling just as uncomfortable when lying on his left side, he turned over again, restless and perspiring, beneath the hot coverlet; and now his head ached.

"Chastity is an ideal, but, to realize this, humanity would perish. Therefore, it is folly. And life? what is life but folly too?" He almost uttered the words in a loud voice, grinding his teeth with such fury that yellow stars flashed before his eyes.

So, till morning, he tossed from side to side, his heart and brain heavy with despairing thoughts. At last, to escape from them, he sought to persuade himself that he, too, was a depraved, sensual egoist, and that his scruples were but the outcome of hidden lust. Yet this only depressed him the more, and relief was finally obtained by the simple question:

"Why, after all, do I torment myself in this way?"

Disgusted at all such futile processes of self-examination, Yourii, nerveless and exhausted, finally fell asleep.

CHAPTER XV

LIALIA wept in her room for such a long while that at last, her face buried in the pillows, she fell asleep. She woke next morning with aching head and swollen eyes, her first thought being that she must not cry, as Riasantzeff, who was coming to lunch, would be shocked to see her looking so plain. Then, suddenly, she recollected that all was over between them, and a sense of bitter pain and burning love caused her to weep afresh.

"How base, how horrible!" she murmured, striving to keep back her tears. "And why? Why?" she repeated, as infinite grief for love that was lost seemed to overwhelm her. It was revolting to think that Riasantzeff had always lied to her in such a facile, heartless way. "And not only he, but all the others lied, too," she thought. "They all of them professed to be so delighted at our marriage, and said that he was such a good, honest fellow! Well, no, they didn't actually lie about it, but they simply didn't think it was wrong. How hateful of them!"

Thus all those who surrounded her seemed odious, evil persons. She leant her forehead against the window-pane and, through her tears, gazed at the garden. It was gloomy, there; and large raindrops beat incessantly against the panes, so that Lialia could not tell if it were these or her tears which hid the garden from her view. The trees looked sad and forlorn, their pale, dripping leaves and black boughs faintly discernible amid the general downpour that converted the lawn into a muddy swamp.

And Lialia's whole life seemed to her utterly unhappy; the future was hopeless, the past all dark.

When the maid-servant came to call her to breakfast, Lialia, though she heard the words, failed to understand their meaning. Afterwards, at table, she felt confused when her father spoke to her. It was as if he spoke with special pity in his voice; no doubt, everyone knew by this time how abominably false to her the beloved one had been. She hastily returned to her room and once more sat down and gazed at the grey, dreary garden.

"Why should he be so false? Why should he have hurt me like this? Is it that he does not love me? No, Tolia loves me, and I love him. Well, then, what is wrong? Why, it's this; he's deceived me; he's been making love to all sorts of nasty women. I wonder if they loved him as I love him?" she asked herself, naïvely, ardently. "Oh! how silly I am, to be sure! What's the good of worrying about that? He has been false to me, and everything now is at an end. Oh! how perfectly miserable I am! Yes, I ought to worry about it! He was false to me! At least, he might have confessed it to me! But he didn't! Oh! it's abominable! Kissing a lot of other women, and perhaps, even . . . It's awful. Oh! I'm so wretched!"

A little frog hopped across the path,
With legs outstretched!

Thus sang Lialia, mentally, as she spied a little grey ball hopping timidly across the slippery foot-path.

"Yes, I am miserable, and it is all over," thought she, as the frog disappeared in the long grass. "For me it was all so beautiful, so wonderful, and for him, well—just an ordinary, commonplace affair! That is why he always avoided speaking to me of his past life! That is why he always looked so strange, as if he were thinking of something; as if he were thinking 'I know all about that; I know exactly what you feel and what the result of it will be.' While all the time, I was . . . Oh! it's horrible! It's shameful! I'll never, never, never love anybody again!"

And she wept again, her cheek pressed against the cool window-pane, as she watched the drifting clouds.

"But Tolia is coming to lunch to-day!" The thought of it made her shiver. "What am I to say to him? What ought one to say in cases of this kind?"

Lialia opened her mouth and stared anxiously at the wall.

"I must ask Yourii about it. Dear Yourii, He's so good and upright!" she thought, as tears of sympathy filled her eyes. Then, being never wont to postpone matters, she hastened to her brother's room. There she found Schafroff, who was discussing something with Yourii. She stood, irresolute, in the doorway.

"Good morning," she said absently.

"Good morning!" replied Schafroff. "Pray come in, Ludmilla Nicolaijevna; your help is absolutely necessary in this matter."

Still somewhat embarrassed, Lialia sat down obediently at the table and began fingering in desultory fashion some of the green and red pamphlets which were heaped upon it.

"You see, it's like this," began Schafroff, turning towards her as if he were about to explain something extremely complicated, "several of our comrades at Koursk are very hard up, and we must absolutely do what we can to help them. So I think of getting up a concert, eh, what?"

This favourite expression of Schafroff's, "eh, what?" reminded Lialia of her object in coming to her brother's room, and she glanced hopefully at Yourii.

"Why not? It's a very good idea!" she replied, wondering why Yourii avoided her glance.

After Lialia's torrent of tears and the gloomy thoughts which had harrassed him all night long, Yourii felt too depressed to speak to his sister. He had expected that she would come to him for advice, yet to give this in a satisfactory way seemed impossible. So, too, it was impossible to take back what he had said in order to comfort Lialia, and thrust her back into Riasantzeff's arms; nor had he the heart to give the death-blow to her childish happiness.

"Well, this is what we have decided to do," continued Schafroff, moving nearer to Lialia, as if the matter were becoming much more complex, "we mean to ask Lida Sanina and Sina Karsavina to sing. Each a solo, first of all, and afterwards a duet. One is a contralto, and the other, a soprano, so that will do nicely. Then I shall play the violin, and afterwards Sarudine might sing, accompanied by Tanaroff."

"Oh! then, officers are to take part in the concert, are they?" asked Lialia mechanically, thinking all the while of something quite different.

"Why, of course!" exclaimed Schafroff, with a wave of his hand. "Lida has only got to accept, and they'll all swarm round her like bees. As for Sarudine, he'll be delighted to sing; it doesn't matter where, so long as he can sing. This will attract a good many of his brother-officers, and we shall get a full house."

"You ought to ask Sina Karsavina," said Lialia, looking wistfully at her brother. "He surely can't have forgotten," she thought. "How can he discuss this stupid concert, whilst I . . ."

"Why, I told you just now we had done so!" replied Schafroff.

"Oh! yes, so you did," said Lialia, smiling faintly. "Then there's Lida. But you mentioned her, I think?"

"Of course I did! Whom else can we ask, eh?"

"I really . . . don't know!" faltered Lialia. "I've got such a headache."

Yourii glanced hurriedly at his sister, and then continued to pore over his pamphlets. Pale and heavy-eyed, she excited his compassion.

"Oh! why, why did I say all that to her?" he thought. "The whole question is so obscure, to me, as to so many others, and now it must needs trouble her poor little heart! Why, why did I say that!"

He felt as if he could tear his hair.

"If you please, miss," said the maid at the door, "Mr. Anatole Pavlovitch has just come."

Yourii gave another frightened glance at his sister, and met her sad eyes. In confusion he turned to Schafroff, and said hastily:

"Have you read Charles Bradlaugh?"

"Yes, we read some of his works with Dubova, and Sina Karsavina. Most interesting."

"Yes. Oh! have they come back?"

"Yes."

"Since when?" asked Yourii, hiding his emotion.

"Since the day before yesterday."

"Oh! really!" replied Yourii, as he watched Lialia. He felt ashamed and afraid in her presence, as if he had deceived her.

For a moment Lialia stood there irresolute, touching things nervously on the table. Then she approached the door.

"Oh! what have I done!" thought Yourii, as, sincerely grieved, he listened to the sound of her faltering footsteps. As she went towards the other room, Lialia, doubting and distressed, felt as if she were frozen. It seemed as though she were wandering in a dark wood. She glanced at a mirror, and saw the reflection of her own rueful countenance.

"He shall just see me looking like this!" she thought.

Riasantzeff was standing in the dining-room, saying in his remarkably pleasant voice to Nicolai Yegorovitch:

"Of course, it's rather strange, but quite harmless."

At the sound of his voice Lialia felt her heart throb violently, as if it must break. When Riasantzeff saw her, he suddenly stopped talking and came forward to meet her with outstretched arms. She alone knew that this gesture signified his desire to embrace her.

Lialia looked up shyly at him, and her lips trembled. Without a word she pulled her hand away, crossed the room and opened the glass door leading to the balcony. Riasantzeff watched her, calmly, but with slight astonishment.

"My Ludmilla Nicolaijevna is cross," he said to Nicolai Yegorovitch with serio-comic gravity of manner. The latter burst out laughing.

"You had better go and make it up."

"There's nothing else to be done!" sighed Riasantzeff, in droll fashion, as he followed Lialia on to the balcony.

It was still raining. The monotonous sound of falling drops filled the air; but the sky seemed clearer now, and there was a break in the clouds.

Lialia, her cheek propped against one of the cold, damp pillars of the veranda, let the rain beat upon her bare head, so that her hair was wet through.

"My princess is displeased . . . Lialitschka!" said Riasantzeff, as he drew her closer to him, and lightly kissed her moist, fragrant hair.

At this touch, so intimate and familiar, something seemed to melt in Lialia's breast, and without knowing what she did, she flung her arms round her lover's strong neck as, amid a shower of kisses, she murmured:

"I am very, very angry with you! You're a bad man!"

All the while she kept thinking that after all there was nothing so bad, or awful, or irreparable as she had supposed. What did it matter? All that she wanted was to love and be loved by this big, handsome man.

Afterwards, at table, it was painful to her to notice Yourii's look of amazement, and, when the chance came, she whispered to him, "It's awful of me, I know!" at which he

only smiled awkwardly. Yourii was really pleased that the
matter should have ended happily like this, while yet affecting to despise such an attitude of bourgeois complacency
and toleration. He withdrew to his room, remaining there
alone until evening, and as, before sunset, the sky grew clear,
he took his gun, intending to shoot in the same place where
he and Riasantzeff had been yesterday.

After the rain, the marsh seemed full of new life. Many
strange sounds were now audible, and the grasses waved as
if stirred by some secret vital force. Frogs croaked lustily in
a chorus; now and again some birds uttered a sharp discordant cry; while at no great distance, yet out of range, ducks
could be heard cackling in the wet reeds. Yourii, however,
felt no desire to shoot, but he shouldered his gun and turned
homeward, listening to sounds of crystalline clearness in
the grey calm twilight.

"How beautiful!" thought he. "All is beautiful; man alone
is vile!"

Far away he saw the little fire burning in the melon-field,
and ere long by its light he recognized the faces of Kousma
and Sanine.

"What does he always come here for?" thought Yourii,
surprised and curious.

Seated by the fire, Kousma was telling a story, laughing
and gesticulating meanwhile. Sanine was laughing, too.
The fire burned with a slender flame, as that of a taper, the
light being rosy, not red as at night-time, while overhead,
in the blue dome of heaven, the first stars glittered. There
was an odour of fresh mould and rain-drenched grass.

For some reason or other Yourii felt afraid lest they

should see him, yet at the same time it saddened him to think that he could not join them. Between himself and them there seemed to be a barrier incomprehensible and yet unreal; a space devoid of atmosphere, a gulf that could never be bridged.

This sense of utter isolation depressed him greatly. He was alone; from this world with its vesper lights and hues, and fires, and stars, and human sounds, he stood aloof and apart, as though shut close within a dark room. So distressful was this sense of solitude, that as he crossed the melon-field where hundreds of melons were growing in the gloom, to him they seemed like human skulls that lay strewn upon the ground.

CHAPTER XVI

SUMMER now came on, abounding in light and warmth. Between the luminous blue heaven and the sultry earth there floated a tremulous veil of golden haze. Exhausted with the heat, the trees seemed asleep; their leaves, drooping and motionless, cast short, transparent shadows on the parched, arid turf. Indoors it was cool. Pale green reflections from the garden quivered on the ceiling, and while everything else stirred not, the curtains by the window waved.

His linen jacket all unbuttoned, Sarudine slowly paced up and down the room languidly smoking a cigarette, and displaying his large white teeth. Tanaroff, in just his shirt and riding-breeches, lay at full length on the sofa, furtively watching Sarudine with his little black eyes. He was in urgent need of fifty roubles, and had already asked his friend twice for them. He did not venture to do this a third time, and so was anxiously waiting to see if Sarudine himself would return to the subject. The latter had not forgotten by any means, but, having gambled away seven hundred roubles last month, begrudged any further outlay.

"He already owes me two hundred and fifty," thought he, as he glanced at Tanaroff in passing. Then, more irritably, "It's astonishing, upon my word! Of course we're good friends, and all that, but I wonder that he's not the least bit ashamed of himself. He might at any rate make some excuse for owing me all that money. No, I won't lend him another penny," he thought maliciously.

The orderly now entered the room, a little freckled fellow who in slow, clumsy fashion stood at attention, and, without looking at Sarudine, said,

"If you please, sir, you asked for beer, but there isn't any more."

Sarudine's face grew red, as involuntarily he glanced at Tanaroff.

"Well, this is really a bit too much!" he thought. "He knows that I am hard up, yet beer has to be sent for."

"There's very little vodka left, either," added the soldier.

"All right! Damn you! You've still got a couple of roubles. Go and buy what is wanted."

"Please sir, I haven't got any money at all."

"How's that? What do you mean by lying?" exclaimed Sarudine, stopping short.

"If you please, sir, I was told to pay the washerwoman one rouble and seventy copecks, which I did, and I put the other thirty copecks on the dressing-table, sir."

"Yes, that's right," said Tanaroff, with assumed carelessness of manner, though blushing for very shame, "I told him to do that yesterday . . . the woman had been worrying me for a whole week, don't you know."

Two red spots appeared on Sarudine's scrupulously shaven cheeks, and the muscles of his face worked convulsively. He silently resumed his walk up and down the room and suddenly stopped in front of Tanaroff.

"Look here," he said, and his voice trembled with anger,

"I should be much obliged if, in future, you would leave me to manage my own money-affairs."

Tanaroff's face flushed crimson.

"H'm! A trifle like that!" he muttered, shrugging his shoulders.

"It is not a question of trifles," continued Sarudine, bitterly, "it is the principle of the thing. May I ask what right you . . ."

"I . . ." stammered Tanaroff.

"Pray don't explain," said Sarudine, in the same cutting tone. "I must beg you not to take such liberty again."

Tanaroff's lips quivered. He hung his head, and nervously fingered his mother-of-pearl cigarette-holder. After a moment's pause, Sarudine turned sharply round, and, jingling the keys loudly, opened the drawer of his bureau.

"There, go and buy what is wanted!" he said irritably, but in a calmer tone, as he handed the soldier a hundred-rouble note.

"Very good, sir," replied the soldier, who saluted and withdrew.

Sarudine pointedly locked his cash-box and shut the drawer of the bureau. Tanaroff had just time to glance at the box containing the fifty roubles which he needed so much, and then, sighing, lit a cigarette. He felt deeply mortified, yet he was afraid to show this, lest Sarudine should become more angry.

"What are two roubles to him?" he thought. "He knows very well that I am hard up."

Sarudine continued walking up and down obviously irritated, but gradually growing calmer. When the servant brought in the beer, he drank off a tumbler of the ice-cold foaming beverage with evident gusto. Then as he sucked the end of his moustache, he said, as if nothing had happened:

"Lida came again to see me yesterday. A fine girl, I tell you! As hot as they make them."

Tanaroff, still smarting, made no reply.

Sarudine, however, did not notice this, and slowly crossed the room, his eyes laughing as if at some secret recollection. His strong, healthy organism, enervated by the heat, was the more sensitive to the influence of exciting thought. Suddenly he laughed, a short laugh; it was as if he had neighed. Then he stopped.

"You know yesterday I tried to . . ." (here he used a coarse, and in reference to a woman, a most humiliating, expression). "She jibbed a bit, at first; that wicked look in her eyes; you know the sort of thing!"

His animal instincts roused in their turn, Tanaroff grinned lecherously.

"But afterwards, it was all right; never had such a time in my life!" said Sarudine, and he shivered at the recollection.

"Lucky chap!" exclaimed Tanaroff, enviously.

"Is Sarudine at home?" cried a loud voice from the street. "May we come in?" It was Ivanoff.

Sarudine started, fearful lest his words about Lida Sanina should have been heard by some one else. But Ivanoff had hailed him from the roadway, and was not even visible.

"Yes, yes, he's at home!" cried Sarudine from the window.

In the ante-room there was a noise of laughter and clattering of feet, as if the house were being invaded by a merry crowd. Then Ivanoff, Novikoff, Captain Malinowsky, two other officers, and Sanine all appeared.

"Hurrah!" cried Malinowsky, as he pushed his way in. His face was purple, he had fat, flabby cheeks and a moustache like two wisps of straw. "How are you, boys?"

"Bang goes another twenty-five-rouble note!" thought Sarudine with some irritation.

As he was mainly anxious, however, not to lose his reputation for being a wealthy, open-handed fellow, he exclaimed, smiling:

"Hallo! Where are you all going? Here, Tcherepanoff! get some vodka, and whatever's wanted. Run across to the club and order some beer. You will like some beer, gentlemen, eh? A hot day like this?"

When beer and vodka had been brought, the din grew greater. All were laughing, and shouting and drinking, apparently bent on making as much noise as possible. Only Novikoff seemed moody and depressed; his good-tempered face wore an evil expression.

It was not until yesterday that he had discovered what the whole town had been talking about; and at first a sense of humiliation and jealousy utterly overcame him.

"It's impossible! It's absurd! Silly gossip!" he said to himself, refusing to believe that Lida, so fair, so proud, so unapproachable, Lida whom he so deeply loved, could possibly have scandalously compromised herself with such a creature as Sarudine whom he looked upon as infinitely inferior and more stupid than himself. Then wild, bestial jealousy took possession of his soul. He had moments of the

bitterest despair, and anon he was consumed by fierce hatred
of Lida, and specially of Sarudine. To his placid, indolent
temperament this feeling was so strange that it craved an
outlet. All night long he had pitied himself, even thinking
of suicide; but when morning came he only longed with a
wild, inexplicable longing to set eyes upon Sarudine.

Now amid the noise and drunken laughter, he sat apart,
drinking mechanically glass after glass, while intently watching every movement of Sarudine's, much as some wild beast
in a wood watches another wild beast, pretending to see
nothing, yet ever ready to spring. Everything about Sarudine, his smile, his white teeth, his good looks, his voice, were,
for Novikoff, all so many daggers thrust into an open wound.

"Sarudine," said a tall lean officer with exceptionally long,
unwieldy arms, "I've brought you a book."

Above the general clamour Novikoff instantly caught the
name, Sarudine, and the sound of his voice, as well, all other
voices seeming mute.

"What sort of book?"

"It's about women, by Tolstoi," replied the lanky officer,
raising his voice as if he were making a report. On his long
sallow face there was a look of evident pride at being able to
read and discuss Tolstoi.

"Do you read Tolstoi?" asked Ivanoff, who had noticed
this naïvely complacent expression.

"Von Deitz is mad about Tolstoi," exclaimed Malinowsky,
with a loud guffaw.

Sarudine took the slender red-covered pamphlet, and, turning over a few pages, said:

"Is it interesting?"

"You'll see for yourself," replied Von Deitz with enthusiasm. "There's a brain for you, my word! It's just as if one had known it all one's self!"

"But why should Victor Sergejevitsch read Tolstoi when he has his own special views concerning women?" asked Novikoff, in a low tone, not taking his eyes off his glass.

"What makes you think that?" rejoined Sarudine warily, scenting an attack.

Novikoff was silent. With all that was in him, he longed to hit Sarudine full in the face, that pretty self-satisfied-looking face, to fling him to the ground, and kick him, in a blind fury of passion. But the words that he wanted would not come; he knew, and it tortured him the more to know, that he was saying the wrong thing, as, with a sneer, he replied:

"It is enough to look at you to know that."

The strange, menacing tone of his voice produced a sudden lull, almost as if a murder had been committed. Ivanoff guessed what was the matter.

"It seems to me that . . ." began Sarudine coldly. His manner had changed somewhat, though he did not lose his self-control.

"Come, come, gentlemen! What's the matter?" cried Ivanoff.

"Don't interfere! Let them fight it out!" interposed Sanine, laughing.

"It does not seem, but it is so!" said Novikoff, in the same tone, his eyes still fixed on his glass.

Instantly, as it were, a living wall rose up between the rivals, amid much shouting, waving of arms, and expressions of amusement or of surprise. Sarudine was held back by Malinowsky and Von Deitz, while Ivanoff and the other officers kept Novikoff in check. Ivanoff filled up the glasses, and shouted out something, addressing no one in particular. The gaiety was now forced and insincere, and Novikoff felt suddenly that he must get away.

He could bear it no longer. Smiling foolishly, he turned to Ivanoff and the officers who were trying to engage his attention.

"What is the matter with me?" he thought, half-dazed. "I suppose I ought to strike him . . . rush at him, and give him one in the eye! Otherwise, I shall look such a fool, for they must all have guessed that I wanted to pick a quarrel . . ."

But, instead of doing this, he pretended to be interested in what Ivanoff and Von Deitz were saying.

"As regards women, I don't altogether agree with Tolstoi," said the officer complacently.

"A woman's just a female," replied Ivanoff. "In every thousand men you might find one worthy to be called a man. But women, bah! They're all alike—just little naked, plump, rosy apes without tails!"

"Rather smart, that!" said Von Deitz, approvingly.

"And true, too," thought Novikoff, bitterly.

"My dear fellow," continued Ivanoff, waving his hands close to the other's nose, "I'll tell you what, if you were to go to people and say, 'Whatsoever woman looketh on a man to lust after him hath committed adultery with him already in her heart,' most of them would probably think that you had made a most original remark."

Von Deitz burst into a fit of hoarse laughter that sounded like the barking of a dog. He had not understood Ivanoff's joke, but felt sorry not to have made it himself.

Suddenly Novikoff held out his hand to him.

"What? Are you off" asked Von Deitz in surprise.

Novikoff made no reply.

"Where are you going?" asked Sanine.

Still Novikoff was silent. He felt that in another moment the grief pent up within his bosom must break forth in a flood of tears.

"I know what's wrong with you," said Sanine. "Spit on it all!"

Novikoff glanced piteously at him. His lips trembled and with a deprecating gesture, he silently went out, feeling utterly overcome at his own helplessness. To soothe himself, he thought:

"Of what good would it have been to hit that blackguard in the face? It would have only led to a stupid fight. Better not soil my hands!"

But the sense of jealousy unsatisfied and of utter impotence still oppressed him, and he returned home in deep dejection. Flinging himself on his bed, he buried his face in the pillows and lay thus almost the whole day long, bitterly conscious that he could do nothing.

"Shall we play makao?" asked Malinowsky.

"All right!" said Ivanoff.

The orderly at once opened the card-table and gaily the green cloth beamed upon them all. Malinowsky's suggestion had roused the company, and he now began to shuffle the cards with his short, hairy fingers. The bright coloured cards were now scattered circlewise on the green table as the chink of silver roubles was heard after each deal, while on all sides fingers like spiders closed greedily on the coin. Only brief, hoarse ejaculations were audible, expressing either vexation or pleasure. Sarudine had no luck. He obstinately made a point of staking fifteen roubles, and lost every time. His handsome face wore a look of extreme irritation. Last month he had gambled away seven hundred roubles, and now there was all this to add to his previous loss. His ill-humour was contagious, for soon between Von Deitz and Malinowsky there was an interchange of high words.

"I have staked on the side, there," exclaimed Von Deitz irritably.

It amazed him that this drunken boor, Malinowsky, should dare to dispute with such a clever, accomplished person as himself.

"Oh! so you say!" replied Malinowsky, rudely. "Damnation, take it! when I win, then you tell me you've staked on the side, and when I lose . . ."

"I beg your pardon," said Von Deitz, dropping his Russian accent, as he was wont to do when angry.

"Pardon be hanged! Take back your stake! No! No! Take it back, I say!"

"But let me tell you, sir, that . . ."

"Good God, gentlemen, what the devil does all this mean?" shouted Sarudine, as he flung down his cards.

At this juncture a new-comer appeared in the doorway, Sarudine was ashamed of his own vulgar outburst, and of his noisy, drunken guests, with their cards and bottles, for the whole scene suggested a low tavern.

The visitor was tall and thin, and wore a loosely-fitting white suit, and an extremely high collar. He stood on the threshold amazed, endeavouring to recognize Sarudine.

"Hallo! Pavel Lvovitsch! What brings you here?" cried Sarudine, as, crimson with annoyance, he advanced to greet him.

The new-comer entered in hesitating fashion, and the eyes of all were fixed on his dazzling white shoes picking their way through the beer-bottles, corks and cigarette-ends. So white and neat and scented was he, that, in all these clouds of smoke, and amid all these flushed, drunken fellows, he might have been likened to a lily in the marsh, had he not looked so frail and worn-out, and if his features had not been so puny, nor his teeth so decayed under his scanty, red moustache.

"Where have you come from? Have you been away a long while from Pitjer?" * said Sarudine, somewhat flurried, as he feared that "Pitjer" was not exactly the word which he ought to have used.

"I only got here yesterday," said the gentleman in white, in a determined tone, though his voice sounded like the suppressed crowing of a cock. "My comrades," said Sarudine, introducing the others. "Gentlemen, this is Mr. Pavel Lvovitsch Volochine."

Volochine bowed slightly.

"We must make a note of that!" observed the tipsy Ivanoff, much to Sarudine's horror.

"Pray sit down, Pavel Lvovitsch. Would you like some

---

* A slang term for St. Petersburg.

wine or some beer?"

Volochine sat down carefully in an arm-chair and his
white, immaculate form stood out sharply against the dingy
oil-cloth cover.

"Please don't trouble. I just came to see you for a moment,"
he said, somewhat coldly, as he surveyed the company.

"How's that? I'll send for some white wine. You like
white wine, don't you?" asked Sarudine, and he hurried
out.

"Why on earth does the fool want to come here to-day?"
he thought, irritably, as he sent the orderly to fetch wine.
"This Volochine will say such things about me in Petersburg
that I shan't be able to get a footing in any decent house."

Meanwhile Volochine was taking stock of the others with
undisguised curiosity, feeling that he himself was immeas-
urably superior. There was a look in his little glassy, grey
eyes of unfeigned interest, as if he were being shown a collection of wild beasts. He was specially attracted by Sanine's
height, his powerful physique, and his dress.

"An interesting type, that! He must be pretty strong!" he
thought, with the genuine admiration of the weakling for
the athlete. In fact, he began to speak to Sanine, but the latter
leaning against the window-sill, was looking out at the garden. Volochine stopped short; the very sound of his own
squeaky voice vexed him.

"Hooligans!" he thought.

At this moment Sarudine came back. He sat down next to
Volochine and asked questions about St. Petersburg, and also
about the latter's factory, so as to let the others know what a
very wealthy and important person his visitor was. The

handsome face of this sturdy animal now wore an expression of petty vanity and self-importance.

"Everything's the same with us, just the same!" replied Volochine, in a bored tone of voice. "How is it with you?"

"Oh! I'm just vegetating," said Sarudine with a mournful sigh.

Volochine was silent, and looked up disdainfully at the ceiling where the green reflections from the garden wavered.

"Our one and only amusement is this," continued Sarudine, as with a gesture he indicated the cards, the bottles, and his guests.

"Yes, yes!" drawled Volochine; to Sarudine his tone seemed to say, "and you're no better, either."

"I think I must be going now. I'm staying at the hotel on the boulevard. I may see you again!" Volochine rose to take his leave.

At this moment the orderly entered and saluting in slovenly fashion, said,

"The young lady is there, sir."

Sarudine started. "What?" he cried.

"She has come, sir."

"Ah! yes, I know," said Sarudine. He glanced about him nervously, feeling a sudden presentiment.

"I wonder if it's Lida?" he thought. "Impossible!"

Volochine's inquisitive eyes twinkled. His puny little body in its loose white clothes seemed to acquire new vitality.

"Well, good-bye!" he said, laughing. "Up to your old tricks, as usual! Ha! Ha!"

Sarudine smiled uneasily, as he accompanied his visitor to the door, and with a parting stare the latter in his immaculate shoes hurried off.

"Now, sirs," said Sarudine, on his return, "how's the game going? Take the bank for me, will you, Tanaroff? I shall be back directly." He spoke hastily; his eyes were restless.

"That's a lie!" growled the drunken, bestial Malinowsky. "We mean to have a good look at that young lady of yours."

Tanaroff seized him by the shoulders and forced him back into his chair. The others hurriedly resumed their places at the card-table, not looking at Sarudine. Sanine also sat down, but there was a certain seriousness in his smile. He had guessed that it was Lida who had come, and a vague sense of jealousy and pity was roused within him for his handsome sister, now obviously in great distress.

CHAPTER XVII

SIDEWAYS, on Sarudine's bed, sat Lida, in despair, convulsively twisting her handkerchief. As he came in he was struck by her altered appearance. Of the proud, high-spirited girl there was not a trace. He now saw before him a dejected woman, broken by grief, with sunken cheeks and lifeless eyes. These dark eyes instantly met his, and then as swiftly shunned his gaze. Instinctively he knew that Lida feared him, and a feeling of intense irritation suddenly arose within him. Closing the door with a bang, he walked straight up to her.

"You really are a most extraordinary person," he began, with difficulty checking his fierce wish to strike her. "Here am I, with a room full of people; your brother's there, too! Couldn't you have chosen some other time to come? Upon my word, it is too provoking!"

From the dark eyes there shot such a strange flash that Sarudine quailed. His tone changed. He smiled, showing his white teeth, and taking Lida's hand, sat down beside her on the bed.

"Well, well, it doesn't matter. I was only anxious on your account. I am ever so glad that you've come. I was longing to see you."

Sarudine raised her hot, perfumed hand to his lips and kissed it just above the glove.

"Is that the truth?" asked Lida. The curious tone of her
voice surprised him. Again she looked up at him, and her
eyes said plainly, "Is it true that you love me? You see how
wretched I am, now. Not like I was once. I am afraid of
you, and I feel all the humiliation of my present state, but I
have no one except you that can help me."

"How can you doubt it?" replied Sarudine. The words
sounded insincere, almost cold.

Again he took her hand and kissed it. He was entangled
in a strange coil of sensations and of thoughts. Only two
days ago on this very pillow had lain the dark tresses of Lida's
dishevelled hair as he held her in his arms and their lips had
met in a frenzy of passion uncontrolled. In that moment of
desire the whole world and all his countless sensuous schemes
of enjoyment with other women seemed realized and at-
tained; the desire in deliberate and brutal fashion deeply to
wrong this nature placed by passion within his power. And
now, all at once, his feeling for her was one of loathing. He
would have liked to thrust her from him; he wished never
to see her or hear her again. So overpowering was this desire, that to sit beside her became positive torture. At the
same time a vague dread of her deprived him of will-power
and forced him to remain. He was perfectly aware that there
was nothing whatever to bind him to her, and that it was with
her own consent that he had possessed her, without any
promise on his part. Each had given just as each had taken.
Nevertheless he felt as if caught in some sticky substance
from which he could not free himself. He foresaw that Lida
would make some claim upon him, and that he must either
consent, or else commit a base, vile act. He appeared to be

as utterly powerless as if the bones had been removed from
his legs and arms, and as if, instead of a tongue in his mouth,
there were a moist rag. He wanted to shout at her, and let
her know once for all that she had no right to ask anything
of him, but his heart was benumbed by craven fear, and to
his lips there rose a senseless phrase which he knew to be
absolutely unfitting.

"Oh! women, women!"

Lida looked at him in horror. A pitiless light seemed to
flash across her mind. In one instant she realized that she
was lost. What she had given that was noble and pure, she
had given to a man that did not exist. Her fair young life,
her purity, her pride, had all been flung at the feet of a base,
cowardly brute who instead of being grateful to her had
merely soiled her by acts of coarse lubricity. For a moment
she felt ready to wring her hands and fall to the ground in
an agony of despair, but lightning-swift her mood changed
to one of revenge and bitter hatred.

"Can't you really see how intensely stupid you are?" she
hissed through her clenched teeth, as she looked straight into
his eyes.

The insolent words and the look of hatred were so unsuited
to Lida, gracious, feminine Lida, that Sarudine instinctively
recoiled. He had not quite understood their import, and
sought to pass them by with a jest.

"What words to use!" he said, surprised and annoyed.

"I'm not in a mood to choose my words," replied Lida
bitterly, as she wrung her hands. Sarudine frowned.

"Why all these tragic airs?" he asked. Unconsciously al-
lured by their beauty of outline, he glanced at her soft shoul-

ders and exquisitely moulded arms. Her gesture of helplessness and despair made him feel sure of his superiority. It
was as if they were being weighed in scales, one sinking when
the other rose. Sarudine felt a cruel pleasure in knowing that
this girl whom instinctively he had considered superior to
himself was now made to suffer through him. In the first
stage of their intimacy he had feared her. Now she had been
brought to shame and dishonour; at which he was glad.

He grew softer. Gently he took her strengthless hands in
his, and drew her closer to him. His senses were roused; his
breath came quicker.

"Never mind! It'll be all right! There is nothing so dreadful about it, after all!"

"So you think, eh?" replied Lida scornfully. It was scorn
that helped her to recover herself, and she gazed at him with
strange intensity.

"Why, of course I do," said Sarudine, attempting to embrace her in a way that he knew to be effective. But she remained cold and lifeless.

"Come, now, why are you so cross, my pretty one?" he
murmured in a gentle tone of reproof.

"Let me go! Let me go, I say!" exclaimed Lida, as she
shook him off. Sarudine felt physically hurt that his passion
should have been roused in vain.

"Women are the very devil!" he thought.

"What's the matter with you?" he asked testily, and his
face flushed.

As if the question had brought something to her mind,
she suddenly covered her face with both hands and burst into
tears. She wept just as peasant-women weep, sobbing loudly,

her face buried in her hands, her body being bent forward, while her dishevelled hair drooped over her wet, distorted countenance. Sarudine was utterly nonplussed. He smiled, though yet afraid that this might give offence, and tried to pull away her hands from her face. Lida stubbornly resisted, weeping all the while.

"Oh! my God!" he exclaimed. He longed to shout at her, to wrench her hands aside, to call her hard names.

"What are you whining for like this? You've gone wrong with me, worse luck, and there it is! Why all this weeping just to-day? For Heaven's sake, stop!" Speaking thus roughly, he caught hold of her hand.

The jerk caused her head to oscillate to and fro. She suddenly stopped crying, and removed her hands from her tear-stained face, looking up at him in childish fear. A crazy thought flashed through her mind that anybody might strike her now. But Sarudine's manner again softened, and he said in a consoling voice:

"Come, my Lidotschka, don't cry any more! You're to blame, as well! Why make a scene? You've lost a lot, I know; but, still, we had so much happiness, too, didn't we? And we must just forget. . . ."

Lida began to sob once more.

"Oh! stop it, do!" he shouted. Then he walked across the room, nervously pulling his moustache, and his lips quivered.

In the room it was quite still. Outside the window the slender boughs of a tree swayed gently, as if a bird had just perched thereon. Sarudine, endeavouring to check himself, approached Lida, and gently placed his arm round her waist. But she instantly broke away from him and in so doing struck him violently on the chin, so that his teeth rattled.

"Devil take it!" he exclaimed angrily. It hurt him considerably, and the droll sound of his rattling teeth annoyed him even more. Lida had not heard this, yet instinctively she felt that Sarudine's position was a ridiculous one, and with feminine cruelty she took advantage of it.

"What words to use!" she said, imitating him.

"It's enough to make anyone furious," replied Sarudine peevishly.

"If only I knew what was the matter!"

"You mean to say that you still don't know?" said Lida in a cutting tone.

There was a pause. Lida looked hard at him, her face red as fire. Sarudine turned pale, as if suddenly covered by a grey veil.

"Well, why are you silent? Why don't you speak? Speak! Say something to comfort me!" she shrieked, her voice becoming hysterical in tone. The very sound of it alarmed her.

"I . . ." began Sarudine, and his under-lip quivered.

"Yes, you, and nobody else but you, worse luck!" she screamed, almost stifled with tears of rage and despair.

From him as from her the mask of comeliness and good manners had fallen. The wild untrammelled beast became increasingly evident in each.

Ideas like scurrying mice rushed through Sarudine's mind. His first thought was to give Lida money, and persaude her to get rid of the child. He must break with her at once, and for ever. That would end the whole business. Yet though he considered this to be the best way, he said nothing.

"I really never thought that . . ." he stammered.

"You never thought!" exclaimed Lida wildly. "Why didn't you? What right had you not to think?"

"But, Lida, I never told you that I . . ." he faltered, feeling afraid of what he was going to say, yet conscious that he would yet do so, all the same.

Lida, however, had understood, without waiting for him to speak. Her beautiful face grew dark, distorted by horror and despair. Her hands fell limply to her side as she sat down on the bed.

"What shall I do?" she said, as if thinking aloud. "Drown myself?"

"No, no! Don't talk like that!"

Lida looked hard at him.

"Do you know, Victor Sergejevitsch, I feel pretty sure that such a thing would not displease you," she said.

In her eyes and in her pretty quivering mouth there was something so sad, so pitiful, that Sarudine involuntarily turned away.

Lida rose. The thought, consoling at first, that she would find in him her saviour with whom she would always live, now inspired her with horror and loathing. She longed to shake her fist at him, to fling her scorn in his face, to revenge herself on him for having humiliated her thus. But she felt that at the very first words she would burst into tears. A last spark of pride, all that remained of the handsome, dashing Lida, deterred her. In a tone of such intense scorn that it surprised herself as much as Sarudine, she hissed out:

"You brute!"

Then she rushed out of the room, tearing the lace trimming of her sleeve which caught on the bolt of the door.

Sarudine flushed to the roots of his hair. Had she called him "wretch," or "villain," he could have borne that calmly, but "brute" was such a coarse word, so absolutely opposed to his conception of his own engaging personality, that it utterly stunned him. Even the whites of his eyes became bloodshot. He sniggered uneasily, shrugged his shoulders, buttoned and then unbuttoned his jacket, feeling thoroughly upset. But simultaneously a sense of satisfaction and relief waxed greater within him. All was at an end. It irked him to think that he would never again possess such a woman as Lida, that he had lost so comely and desirable a mistress. But he dismissed all such regret with a gesture of disdain.

"Devil take the lot! I can get hold of as many as I please!"

He put his jacket straight, and, his lips still quivering, lit a cigarette. Then assuming his wonted air of nonchalance, he returned to his guests.

CHAPTER XVIII

ALL the gamblers except the drunken Malinowsky had lost their interest in the game. They were intensely curious to know who the lady was that had come to see Sarudine. Those who guessed that it was Lida Sanina felt instinctively jealous, picturing to themselves her white body in Sarudine's embrace. After a while Sanine got up from the table and said:

"I shall not play any more. Good-bye."

"Wait a minute, my friend, where are you going?" asked Ivanoff.

"I'm going to see what they are about, in there," replied Sanine, pointing to the closed door.

"Don't be a fool! Sit down and have a drink!" said Ivanoff.

"You're the fool!" rejoined Sanine, as he went out.

On reaching a narrow side-street where nettles grew in profusion, Sanine bethought himself of the exact spot which Sarudine's windows overlooked. Carefully treading down the nettles, he climbed the wall. When on the top, he almost forgot why he had got up there at all, so charming was it to look down on the green grass and the pretty garden, and to feel the soft breeze blowing pleasantly on his hot, muscular limbs. Then he dropped down into the nettles on the other side, irritably rubbing the places where they had stung

him. Crossing the garden, he reached the window just as
Lida said:

"You mean to say that you still don't know?"

By the strange tone of her voice Sanine instantly guessed
what was the matter. Leaning against the wall and looking
at the garden, he eagerly listened. He felt pity for his handsome sister, for whose beautiful personality the gross term
"pregnant" seemed so unfitting. What impressed him even
more than the conversation was the singular contrast between
these furious human voices and the sweet silence of the
verdurous garden.

A white butterfly fluttered across the grass, revelling in the
sunlight. Sanine watched its progress just as intently as he
listened to the talking.

When Lida exclaimed "You brute!" Sanine laughed merrily, and slowly crossed the garden, careless as to who should
see him.

A lizard darted across his path, and for a long while he
followed the swift movements of its little supple green body
in the long grass.

CHAPTER XIX

L<small>IDA</small> did not go home, but hurriedly turned her steps in an opposite direction. The streets were empty, the air stifling. Close to the wall and fence lay the short shadows, vanquished by the triumphant sun. Through mere force of habit, Lida opened her parasol. She never noticed if it was cold or hot, light or dark. She walked swiftly past the fences all dusty and overgrown with weeds, her head bowed, her eyes downcast. Now and again she met a few gasping pedestrians half-suffocated by the heat. Over the town lay silence, the oppressive silence of a summer afternoon.

A little white puppy had followed Lida. After eagerly sniffing her dress, it ran on in front, and, looking round, wagged its tail, as if to say that they were comrades. At the corner of a street stood a funny little fat boy, a portion of whose shirt peeped out at the back of his breeches. With cheeks distended and fruit-stained, he was vigorously blowing a wooden pipe.

Lida beckoned to the little puppy and smiled at the boy. Yet she did so almost unconsciously; her soul was imprisoned. An obscure force, separating her from the world, swept her onward, past the sunlight, the verdure, and all the joy of life, towards a black gulf that by the dull anguish within her she knew to be near.

An officer of her acquaintance rode by. On seeing Lida he

175

reined in his horse, a roan, whose glossy coat shone in the
sunlight.

"Lidia Petrovna!" he cried, in a pleasant, cheery voice.
"Where are you going in all this heat?"

Mechanically her eyes glanced at his forage-cap, jauntily
poised on his moist, sunburnt brow. She did not speak, but
merely smiled her habitual, coquettish smile.

At that moment, ignorant herself as to what might happen, she echoed his question:

"Ah! where, indeed?"

She no longer felt angry with Sarudine, hardly knowing
why she had gone to him, for it seemed impossible to live
without him, or bear her grief alone. Yet now it was as if
he had just vanished from her life. The past was dead. That
which remained concerned her alone; and as to that, she
alone could decide.

Her brain worked with feverish haste, her thoughts being
yet clear and plain. The most dreadful thing was, that the
proud, handsome Lida would disappear, and in her stead
there would be a wretched being, persecuted, besmirched,
defenceless. Pride and beauty must be retained. Therefore,
she must go, she must get away to some place where the mud
could not touch her.

This fact clearly established, Lida suddenly imagined herself encircled by a void; life, sunlight, human beings, no
longer existed; she was alone in their midst, absolutely alone.
There was no escape; she must die, she must drown herself.
In a moment this became such a certainty that it was as if
round her a wall of stone had arisen to shut her off from all
that had been, and from all that might be.

"How simple it really is!" she thought, looking round, yet seeing nothing.

She walked faster now; and though hindered by her wide skirts, she almost ran, it seemed to her as if her progress were intolerably slow.

"Here's a house, and yonder there's another one, with green shutters; and then, an open space."

The river, the bridge, and what was to happen there—she had no clear conception of this. It was as a cloud, a mist that covered all. But such a state of mind only lasted until she reached the bridge.

As she leant over the parapet and saw the greenish, turbid water, her confidence instantly forsook her. She was seized with fear and a wild desire to live. Now her perception of living things came back to her. She heard voices, and the twittering of sparrows; she saw the sunlight, the daisies in the grass, and the little white dog, that evidently looked upon her as his rightful mistress. It sat opposite to her, put up a tiny paw, and beat the ground with its tail.

Lida gazed at it, longing to hug it convulsively, and large tears filled her eyes. Infinite regret for her beautiful, ruined life overcame her. Half fainting, she leant forward, over the edge of the sun-baked parapet, and the sudden movement caused her to drop one of her gloves into the water. In mute horror she watched it fall noiselessly on the smooth surface of the water, making large circles. She saw her pale yellow glove become darker and darker, and then filling slowly with water, and turning over once, as in its death-agony, sink down gradually with a spiral movement to the green depths of the stream. Lida strained her eyes to mark its descent, but the yellow spot grew ever smaller and more indistinct, and at last disappeared. All that met her gaze was the smooth, dark surface of the water.

"How did that happen, miss?" asked a female voice, close to her.

Lida started backwards, and saw a fat, snub-nosed peasant-woman who looked at her with sympathetic curiosity.

Although such sympathy was only intended for the lost glove, to Lida it seemed as if the good-natured, fat woman knew all, and pitied her. For a moment she was minded to tell her the whole story, and thus gain some relief, but she swiftly rejected the idea as foolish. She blushed, and stammered out:"Oh, it's nothing!" as she reeled backwards from the bridge.

"Here it's impossible! They would pull me out!" she thought.

She walked farther along the river-bank and followed a smooth foot-path to the left between the river and a hedge. On either side were nettles and daisies, sheep's parsley and ill-smelling garlic. Here it was calm and peaceful as in some village church. Tall willows bent dreamily over the stream; the steep, green banks were bathed in sunlight; tall burdocks flourished amid the nettles, and prickly thistles became entangled in the lace trimming of Lida's dress. One huge plant powdered her with its white seeds.

Lida had now to force herself to go farther, striving to overcome a mighty power within which held her back. "It must be! It must! It must!" she repeated, as, dragging herself along, her feet seemed to break their bonds at every step which took her farther from the bridge and nearer to the place at which unconsciously she had determined to stop.

On reaching it, when she saw the black, cold water underneath over-arching boughs, and the current swirling past a corner of the steep bank, then she realized for the first time how much she longed to live, and how awful it was to die. Yet die she must, for to live on was impossible. Without looking round, she flung down her other glove and her parasol, and, leaving the path, walked through the tall grasses to the water. In that moment a thousand thoughts passed through her brain. Deep in her soul, where long it had lain dormant, her childish faith awoke, as with simple fervour she repeated this short prayer: "Lord, save me! Lord, help me!" She suddenly recollected the refrain of a song that latterly she had been studying; for an instant she thought of Sarudine, and then she saw the face of her mother who seemed doubly dear to her in this awful moment. Indeed it was this last recollection which drove her faster to the river. Never till then had Lida so keenly realized that her mother and all those who loved her, did not love her for what she really was, with all her defects and desires, but only for that which they wished her to be. Now that she had strayed from the path that according to them was the only right one, these persons, and especially her mother, having loved her much, would now prove proportionately severe.

Then, as in a delirious dream, all became confused; fear, the longing to live, the sense of the inevitable, unbelief, the conviction that all was at an end, hope, despair, the horrible consciousness that this was the spot where she must die, and then the vision of a man strangely like her brother who leapt over a hedge and rushed towards her.

"You could not have thought of anything sillier!" cried Sanine, breathless.

By a strange coincidence it so happened that Lida had reached the very spot adjoining Sarudine's garden where first she had surrendered to him, a place screened by dark trees from the light of the moon. Sanine had seen her in the distance, and had guessed her intention. At first he was for letting her have her way, but her wild, convulsive movements aroused his pity, and vaulting the garden-seats and the bushes he hastened to her rescue.

Her brother's voice had an alarming effect upon Lida. Her nerves, wrought to the utmost pitch by her inward conflict, suddenly gave way. She became giddy; everything swam before her eyes, and she no longer knew if she were in the water or on the river-bank. Sanine had just time to seize her firmly and drag her backwards, secretly pleased at his own strength and adroitness.

"There!" he said.

He placed her in a sitting posture against the hedge, and then looked about him.

"What shall I do with her?" he thought. Lida in that moment recovered consciousness, as, pale and confused, she began to weep piteously. "My God! My God!" she sobbed, like a child.

"Silly thing!" said Sanine, chiding her good-humouredly.

Lida did not hear him, but, as he moved, she clutched at his arm, sobbing more violently.

"Ah! what am I doing?" she thought fearfully. "I ought not to weep; I must try and laugh it off, or else he'll guess what is wrong."

"Well, why are you so upset?" asked Sanine, as he patted her shoulder tenderly.

Lida looked up at him under her hat, timidly as a child, and stopped crying.

"I know all about it," said Sanine; "the whole story. I've done so for ever so long."

Though Lida was aware that several persons suspected the nature of her relations with Sarudine, yet when Sanine said this, it was as if he had struck her in the face. Her supple form recoiled in horror; she gazed at him dry-eyed, like some wild animal at bay.

"What's the matter, now? You behave as if I had trodden on your foot," laughed Sanine. Taking hold of her round, soft shoulders, which quivered at his touch, he tenderly drew her back to her former place by the hedge, and she obediently submitted.

"Come now, what is it that distresses you so?" he said. "Is it because I know all? Or do you think your misconduct with Sarudine so dreadful that you are afraid to acknowledge it? I really don't understand you. But, if Sarudine won't marry you, well—that is a thing to be thankful for. You know now, and you must have known before, what a base, common fellow he really is, in spite of his good looks and his fitness for amours. All that he has is beauty, and you have now had your fill of that."

"He of mine, not I of his!" she faltered. "Ah! well yes, perhaps I had! Oh! my God, what shall I do?"

"And now you are pregnant . . ."

Lida shut her eyes and bowed her head.

"Of course, it's a bad business," continued Sanine gently.

"In the first place, giving birth to children is a nasty, painful affair; in the second place, and what really matters, people would persecute you incessantly. After all, Lidotschka, my Lidotschka," he said with a sudden access of affection, "you've not done harm to anybody; and, if you were to bring a dozen babies into the world, the only person to suffer thereby would be yourself."

Sanine paused to reflect, as he folded his arms across his chest and bit the ends of his moustache.

"I could tell you what you ought to do, but you are too weak and too foolish to follow my advice. You are not plucky enough. Anyhow, it is not worth while to commit suicide. Look at the sun shining, at the calm, flowing stream. Once dead, remember, everyone would know what your condition had been. Of what good, then, would that be to you? It is not because you are pregnant that you want to die, but because you are afraid of what other folk will say. The terrible part of your trouble lies, not in the actual trouble itself, but because you put it between yourself and your life which, as you think, ought to end. But, in reality, that will not alter life a jot. You do not fear folk who are remote, but those who are close to you, especially those who love you and who regard your surrender as utterly shocking because it was made in a wood, or a meadow, instead of in a lawful marriage-bed. They will not be slow to punish you for your offence, so, of what good are they to you? They are stupid, cruel, brainless people. Why should you die because of stupid, cruel, brainless people?"

Lida looked up at him with her great questioning eyes in which Sanine could detect a spark of comprehension.

"But what am I to do? Tell me, what . . . what . . ." she murmured huskily.

"For you there are two ways open: you must get rid of this child that nobody wants, and whose birth, as you must see yourself, will only bring trouble."

Lida's eyes expressed wild horror.

"To kill a being that knows the joy of living and the terror of death is a grave injustice," he continued; "but a germ, an unconscious mass of flesh and blood . . ."

Lida experienced a strange sensation. At first shame overwhelmed her, such shame as if she were completely stripped, while brutal fingers touched her. She dared not look at her brother, fearing that for very shame they would both expire. But Sanine's grey eyes wore a calm expression, and his voice was firm and even in tone, as if he were talking of ordinary matters. It was this quiet strength of utterance and the profound truth of his words that removed Lida's shame and fear. Yet suddenly despair prevailed, as she clasped her forehead, while the flimsy sleeves of her dress fluttered like the wings of a startled bird.

"I cannot, no, I cannot!" she faltered. "I dare say you're right, but I cannot! It is so awful!"

"Well, well, if you can't," said Sanine, as he knelt down, and gently drew away her hands from her face, "we must contrive to hide it somehow. I will see to it that Sarudine has to leave the town, and you—well, you shall marry Novikoff, and be happy. I know that if you had never met this dashing young officer, you would have accepted Sascha Novikoff. I am certain of it."

At the mention of Novikoff's name Lida saw light through

the gloom. Because Sarudine had made her unhappy, and she was convinced that Novikoff would never have done so, for an instant it seemed to her that all could easily be set right. She would at once get up, go back, say something or other, and life in all its radiant beauty would again lie before her. Again she would live, again she would love, only this time it would be a better life, a deeper, purer love. Yet immediately afterwards she recollected that this was impossible, for she had been soiled and degraded by an ignoble, senseless amour.

A gross word, which she scarcely knew and had never uttered, suddenly came into her mind. She applied it to herself. It was as if she had received a box on the ears.

"Great heavens! Am I really a . . .? Yes, yes, of course, I am!"

"What did you say?" she murmured, ashamed of her own resonant voice.

"Well, what is it to be?" asked Sanine, as he glanced at her pretty hair falling in disorder about her white neck flecked by sunlight breaking through the net work of leaves. A sudden fear seized him that he would not succeed in persuading her, and that this young, beautiful woman, fitted to bestow such joy upon others, might vanish into the dark, senseless void. Lida was silent. She strove to repress her longing to live, which, despite her will, had mastered her whole trembling frame. After all that had occurred, it seemed to her shameful not only to live, but to wish to live. Yet her body, strong and full of vitality, rejected so distorted an idea as if it were poison.

"Why this silence?" asked Sanine.

"Because it is impossible. . . . It would be a vile thing to do! . . . I . . ."

"Don't talk such nonsense!" retorted Sanine impatiently.

Lida looked up at him again, and in her tearful eyes there was a glimmer of hope.

Sanine broke off a twig, which he bit and then flung away.

"A vile thing!" he went on. "A vile thing! My words amaze you. Yet why? The question is one that neither you nor I can ever rightly answer. Crime! What is a crime? If a mother's life is in danger when giving birth to a child, and that living child, to save its mother, is destroyed, that is not a crime, but an unfortunate necessity! But to suppress something that does not yet exist, that is called a crime, a horrible deed. Yes, a horrible deed, even though the mother's life, and, what is more, her happiness, depends upon it! Why must it be so? Nobody knows, but everybody loudly maintains that view, crying, 'Bravo!' " Sanine laughed sarcastically. "Oh! you men, you men! Men create for themselves phantoms, shadows, illusions, and are the first to suffer by them. But they all exclaim, 'Oh! Man is a masterpiece, noblest of all; man is the crown, the King of creation'; but a king that has never yet reigned, a suffering king that quakes at his own shadow."

For a moment, Sanine paused.

"After all, that is not the main point. You say that it is a vile thing. I don't know; perhaps it is. If Novikoff were to hear of your trouble, it would grieve him terribly; in fact, he might shoot himself, but yet he would love you, just the same. In that case the blame would be his. But if he were a really intelligent man, he would not attach the slightest importance

to the fact that you had already (excuse the expression!) slept
with somebody else. Neither your body nor your soul has
suffered thereby. Good Lord! Why, he might marry a
widow himself, for instance! Therefore it is not that which
prevents him, but the confused notions with which his head
is filled. And, as regards yourself, if it were only possible for
human beings to love once in their lives, then, a second attempt to do so would certainly prove futile and unpleasant.
But this is not so. To fall in love, or to be loved, is just as
delightful and desirable. You will get to love Novikoff, and
if you don't, well, we'll travel together, my Lidotschka; one
can live, can't one, anywhere, after all?"

Lida sighed and strove to overcome her final scruples.

"Perhaps . . . everything will come right again," she murmured. "Novikoff . . . he's so good and kind . . . nice-look-
ing, too, isn't he? Yes . . . no . . . I don't know what to say."

"If you had drowned yourself, what then? The powers of
good and evil would have neither gained nor lost thereby.
Your corpse, bloated, disfigured, and covered with slime,
would have been dragged from the river, and buried. That
would have been all!"

Lida had a lurid vision of greenish, turbid water with
slimy trailing weeds and gruesome bubbles floating round
her.

"No, no, never!" she thought, turning pale. "I would
rather bear all the shame of it . . . and Novikoff . . . everything . . . anything but that."

"Ah! look how scared you are!" said Sanine, laughing.

Lida smiled through her tears, and her very smile consoled
her.

"Whatever happens, I mean to live!" she said with passionate energy.

"Good!" exclaimed Sanine, as he jumped up. "Nothing is more awful than the thought of death. But so long as you can bear the burden without losing perception of the sights and sounds of life, I say live! Am I not right? Now, give me your paw!"

Lida held out her hand. The shy, feminine gesture betokened childish gratitude.

"That's right . . . What a pretty little hand you've got."

Lida smiled and said nothing.

But Sanine's words had not proved ineffectual. Hers was a vigorous, buoyant vitality; the crisis through which she had just passed had strained that vitality to the utmost. A little more pressure, and the string would have snapped. But the pressure was not applied, and her whole being vibrated once more with an impetuous, turbulent desire to live. She looked above, around her, in ecstasy, listening to the immense joy pulsating on every side; in the sunlight, in the green meadows, the shining stream, the calm, smiling face of her brother, and in herself. It was as if she could see and hear all this for the first time. "To be alive!" cried a gladsome voice within her.

"All right!" said Sanine. "I will help you in your trouble, and stand by you when you fight your battles. And now, as you're such a beauty, you must give me a kiss."

Lida smiled; a smile mysterious as that of a wood-nymph. Sanine put his arms round her waist, and, as her warm supple form thrilled at his touch, his fond embrace became almost vehement. A strange, indefinable sense of joy overcame

Lida, as she yearned for life ampler and more intense. It
mattered not to her what she did. She slowly put both arms
round her brother's neck and, with half-closed eyes, set her
lips tight to give the kiss.

She felt unspeakably happy beneath Sanine's burning caress, and in that moment cared not who it was that kissed her,
just as a flower warmed by the sun never asks whence cometh
such warmth.

"What is the matter with me?" she thought, pleasurably
alarmed. "Ah! yes! I wanted to drown myself . . . how
silly! And for what? Oh! that's nice! Again! Again!
Now, I'll kiss you! It's lovely! And I don't care what happens so long as I'm alive, alive!"

"There, now, you see," said Sanine, releasing her. "All
good things are just good, and one mustn't make them out
to be anything else."

Lida smiled absently, and slowly re-arranged her hair.
Sanine handed her the parasol and glove. To find the other
glove was missing at first surprised her, but instantly recollecting the reason, she felt greatly amused at the absurd importance which she had given to that trifling incident.

"Ah! well, that's over!" she thought, and walked with her
brother along the river-bank. Fiercely the sun's rays beat
upon her round, ripe bosom.

CHAPTER XX

Novikoff, when he opened the door himself to Sanine, looked far from pleased at the prospect of such a visit. Everything that reminded him of Lida and of his shattered dream of bliss caused him pain.

Sanine noticed this, and came into the room smiling affably. All there was in disorder, as if scattered by a whirlwind. Scraps of paper, straw, and rubbish of all sorts covered the floor. On the bed and the chairs lay books, linen, surgical instruments and a portmanteau.

"Going away?" asked Sanine, in surprise. "Where?"

Novikoff avoided the other's glance and continued to overhaul the things, vexed at his own confusion. At last he said:

"Yes, I've got to leave this place. I've had my official notice."

Sanine looked at him and then at the portmanteau. After another glance his features relaxed in a broad smile.

Novikoff was silent, oppressed by his sense of utter loneliness and inconsolable grief. Lost in his thoughts, he proceeded to wrap up a pair of boots together with some glass tubes.

"If you pack like that," said Sanine, "when you arrive you'll find yourself minus either tubes or boots."

Novikoff's tear-stained eyes flashed back a reply. They

said, "Ah! leave me alone! Surely you can see how sad I am!"

Sanine understood and was silent.

The dreamy summer twilight-hour had come, and above the verdant garden the sky, clear as crystal, grew paler. At last Sanine spoke.

"Instead of going the deuce knows where, I think it would be much more sensible if you were to marry Lida!"

Novikoff turned round trembling.

"I must ask you to stop making such stupid jokes!" he said in a shrill, hard voice. It rang out through the dusk, and echoed among the dreaming garden-trees.

"Why so furious?" asked Sanine.

"Look here!" began Novikoff hoarsely. In his eyes there was a such an expression of rage that Sanine scarcely recognized him.

"Do you mean to say that it wouldn't be a lucky thing for you to marry Lida?" continued Sanine merrily.

"Shut up!" cried the other, staggering forward, and brandishing an old boot over Sanine's head.

"Now then! Gently! Are you mad?" said Sanine sharply, as he stepped backwards.

Novikoff flung the boot away in disgust, breathing hard.

"With that boot you were actually going to . . ." Sanine stopped, and shook his head. He pitied his friend, though such behaviour seemed to him utterly ridiculous.

"It's your fault," stammered Novikoff in confusion.

And then, suddenly, he felt full of trust and sympathy for Sanine, strong and calm as he was. He himself resembled a little school-boy, eager to tell some one of his troubles. Tears filled his eyes.

"If you only knew how sad at heart I am," he murmured, striving to conquer his emotion.

"My dear fellow, I know all about it—everything," said Sanine kindly.

"No! You can't know all!" said Novikoff, as he sat down beside the other. He thought that no one could possibly feel such sorrow as his.

"Yes, yes, I do," replied Sanine, "I swear that I do; and if you'll promise not to attack me with your old boot, I will prove what I say. Promise?"

"Yes, yes! Forgive me, Volodja!" said Novikoff, calling Sanine by his first name which he had never done before. This touched Sanine, and he felt the more anxious to help his friend.

"Well, then, listen," he began, as he placed his hand in confidential fashion on the other's knee. "Let us be quite frank. You are going away, because Lida refused you, and because, at Sarudine's the other day, you had an idea that it was she who came to see him in private."

Novikoff bent forward, too distressed to speak. It was as if Sanine had re-opened an agonizing wound. The latter, noticing Novikoff's agitation, thought inwardly, "You good-natured old fool!"

Then he continued:

"As to the relation between Lida and Sarudine, I can affirm nothing positively, for I know nothing, but I don't believe that ... " He did not finish the sentence when he saw how dark the other's face became.

"Their intimacy," he went on, "is of such recent date that

nothing serious can have happened, especially if one considers Lida's character. You, of course, know what she is."

There rose up before Novikoff the image of Lida, as he had once known and loved her; of Lida, the proud, high-spirited girl, lustrous-eyed, and crowned with serene, consummate beauty as with a radiant aureole. He shut his eyes and put faith in Sanine's words.

"Well, and if they really did flirt a bit, that's over and ended now. After all, what is it to you if a girl like Lida, young and fancy-free, has had a little amusement of this sort? Without any great effort of memory I expect you could recall at least a dozen such flirtations of a far more dangerous kind, too."

Novikoff glanced trustfully at Sanine, afraid to speak, lest the faint spark of hope within him should be extinguished. At last he stammered out:

"You know, if I . . ."; but he got no further. Words failed him, and tears choked his utterance.

"Well, if you what?" asked Sanine loudly, and his eyes shone. "I can tell you this, that there is not, and there never has been, anything between Lida and Sarudine."

Novikoff looked at him in amazement.

"I . . . well . . . I thought . . ." he began, feeling, to his dismay, that he could no longer believe what Sanine said.

"You thought a lot of nonsense!" replied Sanine sharply. "You ought to know Lida better than that. What sort of love can there be with all that hesitation and shilly-shally-ing?"

Novikoff, overjoyed, grasped the other's hand.

Then, suddenly Sanine's face wore a furious expression as

he closely watched the effect of his words upon his companion.

Novikoff showed obvious pleasure at the thought of the woman he desired being immaculate. Into those honest sorrowful eyes, there came a look of animal jealousy and concupiscence.

"Oho!" exclaimed Sanine threateningly, as he got up. "Then what I have to tell you is this: Lida has not only fallen in love with Sarudine, but she has also had illicit relations with him, and is now *enceinte.*"

There was dead silence in the room. Novikoff smiled a strange, sickly smile and rubbed his hands. From his trembling lips there issued a faint cry. Sanine stood over him, looking straight into his eyes. The wrinkled corners of his mouth showed suppressed anger.

"Well, why don't you speak?" he asked.

Novikoff looked up for a moment, but instantly avoided the other's glance, his features being still distorted by a vacuous smile.

"Lida has just gone through a terrible ordeal," said Sanine in a low voice, as if soliloquizing. "If I had not chanced to overtake her, she would not be living now, and what yesterday was a healthful, handsome girl would now be lying in the river-mud, a bloated corpse, devoured by crabs. The question is not one of her death—we must each of us die some day—yet how sad to think that with her all the brightness and joy created for others by her personality would also have perished. Of course, Lida is not the only one in all the world; but, my God! if there were no girlish loveliness left, it would be as sad and gloomy as the grave.

"For my part, I am eager to commit murder when I see a poor girl brought to ruin in this senseless way. Personally, it is a matter of utter indifference to me whether you marry Lida or go to the devil, but I must tell you that you are an idiot. If you had got one sound idea in your head, would you worry yourself and others so much merely because a young woman, free to pick and choose, had become the mistress of a man who was unworthy of her, and by following her sexual impulse had achieved her own complete development? Nor are you the only idiot, let me tell you. There are millions of your sort who make life into a prison, without sunshine or warmth! How often have you given rein to your lust in company with some harlot, the sharer of your sordid debauch? In Lida's case it was passion, the poetry of youth, and strength, and beauty. By what right, then, do you shrink from her, you that call yourself an intelligent, sensible man? What has her past to do with you? Is she less beautiful? Or less fitted for loving, or for being loved? Is it that you yourself wanted to be the first to possess her? Now then, speak!"

"You know very well that it is not that!" said Novikoff, as his lips trembled.

"Ah! yes, but it is!" cried Sanine. "What else could it be, pray?"

Novikoff was silent. All was darkness within his soul, yet, as a distant ray of light through the gloom there came the thought of pardon and self-sacrifice.

Sanine, watching him, seemed to read what was passing through his mind.

"I see," he began in a subdued tone, "that you contemplate

sacrificing yourself for her. 'I will descend to her level, and
protect her from the mob,' and so on. That's what you are
saying to your virtuous self, waxing big in your own eyes as
a worm does in carrion. But it's all a sham; nothing else but
a lie! You're not in the least capable of self-sacrifice. If,
for instance, Lida had been disfigured by small-pox, perhaps
you might have worked yourself up to such a deed of heroism. But after a couple of days you would have embittered
her life, either by spurning her or deserting her, or over-
whelming her with reproaches. At present your attitude
towards yourself is one of adoration, as if you were an *ikon*.
Yes, yes, your face is transfigured, and everyone would say
'Oh! look, there's a saint.' Yet you have lost nothing which
you desired. Lida's limbs are the same as before; so are her
passion and her splendid vitality. But of course, it is extremely convenient and also agreeable to provide oneself
with enjoyment while piously imagining that one is doing
a noble deed. I should rather say it was!"

At these words, Novikoff's self-pity gave place to a nobler
sentiment.

"You take me to be worse than I am," he said reproach-
fully. "I am not so wanting in feeling as you think. I won't
deny that I have certain prejudices, but I love Lidia Petrovna,
and if I were quite sure that she loved me, do you think that
I should take a long while to make up my mind, because
..."

His voice failed him at this last word.

Sanine suddenly became quite calm. Crossing the room,
he stood at the open window, lost in thought.

"Just now she is very sad," he said, "and will hardly be

thinking of love. If she loves you or not, how can I tell? But it seems to me that if you came to her as the second man who did not condemn her for her brief amour, well ... Anyway, there's no knowing what she'll say!"

Novikoff sat there, as one in a dream. Sadness and joy produced within his heart a sense of happiness as gentle and elusive as the light in an evening sky.

"Let us go to her," said Sanine. "Whatever happens, it will please her to see a human face amid so many false masks that hide grimacing brutes. You're a bit of a fool, my friend, but in your stupidity there is something which others haven't got. And to think that for ever so long the world founded its hopes and happiness upon such folly! Come, let us go!"

Novikoff smiled timidly. "I am very willing to go to her. But will she care to see me?"

"Don't think about that," said Sanine, as he placed both hands on the other's shoulders. "If you are minded to do what's right, then, do it, and the future will take care of itself."

"All right; let us go," exclaimed Novikoff with decision. In the doorway he stopped and looking Sanine full in the face he said with unwonted emphasis:

"Look here, if it is in my power, I will do my best to make her happy. This sounds commonplace, I know, but I can't express my feelings in any other way."

"No matter, my friend," replied Sanine cordially, "I understand."

CHAPTER XXI

THE glow of summer lay on the town. Calm were the nights when the large, lustrous moon shone overhead and the air, heavy with odours from field and garden, pleasurably soothed the languid senses.

In the daytime people worked, or were engaged in politics or art; in eating, drinking, bathing, conversing. Yet, when the heat grew less, and the bustle and turmoil had ceased, while on the dim horizon the moon's round mysterious disc rose slowly above meadow and field, shedding on roofs and gardens a strange, cold light, then folk began to breathe more freely, and to live anew, having cast off, as it were, an oppressive cloak.

And, where youth predominated, life became ampler and more free. The gardens were filled with the melody of nightingales, the meadow-grasses quivered in response to the light touch of a maiden's gown, while shadows deepened, and in the warm dusk eyes grew brighter and voices more tender, for love was in the languid, fragrant air.

Yourii Svarogitsch and Schafroff were both keenly interested in politics, and in a recently formed society for mutual education, Yourii read all the latest books, and believed that he had now found his vocation in life, and a way to end all his doubts. Yet, however much he read, and despite all his activities, life had no charm for him, being barren and dreary. Only when in robust health, and when the physical part of him was roused by the prospect of falling in love, did life seem really desirable. Formerly all pretty young women had interested him in equal measure, yet among the rest he now singled out one in whom the charms of all the others were united, standing apart in her loveliness as a young birch-tree stands in springtime on the border of a wood.

She was tall and shapely, her head was gracefully poised on her white, smooth shoulders, and her voice, in speech sonorous, was in singing sweet. Although her own talents for music and poetry were eminently pleasing to her, it was in physical effort that her intense vitality found its fullest expression. She longed to crush something against her bosom, to stamp her foot on the ground, to laugh and sing, and to contemplate good-looking young men. There were times when, in the blaze of noon or in the pale moonlight, she felt as if she must suddenly take off all clothing, rush across the grass, and plunge into the river to seek some one that with tender accents she longed to allure. Her presence troubled Yourii. In her company he became more eloquent, his pulses beat faster, and his brain was more alert. All day long his thoughts were of her, and in the evening it was she that he sought, though he never admitted to himself that he did so. He was forever analysing his feelings, each sentiment withering as a blossom in the frost. Whenever he asked himself what it was that attracted him to Sina Karsavina, the answer was always "the sexual instinct, and nothing else." Without knowing why, this explanation provoked self-contempt.

Yet a tacit understanding had been established between

them and, like two mirrors, the emotions of the one were reflected in the other.

Sina Karsavina never troubled to analyse her sentiments which, if they caused her slight apprehension, yet pleased her vastly. She jealously hid them from others, being determined to keep them entirely to herself. It distressed her much that she could not discover what was really at work in that handsome young fellow's heart. At times it seemed to her that there was nothing between them, and then she grieved as if for the loss of something precious. Nevertheless she was not averse to receiving the attentions of other men, and her belief that Yourii loved her gave her the elated manner of a bride-elect, making her doubly attractive to other admirers. She was powerfully fascinated by the presence of Sanine, whose broad shoulders, calm eyes, and deliberate manner won her regard. When Sina became aware of his effect upon her, she accused herself of want of self-control if not of modesty; nevertheless she always continued to observe him with great interest.

On the very evening that Lida had undergone such a terrible ordeal, Yourii and Sina met at the library. They merely exchanged greetings, and went about their business, she to choose books, and he to look at the latest Petersburg newspapers. They happened, however, to leave the building together and walked along the lonely, moonlit streets side by side. All was silent as the grave, and one could only hear at intervals the watchman's rattle, and the distant bark of a dog.

On reaching the boulevard they were aware of a merry party sitting under the trees. They heard laughter; and the

gleam of a lighted cigarette revealed for an instant a fair
moustache. Just as they passed a man's voice sang:

> The heart of fair lady
> Is wayward as the wind across the wheat . . .

When they got within a short distance of Sina's home they
sat down on a bench where it was very dark. In front of
them lay the broad street, all white in the moonlight, and
the church topped by a cross that gleamed as a star above
the black linden-trees.

"Look! How pretty that is!" exclaimed Sina, as she pointed
to the church. Yourii glanced admiringly at her white
shoulder which, in the costume of Little Russia that she
wore, was exposed to view. He longed to clasp her in his
arms and kiss her full red lips. It seemed as if he must do
so, and as if she expected and desired this. But he let the
propitious moment pass, laughing gently, almost mockingly,
to himself.

"Why do you laugh?"

"Oh! I don't know!—nothing!" replied Yourii nervously,
trying to appear unmoved.

They were both silent as they listened to faint sounds that
came to them through the darkness.

"Have you ever been in love?" asked Sina, suddenly.

"Yes," said Yourii slowly. "Suppose I tell her?" he thought.
Then, aloud, "I am in love now."

"With whom?" she asked, fearing to hear the answer,
while yet certain that she knew it.

"With you, of course," replied Yourii, vainly assuming a
playful tone as he leant forward and gazed into her eyes, that

shone strangely in the gloom. They expressed surprise and expectancy. Yourii longed to embrace her, yet again his courage failed him, and he pretended to stifle a yawn.

"He's only in fun!" thought Sina, growing suddenly cool.

She felt hurt at such hesitation on Yourii's part. To keep back her tears, she clenched her teeth, and in an altered tone exclaimed "Nonsense!" as she quickly got up.

"I am speaking quite seriously," began Yourii, with unnatural earnestness. "I love you, believe me, I do, passionately!"

Sina took up her books without saying a word.

"Why, why does he talk like this?" she thought to herself. "I've let him see that I care, and now he despises me."

Yourii bent down to pick up a book that had fallen.

"It is time to go home," she said coldly. Yourii felt grieved that she wanted to go just at that moment, but he thought at the same time that he had played his part quite successfully, and without in the least appearing commonplace. Then he said, impressively: "Au revoir!"

She held out her hand. He swiftly bent over it and kissed it. Sina started back, uttering a faint cry: "What are you doing?"

Though his lips had only just touched her soft little hand, his emotion was so great that he could only smile feebly as she hurried away, and soon he heard the click of her garden gate. As he walked homewards his face wore the same silly smile, while he breathed the pure night air, and felt strong, and glad of heart.

CHAPTER XXII

On reaching his room, narrow and stuffy as a prison-cell, Yourii found life as dreary as ever, and his little love-episode seemed to him thoroughly commonplace.

"I stole a kiss from her! What bliss! How heroic of me! How exquisitely romantic! In the moonlight the hero beguiles the fair maid with burning words and kisses! Bah! what rubbish! In such a cursed little hole as this one insensibly becomes a shallow fool!"

When he lived in a city, Yourii imagined that the country was the real place for him where he could associate with peasants and share in their rustic toil beneath a burning sun. Now that he had the chance to do this, village life seemed insufferable to him, and he longed for the stimulus of a town where alone his energies could have scope.

"The stir and bustle of a city! The thrill of passionate eloquence!" so he rapturously phrased it to himself; yet he soon checked such boyish enthusiasm.

"After all, what does it mean? What are politics and science? Great as ideals in the distance, yes! But in the life of each individual they're only a trade, like anything else! Strife! Titanic efforts! The conditions of modern existence make all that impossible. I suffer, I strive, I surmount obstacles! Well, what then? Where's the end of it? Not in my lifetime, at any rate! Prometheus wished to give fire to

202

mankind, and he did so. That was a triumph, if you like! But what about us? The most we do is to throw faggots on a fire that we have never kindled, and which by us will never be put out."

It suddenly struck him that if things were wrong it was because he, Yourii, was not a Prometheus. Such a thought, in itself most distressing, yet gave him another opportunity for morbid self-torture.

"What sort of a Prometheus am I? Always looking at everything from a personal, egotistic point of view. It is I, always I; always for myself. I am every bit as weak and insignificant as the other people that I heartily despise."

This comparison was so displeasing to him that his thoughts became confused, and for a while he sat brooding over the subject, endeavouring to find a justification of some kind.

"No, I am not like the others," he said to himself, feeling, in a sense, relieved, "because I think about these things. Fellows like Riasantzeff and Novikoff and Sanine would never dream of doing so. They have not the remotest intention of criticizing themselves, being perfectly happy and self-satisfied, like Zarathustra's triumphant pigs. The whole of life is summed up in their infinitesimal *ego;* and by their spirit of shallowness it is that I am infected. Ah, well! when you are with wolves you've got to howl. That is only natural."

Yourii began to walk up and down the room, and, as often happens, his change of position brought with it a change in his train of thought.

"Very well. That's so. All the same, a good many things have to be considered. For instance, what is my position with

regard to Sina Karsavina? Whether I love her or not it
doesn't much matter. The question is, what will come of it
all? Suppose I marry her, or become closely attached to her.
Will that make me happy? To betray her would be a crime,
and if I love her . . . Well, then, I can . . . In all prob-
ability she would have children." He blushed at the thought.
"There's nothing wrong about that, only it would be a tie,
and I should lose my freedom. A family man! Domestic
bliss! No, that's not in my line."

"One . . . two . . . three," he counted, as he tried each time
to step across two boards and set his foot on the third one.
"If I could be sure that she would not have children, or that
I should get so fond of them that my whole life would be devoted to them! No; how terribly commonplace! Riasantzeff
would be fond of his children, too. What difference would
there then be between us? A life of self-sacrifice! That is the
real life! Yes, but of sacrifice for whom? And in what way?
No matter what road I choose nor at what goal I aim, show
me the pure and perfect ideal for which it were worth while
to die! No, it is not that I am weak; it is because life itself is
not worthy of sacrifice nor of enthusiasm. Consequently
there is no sense in living at all."

Never before had this conclusion seemed so absolutely con-
vincing to him. On his table lay a revolver, and each time
he passed it, while walking up and down, its polished steel
caught his eye.

He took it up and examined it carefully. It was loaded.
He placed the barrel against his temple.

"There! Like that!" he thought. "Bang! And it's all over.
Is it a wise or a stupid thing to shoot oneself? Is suicide a

cowardly act? Then I suppose that I am a coward!"

The contact of cold steel on his heated brow was at once pleasant and alarming.

"What about Sina?" he asked himself. "Ah! well, I shall never get her, and so I leave to some one else this enjoyment." The thought of Sina awoke tender memories, which he strove to repress as sentimental folly.

"Why should I not do it?" His heart seemed to stop beating. Then once more, and deliberately this time, he put the revolver to his brow and pulled the trigger. His blood ran cold; there was a buzzing in his ears and the room seemed to whirl round.

The weapon did not go off; only the click of the trigger could be heard. Half fainting, his hand dropped to his side. Every fibre within him quivered, his head swam, his lips were parched, and his hand trembled so much that when he laid down the revolver it rattled against the table.

"A fine fellow I am!" he thought as, recovering himself, he went to the glass to see what he looked like.

"Then I'm a coward, am I?" "No," he thought proudly, "I am not! I did it right enough. How could I help it if the thing didn't go off?"

His own vision looked out at him from the mirror; rather a solemn, grave one, he thought. Trying to persuade himself that he attached no importance to what he had just done, he put out his tongue and moved away from the glass.

"Fate would not have it so," he said aloud, and the sound of the words seemed to cheer him.

"I wonder if anyone saw me?" he thought, as he looked round in alarm. Yet all was still, and nothing could be heard moving behind the closed door. To him it was as if nothing in the world existed and suffered in this terrible solitude but himself. He put out the lamp, and to his amazement perceived through a chink in the shutter the first red rays of dawn. Then he lay down to sleep, and in dream was aware of something gigantic that bent over him, exhaling fiery breath.

CHAPTER XXIII

GENTLY, caressingly, the dusk, fragrant with the scent of blossoms, descended. Sanine sat at a table near the window, striving to read in the waning light a favorite tale of his. It described the lonely, tragic death of an old bishop, who, clad in his sacredotal vestments and holding a jewelled cross, expired amid the odour of incense.

In the room the temperature was as cool as that outside, for the soft evening breeze played round Sanine's powerful frame, filling his lungs, and lightly caressing his hair. Absorbed in his book, he read on, while his lips moved from time to time, and he seemed like a big boy devouring some story of adventures among Indians. Yet, the more he read, the sadder became his thoughts. How much there was in this world that was senseless and absurd! How dense and uncivilized men were, and how far ahead of them in ideas he was!

The door opened and some one entered. Sanine looked up. "Aha!" he exclaimed, as he shut the book, "what's the news?"

Novikoff smiled sadly, as he took the other's hand.

"Oh! nothing," he said, as he approached the window. "It's all just the same as ever it was."

From where he sat Sanine could only see Novikoff's tall figure silhouetted against the evening sky, and for a long while he gazed at him without speaking.

When Sanine first took his friend to see Lida, who now no longer resembled the proud, high-spirited girl of heretofore, neither she nor Novikoff said a word to each other about all that lay nearest to their hearts. He knew that, after having spoken, they would be unhappy, yet doubly so if they kept silence. What to him was plain and easy they could only accomplish, he felt sure, after much suffering. "Be it so," thought he, "for suffering purifies and ennobles." Now however, the propitious moment for them had come.

Novikoff stood at the window, silently watching the sunset. His mood was a strange one, begotten of grief for what was lost, and of longing for joy that was near. In this soft twilight he pictured to himself Lida, sad, and covered with shame. If he had but the courage to do it, this very moment he would kneel before her, with kisses warm her cold little hands, and by his great, all-forgiving love rouse her to a new life. Yet the power to go to her failed him.

Of this Sanine was conscious. He rose slowly, and said, "Lida is in the garden. Shall we go to her?"

Novikoff's heart beat faster. Within it, joy and grief seemed strangely blended. His expression changed somewhat, and he nervously fingered his moustache.

"Well, what do you say? Shall we go?" repeated Sanine calmly, as if he had decided to do something important. Novikoff felt that Sanine knew all that was troubling him, and, though in a measure comforted, he was yet childishly abashed.

"Come along!" said Sanine gently, as taking hold of Novikoff's shoulders he pushed him towards the door.

"Yes ... I ..." murmured the latter.

A sudden impulse to embrace Sanine almost overcame him, but he dared not and could but glance at him with tearful eyes. It was dark in the warm, fragrant garden, and the trunks of the trees formed Gothic arches against the pale green of the sky.

A faint mist hovered above the parched surface of the lawn. It was as if an unseen presence wandered along the silent walks and amid the motionless trees, at whose approach the slumbering leaves and blossoms softly trembled. The sunset still flamed in the west behind the river which flowed in shining curves through the dark meadows. At the edge of the stream sat Lida. Her graceful figure bending forward above the water seemed like that of some mournful spirit in the dusk. The sense of confidence inspired by the voice of her brother forsook her as quickly as it had come, and once more shame and fear overwhelmed her. She was obsessed by the thought that she had no right to happiness, nor yet to live. She spent whole days in the garden, book in hand, unable to look her mother in the face. A thousand times she said to herself that her mother's anguish would be as nothing to what she herself was now suffering, yet whenever she approached her parent her voice faltered, and in her eyes was a guilty look. Her blushes and strange confusion of manner at last aroused her mother's suspicion, to avoid whose searching glances and anxious questionings Lida preferred to spend her days in solitude. Thus, on this evening she was seated by the river, watching the sunset and brooding over her grief. Life, as it seemed to her, was still incomprehensible. Her view of it was blurred as by some hideous phantom. A series of books which she had read had served to give her greater freedom of thought. As she believed, her conduct was not only natural but almost worthy of praise. She had brought harm to no one thereby, only providing herself and another with sensual enjoyment. Without such enjoyment there would be no youth, and life itself would be barren and desolate as a leafless tree in autumn.

The thought that her union with a man had not been sanctioned by the church seemed to her ridiculous. By the free mind of man such claims had long been swept aside. She ought really to find joy in this new life, just as a flower on some bright morning rejoices at the touch of the pollen borne to it on the breeze. Yet she felt unutterably degraded, and baser than the basest.

All such grand, noble ideas and eternal verities melted like wax at the thought of her day of infamy that was at hand. And instead of trampling underfoot the folk that she despised, her one thought was how best she might avoid or deceive them.

While concealing her grief from others, Lida felt herself attracted to Novikoff as a flower to the sunlight. The suggestion that he was to save her seemed base, almost criminal. It galled her to think that she should depend upon his affection and forgiveness, yet stronger far than pride was the passionate longing to live.

Her attitude towards human stupidity was one of fear rather than disdain; she could not look Novikoff in the face, but trembled before him, like a slave. Her plight was pitiable as that of a helpless bird whose wings have been clipped, and that can never fly again.

At times, when her suffering seemed intolerable, she thought with naïve astonishment of her brother. She knew that, for him, nothing was sacred, that he looked at her, his sister, with the eyes of a male, and that he was selfish and immoral. Nevertheless he was the only man in whose presence she felt herself absolutely free, and with whom she could openly discuss the most intimate secrets of her life. She had been seduced. Well, what of that? She had had an intrigue. Very good. It was at her own wish. People would despise and humiliate her; what did it matter? Before her lay life, and sunshine, and the wide world; and, as for men, there were plenty to be had. Her mother would grieve. Well, that was her own affair. Lida had never known what her mother's youth had been, and after her death there would be no further supervision. They had met by chance on life's road, and had gone part of the way together. Was that any reason why they should mutually oppose each other?

Lida saw plainly that she would never have the same freedom which her brother possessed. That she had ever thought so was due to the influence of this calm, strong man whom she affectionately admired. Strange thoughts came to her, thoughts of an illicit nature.

"If he were not my brother, but a stranger! . . ." she said to herself, as she hastily strove to suppress the shameful and yet alluring suggestion.

Then she remembered Novikoff and like a humble slave longed for his pardon and his love. She heard steps and looked round. Novikoff and Sanine came to her silently across the grass. She could not discern their faces in the dusk, yet she felt that the dreaded moment was at hand. She turned very pale, and it seemed as if life was about to end.

"There!" said Sanine. "I have brought Novikoff to you. He will tell you himself all that he has to tell. Stay here quietly, while I go and get some tea."

Turning on his heel, he walked swiftly away, and for a moment they watched his white shirt as he disappeared in the gloom. So great was the silence that they could hardly believe that he had gone farther than the shadow of the surrounding trees.

"Lidia Petrovna," said Novikoff gently, in a voice so sad and touching that it went to her heart.

"Poor fellow," she thought, "how good he is."

"I know everything, Lidia Petrovna," continued Novikoff, "but I love you just as much as ever. Perhaps some day you will learn to love me. Tell me, will you be my wife?"

"I had better not say too much about *that*," he thought, "she must never know what a sacrifice I am making for her."

Lida was silent. In such stillness one could hear the rippling of the stream.

"We are both unhappy," said Novikoff, conscious that these words came from the depth of his heart. "Together perhaps we may find life easier."

Lida's eyes were filled with tears of gratitude as she turned towards him and murmured: "Perhaps."

Yet her eyes said, "God knows I will be a good wife to you, and love and respect you."

Novikoff read their message. He knelt down impetuously, and seizing her hand, kissed it passionately. Roused by such emotion, Lida forgot her shame.

"That's over!" she thought, "and I shall be happy again! Dear, good fellow!" Weeping for joy, she gave him both her hands, and bending over his head she kissed his soft, silky hair which she had always admired. A vision rose before her of Sarudine, but it instantly vanished.

When Sanine returned, having given them enough time, as he thought, for a mutual explanation, he found them seated, hand in hand, engaged in quiet talk.

"Aha! I see how it is!" said Sanine gravely.

"Thank God, and be happy."

He was about to say something else, but sneezed loudly instead.

"It's damp out here. Mind you don't catch cold," he added, rubbing his eyes.

Lida laughed. The echo of her voice across the river sounded charming.

"I must go," said Sanine, after a pause.

"Where are you going?" asked Novikoff.

"Svarogitsch and that officer who admires Tolstoi, what's his name? a lanky German fellow, have called for me."

"You mean Von Deitz?" said Lida, laughing.

"That's the man. They wanted us all to come with them to a meeting, but I said that you were not at home."

"Why did you do that?" asked Lida, still laughing; "we might have gone, too."

"No, you stop here," replied Sanine. "If I had anybody to keep me company, I should do the same."

With that he left them.

Night came on apace, and the first trembling stars were mirrored in the swiftly flowing stream.

CHAPTER XXIV

THE evening was dark and sultry. Above the trees clouds chased each other across the sky, hurrying onward as to some mysterious goal. In the pale green spaces overhead faint stars glimmered and then vanished. Above, all was commotion, while the earth seemed waiting, as in breathless suspense. Amid this silence, human voices in dispute sounded harsh and shrill.

"Anyhow," exclaimed Von Deitz, blundering along in unwieldy fashion, "Christianity has enriched mankind with an imperishable boon, being the only system of morals that is complete and comprehensible."

"Quite so," replied Yourii, who walked behind the last speaker tossing his head defiantly, and glaring at the officer's back, "but in its conflict with the bestial instincts of mankind Christianity has proved itself to be as impotent as all the other religions."

"How do you mean, 'proved itself to be'?" exclaimed Von Deitz angrily. "To Christianity belongs the future, and to suggest that it is obsolete . . ."

"There is no future for Christianity," broke in Yourii vehemently. "If at the zenith of its development Christianity could not triumph, but became the tool of a shameless gang of impostors, it would be nothing short of absurd to expect a miracle nowadays, when even the word Christianity sounds grotesque. History is inexorable; what has once disappeared from the scene can never return."

"Do you mean to say that Christianity has disappeared from the scene?" shrieked Von Deitz.

"Certainly, I do," continued Yourii obstinately. "You seem as surprised as if such an idea were utterly impossible. Just as the law of Moses has passed away, just as Buddha and the gods of Greece are dead, so, too, Christ is dead. It is but the law of evolution. Why should you be so amazed? You don't believe in the divinity of his doctrine, do you?"

"No, of course not," retorted Von Deitz, less irritated at the question than at Yourii's offensive tone.

"Then how can you maintain that a man is able to create eternal laws?"

"Idiot!" thought Yourii, agreeably convinced that the other was infinitely less intelligent than he, and would never be able to comprehend what was as plain and clear as noonday.

"Supposing it were so," rejoined Von Deitz, nettled, in his turn. "The future will nevertheless have Christianity as its basis. It has not perished, but like seed in the soil . . ."

"I was not talking about that," said Yourii, confused somewhat, and thus the more excited, "what I meant to say . . ."

"No, excuse me, but that's what you said . . ."

"If I said no, then I meant no! How absurd you are!" interrupted Yourii, rendered more furious by the thought that this stupid Von Deitz should for a moment presume to think himself the cleverer. "I meant to say . . ."

"That may be. I am sorry if I misunderstood you." Von Deitz shrugged his narrow shoulders, with an air of condescension, as much as to say that he had got the best of the argument.

This was not lost upon Yourii, whose fury almost choked him.

"I do not deny that Christianity has played an enormous part . . ."

"Ah! now you contradict yourself," exclaimed Von Deitz, more triumphant than ever, being intensely pleased to feel how incomparably superior he was to Yourii, who obviously had not the remotest conception of what was so neatly and definitely set out in his own brain.

"To *you* it may seem that I am contradicting myself," said Yourii bitterly, "but, as a matter of fact, my contention is a perfectly logical one, and it is not my fault if you don't wish to understand me. I said before, and I say again, that Christianity is played out, and it is vain to look to it for salvation."

"Yes, yes; but do you mean to deny the salutary influence of Christianity, that is to say, as the basis of social order? . . ."

"No, I don't deny that."

"But I do," interposed Sanine, who till now had walked behind them in silence. His voice sounded calm and pleasant, in strange contrast to the harsh accent of the disputants.

Yourii was silent. This good-tempered, mocking tone of voice annoyed him, yet he had no answer ready. He was not fond of arguing with Sanine, for his usual vocabulary proved useless in such an encounter. Every time it seemed as if he were trying to break down a wall while standing on smooth ice.

Von Deitz, however, stumbling along and rattling his

spurs, exclaimed irritably:

"May I ask why?"

"Because I do," replied Sanine coolly.

"Because you do! If one asserts a thing, one ought to prove it."

"Why must I prove it? There is no need to prove anything. It is my own personal conviction, but I have not the slightest wish to convince you. Besides, it would be useless."

"According to your line of reasoning," observed Yourii cautiously, "one had better make a bonfire of all literature."

"Oh no! Why do that?" replied Sanine. "Literature is a very great, and a very interesting thing. Real literature, such as I mean, is not polemical after the manner of some prig who, having nothing to do, endeavours to convince everybody that he is extremely intelligent. Literature reconstructs life, and penetrates even to the very life-blood of humanity, from generation to generation. To destroy literature would be to take away all colour from life and make it insipid."

Von Deitz stopped short, letting Yourii pass him, and then he asked Sanine:

"Oh! pray tell me more! What you were saying just now interests me immensely."

Sanine laughed.

"What I said was simple enough. I can explain my point at greater length, if you wish. In my opinion Christianity has played a sorry part in the life of humanity. At the very moment when human beings felt that their lot was unbearable, and when the down-trodden and oppressed, coming to their senses, had determined to upset the monstrously

unjust order of things, and to destroy all human parasites—
then, I say, Christianity made its appearance, gentle, humble,
and promising much. It condemned strife, held out visions
of eternal bliss, lulled mankind to sweet slumber, and
preached a religion of non-resistance to ill-treatment; in
short, it acted as a safety-valve for all this pent-up wrath.
Those of powerful character, nurtured amid a spirit of revolt,
and longing to shake off the yoke of centuries, lost all their
fire. Like imbeciles, they walked into the arena and, with
courage worthy of a better aim, courted destruction. Naturally, their enemies wished for nothing better. And now it
will need centuries of infamous oppression before the flame
of revolt shall again be lighted. Christianity has clothed human individuality, too obstinate ever to accept slavery, with
a garb of penitence, hiding under it all the colours of liberty.
It deceived the strong who to-day could have captured fortune and happiness, transferring life's centre of gravity to
the future, to a dreamland that does not exist, and that none
of them will ever see. And thus all the charm of life vanished; bravery, passion, beauty, all were dead; duty alone
remained, and the dream of a future golden age—golden
maybe, for others, coming after. Yes, Christianity has
played a sorry part; and the name of Christ . . ."

"Well! I never!" broke in Von Deitz, as he stopped short,
waving his long arms in the dusk. "That's really a bit too
much!"

"Yet, have you never thought what a hideous era of bloodshed would have supervened if Christianity had not averted
it?" asked Yourii nervously.

"Ha! ha!" replied Sanine, with a disdainful gesture, "at

first, under the cloak of Christianity, the arena was drenched
with the blood of the martyrs, and then, later, people were
massacred and shut up in prisons and mad-houses. And now,
every day, more blood is spilt than ever could be shed by a
universal revolution. The worst of it all is that each better-
ment in the life of humanity has always been achieved by
bloodshed, anarchy and revolt, though men always affect
to make humanitarianism and love of one's neighbour the
basis of their lives and actions. The whole thing results in
a stupid tragedy; false, hypocritical, neither flesh nor fowl.
For my part, I should prefer an immediate world-catastro-
phe to a dull, vegetable-existence lasting probably another
two thousand years."

Yourii was silent. Strange to say, his thoughts were not
fixed upon the speaker's words, but upon the speaker's personality. The latter's absolute assurance he considered offensive, in fact insupportable.

"Would you, please, tell me," he began, irresistibly impelled to wound Sanine, "why you always talk as if you were
teaching little children?"

Von Deitz, feeling uneasy at this speech, uttered something conciliatory, and rattled his spurs.

"What do you mean by that?" asked Sanine sharply,
"why are you so angry?"

Yourii felt that his speech was discourteous, and that he
ought not to go any farther, yet his wounded self-respect
drove him to add:

"Such a tone is really most unpleasant."

"It is my usual tone," replied Sanine, partly annoyed, and
partly anxious to appease the other.

"Well, it is not always a suitable one," continued Yourii, raising his voice, "I really fail to see what gives you such assurance."

"Probably the consciousness of being more intelligent than you are," replied Sanine, now quite calm.

Yourii stood still, trembling from head to foot.

"Look here!" he exclaimed hoarsely.

"Don't get angry!" interposed Sanine. "I had no wish to offend you, and only expressed my candid opinion. It is the same opinion that you have of me, and that Von Deitz has of both of us, and so on. It is only natural."

Sanine spoke in such a frank, friendly way that to show further displeasure would have been absurd. Yourii was silent, and Von Deitz, being still concerned on his behalf, again rattled his spurs and breathed hard.

"At any rate I don't tell you my opinion to your face," murmured Yourii.

"No; and that is where you are wrong. I was listening to your discussion just now, and the offensive spirit prompted every word you said. It is merely a question of form. I say what I think, but you don't say what you think; and that is not in the least interesting. If we were all more sincere, it would be far more amusing for everybody."

Von Deitz laughed loudly.

"What an original idea!" he exclaimed.

Yourii did not reply. His anger had subsided, and he felt almost pleased, though it irked him to think that he had got the worst of it, and would not admit this.

"Such a state of things might be somewhat too primitive," added Von Deitz sententiously.

"Then, you had rather that it were complicated and obscure?" asked Sanine.

Von Deitz shrugged his shoulders, lost in thought.

CHAPTER XXV

LEAVING the boulevard behind them, they passed along the dreary streets lying outside the town, though they were better lighted than the boulevard. The wood-pavement stood out clearly against the black ground, and above loomed the pale cloud-covered heaven, where here and there stars gleamed.

"Here we are," said Von Deitz as he opened a low door and disappeared through it. Immediately afterwards they heard the hoarse bark of a dog, and a voice exclaiming, "Lie down, Sultan." Before them lay a large empty courtyard at the farther side of which they discerned a black mass. It was a steam mill, and its narrow chimney pointed sadly to the sky. Round about it were dark sheds, but no trees, except in the small garden in front of the adjoining house. Through an open window a ray of light touched their green leaves.

"A dismal kind of place," said Sanine.

"I suppose the mill has been here a long while?" asked Yourii.

"Oh! yes, for ever so long!" replied Von Deitz who, as he passed, looked through the lighted window, and in a tone of satisfaction said, "Oho! Quite a lot of people, already."

Yourii and Sanine also looked in at the window and saw heads moving in a dim cloud of blue smoke. A broad-

shouldered man with curly hair leant over the sill and called
out, "Who's there?"

"Friends!" replied Yourii.

As they went up the steps they pushed against some one
who shook hands with them in friendly fashion.

"I was afraid that you wouldn't come!" said a cheery voice
in a strong Jewish accent.

"Soloveitchik—Sanine," said Von Deitz, introducing the
two, and grasping the former's cold, trembling hand.

Soloveitchik laughed nervously.

"So pleased to meet you!" he said. "I have heard so much
about you, and, you know——" He stumbled backwards,
still holding Sanine's hand. In doing so he fell against
Yourii, and trod on Von Deitz's foot.

"I beg your pardon, Jakof Adolfovitch!" he exclaimed, as
he proceeded to shake Von Deitz's hand with great energy.
Thus it was some time before in the darkness they could
find the door. In the ante-room, on rows of nails put up
specially for this evening by orderly Soloveitchik, hung hats
and caps, while close to the window were dark green bottles
containing beer. Even the ante-room was filled with smoke.

In the light Soloveitchik appeared to be a young dark-eyed
Jew with curly hair, small features, and bad teeth which, as
he was continually smiling, were always displayed.

The new-comers were greeted with a noisy chorus of welcome. Yourii saw Sina Karsavina sitting on the window-
sill, and instantly everything seemed to him bright and joyous, as if the meeting were not in a stuffy room full of smoke,
but at a festival amid fair green meadows in spring.

Sina, slightly confused, smiled at him pleasantly.

"Well, sirs, I think we are all here, now," exclaimed Solo-veitchik, trying to speak in a loud, cheery way with his feeble, unsteady voice, and gesticulating in ludicrous fashion.

"I beg your pardon, Yourii Nicolaijevitch; I seem to be always pushing against you," he said, laughing, as he lurched forward in an endeavour to be polite.

Yourii good-humoredly squeezed his arm.

"That's all right," he said.

"We're not all here, but deuce take the others!" cried a burly, good-looking student. His loud tradesman's voice made one feel that he was used to ordering others about.

Soloveitchik sprang forward to the table and rang a little bell. He smiled once more, and this time for sheer satisfaction at having thought of using a bell.

"Oh! none of that!" growled the student. "You've always got some silly nonsense of that sort. It's not necessary in the least."

"Well . . . I thought . . . that . . ." stammered Soloveit-chik, as, looking embarrassed, he put the bell in his pocket.

"I think that the table should be placed in the middle of the room," said the student.

"Yes, yes, I am going to move it directly!" replied Solo-veitchik, as he hurriedly caught hold of the edge of the table.

"Mind the lamp!" cried Dubova.

"That's not the way to move it!" exclaimed the student, slapping his knee.

"Let me help you," said Sanine.

"Thank you! Please!" replied Soloveitchik eagerly.

Sanine set the table in the middle of the room, and as he did so, the eyes of all were fixed on his strong back and muscular shoulders which showed through his thin shirt.

"Now, Goschienko, as the initiator of this meeting, it is for you to make the opening speech," said the pale-faced Dubova, and from the expression in her eyes it was hard to say if she were in earnest, or only laughing at the student.

"Ladies and gentlemen," began Goschienko, raising his voice, "everybody knows why we have met here to-night, and so we can dispense with any introductory speech."

"As a matter of fact," said Sanine, "I don't know why I came here, but," he added, laughing, "it may have been because I was told that there would be some beer."

Goschienko glanced contemptuously at him over the lamp, and continued:

"Our association is formed for the purpose of self-education by means of mutual readings, and debates, and independent discussions——"

"Mutual readings? I don't understand," interrupted Dubova in a tone of voice that might have been thought ironical.

Goschienko blushed slightly.

"I meant to say readings in which all take part. Thus, the aim of our association is for the development of individual opinion which shall lead to the formation in this town of a league in sympathy with the social democratic party . . . ."

"Aha!" drawled Ivanoff, as he scratched the back of his head.

"But with that we shall deal later on. At the commencement we shall not set ourselves to solve such great——"

"Or small . . ." prompted Dubova.

"Problems," continued Goschienko, affecting not to hear. "We shall begin by making out a programme of such works as we intend to read, and I propose to devote the present evening to this purpose."

"Soloveitchik, don't shout like that!" exclaimed Goschienko.

"Yes, of course they are!" replied Soloveitchik, jumping up as if he had been stung. "We have already sent to fetch them."

"Soloveitchik, don't shout like that!" exclaimed Goschienko.

"Here they are!" said Schafroff, who was listening to Goschienko's words with almost reverent attention.

Outside, the gate creaked, and again the dog's gruff bark was heard.

"They've come!" cried Soloveitchik as he rushed out of the room.

"Lie down, Sultan!" he shouted from the house-door.

There was a sound of heavy footsteps, of coughing, and of men's voices. Then a young student from the Polytechnic School entered, very like Goschienko, except that he was dark and plain. With him, looking awkward and shy, came two workmen, with grimy hands, and wearing short jackets over their dirty red shirts. One of them was very tall and gaunt, whose clean-shaven, sallow face bore the mark of years of semi-starvation, perpetual care and suppressed hatred. The other had the appearance of an athlete, being broad-shouldered and comely, with curly hair. He looked about him as a young peasant might do when first coming to a town. Pushing past them, Soloveitchik began solemnly, "Gentlemen, these are——"

"Oh! that'll do!" cried Goschienko, interrupting him, as usual. "Good evening, comrades."

"Pistzoff and Koudriavji," said the Polytechnic student.

The men strode cautiously into the room, stiffly grasping the hands held out to give them a singularly courteous welcome. Pistzoff smiled confusedly, and Koudriavji moved his long neck about as if the collar of his shirt were throttling him. Then they sat down by the window, near Sina.

"Why hasn't Nicolaieff come?" asked Goschienko sharply.

"Nicolaieff was not able to come," replied Pistzoff.

"Nicolaieff is blind drunk," added Koudriavji in a dry voice.

"Oh! I see," said Goschienko, as he shook his head. This movement on his part, which seemed to express compassion, exasperated Yourii, who saw in the big student a personal enemy.

"He chose the better part," observed Ivanoff.

Again the dog barked in the courtyard.

"Some one else is coming," said Dubova.

"Probably, the police," remarked Goschienko with feigned indifference.

"I am sure that you would not mind if it were the police," cried Dubova.

Sanine looked at her intelligent eyes, and the plait of fair hair falling over her shoulder, which almost made her face attractive.

"A smart girl, that!" he thought.

Soloveitchik jumped up as if to run out, but, recollecting himself, pretended to take a cigarette from the table. Goschienko noticed this, and, without replying to Dubova, said:

"How fidgety you are, Soloveitchik!"

Soloveitchik turned crimson and blinked his eyes ruefully.

He felt vaguely conscious that his zeal did not deserve to be so severely rebuked. Then Novikoff noisily entered.

"Here I am!" he exclaimed, with a cheery smile.

"So I see," replied Sanine.

Novikoff shook the other's hand and whispered hurriedly, as if by way of excuse, "Lidia Petrovna has got visitors."

"Oh! yes."

"Have we only come here to talk?" asked the Polytechnic student with some irritation. "Do let us make a start."

"Then you have not begun yet?" said Novikoff, evidently pleased. He shook hands with the two workmen, who hastily rose from their seats. It was embarrassing to meet the doctor as a fellow-comrade, when at the hospital he was wont to treat them as his inferiors.

Goschienko, looking rather annoyed, then began.

"Ladies and gentlemen, we are naturally all desirous to widen our outlook, and to broaden our views of life; and, believing that the best method of self-culture and of self-development lies in a systematic course of reading and an interchange of opinions regarding the books read, we have decided to start this little club . . . "

"That's right," sighed Pistzoff approvingly, as he looked round at the company with his bright, dark eyes.

"The question now arises: What books ought we to read? Possibly some one here present could make a suggestion regarding the programme that should be adopted?"

Schafroff put on his glasses and slowly stood up. In his hand he held a small note-book.

"I think," he began in his dry, uninteresting voice, "I think that our programme should be divided into two parts. For

the purpose of intellectual development two elements are un-
doubtedly necessary; the study of life from its earliest stages,
and the study of life as it actually is."

"Schafroff's getting quite eloquent," cried Dubova.

"Knowledge of the former can be gained by reading
standard books of historical and scientific value, and knowledge of the latter, by *belles lettres,* which bring us face to
face with life."

"If you go on talking to us like this, we shall soon fall fast
asleep." Dubova could not resist making this remark, and
in her eyes there was a roguish twinkle.

"I am trying to speak in such a way as to be understood by
all," replied Schafroff gently.

"Very well! Speak as best you can!" said Dubova with a
gesture expressing her resignation.

Sina Karsavina laughed at Schafroff, too, in her pretty
way, tossing back her head and showing her white, shapely
throat. Hers was a rich, musical laugh.

"I have drawn up a programme—but perhaps it would bore
you if I read it out?" said Schafroff, with a furtive glance at
Dubova. "I propose to begin with 'The Origin of the Family'
side by side with Darwin's works, and, in literature, we could
take Tolstoi."

"Of course, Tolstoi!" said Von Deitz, looking extremely
pleased with himself as he proceeded to light a cigarette.

Schafroff paused until the cigarette was lighted, and then
continued his list:

"Tchekhof, Ibsen, Knut Hamsun——"

"But we've read them all!" exclaimed Sina Karsavina.

Her delightful voice thrilled Yourii, and he said:

"Of course! Schafroff forgets that this is not a Sunday school. What a strange jumble, too! Tolstoi and Knut Hamsun——"

Schafroff blandly adduced certain arguments in support of his programme, yet in so diffuse a way that no one could understand him.

"No," said Yourii with emphasis, delighted to observe Sina Karsavina looking at him, "No, I don't agree with you." He then proceeded to expound his own views on the subject, and the more he spoke, the more he strove to win Sina's approval, mercilessly attacking Schafroff's scheme, and even those points with which he himself was in sympathy.

The burly Goschienko now gave his views on the subject. He considered himself the cleverest, most eloquent and most cultured of them all; moreover in a little club like this, which he had organized, he expected to play first fiddle. Yourii's success annoyed him, and he felt bound to go against him. Being ignorant of Svarogitsch's opinions, he could not oppose them *en bloc,* but only fixed upon certain weak points in his argument with which he stubbornly disagreed.

Thereupon a lengthy and apparently interminable discussion ensued. The Polytechnic student, Ivanoff, and Novikoff all began to argue at once, and through clouds of tobacco-smoke hot, angry faces could be seen, while words and phrases were hopelessly blent in a bewildering chaos devoid at last of all meaning.

Dubova gazed at the lamp, listening and dreaming. Sina Karsavina paid no attention, but opened the window facing the garden, and, folding her arms, leaned over the sill and looked out at the night. At first she could distinguish noth-

ing, but gradually out of the gloom the dark trees emerged
and she saw the light on the garden-fence and the grass.
A soft, refreshing breeze fanned her shoulders and lightly
touched her hair.

Looking upwards, Sina could watch the swift procession of
the clouds. She thought of Yourii and of her love. Her
mood, if pleasurably pensive, was yet a little sad. It was so
good to rest there, exposed to the cool night wind, and listen
with all her heart to the voice of one man which to her ears
sounded clearer and more masterful than the rest. Meanwhile the din grew greater, and it was evident that each
person thought himself more cultivated and intelligent than
his neighbours and was striving to convert them. Matters at
last became so unpleasant that the most peaceable among
them lost their tempers.

"If you judge like that," shouted Yourii, his eyes flashing,
for he was anxious not to yield in the presence of Sina though
she could only hear his voice, "then we must go back to the
origin of all ideas . . ."

"What ought we, then, in your opinion, to read?" said the
hostile Goschienko.

"What you ought to read? Why, Confucius, the Gospels,
Ecclesiastes . . ."

"The Psalms and the Apocrypha," was the Polytechnic
student's mocking interruption.

Goschienko laughed maliciously, oblivious of the fact that
he himself had never read one of these works.

"Of what good would that be?" asked Schafroff in a tone
of disappointment.

"It's like they do in church!" tittered Pistzoff.

Yourii's face flushed.

"I am not joking. If you wish to be logical, then . . ."

"Ah! but what did you say to me just now about Christ?" cried Von Deitz exultantly.

"What did I say? . . . If one wishes to study life, and to form some definite conception of the mutual relationship of man to man, surely the best way is to get a thorough knowledge of the titanic work of those who, representing the best models of humanity, devoted their lives to the solution of the simplest and most complex problems with regard to human relationships."

"There I don't agree with you," retorted Goschienko.

"But I do," cried Novikoff hotly.

Once more all was confusion and senseless uproar, during which it was impossible to hear either the beginning or the end of any utterance.

Reduced to silence by this war of words, Soloveitchik sat in a corner and listened. At first the expression on his face was one of intense, almost childish interest, but after a while his doubt and distress were shown by lines at the corners of his mouth and of his eyes.

Sanine drank, smoked, and said nothing. He looked thoroughly bored, and when amid the general clamour some of the voices became unduly violent, he got up, and extinguishing his cigarette, said: .

"I say, do you know, this is getting uncommonly boring!"

"Yes, indeed!" cried Dubova.

"Sheer vanity and vexation of spirit!" said Ivanoff, who had been waiting for a fitting moment to drag in this favourite phrase of his.

"In what way?" asked the Polytechnic student, angrily.

Sanine took no notice of him, but, turning to Yourii, said:

"Do you really believe that you can get a conception of life from any book?"

"Most certainly I do," replied Yourii, in a tone of surprise.

"Then you are wrong," said Sanine. "If this were really so, one could mould the whole of humanity according to one type by giving people works to read of one tendency. A conception of life is only obtained from life itself, in its entirety, of which literature and human thought are but an infinitesimal part. No theory of life can help one to such a conception, for this depends upon the mood or frame of mind of each individual, which is consequently apt to vary so long as man lives. Thus, it is impossible to form such a hard and fast conception of life as you seem anxious to . . ."

"How do you mean—'impossible'?" cried Yourii angrily.

Sanine again looked bored, as he answered:

"Of course it's impossible. If a conception of life were the outcome of a complete, definite theory, then the progress of human thought would soon be arrested; in fact it would cease. But such a thing is inadmissible. Every moment of life speaks its new word, its new message to us, and this we must listen to and understand, without first of all fixing limits for ourselves. After all, what's the good of discussing it? Think what you like. I would merely ask why you, who have read hundreds of books from Ecclesiastes to Marx, have not yet been able to form any definite conception of life?"

"Why do you suppose that I have not?" asked Yourii, and his dark eyes flashed menacingly. "Perhaps my conception of life may be a wrong one, but I have it."

"Very well, then," said Sanine, "why seek to acquire another?"

Pistzoff tittered.

"Hush!" cried Koudriavji contemptuously, as his neck twitched.

"How clever he is!" thought Sina Karsavina, full of naïve admiration for Sanine. She looked at him, and then at Svarogitsch, feeling almost bashful, and yet strangely glad. It was as if the two disputants were arguing as to who should possess her.

"Thus, it follows," continued Sanine, "that you do not need what you are vainly seeking. To me it is evident that every person here to-night is endeavouring to force the others to accept his views, being himself mortally afraid lest others should persuade him to think as they do. Well, to be quite frank, that is boring."

"One moment! Allow me!" exclaimed Goschienko.

"Oh! that will do!" said Sanine, with a gesture of annoyance. "I expect that you have a most wonderful conception of life, and have read heaps of books. One can see that directly. Yet you lose your temper because everybody doesn't agree with you; and, what is more, you behave rudely to Soloveitchik, who has certainly never done you any harm."

Goschienko was silent, looking utterly amazed, as if Sanine had said something most extraordinary.

"Yourii Nicolaijevitch," said Sanine cheerily, "you must not be angry with me because I spoke somewhat bluntly just now. I can see that in your soul discord reigns."

"Discord?" exclaimed Yourii, reddening. He did not know whether he ought to be angry or not. Just as it had done during their walk to the meeting, Sanine's calm, friendly voice pleasantly impressed him.

"Ah! you know yourself that it is so!" replied Sanine, with a smile. "But it won't do to pay any attention to such childish nonsense. Life's really too short."

"Look here," shouted Goschienko, purple with rage. "You take far too much upon yourself!"

"Not more than you do."

"How's that?"

"Think it out for yourself," said Sanine. "What you say and do is far ruder and more unamiable than anything that I say."

"I don't understand you!"

"That's not my fault."

"What?"

To this Sanine made no reply, but taking up his cap, said: "I'm off. It's getting a bit too dull for me."

"You're right! And there's no more beer!" added Ivanoff, as he moved towards the ante-room.

"We shan't get along like this; that's very clear," said Dubova.

"Walk back with me, Yourii Nicolaijevitch," cried Sina. Then, turning to Sanine, she said "Au revoir!"

For a moment their eyes met. Sina felt pleasurably alarmed.

"Alas!" cried Dubova, as she went out, "our little club has collapsed before it has even been properly started."

"But why is that?" said a mournful voice, as Soloveitchik,

who was getting in everyone's way, stumbled forward.

Until this moment his existence had been ignored, and many were struck by the forlorn expression of his countenance.

"I say, Soloveitchik," said Sanine pensively, "one day I must come and see you, and we'll have a chat."

"By all means! Pray do so!" said Soloveitchik, bowing effusively.

On coming out of the lighted room, the darkness seemed so intense that nobody was able to see anybody else, and only voices were recognizable. The two workmen kept aloof from the others, and, when they were at some distance, Pistzoff laughed and said:

"It's always like that, with them. They meet together, and are going to do such wonders, and then each wants to have his own way. That big chap was the only one I liked."

"A lot you understand when clever folk of that sort talk together!" replied Koudriavji testily, twisting his neck about as if he were being throttled.

Pistzoff whistled mockingly in lieu of answer.

CHAPTER XXVI

Soloveitchik stood at the door for some time, looking up to the starless sky and rubbing his thin fingers.

The wind whistled round the gloomy tin-roofed sheds, bending the tree-tops that were huddled together like a troop of ghosts. Overhead, as if driven by some resistless force, the clouds raced onward, ever onward. They formed black masses against the horizon, some being piled up to insuperable heights. It was as though, far away in the distance, they were awaited by countless armies that, with sable banners all unfurled, had gone forth in their dreadful might to some wild conflict of the elements. From time to time the restless wind seemed to bring with it the clamour of the distant fray.

With childish awe Soloveitchik gazed upwards. Never before had he felt how small he was, how puny, how almost infinitesimal when confronted with this tremendous chaos.

"My God! My God!" he sighed.

In the presence of the sky and the night he was not the same man as when among his fellows. There was not a trace of that restless, awkward manner, now; the unsightly teeth were concealed by the sensitive lips of a youthful Jew in whose dark eyes the expression was grave and sad.

He went slowly indoors, extinguished an unnecessary lamp, and clumsily set the table and the chairs in their places again. The room was still full of tobacco-smoke, and the floor was covered with cigarette ends and matches.

Soloveitchik at once fetched a broom and began to sweep out the rooms, for he took pride in keeping his little home clean and neat. Then he got a bucket of water from a cupboard, and broke bread into it. Carrying this in one hand, the other being outstretched to maintain his balance, he walked across the yard, taking short steps. In order to see better, he had placed a lamp close to the window, yet it was so dark in the yard that Soloveitchik felt relieved when he reached the dog's kennel. Sultan's shaggy form, invisible in the gloom, advanced to meet him, and a chain rattled ominously.

"Ah! Sultan! Kusch! Kusch!" exclaimed Soloveitchik, in order to give himself courage. In the darkness, Sultan thrust his cold, moist nose into his master's hand.

"There you are!" said Soloveitchik, as he sat down the bucket.

Sultan sniffed, and began to eat voraciously, while his master stood beside him and gazed mournfully at the surrounding gloom.

"Ah! what can I do?" he thought. "How can I force people to alter their opinions? I myself expected to be told how to live, and how to think. God has not given me the voice of a prophet, so, in what way can I help?"

Sultan gave a grunt of satisfaction.

"Eat away, old boy, eat away!" said Soloveitchik. "I would let you loose for a little run, but I haven't got the key and I'm so tired." Then to himself, "What clever, well-informed people those are! They know such a lot; good Christians, very likely; and here am I .... Ah! well, perhaps it's my own fault. I should have liked to say a word to them, but I didn't know how to do it."

From the distance, beyond the town, there came the sound of a long, plaintive whistle. Sultan raised his head, and listened. Large drops fell from his muzzle into the pail.

"Eat away," said Soloveitchik. "That's the train!"

Sultan heaved a sigh.

"I wonder if men will ever live like that! Perhaps they can't," said Soloveitchik aloud, as he shrugged his shoulders, despairingly. There, in the darkness he imagined that he could see a multitude of men, vast, unending as eternity, sinking ever deeper in the gloom; a succession of centuries without beginning and without end; an unbroken chain of wanton suffering for which remedy there was none; and, on high, where God dwelt, silence, eternal silence.

Sultan knocked against the pail, and upset it. Then, as he wagged his tail, the chain rattled slightly.

"Gobbled it all up, eh?"

Soloveitchik patted the dog's shaggy coat and felt its warm body writhe in joyous response to his touch. Then he went back to the house.

He could hear Sultan's chain rattle, and the yard seemed less gloomy than before, while blacker and more sinister was the mill with its tall chimney and narrow sheds that looked like coffins. From the window a broad ray of light fell across the garden, illuminating in mystic fashion the frail little flowers that shrank beneath the turbulent heaven with its countless banners, black and ominous, unfolded to the night.

Overcome by grief, unnerved by a sense of solitude and of some irreparable loss, Soloveitchik went back into his room, sat down at the table, and wept.

CHAPTER XXVII

VOLOCHINE owned immense works in St. Petersburg upon which the existence of thousands of his employés depended.

At the present time, while a strike was in progress, he had turned his back upon the crowd of hungry, dirty malcontents, and was enjoying a trip in the provinces. Libertine as he was, he thought of nothing but women, and in young, fresh, provincial women he displayed an intense, in fact, an absorbing interest. He pictured them as delightfully shy and timid, yet sturdy as a woodland mushroom, and their provocative perfume of youth and purity he scented from afar.

Volochine had clothed his puny little body in virgin white, after sprinkling himself from head to foot with various essences; and, although he did not exactly approve of Sarudine's society, he hailed a *droschky* and hastened to the latter's rooms.

Sarudine was sitting at the window, drinking cold tea.

"What a lovely evening!" he kept saying to himself, as he looked out on the garden. But his thoughts were elsewhere. He felt ashamed and afraid.

He was afraid of Lida. Since their interview, he had not set eyes on her. To him she seemed another Lida now, unlike the one that had surrendered to his passion.

"Anyhow," he thought, "the matter is not at an end yet. The child must be got rid of . . . or shall I treat the whole thing as a joke? I wonder what she is doing now?"

He seemed to see before him Lida's handsome, inscrutable eyes, and her lips tightly compressed, vindictive, menacing.

"She may be going to pay me out? A girl of that sort isn't one to be trifled with. At all costs I shall have to . . ."

The prospect of a huge scandal vaguely suggested itself, striking terror to his craven heart.

"After all," he thought, "what could she possibly do?" Then suddenly it all seemed quite clear and simple. "Perhaps she'll drown herself? Let her go to the deuce! I didn't force her to do it! They'll say that she was my mistress—well, what of that? It only proves that I am a good-looking fellow. I never said that I would marry her. Upon my word, it's too silly!" Sarudine shrugged his shoulders, yet the sense of oppression was not lessened. "People will talk, I expect, and I shan't be able to show myself," he thought, while his hand trembled slightly as he held the glass of cold over-sweetened tea to his lips.

He was as smart and well-groomed and scented as ever, yet it seemed as if, on his face, his white jacket, and his hands, and even on his heart, there was a foul stain which became even greater.

"Bah! After a while it will all blow over. And it's not the first time, either!" Thus he sought to soothe his conscience, but an inward voice refused to accept such consolation.

Volochine entered gingerly, his boots creaking loudly, and his discoloured teeth revealed by a condescending smile.

The room was instantly filled with an odour of musk and of tobacco, quite overpowering the fresh scents of the garden.

"Ah! how do you do, Pavel Lvovitsch!" cried Sarudine as he hastily rose.

Volochine shook hands, sat down by the window and proceeded to light a cigar. He looked so elegant and self-possessed, that Sarudine felt somewhat envious, and endeavoured to assume an equally careless demeanour; but ever since Lida had flung the word "brute" in his face, he had felt ill at ease, as if everyone had heard the insult and was secretly mocking him.

Volochine smiled, and chatted about various trifling matters. Yet he found it difficult to keep up such superficial conversation. "Woman" was the theme that he longed to approach, and it underlay all his stale jokes and stories of the strike at his St. Petersburg factory.

As he lighted another cigar he took the opportunity of looking hard at Sarudine. Their eyes met, and they instantly understood each other. Volochine adjusted his *pince-nez* and smiled a smile that found its reflection in Sarudine's face, which suddenly acquired a look of lust.

"I don't expect you waste much of your time, do you?" said Volochine, with a knowing wink.

"Oh! as for that, well, what else is there to do?" replied Sarudine, shrugging his shoulders slightly.

Then they both laughed, and for a while were silent. Volochine was eager to have details of the other's conquests. A little vein just below his left knee throbbed convulsively. Sarudine, however, was not thinking of such piquant details, but of the distressing events of the last few days. He turned towards the garden and drummed with his fingers on the window-sill.

Yet Volochine was evidently waiting, and Sarudine felt that he must keep to the desired theme of conversation.

"Of course, I know," he began, with an exaggerated air of nonchalance, "I know that to you men-about-town these country wenches are extraordinarily attractive. But you're wrong. They're fresh and plump, it's true, but they've no *chic*; they don't know how to make love artistically."

In a moment Volochine was all animation. His eyes sparkled, and there was a change in the tone of his voice.

"No, that's quite true. But after a while all that sort of thing is apt to become boring. Our Petersburg women are not well made. You know what I mean? They're just bundles of nerves; they've no limbs on them. Now here . . ."

"Yes, you're right," said Sarudine, growing interested in his turn, as he twirled his moustache complacently.

"Take off her corset, and the smartest Petersburg woman becomes— Oh! by the way, have you heard the latest?" said Volochine, interrupting himself.

"No, I dare say not," replied Sarudine, leaning forward, eagerly.

"Well," said the other, "it's an awfully good story about a Parisian *cocotte*." Then, with much wealth of detail, Volochine proceeded to relate a spicy anecdote that pleased his companion vastly.

"Yes," said Volochine in conclusion, as he rolled his eyes, "shape's everything in a woman. If she hasn't got that, well, for me she simply doesn't exist."

Sarudine thought of Lida's beauty, and he shrank from discussing it with Volochine. However, after a pause, he observed with much affectation:

"Everyone to his taste. What I like most in a woman is the back; that sinuous line, don't you know . . . ."

"Yes," drawled Volochine nervously.

"Some women, especially very young ones, have got . . ."

The orderly now entered, treading clumsily in his heavy boots. He had come to light the lamp, and during the process of striking matches and jingling the glass shade, Sarudine and Volochine were silent.

As the flame of the lamp rose, only their glittering eyes and the glowing cigarette-ends could be seen. When the soldier had gone out, they returned to their subject, the word "Woman" forming the theme of talk that became at times grotesque in its obscenity. Sarudine's instinctive longing to boast, and to eclipse Volochine, led him at last to speak of the splendid woman who had yielded to his charms, and gradually to reveal his own secret lasciviousness. Before the eyes of Volochine, Lida was exhibited as in a state of nudity, her physical attributes and her passion all being displayed as though she were some animal for sale at a fair. By their filthy thoughts she was touched and polluted and held up to ridicule. Their love of woman knew no gratitude for the enjoyment given them; they merely strove to humiliate and insult the sex, to inflict upon it indescribable pain.

The smoke-laden atmosphere of the room had become stifling. Their bodies, at fever heat, exhaled an unwholesome odour, as their eyes gleamed and their voices sounded shrill and rabid as those of wild beasts.

Beyond the window lay the calm, clear moonlit night. But
for them the world with all its wealth of colour and sound
had vanished: all that their eyes beheld was a vision of
woman in her nude loveliness. Soon their imagination became so heated that they felt a burning desire to see Lida,
whom now they had dubbed Lidka, by way of being
familiar. Sarudine had the horses harnessed, and they drove
to a house situated on the outskirts of the town.

CHAPTER XXVIII

A LETTER sent by Sarudine to Lida on the day following their interview fell by chance into Maria Ivanovna's hands. It contained a request for the permission to see her, and awkwardly suggested that sundry matters might be satisfactorily arranged. Its pages cast, so Maria Ivanovna thought, an ugly, shameful shadow upon the pure image of her daughter. In her first perplexity and distress, she remembered her own youth with its love, its deceptions, and the grievous episodes of her married life. A long chain of suffering forged by a life based on rigid laws of morality dragged its slow length along, even to the confines of old age. It was like a grey band, marred in places by monotonous days of care and disappointment.

Yet the thought that her daughter had broken through the solid wall surrounding this grey, dusty life, and had plunged into the lurid whirlpool where joy and sorrow and death were mingled, filled the old woman with horror and rage.

"Vile, wicked girl!" she thought, as despairingly she let her hands fall into her lap. Suddenly it consoled her to imagine that possibly things had not gone too far, and her face assumed a dull, almost a cunning expression. She read and re-read the letter, yet could gather nothing from its frigid, affected style.

Feeling how helpless she was the old woman wept bitterly;

and then, having set her cap straight, she asked the maid-servant:

"Dounika, is Vladimir Petrovitch at home?"

"What?" shouted Dounika.

"Fool! I asked if the young gentleman was at home."

"He's just gone into the study. He's writing a letter!" replied Dounika, looking radiant, as if this letter were the reason for unusual rejoicing.

Maria Ivanovna looked hard at the girl and an evil light flashed from her faded eyes.

"Toad! if you dare to fetch and carry letters again, I'll give you a lesson that you'll never forget."

Sanine was seated at the table writing. His mother was so little used to seeing him write, that, in spite of her grief, she was interested.

"What's that you're writing?"

"A letter," replied Sanine, looking up, gaily.

"To whom?"

"Oh! to a journalist I know. I think of joining the staff of his paper."

"So you write for the papers?"

Sanine smiled. "I do everything."

"But why do you want to go there?"

"Because I'm tired of living here with you, mother," said Sanine frankly.

Maria Ivanovna felt somewhat hurt.

"Thank you," she said.

Sanine looked attentively at her, and felt inclined to tell her not to be so silly as to imagine that a man, especially one who had no employment, could care to remain always in the

same place. But it irked him to have to say such a thing; and
he was silent.

Maria Ivanovna took out her pocket-handkerchief and
crumpled it nervously in her fingers. If it had not been for
Sarudine's letter and her consequent distress and anxiety, she
would have bitterly resented her son's rudeness. But, as it
was, she merely said:

"Ah! yes, the one slinks out of the house like a wolf, and
the other . . ."

A gesture of resignation completed the sentence.

Sanine looked up quickly, and put down his pen.

"What do you know about it?" he asked.

Suddenly Maria Ivanovna felt ashamed that she had read
the letter to Lida. Turning very red, she replied unsteadily,
but with some irritation:

"Thank God, I am not blind! I can see."

"See? You can see nothing," said Sanine, after a moment's
reflection, "and, to prove it, allow me to congratulate you on
the engagement of your daughter. She was going to tell
you herself, but, after all, it comes to the same thing."

"What!" exclaimed Maria Ivanovna, drawing herself up.

"Lida is going to be married!"

"To whom?"

"To Novikoff, of course."

"Yes, but what about Sarudine?"

"Oh! he can go to the devil!" exclaimed Sanine angrily.
"What's that to do with you? Why meddle with other
people's affairs?"

"Yes, but I don't quite understand, Volodja!" said his
mother, bewildered, while yet in her heart she could hear

the joyous refrain, "Lida's going to be married, going to be married!"

Sanine shrugged his shoulders.

"What is that you don't understand? She was in love with one man, and now she's in love with another; and to-morrow she'll be in love with a third. Well, God bless her!"

"What's that you say?" cried Maria Ivanovna indignantly.

Sanine leant against the table and folded his arms.

"In the course of your life did you yourself only love one man?" he asked angrily.

Maria Ivanovna rose. Her wrinkled face wore a look of chilling pride.

"One shouldn't speak to one's mother like that," she said sharply.

"Who?"

"How do you mean, who?"

"Who shouldn't speak?" said Sanine, as he looked at her from head to foot. For the first time he noticed how dull and vacant was the expression in her eyes, and how absurdly her cap was placed upon her head, like a cock's comb.

"Nobody ought to speak to me like that!" she said huskily.

"Anyhow, I've done so!" replied Sanine, recovering his good temper, and resuming his pen.

"You've had your share of life," he said, "and you've no right to prevent Lida from having hers."

Maria Ivanovna said nothing, but stared in amazement at her son, while her cap looked droller than ever.

She hastily checked all memories of her past youth with its joyous nights of love, fixing upon this one question in her

mind: "How dare he speak thus to his mother?" Yet before
she could come to any decision, Sanine turned round, and
taking her hand said kindly:

"Don't let that worry you, but, you must keep Sarudine
out of the house, for the fellow's quite capable of playing us
a dirty trick."

Maria Ivanovna was at once appeased.

"God bless you, my boy," she said. "I am very glad, for
I have always liked Sascha Novikoff. Of course, we can't receive Sarudine; it wouldn't do, because of Sascha."

"No, just that! Because of Sascha," said Sanine with a
humorous look in his eyes.

"And where is Lida?" asked his mother.

"In her room."

"And Sascha?" She pronounced the pet name lovingly.

"I really don't know. He went to . . ." At that moment
Dounika appeared in the doorway, and said:

"Victor Sergejevitsch is here, and another gentleman."

"Turn them out of the house," said Sanine.

Dounika smiled sheepishly.

"Oh! Sir, I can't do that, can I?"

"Of course you can! What business brings them here?"

Dounika hid her face, and went out.

Drawing herself up to her full height, Maria Ivanovna
seemed almost younger, though her eyes looked malevolent.
With astonishing ease her point of view had undergone a
complete change, as if by playing a trump card she had suddenly scored. Kindly as her feelings for Sarudine had been
while she hoped to have him as a son-in-law, they swiftly
cooled when she realized that another was to marry Lida,

and that Sarudine had only made love to her.

As his mother turned to go, Sanine, who noticed her stony profile and forbidding expression, said to himself, "There's an old hen for you!" Folding up his letter he followed her out, curious to see what turn matters would take.

With exaggerated politeness Sarudine and Volochine rose to salute the old lady, yet the former showed none of his wonted ease of manner when at the Sanines'. Volochine indeed felt slightly uncomfortable, because he had come expressly to see Lida, and was obliged to conceal his intention.

Despite his simulated ease, Sarudine looked obviously anxious. He felt that he ought not to have come. He dreaded meeting Lida, yet he could on no account let Volochine see this, to whom he wished to pose as a gay Lothario.

"Dear Maria Ivanovna," began Sarudine, smiling affectedly, "allow me to introduce to you my good friend, Pavel Lvovitsch Volochine."

"Charmed!" said Maria Ivanovna, with frigid politeness, and Sarudine observed the hostile look in her eyes, which somewhat unnerved him. "We ought not to have come," he thought, at last aware of the fact, which in Volochine's society he had forgotten. Lida might come in at any moment, Lida, the mother of his child; what should he say to her? How should he look her in the face? Perhaps her mother knew all? He fidgeted nervously on his chair; lit a cigarette, shrugged his shoulders, moved his legs, and looked about him right and left.

"Are you making a long stay?" asked Maria Ivanovna of Volochine, in a cold, formal voice.

"Oh! no," he replied, as he stared complacently at this

provincial person, thrusting his cigar into the corner of his mouth so that the smoke rose right into her face.

"It must be rather dull for you, here, after Petersburg."

"On the contrary, I think it is delightful. There is something so patriarchal about this little town."

"You ought to visit the environs, which are charming for excursions and picnics. There's boating and bathing, too."

"Of course, madam, of course!" drawled Volochine, who was already somewhat bored.

The conversation languished, and they all seemed to be wearing smiling masks behind which lurked hostile eyes. Volochine winked at Sarudine in the most unmistakable manner; and this was not lost upon Sanine, who from his corner was watching them closely.

The thought that Volochine would no longer regard him as a smart, dashing, dare-devil sort of fellow gave Sarudine some of his old assurance.

"And where is Lidia Petrovna?" he asked carelessly.

Maria Ivanovna looked at him in surprise and anger. Her eyes seemed to say: "What is that to you, since you are not going to marry her?"

"I don't know. Probably in her room," she coldly replied.

Volochine shot another glance at his companion.

"Can't you manage to make Lida come down quickly?" it said. "This old woman's becoming a bore."

Sarudine opened his mouth and feebly twisted his moustache.

"I have heard so many flattering things about your daughter," began Volochine, smiling, and rubbing his hands, as he bent forward to Maria Ivanovna, "that I hope to have the honour of being introduced to her."

Maria Ivanovna wondered what this insolent little *roué* could have heard about her own pure Lida, her darling child, and again she had a terrible presentiment of the latter's downfall. It utterly unnerved her, and for the moment her eyes had a softer, more human expression.

"If they are not turned out of the house," thought Sanine, at this juncture, "they will only cause further distress to Lida and Novikoff."

"I hear that you are going away!" he suddenly said, looking pensively at the floor.

Sarudine wondered that so simple an expedient had not occurred to him before. "That's it! A good idea. Two months' leave!" he thought, before hastily replying:

"Yes, I was thinking of doing so. One wants a change, you know. By stopping too long in one place, you are apt to get rusty."

Sanine laughed outright. The whole conversation, not one word of which expressed their real thoughts and feelings, all this deceit, which deceived nobody, amused him immensely; and with a sudden sense of gaiety and freedom he got up, and said:

"Well, I should think that the sooner you went, the better!"

In a moment as if from each a stiff, heavy garb had fallen off, the other three persons became changed. Maria Ivanovna looked pale and shrunken, Volochine's eyes expressed animal fear, and Sarudine slowly and irresolutely rose.

"What do you mean?" he asked in a hoarse voice.

Volochine tittered, and looked about nervously for his hat. Sanine did not reply to the question, but maliciously

handed Volochine the hat. From the latter's open mouth a
stifled sound escaped like a plaintive squeak.

"What do you mean by that?" cried Sarudine angrily,
aware that he was losing his temper. "A scandal!" he thought
to himself.

"I mean what I say," replied Sanine. "Your presence here
is utterly unnecessary, and we shall all be delighted to see the
last of you."

Sarudine took a step forward. He looked extremely uncomfortable, and his white teeth gleamed threateningly, like
those of a wild beast.

"Aha! That's it, is it?" he muttered, breathing hard.

"Get out!" said Sanine contemptuously, yet in so terrible a
tone that Sarudine glared, and involuntarily drew back.

"I don't know what the deuce it all means!" said Volochine, under his breath, as with shoulders raised he hurried
to the door.

But there, in the door-way, stood Lida. She was dressed
in a style quite different from her usual one. Instead of a
fashionable coiffure, she wore her hair in a thick plait hanging down her back. Instead of an elegant costume she was
wearing a loose gown of diaphanous texture, the simplicity
of which alluringly heightened the beauty of her form.

As she smiled, her likeness to Sanine became more re-
markable, and, in her sweet, girlish voice she said calmly:

"Here I am. Why are you hurrying away? Victor Sergejevitsch, do put down your cap!"

Sanine was silent, and looked at his sister in amazement.
"Whatever does she mean?" he thought to himself.

As soon as she appeared, a mysterious influence, at once

irresistible and tender, seemed to make itself felt. Like a lion-
tamer in a cage filled with wild beasts, Lida stood there, and
the men at once became gentle and submissive.

"Well, do you know, Lidia Petrovna . . ." stammered
Sarudine.

At the sound of his voice, Lida's face assumed a plaintive,
helpless expression, and as she glanced swiftly at him there
was great grief at her heart not unmixed with tenderness and
hope. Yet in a moment such feelings were effaced by a fierce
desire to show Sarudine how much he had lost in losing her;
to let him see that she was still beautiful, in spite of all the
sorrow and shame that he had caused her to endure.

"I don't want to know anything," she replied in an im-
perious, almost a stagy voice, as for a moment she closed her
eyes.

Upon Volochine, her appearance produced an extraordinary effect, as his sharp little tongue darted out from his dry
lips, and his eyes grew smaller and his whole frame vibrated
from sheer physical excitement.

"You haven't introduced us," said Lida, looking round at
Sarudine.

"Volochine . . . Pavel Lvovitsch . . ." stammered the officer.

"And this beauty," he said to himself, "was my mistress."
He felt honestly pleased to think this, at the same time being
anxious to show off before Volochine, while yet bitterly conscious of an irrevocable loss.

Lida languidly addressed her mother.

"There is some one who wants to speak to you," she said.

"Oh! I can't go now," replied Maria Ivanovna.

"But they are waiting," persisted Lida, almost hysterically.

Maria Ivanovna got up quickly.

Sanine watched Lida, and his nostrils were dilated.

"Won't you come into the garden? It's so hot in here," said Lida, and without looking round to see if they were coming, she walked out through the veranda.

As if hypnotized, the men followed her, bound, seemingly, with the tresses of her hair, so that she could draw them whither she wished. Volochine walked first, ensnared by her beauty, and apparently oblivious of aught else.

Lida sat down in the rocking-chair under the linden-tree and stretched out her pretty little feet clad in black open-work stockings and tan shoes. It was as if she had two natures; the one overwhelmed with modesty and shame, the other, full of self-conscious coquetry. The first nature prompted her to look with disgust upon men, and life, and herself.

"Well, Pavel Lvovitsch," she asked, as her eyelids drooped, "What impression has our little out-of-the-way town made upon you?"

"The impression which probably he experiences who in the depth of the forest suddenly beholds a radiant flower," replied Volochine, rubbing his hands.

Then began talk which was thoroughly vapid and insincere, the spoken being false, and the unspoken, true. Sanine sat silently listening to this mute but sincere conversation, as expressed by faces, hands, feet, and tremulous accents. Lida was unhappy, Volochine longed for all her beauty, while Sarudine loathed Lida, Sanine, Volochine, and the world generally. He wanted to go, yet he could not make a move. He was for doing something outrageous, yet he could only smoke cigarette after cigarette, while dominated by the desire to proclaim Lida his mistress to all present.

"And how do you like being here? Are you not sorry to have left Petersburg behind you?" asked Lida, suffering meanwhile intense torture, and wondering why she did not get up and go.

"*Mais au contraire!*" lisped Volochine, as he waved his hand in a finicking fashion and gazed ardently at Lida.

"Come! come! no pretty speeches!" said Lida, coquettishly, while to Sarudine her whole being seemed to say:

"You think that I am wretched, don't you? and utterly crushed? But I am nothing of the kind, my friend. Look at me!"

"Oh, Lidia Petrovna!" said Sarudine, "you surely don't call that a pretty speech!"

"I beg your pardon?" asked Lida drily, as if she had not heard, and then, in a different tone, she again addressed Volochine.

"Do tell me something about life in Petersburg. Here, we don't live, we only vegetate."

Sarudine saw that Volochine was smiling to himself, as if he did not believe that the former had even been on intimate terms with Lida.

"Ah! Ah! Ah! Very good!" he said to himself, as he bit his lip viciously.

"Oh! our famous Petersburg life!" Volochine, who chattered with ease, looked like a silly little monkey babbling of things that it did not comprehend.

"Who knows?" he thought to himself, his gaze riveted on Lida's beautiful form.

"I assure you on my word of honour that our life is extremely dull and colourless. Until to-day I thought that life, generally, was always dull, whether in the town or in the country."

"Not really!" exclaimed Lida, as she half closed her eyes.

"What makes life worth living is . . . a beautiful woman! And the women in big towns! If you could only see what they are like! Do you know, I feel convinced that if the world is ever saved it will be by beauty." This last phrase Volochine unexpectedly added, believing it to be most apt and illuminating. The expression of his face was one of stupidity and greed, as he kept reverting to his pet theme, Woman. Sarudine, alternately flushed and pale with jealousy, found it impossible to remain in one place, but walked restlessly up and down the path.

"Our women are all alike . . . stereotyped and made-up. To find one whose beauty is worthy of adoration, it is to the provinces that one must go, where the soil, untilled as yet, produces the most splendid flowers."

Sanine scratched the nape of his neck, and crossed his legs.

"Ah! of what good is it if they bloom here, since there is no one worthy to pluck them?" replied Lida.

"Aha!" thought Sanine, suddenly becoming interested, "so that's what she's driving at!"

This word-play, where sentiment and grossness were so obviously involved, he found extremely diverting.

"Is it possible?"

"Why of course! I mean what I say, who is it that plucks our unfortunate blossoms? What men are those whom we set up as heroes?" rejoined Lida bitterly.

"Aren't you rather too hard upon us?" asked Sarudine.

"No, Lidia Petrovna is right!" exclaimed Volochine, but, glancing at Sarudine, his eloquence suddenly subsided. Lida laughed outright. Filled with shame and grief and revenge, her burning eyes were set on her seducer, and seemed to pierce him through and through. Volochine again began to babble, while Lida interrupted him with laughter that concealed her tears.

"I think that we ought to be going," said Sarudine, at last, who felt the situation was becoming intolerable. He could not tell why, but everything, Lida's laughter, her scornful eyes and trembling hands were all to him as so many secret boxes on the ear. His growing hatred of her, and his jealousy of Volochine as well as the consciousness of all that he had lost, served to exhaust him utterly.

"Already?" asked Lida.

Volochine smiled sweetly, licking his lips with the tip of his tongue.

"It can't be helped! Victor Sergejevitsch apparently is not quite himself," he said in a mocking tone, proud of his conquest.

So they took their leave; and, as Sarudine bent over Lida's hand, he whispered:

"This is good-bye!"

Never had he hated Lida as much as at this moment.

In Lida's heart there arose a vague, fleeting desire to bid tender farewell to all those bygone hours of love which had once been theirs. But this feeling she swiftly repressed, as she said in a loud, harsh voice:

"Good-bye! *Bon voyage!* Don't forget us, Pavel Lvovitsch!"

As they were going, Volochine's remark could be distinctly heard.

"How charming she is! She intoxicates one, like champagne!"

When they had gone, Lida sat down again in the rocking-chair. Her position was a different one, now, for she bent forward, trembling all over, and her silent tears fell fast.

"Come, come! What's the matter?" said Sanine, as he took hold of her hand.

"Oh! don't! What an awful thing life is!" she exclaimed, as her head sank lower, and she covered her face with her hands, while the soft plait of hair, slipping over her shoulder, hung down in front.

"For shame!" said Sanine. "What's the use of crying about such trifles?"

"Are there really no other . . . better men, then?" murmured Lida.

Sanine smiled.

"No, certainly not. Man is vile by nature. Expect nothing good from him. . . . And then the harm that he does to you will not make you grieve."

Lida looked up at him with beautiful tear-stained eyes.

"Do you expect nothing good from your fellow-men, either?"

"Of course not," replied Sanine, "I live alone."

CHAPTER XXIX

On the following day Dounika, bare-headed and bare-footed, came running to Sanine who was gardening.

"Vladimir Petrovitch," she exclaimed, and her silly face had a scared look, "the officers have come, and they wish to speak to you." She repeated the words like a lesson that she had learnt by heart.

Sanine was not surprised. He had been expecting a challenge from Sarudine.

"Are they very anxious to see me?" he asked in a jocular tone.

Dounika, however, must have had an inkling of something dreadful, for instead of hiding her face she gazed at Sanine in sympathetic bewilderment.

Sanine propped his spade against a tree, tightened his belt and walked towards the house with his usual jaunty step.

"What fools they are! What absolute idiots!" he said to himself, as he thought of Sarudine and his seconds. By this no insult was intended; it was just the sincere expression of his own opinion.

Passing through the house he saw Lida coming out of her room. She stood on the threshold; her face white as a shroud, and her eyes anxious and distrustful. Her lips moved, yet no sound escaped from them. At that moment she felt that she was the guiltiest, most miserable woman in all the world.

In an arm-chair in the morning-room sat Maria Ivanovna, looking utterly helpless and panic-stricken. Her cap that resembled a cock's comb was poised sideways on her head, and she gazed in terror at Sanine, unable to utter a word. He smiled at her and was inclined to stop for a moment, yet he preferred to proceed.

Tanaroff and Von Deitz were sitting in the drawing-room bolt upright, with their heads close together, as if in their white tunics and tight riding-breeches they felt extremely uncomfortable. As Sanine entered they both rose slowly and with some hesitation, apparently uncertain how to behave.

"Good day, gentlemen," said Sanine in a loud voice, as he held out his hand.

Von Deitz hesitated, but Tanaroff bowed in such an exaggerated way that for an instant Sanine caught sight of the closely cropped hair at the back of his neck.

"How can I be of service to you?" continued Sanine, who had noticed Tanaroff's excessive politeness, and was surprised at the assurance with which he played his part in this absurd comedy.

Von Deitz drew himself up and sought to give an expression of *hauteur* to his horse-like countenance; unsuccessfully however, owing to his confusion. Strange to say, it was Tanaroff, usually so stupid and shy, who addressed Sanine in firm, decisive fashion.

"Our friend, Victor Sergejevitsch Sarudine, has done us the honour of asking us to represent him in a certain matter which concerns you and himself." The sentence was delivered with automatic precision.

"Oho!" said Sanine with comic gravity, as he opened his mouth wide.

"Yes, sir," continued Tanaroff, frowning slightly. "He considers that your behaviour towards him was not—er— quite ..."

"Yes, yes, I understand," interrupted Sanine, losing patience. "I very nearly kicked him out of the house, so that 'not—er—quite' is hardly the right way of putting it."

The speech was lost upon Tanaroff, who went on:

"Well, sir, he insists on your taking back your words."

"Yes, yes," chimed in the lanky Von Deitz, who kept shifting the position of his feet, like a stork.

Sanine smiled.

"Take them back? How can I do that? 'As uncaged bird is spoken word!'"

Too perplexed to reply, Tanaroff looked Sanine full in the face.

"What evil eyes he has!" thought the latter.

"This is no joking matter," began Tanaroff, looking flushed and angry. "Are you prepared to retract your words, or are you not?"

Sanine at first was silent.

"What an utter idiot!" he thought, as he took a chair and sat down.

"Possibly I might be willing to retract my words in order to please and pacify Sarudine," he began, speaking seriously, "the more so as I attach not the slightest importance to them. But, in the first place, Sarudine, being a fool, would not understand my motive, and, instead of holding his tongue, would brag about it. In the second place, I thoroughly dislike Sarudine, so that, under these circumstances, I don't see that there is any sense in my retraction."

"Very well, then . . ." hissed Tanaroff through his teeth.

Von Deitz stared in amazement, and his long face turned yellow.

"In that case . . ." began Tanaroff, in a louder and would-be threatening tone.

Sanine felt fresh hatred for the fellow as he looked at his narrow forehead and his tight breeches.

"Yes, yes, I know all about it," he interrupted. "E thing, let me tell you; I don't intend to fight Sarudine."

Von Deitz turned round sharply.

Tanaroff drew himself up, and said in a tone of contempt, "Why not, pray?"

Sanine burst out laughing. His hatred had vanished as swiftly as it had come.

"Well, this is why. First of all, I have no wish to kill Sarudine, and secondly, I have even less desire to be killed myself."

"But . . ." began Tanaroff scornfully.

"I won't, and there's an end of it!" said Sanine, as he rose. "Why, indeed? I don't feel inclined to give you any explanation. That were too much to expect, really!"

Tanaroff's profound contempt for the man who refused to fight a duel was blended with implicit belief that only an officer could possibly possess the pluck and the fine sense of honour necessary to do such a thing. That is why Sanine's refusal did not surprise him in the least; in fact, he was secretly pleased.

"That is your affair," he said, in an unmistakably contemptuous tone, "but I must warn you that . . ."

Sanine laughed.

"Yes, yes, I know, but I advise Sarudine not to . . ."

"Not to—what?" asked Tanaroff, as he picked up his cap from the window-sill.

"I advise him not to touch me, or else I'll give him such a thrashing that . . ."

"Look here!" cried Von Deitz, in a fury. "I'm not going to stand this . . . You . . . you are simply laughing at us.)on't you understand that to refuse to accept a challenge is . . . is . . ."

He was as red as a lobster, his eyes were starting from his head, and there was foam on his lips.

Sanine looked curiously at his mouth, and said:

"And this is the man who calls himself a disciple of Tolstoi!"

Von Deitz winced, and tossed his head.

"I must beg of you," he spluttered, ashamed all the while at thus addressing a man with whom till now he had been on friendly terms. "I must beg of you not to mention that. It has nothing whatever to do with this matter."

"Hasn't it though?" replied Sanine. "It has a great deal to do with it."

"Yes, but I must ask you," croaked Von Deitz, becoming hysterical.

"Really, this is too much! In short . . ."

"Oh! That'll do!" replied Sanine, drawing back in disgust from Von Deitz, from whose mouth saliva spurted. "Think what you like; I don't care. And tell Sarudine that he is an ass!"

"You've no right, sir, I say, you've no right," shouted Von Deitz.

"Very good, very good," said Tanaroff, quite satisfied. "Let us go."

"No!" cried the other, plaintively, as he waved his lanky arms. "How dare he? . . . What business! . . . It's simply . . ."

Sanine looked at him, and, making a contemptuous gesture, walked out of the room.

"We will deliver your message to our brother-officer," said Tanaroff, calling after him.

"As you please," said Sanine, without looking round. He could hear Tanaroff trying to pacify the enraged Von Deitz, and thought to himself, "As a rule the fellow's an utter fool, but put him on his hobby-horse, and he becomes quite sensible."

"The matter cannot be allowed to rest thus!" cried the implacable Von Deitz, as they went out.

From the door of her room, Lida gently called "Volodja!"

Sanine stood still.

"What is it?"

"Come here; I want to speak to you."

Sanine entered Lida's little room where, owing to the trees in front of the window, soft green twilight reigned. There was a feminine odour of perfume and powder.

"How nice it is in here," said Sanine, with a sigh of relief.

Lida stood facing the window, and green reflected lights from the garden flickered round her cheeks and shoulders.

"What do you want with me?" he asked kindly.

Lida was silent, and she breathed heavily.

"Why, what is the matter?"

"Are you—not going to fight a duel?" she asked hoarsely, without looking round.

"No."

Lida was silent.

"Well, what of that?" said Sanine.

Lida's chin trembled. She turned sharply round and murmured quickly:

"I can't understand that, I can't . . ."

"Oh!" exclaimed Sanine, frowning. "Well, I'm very sorry for you."

Human stupidity and malice surrounded him on all sides. To find such qualities alike in bad folk and good folk, in handsome people as in ugly, proved utterly disheartening.

He turned on his heels and went out.

Lida watched him go, and then, holding her head with both hands, she flung herself upon the bed. The long black plait lay at full length along the white coverlet. At this moment Lida, strong, supple and beautiful in spite of her despair, looked younger, more full of life than ever. Through the window came warmth and radiance from the garden, and the room was bright and pleasant. Yet of all this Lida saw nothing.

CHAPTER XXX

It was one of those strangely beautiful evenings in late summer that descend upon earth from the majestic azure vaults of heaven. The sun had set, but the light was still distinct, and the air pure and clear. There was a heavy dew, and the dust which had slowly risen formed long gauze-like strips of cloud against the sky. The atmosphere was sultry and yet fresh. Sounds floated hither and thither, as if borne on rapid wings.

Sanine, hatless, and wearing his blue shirt that at the shoulders was slightly faded, sauntered along the dusty road and turned down the little grass-grown side-street leading to Ivanoff's lodging.

At the window, making cigarettes, sat Ivanoff, broad-shouldered and sedate, with his long, straw-coloured hair carefully brushed back. Humid airs floated towards him from the garden where grass and foliage gained new lustre in the evening dew. The strong odour of tobacco was an inducement to sneeze.

"Good evening," said Sanine, leaning on the window-sill.

"Good evening."

"To-day I have been challenged to fight a duel," said Sanine.

"What fun!" replied Ivanoff carelessly. "With whom, and why?"

"With Sarudine. I turned him out of the house, and he considers himself insulted."

"Oho! Then you'll have to meet him," said Ivanoff. "I'll be your second, and you shall shoot his nose off."

"Why? The nose is a noble part of one's physiognomy. I am not going to fight," rejoined Sanine, laughing.

Ivanoff nodded.

"A good thing, too. Duelling is quite unnecessary."

"My sister Lida doesn't think so," said Sanine.

"Because she's a goose," replied Ivanoff. "What a lot of tomfoolery people choose to believe, don't they?"

So saying, he finished making the last cigarette, which he lighted, putting the others in his leather cigarette-case.

Then he blew away the tobacco left on the window-sill, and, vaulting over it, joined Sanine.

"What shall we do this evening?" he asked.

"Let us go see Soloveitchik," suggested Sanine.

"Oh! no!"

"Why not?"

"I don't like him. He's such a worm."

Sanine shrugged his shoulders.

"Not worse than others. Come along."

"All right," said Ivanoff, who always agreed to anything that Sanine proposed. So they both went along the street together.

Soloveitchik, however, was not at home. The door was shut, and the courtyard dreary and deserted. Only Sultan rattled his chain and barked at these strangers who had invaded his yard. "What a ghastly place!" exclaimed Ivanoff. "Let us go to the boulevard."

They turned back, shutting the gate after them. Sultan barked two or three times and then sat in front of his kennel, sadly gazing at the desolate yard, the silent mill and the little white footpaths across the dusty turf.

In the public garden the band was playing, as usual, and there was a pleasant breeze on the boulevard, where promenaders abounded. Lit up by bright feminine toilettes, the dark throng moved now in the direction of the shady gardens, and now towards the main entrance of massive stone.

On entering the garden arm-in-arm, Sanine and Ivanoff instantly encountered Soloveitchik who was walking pensively along, his hands behind his back, and his eyes on the ground.

"We have just been to your place," said Sanine.

Soloveitchik blushed and smiled, as he timidly replied:

"Oh! I beg your pardon! I am so sorry, but I never thought that you were coming, or else I would have stayed at home. I am just out for a little walk." His wistful eyes shone.

"Come along with us," said Sanine, kindly, as he took hold of his arm.

Soloveitchik, apparently delighted, accepted the proffered arm, thrust his cap on the back of his head, and walked along as if, instead of Sanine's arm, it was something precious that he was holding. His mouth seemed to reach from ear to ear.

Purple-faced, and with distended cheeks, the members of the regimental band flung out their deafening notes upon the air, stimulated in their efforts by a smartly-dressed bandmaster who looked like a pert little sparrow, and who zealously flourished his *bâton*. Grouped round the band-stand

were clerks, shopmen, schoolboys in Hessian boots, and little girls wearing brightly-coloured handkerchiefs round their
heads. In the main walks and side-walks, as if engaged in
an endless quadrille, there moved a vivacious throng, com-
posed of officers, students, and ladies.

They soon met Dubova, Schafroff, and Yourii Svarogitsch,
and exchanged smiles as they passed. Then, after they had
strolled through the entire garden, they again met, Sina
Karsavina being now one of the party, looking charmingly
graceful in her light summer dress.

"Why are you walking by yourselves, like that?" asked
Dubova.

"Come; and join us."

"Let us go down one of the side-walks," suggested Schafroff. "Here, it's so terribly crowded."

Laughing and chatting, the young people accordingly
turned aside into a more shady, quieter avenue. As they
reached the end of it and were about to turn, Sarudine,
Tanaroff and Volochine suddenly came round the corner.
Sanine saw at once that Sarudine had not expected to meet
him here, and that he was considerably disconcerted. His
handsome face grew dark, and he drew himself up to his full
height. Tanaroff laughed contemptuously.

"That little jackanapes is still here," said Ivanoff, as he
stared at Volochine. The latter had not noticed them, being
so much interested in Sina, who walked first, that he turned
round in passing to look at her.

"So he is!" said Sanine, laughing.

Sarudine thought that this laughter was meant for him,
and he winced, as if struck by a whip. Flushed with anger,

and impelled as by some irresistible force, he left his companions, and rapidly approached Sanine.

"What is it?" said the latter, suddenly becoming serious, while his eyes were fixed on the little riding-whip in Sarudine's trembling hand.

"You fool!" he thought to himself, as much in pity as in anger.

"I should like a word with you," began Sarudine, hoarsely. "Did you receive my challenge?"

"Yes," replied Sanine, intently watching every movement of the officer's hands.

"And you have decided to refuse ... er ... to act as any decent man is bound to act under the circumstances?" asked Sarudine. His voice was muffled, though loud in tone. To himself it seemed a strange one, as uncanny as the cold handle of the whip in his moist fingers. But he had not the strength to turn aside from the path that lay before him. Suddenly in the garden there seemed to be no air whatever. All the others stood still, perplexed, and expectant.

"Oh! what the deuce——" began Ivanoff, endeavouring to interpose.

"Of course I refuse," said Sanine in a strangely calm voice, looking the other straight in the eyes.

Sarudine breathed hard, as if he were lifting a heavy weight.

"Once more I ask you—do you refuse?" His voice had a hard, metallic ring.

Soloveitchik turned very pale. "Oh, dear! Oh! dear! He's going to hit him!" he thought.

"What ... what is the matter?" he stammered, as he endeavoured to protect Sanine.

Scarcely noticing him, Sarudine roughly pushed him aside. He saw nothing else in front of him but Sanine's cold, calm eyes.

"I have already told you so," said Sanine, in the same tone.

To Sarudine everything seemed whirling round. He heard behind him hasty footsteps, and the startled cry of a woman. With a sense of despair such as one who falls headlong into a chasm might feel, he clumsily and threateningly flourished the whip.

At that same moment Sanine, using all his strength, struck him full in the face with his clenched fist.

"Good!" exclaimed Ivanoff involuntarily.

Sarudine's head hung limply on one side. Something hot that stabbed his brain and eyes like sharp needles flooded his mouth and nose.

"Ah!" he groaned, and sank helplessly forward on his hands, dropping the whip, while his cap fell off. He saw nothing, he heard nothing, being only conscious of the horrible disgrace, and of a dull burning pain in his eye.

"Oh! God!" screamed Sina Karsavina, holding her head with both hands, and shutting her eyes tightly.

Horrified and disgusted at the sight of Sarudine crouching there on all fours, Yourii, followed by Schafroff, rushed at Sanine. Volochine, losing his *pince-nez* as he stumbled over a bush, ran away as fast as he could across the damp grass, so that his spotless trousers instantly became black up to the knees.

Tanaroff ground his teeth with fury, and also dashed forward, but Ivanoff caught him by the shoulders and pulled him back.

"That's all right!" said Sanine scornfully. "Let him come."
He stood with legs apart, breathing hard, and big drops of
sweat were on his brow.

Sarudine slowly staggered to his feet. Faint, incoherent
words escaped from his quivering, swollen lips, vague words
of menace that to Sanine sounded singularly ridiculous.
The whole left side of Sarudine's face had instantly become
swollen. His eye was no longer visible; blood was flowing
from his nose and mouth, his lips twitched, and his whole
body shook as if in the grip of a fever. Of the smart, handsome officer nothing remained. That awful blow had robbed
him of all that was human; it had left only something piteous, terrifying, disfigured. He made no attempt to go away
nor to defend himself. His teeth rattled, and, while he spat
blood, he mechanically brushed the sand from his knees.
Then, reeling forward, he fell down again.

"Oh! how horrible! How horrible!" exclaimed Sina Karsavina, hurrying away from the spot.

"Come along!" said Sanine to Ivanoff, looking upwards
to avoid so revolting a sight.

"Come along, Soloveitchik."

But Soloveitchik did not stir. Wide-eyed he stared at Sarudine, at the blood, and the dirty sand on the snow-white
tunic, trembling all the while, as his lips moved feebly.

Ivanoff angrily pulled him along, but Soloveitchik shook
him off with surprising vehemence, and he then clung to the
trunk of a tree, as if he wished to resist being dragged away
by main force.

"Oh! why, why, did you do that?" he whimpered.

"What a blackguardly thing to do!" shouted Yourii in Sanine's face.

"Yes, blackguardly!" rejoined Sanine, with a scornful smile. "Would it have been better, do you suppose, to have let him hit me?"

Then, with a careless gesture, he walked rapidly along the avenue. Ivanoff looked at Yourii in disdain, lit a cigarette, and slowly followed Sanine. Even his broad back and smooth hair told one plainly how little such a scene as this affected him.

"How stupid and brutal man can be!" he murmured to himself.

Sanine glanced round once, and then walked faster.

"Just like brutes," said Yourii, as he went away. He looked back, and the garden which he had always thought beautiful, and dim, and mysterious, seemed now, after what had happened, to have been shut off from the rest of the world, a sombre, dreary place.

Schafroff breathed hard, and looked nervously over his spectacles in all directions, as if he thought that at any moment something equally dreadful might again occur.

CHAPTER XXXI

In a moment Sarudine's life had undergone a complete change. Careless, easy, and gay as it had been before, so now it seemed to him distorted, dire, and unendurable. The laughing mask had fallen; the hideous face of a monster was revealed.

Tanaroff had taken him home in a *droschky*. On the way he exaggerated his pain and weakness so not to have to open his eyes. In this way he thought that he would avoid the shame levelled at him by thousands of eyes so soon as they encountered his.

The slim, blue back of the *droschky* driver, the passers-by, malicious, inquisitive faces at windows, even Tanaroff's arm round his waist were all, as he imagined, silent expressions of undisguised contempt. So intensely painful did this sensation become, that at last Sarudine almost fainted. He felt as if he were losing his reason, and he longed to die. His brain refused to recognize what had happened. He kept thinking that there was a mistake, some misunderstanding, and that his plight was not as desperate and deplorable as he imagined. Yet the actual fact remained, and ever darker grew his despair.

Sarudine felt that he was being supported, that he was in pain, and that his hands were blood-stained and dirty. It really surprised him to know that he was still conscious of it

277

all. At times, when the vehicle turned a sharp corner, and swayed to one side, he partially opened his eyes, and perceived, as if through tears, familiar streets, and houses, and people, and the church. Nothing had become changed, yet all seemed hostile, strange, and infinitely remote.

Passers-by stopped and stared. Sarudine instantly shut his eyes in shame and despair. The drive seemed endless. "Faster! Faster!" he thought anxiously. Then, however, he pictured to himself the faces of his man-servant, of his land-lady, and of the neighbours, which made him wish that the journey might never end. Just to drive on, drive on, anywhere, like that, with eyes closed!

Tanaroff was horribly ashamed of this procession. Very red and confused, he looked straight in front of him, and strove to give the onlookers the impression that he had nothing whatever to do with the affair.

At first he professed to sympathize with Sarudine, but soon relapsed into silence, occasionally through his clenched teeth urging the coachman to drive quicker. From this, as also from the irresolute support of his arm, which at times almost pushed him away, Sarudine knew exactly what Tanaroff felt. It was this knowledge that a man whom he held to be so absolutely his inferior should feel ashamed of him, which convinced Sarudine that all was now at an end.

He could not cross the courtyard without assistance. Tanaroff and the scared, trembling orderly almost had to carry him. If there were other onlookers, Sarudine did not see them. They made up a bed for him on the sofa and stood there, helpless and irresolute. This irritated him intensely. At last, recovering himself, the servant fetched some hot water and a towel, and carefully washed the blood from Sarudine's face and hands. His master avoided his glance, but in the soldier's eyes there was nothing malicious or scornful; only such fear and pity as some kind-hearted old nurse might feel.

"Oh! however did this happen, your Excellency? Oh, dear! Oh, dear! What have they been doing to him?" he murmured.

"It's no business of yours!" hissed Tanaroff angrily, glancing round immediately afterwards in confusion. He went to the window and mechanically took out a cigarette, but uncertain if, while Sarudine lay there, he ought to smoke, he hurriedly thrust his cigarette-case into his pocket.

"Shall I fetch the doctor?" asked the orderly, standing at attention, and unabashed by the rude answer that he had received.

Tanaroff stretched out his fingers irresolutely.

"I don't know," he said in an altered voice, as he again looked round.

Sarudine had heard these words, and was horrified to think that the doctor would see his battered face.

"I don't want anybody," he murmured feebly, trying to persuade himself and the others that he was going to die.

Cleansed now from blood and dirt, his face was no longer horrible to behold, but called rather for compassion.

From mere animal curiosity Tanaroff hastily glanced at him, and then, in a moment, looked elsewhere. Almost imperceptible as this movement had been, Sarudine noticed it with unutterable anguish and despair. He shut his eyes tighter, and exclaimed, in a broken, tearful voice:

"Leave me! Leave me! Oh! Oh!"

Tanaroff glanced again at him. Suddenly a feeling of irritation and contempt possessed him.

"He's actually going to cry now!" he thought, with a certain malicious satisfaction.

Sarudine's eyes were closed, and he lay quite still. Tanaroff drummed lightly on the window-sill with his fingers, twirled his moustache, looked round first, and then out of the window, feeling selfishly eager to get away.

"I can't very well, just yet," he thought. "What a damned bore! Better wait until he goes to sleep."

Another quarter of an hour passed, and Sarudine appeared to be restless. To Tanaroff such suspense was intolerable. At last the sufferer lay motionless.

"Aha! he's asleep," thought Tanaroff, inwardly pleased. "Yes, I'm sure that he is."

He moved cautiously across the room so that the jingling of his spurs was scarcely audible. Suddenly Sarudine opened his eyes. Tanaroff stood still, but Sarudine had already guessed his intention, and the former knew that he had been detected in the act. Now something strange occurred. Sarudine shut his eyes and pretended to be asleep. Tanaroff tried to persuade himself that this was the case, while yet perfectly well aware that each was watching the other; and so, in an awkward, stooping posture, he crept out of the room on tiptoe, feeling like a convicted traitor.

The door closed gently behind him. In such wise were the bonds of friendship that had bound these two men together broken once and for all. They both felt that a gulf now lay between them that could never be bridged; in this world henceforth they could be nothing to each other.

In the outer room Tanaroff breathed more freely. He had no regret that all was at an end between himself and the man with whom for many years his life had been spent.

"Look here!" said he to the servant as if, for form's sake, it behoved him to speak. "I am now going. If anything should happen—well . . . you understand . . ."

"Very good, sir," replied the soldier, looking scared.

"So now you know. . . . And see that the bandage is frequently changed."

He hurried down the steps, and, after closing the garden-gate, he drew a deep breath when he saw before him the broad, silent street. It was now nearly dark, and Tanaroff was glad that no one could notice his flushed face.

"I may even be mixed up in this horrid affair myself," he thought, and his heart sank as he approached the boulevard. "After all, what have I got to do with it?"

Thus he sought to pacify himself, endeavouring to forget how Ivanoff had flung him aside with such force that he almost fell down.

"Deuce take it! What a nasty business! It's all that fool of a Sarudine! Why did he ever associate with such *canaille?*"

The more he brooded over the whole unpleasantness of this incident, the more his commonplace figure, as he strutted along in his tightly-fitting breeches, smart boots, and white tunic, assumed a threatening aspect.

In every passer-by he was ready to detect ridicule and scorn; indeed, at the slightest provocation he would have wildly drawn his sword. However, he met but few folk, who, like furtive shadows, passed swiftly along the outskirts of the darkening boulevard. On reaching home he became somewhat calmer, and then he thought again of what Ivanoff had done.

"Why didn't I hit him? I ought to have given him one in the jaw. I might have used my sword. I had my revolver, too, in my pocket. I ought to have shot him like a dog. How came I to forget the revolver? Well, after all, perhaps it's just as well that I didn't. Suppose I had killed him? It would have been a matter for the police. One of those other fellows might have had a revolver, too! A pretty state of things, eh? At all events, nobody knows that I had a weapon on me, and by degrees the whole thing will blow over."

Tanaroff looked cautiously round before he drew out his revolver and placed it in the table drawer.

"I shall have to go to the colonel at once, and explain to him that I had nothing whatever to do with the matter," he thought, as he locked the drawer. Then an irresistible impulse seized him to go to the officers' mess, and, as an eyewitness, describe exactly what took place. The officers had already heard about the affair in the public gardens, and they hurried back to the brilliantly lighted mess-rooms to give vent in heated language to their indignation. They were really rather pleased at Sarudine's discomfiture, since often enough his smartness and elegance in dress and demeanour had served to put them in the shade.

Tanaroff was hailed with undisguised curiosity. He felt that he was the hero of the hour as he began to give a detailed account of the whole incident. In his narrow black eyes there was a look of hatred for the friend who had always

been his superior. He thought of the money incident, and
of Sarudine's condescending attitude towards him, and he
revenged himself for past slights by a minute description of
his comrade's defeat.

Meanwhile, forsaken and alone, Sarudine lay there upon
his couch.

His soldier-servant, who had learnt the whole truth elsewhere, moved noiselessly about, looking sad and anxious as
before. He set the tea-things ready, fetched some wine, and
drove the dog out of the room as it leapt about for joy at the
sight of its master.

After a while the man came back on tiptoe. "Your Excellency had better have a little wine," he whispered.

"Eh? What?" exclaimed Sarudine, opening his eyes and
shutting them again instantly. In a tone which he thought
severe, but which was really piteous, he could just move his
swollen lips sufficiently to say: "Bring me the looking-
glass."

The servant sighed, brought the mirror, and held a candle
close to it.

"Why does he want to look at himself?" he thought.

When Sarudine looked in the glass he uttered an involuntary cry. In the dark mirror a terribly disfigured face confronted him. One side of it was black and blue, his eye
was swollen, and his moustache stuck out like bristles on his
puffy cheek.

"Here! Take it away!" murmured Sarudine, and he
sobbed hysterically. "Some water!"

"Your Excellency mustn't take it so to heart. You'll soon
be all right again," said the kindly soldier, as he proffered

water in a sticky glass which smelt of tea.

Sarudine could not drink; his teeth rattled helplessly against the rim of the glass, and the water was spilt over his coat.

"Go away!" he feebly moaned.

His servant, so he thought, was the only man in the world who sympathized with him, yet that kindlier feeling towards him was speedily extinguished by the intolerable conscious- ness that his serving-man had cause to pity him.

Almost in tears, the soldier blinked his eyes and, going out, sat down on the steps leading to the garden. Fawning upon him, the dog thrust its pretty nose against his knee and looked up at him gravely with dark, questioning eyes. He gently stroked its soft, wavy coat. Overhead shone the silent stars. A sense of fear came over him, as the presage of some great, inevitable mischance.

"Life's a sad thing!" he thought bitterly, remembering for a moment his own native village.

Sarudine turned hastily over on the sofa and lay motion- less, without noticing that the compress, now grown warm, had slipped off his face.

"Now all is at an end!" he murmured hysterically, "What is at an end? Everything! My whole life—done for! Why? Because I've been insulted—struck like a dog! My face struck with a fist! I can never remain in the regiment, never!"

He could clearly see himself there, in the avenue, hobbling on all fours, cowed and ridiculous, as he uttered feeble, sense- less threats. Again and again he mentally rehearsed that awful incident with ever increasing torture and, as if illuminated, all the details stood out vividly before his eyes. That which most irritated him was his recollection of Sina Karsavina's white dress, of which he caught a glimpse at the very moment when he was vowing futile vengeance.

"Who was it that lifted me up?" He tried to turn his thoughts into another channel. "Was it Tanaroff? Or that Jew boy who was with them! It must have been Tanaroff. Anyhow it doesn't matter in the least. What matters is that my whole life is ruined, and that I shall have to leave the regiment. And the duel? What about that? He won't fight. I shall have to leave the regiment."

Sarudine recollected how a regimental committee had forced two brother-officers, married men, to resign because they had refused to fight a duel.

"I shall be asked to resign in the same way. Quite civilly without shaking hands . . . the very fellows that . . . Nobody will feel flattered now to be seen walking arm-in-arm with me in the boulevard, or envy me, or imitate my manner. But, after all, that's nothing. It's the shame, the dishonour of it. Why? Because I was struck in the face? It has happened to me before when I was a cadet. That big fellow, Schwartz, gave me a hiding, and knocked out one of my teeth. Nobody thought anything about it, but we shook hands afterwards, and became the best of friends. Nobody despised me then. Why should it be different now? Surely it is just the same thing! On that occasion, too, blood was spilt, and I fell down. So that . . ."

To these despairing questions Sarudine could find no answer.

"If he had accepted my challenge and had shot me in the

face, that would have been worse, and much more painful.
Yet no one would have despised me in that case; on the contrary, I should have had sympathy and admiration. Thus
there is a difference between a bullet and the fist. What
difference is there, and why should there be any?"

His thoughts came swiftly, incoherently, yet his suffering
and irreparable misfortune would seem to have roused something new and latent within him of which in his careless
years of selfish enjoyment he had never been conscious.

"Von Deitz, for instance, was always saying, 'If one smite
thee on the right cheek, turn to him the left.' But how did
he come back that day from Sanine's? Shouting angrily, and
waving his arms because the fellow wouldn't accept my
challenge! The others are really to blame for my wanting to
hit him with the riding-whip. My mistake was that I didn't
do it in time. The whole thing's absurdly unjust. However,
there it is; the disgrace remains; and I shall have to leave the
regiment."

With both hands pressed to his aching brow, Sarudine
tossed from side to side, for the pain in his eye was excruciat-
ing. Then, in a fit of fury, he muttered:

"Get a revolver, rush at him, and put a couple of bullets
through his head . . . and then, as he lies there, stamp on
his face, on his eyes, on his teeth! . . ."

The compress fell to the floor with a dull thud. Sarudine,
startled, opened his eyes and, in the dimly-lighted room, saw
a basin of water, a towel, and the dark window, that like an
awful eye, stared at him mysteriously.

"No, no, there's no help for it now," he thought, in dull
despair. "They all saw it; saw I was struck in the face,

and how I crawled along on all fours. Oh! the shame of it! Struck like that, in the face! No, it's too much! I shall never be free or happy again!"

And again through his mind there flashed a new, keen thought.

"After all, have I ever been free? No. That's just why I've come to grief now, because my life has never been free; because I've never lived it in my own way. Of my own free will should I ever have wanted to fight a duel, or to hit him with the whip? Nobody would have struck me, and everything would have been all right. Who first imagined, and when, that an insult could only be wiped out with blood? Not I, certainly. Well, I've wiped it out, or rather, it's been wiped out with my blood, hasn't it? I don't know what it all means, but I know this, that I shall have to leave the regiment!"

His thoughts would fain have taken another direction, yet, like birds with clipped wings, they always fell back again, back to the one central fact that he had been grossly insulted, and would be obliged to leave the regiment.

He remembered having once seen a fly that had fallen into syrup crawling over the floor, dragging its sticky legs and wings along with the utmost difficulty. It was plain that the wretched insect must die, though it still struggled, and made frantic efforts to regain its feet. At the time he had turned away from it in disgust, and now he saw it again, as in a feverish dream. Then he suddenly thought of a fight that he had once witnessed between two peasants, when one, with a terrific blow in the face, felled the other, an elderly, grey-haired man. He got up, wiped his bloody nose on his sleeve, exclaiming with emphasis, "What a fool!"

"Yes, I remember seeing that," thought Sarudine, "and then they had drinks together at the 'Crown.'"

The night drew near to its end. In silence so strange, so oppressive, it seemed as if Sarudine were the one living, suffering soul left on earth. On the table the guttering candle was still burning with a faint, steady flame. Lost in the gloom of his disordered thoughts Sarudine stared at it with glittering, feverish eyes.

Amid the wild chaos of impressions and recollections there was one thing which stood out clearly from all others. It was the sense of his utter solitude that stabbed his heart like a dagger. Millions of men at that moment were merrily enjoying life, laughing and joking; some, it might be, were even talking about him. But he, only he, was alone. Vainly he sought to recall familiar faces. Yet pale, and strange, and cold, they appeared to him, and their eyes had a look of curiosity and malevolent glee. Then, in his dejection, he thought of Lida.

He pictured her as he had seen her last; her large, sad eyes; the thin blouse that lightly veiled her soft bosom; her hair in a single loose plait. In her face Sarudine saw neither malice nor contempt. Those dark eyes gazed at him in sorrowful reproach. He remembered how he had repulsed her at the moment of her supreme distress. The sense of having lost her wounded him like a knife.

"She suffered then far more than I do now . . . . I thrust her from me. . . . I almost wanted her to drown herself; wanted her to die."

As to a last anchor that should save him, his whole soul

turned to her. He yearned for her caresses, her sympathy. For an instant it seemed to him as if all his actual sufferings would efface the past; yet he knew, alas! that Lida would never, never come back to him, and that all was at an end. Before him lay nothing but the black, abysmal void!

Raising his arm, Sarudine pressed his hand against his brow. He lay there, motionless, with eyes closed and teeth clenched, striving to see nothing, to hear nothing, to feel nothing. But after a little while his hand dropped, and he sat up. His head ached terribly, his tongue seemed on fire, and he trembled from head to foot. Then he rose and staggered to the table.

"I have lost everything; my life, Lida, everything!"

It flashed across him that this life of his, after all, had not been either good, or glad, or sane, but foolish, perverted and base. Sarudine, the handsome Sarudine, entitled to all that was best and most enjoyable in life, no longer existed. There was only a feeble, emasculated body left to bear all this pain and dishonour.

"To live on is impossible," he thought, "for that would mean the entire effacement of the past. I should have to begin a new life, to become quite a different man, and that I cannot do!"

His head fell forward on the table, and in the weird, flickering candlelight he lay there, motionless.

CHAPTER XXXII

On that same evening Sanine went to see Soloveitchik. The little Jew was sitting alone on the steps of his house, gazing at the bare, deserted space in front of it where several disused pathways crossed the withered grass. Depressing indeed was the sight of the vacant sheds, with their huge, rusty locks, and of the black windows of the mill. The whole scene spoke mournfully of life and activity that long had ceased.

Sanine instantly noticed the changed expression of Soloveitchik's face. He no longer smiled, but seemed anxious and worried, His dark eyes had a questioning look.

"Ah! good evening," he said, as in apathetic fashion he took the other's hand. Then he continued gazing at the calm evening sky, against which the black roofs of the sheds stood out in ever sharper relief.

Sanine sat down on the opposite side of the steps, lighted a cigarette, and silently watched Soloveitchik, whose strange demeanour interested him.

"What do you do with yourself here?" he asked, after a while.

Languidly the other turned to him his large, sad eyes.

"I just live here, that's all. When the mill was at work, I used to be in the office. But now it's closed, and everybody's gone away except myself."

"Don't you find it lonely, to be all by yourself, like this?"

Then, shrugging his shoulders, he said: "It's all the same
to me."

They remained silent. There was no sound but the rattling
of the dog's chain.

"It's not the place that's lonely," exclaimed Soloveitchik
with sudden vehemence. "But it's here I feel it, and here."
He touched his forehead and his breast.

"What's the matter with you?" asked Sanine calmly.

"Look here," continued Soloveitchik, becoming more excited, "you struck a man to-day, and smashed his face in.
Perhaps you have ruined his whole life. Pray don't be offended at my speaking to you like this. I have thought a
great deal about it all, sitting here, as you see, and wondering,
wondering. Now, if I ask you something, will you answer
me?"

For a moment his features were contorted by his usual set
smile.

"Ask me whatever you like," replied Sanine, kindly.
"You're afraid of offending me, eh? That won't offend me,
I assure you. What's done is done; and if I thought that I
had done wrong, I should be the first to say so."

"I wanted to ask you this," said Soloveitchik, quivering
with excitement. "Do you realize that perhaps you might
have killed that man?"

"There's not much doubt about that," replied Sanine. "It
would have been difficult for a man like Sarudine to get out
of the mess unless he killed me, or I killed him. But, as regards killing me, he missed the psychological moment, so to
speak; and at present he's not in a fit condition to do me

harm. Later on he won't have the pluck. He's played his part."

"And you calmly tell me all this?"

"What do you mean by 'calmly'?" asked Sanine. "I couldn't look on calmly and see a chicken killed, much less a man. It was painful to me to hit him. To be conscious of one's own strength is pleasant, of course, but it was nevertheless a horrible experience—horrible, because such an act in itself was brutal. Yet my conscience is calm. I was but the instrument of fate. Sarudine has come to grief because the whole bent of his life was bound to bring about a catastrophe; and the marvel is that others of his sort do not share his fate. These are the men who learn to kill their fellow-creatures and to pamper their own bodies, not knowing why or wherefore. They are lunatics, idiots! Let them loose, and they would cut their own throats and those of other folk as well. Am I to blame because I protected myself from a madman of this type?"

"Yes, but you have killed him," was Soloveitchik's obstinate reply.

"In that case you had better appeal to the good God who made us meet."

"You could have stopped him by seizing hold of his hands."

Sanine raised his head.

"In a moment like that one doesn't reflect. And how would that have helped matters? His code of honour demanded revenge at any price. I could not have held his hands for ever. It would only have been an additional insult, nothing more."

Soloveitchik limply waved his hand, and did not reply.

Imperceptibly the darkness closed round them. The fires of sunset paled, and beneath the deserted sheds the shadows grew deeper, as if in these lonely places mysterious, dreadful beings were about to take up their abode during the night. Their noiseless footsteps may have made Sultan uneasy, for he suddenly crept out of his kennel and sat in front of it, rattling his chain.

"Perhaps you're right," observed Soloveitchik sadly, "but was it absolutely necessary? Would it not have been better if you had borne the blow?"

"Better?" said Sanine. "A blow's always a painful thing. And why? For what reason?"

"Oh! do, please, hear me out," interrupted Soloveitchik, with a pleading gesture. "It might have been better——"

"For Sarudine, certainly."

"No, for you, too; for you, too."

"Oh! Soloveitchik," replied Sanine, with a touch of annoyance, "a truce to that silly old notion about moral victory; and a false notion, too. Moral victory does not consist in offering one's cheek to the smiter, but in being right before one's conscience. How this is achieved is a matter of chance, of circumstances. There is nothing so horrible as slavery. Yet most horrible of all is it when a man whose inmost soul rebels against coercion and force yet submits thereto in the name of some power that is mightier than he."

Soloveitchik clasped his head with both hands, as one distraught.

"I've not got the brains to understand it all," he said plaintively. "And I don't in the least know how I ought to live."

"Why should you know? Live as the bird flies. If it wants to move its right wing, it moves it. If it wants to fly round a tree, it does so."

"Yes, a bird may do that, but I'm not a bird; I'm a man," said Soloveitchik with naïve earnestness.

Sanine laughed outright, and for a moment the merry sound echoed through the gloomy courtyard.

Soloveitchik shook his head. "No," he murmured sadly, "all that's only talk. You can't tell me how I ought to live. Nobody can tell me that."

"That's very true. Nobody can tell you that. The art of living implies a talent; and he who does not possess that talent perishes or makes shipwreck of his life."

"How calmly you say that! As if you knew everything! Pray don't be offended, but have you always been like that— always so calm?" asked Soloveitchik, keenly interested.

"Oh! no; though certainly my temperament has usually been calm enough, but there were times when I was harassed by doubts of all kinds. At one time, indeed, I dreamed that the ideal life for me was the Christian life."

Sanine paused, and Soloveitchik leaned forward eagerly as if to hear something of the utmost importance.

"At that time I had a comrade, a student of mathematics, Ivan Lande by name. He was a wonderful man, of indomitable moral force; a Christian, not from conviction, but by nature. In his life all Christianity was mirrored. If struck, he did not strike back; he treated every man as his brother, and in woman he did not recognize the sexual attraction. Do you remember Semenoff?"

Soloveitchik nodded, as with childish pleasure.

"Well, at that time Semenoff was very ill. He was living in the Crimea, where he gave lessons. There, solitude and the presentiment of his approaching death drove him to despair. Lande heard of this, and determined to go thither and save this lost soul. He had no money, and no one was willing to lend any to a reputed madman. So he went on foot, and, after walking over a thousand versts, died on the way, and thus sacrificed his life for others."

"And you, oh! do tell me," cried Soloveitchik with flashing eyes, "do you recognize the greatness of such a man?"

"He was much talked about at the time," replied Sanine thoughtfully. "Some did not look upon him as a Christian, and for that reason condemned him. Others said that he was mad and not devoid of self-conceit, while some denied that he had any moral force; and, since he would not fight, they declared that he was neither prophet nor conqueror. I judge him otherwise. At that time he influenced me to the point of folly. One day a student boxed my ears, and I became almost mad with rage. But Lande stood there, and I just looked at him and—— Well, I don't know how it was, but I got up without speaking, and walked out of the room. First of all I felt intensely proud of what I had done, and secondly I hated the student from the bottom of my heart. Not because he had struck me, but because to him my conduct must have been supremely gratifying. By degrees the falseness of my position became clear to me, and this set me thinking. For a couple of weeks I was like one demented, and after that I ceased to feel proud of my false moral victory. At the first ironical remark on the part of my adversary I thrashed him until he became unconscious. This brought about an estrangement between Lande and myself. When I came to examine his life impartially, I found it astonishingly poor and miserable."

"Oh! how can you say that?" cried Soloveitchik. "How was it possible for you to estimate the wealth of his spiritual emotions?"

"Such emotions were very monotonous. His life's happiness consisted in the acceptance of every misfortune without a murmur, and its wealth, in the total renunciation of life's joys and material benefits. He was a beggar by choice, a fantastic personage whose life was sacrificed to an idea of which he himself had no clear conception."

Soloveitchik wrung his hands.

"Oh! you cannot imagine how it distresses me to hear this!" he exclaimed.

"Really, Soloveitchik, you're quite hysterical," said Sanine, in surprise. "I have not told you anything extraordinary. Possibly the subject is, to you, a painful one?"

"Oh! most painful. I am always thinking, thinking, till my head seems as if it would burst. Was all that really an error, nothing more? I grope about, as in a dark room, and there is no one to tell me what I ought to do. Why do we live? Tell me that."

"Why? That nobody knows."

"And should we not live for the future, so that later on, at least, mankind may have a golden age?"

"There will never be a golden age. If the world and mankind could become better all in a moment, then, perhaps, a golden age would be possible. But that cannot be. Progress towards improvement is slow, and man can only see the step in front of him, and that immediately behind him. You and I have not lived the life of a Roman slave, nor that of some savage of the Stone Age, and therefore we cannot appreciate the boon of our civilization. Thus, if there should ever be a golden age, the men of that period will not perceive any difference between their lives and those of their ancestors. Man moves along an endless road, and to wish to level the road to happiness would be like adding new units to a number that is infinite."

"Then you believe that it all means nothing—that all is of no avail?"

"Yes, that is what I think."

"But what about your friend Lande? You yourself were——"

"I loved Lande," said Sanine gravely, "not because he was a Christian, but because he was sincere, and never swerved from his path, being undaunted by obstacles either ridiculous or formidable. It was as a personality that I prized Lande. When he died, his worth ceased to exist."

"And don't you think that such men have an ennobling influence upon life? Might not such men have followers or disciples?"

"Why should life be ennobled? Tell me that, first of all. And, secondly, one doesn't want disciples. Men like Lande are born so. Christ was splendid; Christians, however, are but a sorry crew. The idea of his doctrine was a beautiful one, but they have made of it a lifeless dogma."

Tired with talking, Sanine said no more. Soloveitchik remained silent also. There was great stillness around them, while overhead the stars seemed to maintain a conversation wordless and unending. Then Soloveitchik suddenly whispered something that sounded so weird that Sanine, shuddering, exclaimed:

"What's that you said?"

"Tell me," muttered Soloveitchik, "tell me what you think. Suppose a man can't see his way clear, but is always thinking and worrying, as everything only perplexes and terrifies him—tell me, wouldn't it be better for him to die?"

"Well," replied Sanine, who clearly read the other's thoughts, "perhaps death in that case would be better. Thinking and worrying are of no avail. He only ought to live who finds joy in living; but for him who suffers, death is best."

"That is what I thought, too," exclaimed Soloveitchik, and he excitedly grasped Sanine's hand. His face looked ghastly in the gloom; his eyes were like two black holes.

"You are a dead man," said Sanine with inward apprehension as they rose to go; "and for a dead man the best place is the grave. Good-bye."

Soloveitchik apparently did not hear him, but sat there motionless. Sanine waited for a while and then slowly walked away. At the gate he stopped to listen, but could hear nothing. Soloveitchik's figure looked blurred and indistinct in the darkness. Sanine, as if in response to a strange presentiment, said to himself:

"After all, it comes to the same thing whether he lives on like this or dies. If it's not to-day, then it will be to-morrow." He turned sharply round; the gate creaked on its hinges, and he found himself in the street.

On reaching the boulevard he heard, at a distance, some

one running along and sobbing as if in great distress. Sanine stood still. Out of the gloom a figure emerged, and rapidly approached him. Again Sanine felt a sinister presentiment.

"What's the matter?" he called out.

The figure stopped for a moment, and Sanine was confronted by a soldier whose dull face showed great distress.

"What has happened?" exclaimed Sanine.

The soldier murmured something and ran on, wailing as he went. As a phantom he vanished in the night.

"That was Sarudine's servant," thought Sanine, and then it flashed across him:

"Sarudine has shot himself!"

For a moment he peered into the darkness, and his brow grew cold. Between the dread mystery of night and the soul of this stalwart man a conflict, brief yet terrible, was in progress.

The town was asleep; the glimmering roadways lay bare and white beneath the sombre trees; the windows were like dull, watchful eyes glaring at the gloom. Sanine tossed his head and smiled, as he looked calmly in front of him.

"I am not guilty," he said aloud. "One more or less——"

Erect and resolute, he strode onward, an imposing spectre in the silent night.

CHAPTER XXXIII

THE news that two persons had committed suicide on the same night spread rapidly through the little town. It was Ivanoff who told Yourii. The latter had just come back from a lesson, and was at work upon a portrait of Lialia. She posed for him in a light-coloured blouse, open at the neck, and her pretty shell-pink arms showed through the semi-transparent stuff. The room was filled with sunlight which lit up her golden hair, and heightened the charm of her girlish grace.

"Good day," said Ivanoff, as, entering, he flung his hat on to a chair.

"Ah! it's you. Well, what's the news?" asked Yourii, smiling.

He was in a contented, happy mood, for at last he had got some teaching which made him less dependent upon his father, and the society of his bright, charming sister served to cheer him, also.

"Oh! lots of news," said Ivanoff, with a vague look in his eyes. "One man has hanged himself, and another has blown his brains out, and the devil's got hold of a third."

"What on earth do you mean?" exclaimed Yourii.

"The third catastrophe is my own invention, just to heighten the effect; but as regards the other two, the news is correct. Sarudine shot himself last night, and I have just

300

heard that Soloveitchik has committed suicide by hanging."

"Impossible!" cried Lialia, jumping up. Her eyes expressed horror and intense curiosity.

Yourii hurriedly laid aside his palette, and approached Ivanoff.

"You're not joking?"

"No, indeed."

As usual, he put on an air of philosophic indifference, yet evidently he was much shocked at what had happened.

"Why did he shoot himself? Because Sanine struck him?"

"Does Sanine know?" asked Lialia anxiously.

"Yes. Sanine heard about it last night," replied Ivanoff.

"And what does he say?" exclaimed Yourii.

Ivanoff shrugged his shoulders. He was in no mood to discuss Sanine with Yourii, and he answered, not without irritation:

"Nothing. What has it to do with him?"

"Anyhow, he was the cause of it," said Lialia.

"Yes, but what business had that fool to attack him? It is not Sanine's fault. The whole affair is deplorable, but it is entirely due to Sarudine's stupidity."

"Oh! I think that the real reason lies deeper," said Yourii sadly. "Sarudine lived in a certain set that . . ."

Ivanoff shrugged his shoulders.

"Yes, and the very fact that he lived in, and was influenced by, such an idiotic set is only proof positive that he was a fool."

Yourii rubbed his hands and said nothing. It pained him to hear the dead man spoken of thus.

"Well, I can understand why Sarudine did it," said Lialia,

"but Soloveitchik? I never would have thought it possible! What was the reason?"

"God knows!". replied Ivanoff. "He was always a bit queer."

At that moment Riasantzeff drove up, and meeting Sina Karsavina on the doorstep, they came upstairs together. Her voice, high-pitched and anxious, could be heard, and also his jovial, bantering tones that talk with pretty girls always evoked.

"Anatole Pavlovitch has just come from there," said Sina excitedly.

Riasantzeff followed her, laughing as usual, and endeavouring to light a cigarette as he entered.

"A nice state of things!" he said gaily. "If this goes on we soon shan't have any young people left."

Sina sat down without speaking. Her pretty face looked sad and dejected.

"Now then, tell us all about it," said Ivanoff.

"As I came out of the club last night," began Riasantzeff, "a soldier rushed up to me and stammered out, 'His Excellency's shot himself!' I jumped into a *droschky* and got there as fast as I could. I found nearly the whole regiment at the house. Sarudine was lying on the bed, and his tunic was unbuttoned."

"And where did he shoot himself?" asked Lialia, clinging to her lover's arm.

"In the temple. The bullet went right through his head and hit the ceiling."

"Was it a Browning?" Yourii asked this.

"Yes. It was an awful sight. The wall was splashed with

blood and brains, and his face was utterly disfigured. Sanine
must have given him a teaser." He laughed. "A tough
customer is that lad!"

Ivanoff nodded approvingly.

"He's strong enough, I warrant you."

"Coarse brute!" said Yourii, in disgust.

Sina glanced timidly at him.

"In my opinion it was not his fault," she said. "He couldn't
possibly wait until . . ."

"Yes, yes," replied Riasantzeff, "but to hit a fellow like
that! Sarudine challenged him."

"There you go!" exclaimed Ivanoff irritably, as he
shrugged his shoulders.

"If you come to think of it, duelling is absurd!" said
Yourii.

"Of course it is!" chimed in Sina.

To his surprise, Yourii noticed that Sina seemed pleased
to take Sanine's part.

"At any rate, it's . . ." The right phrase failed him where-
with to disparage Sanine.

"A brutal thing," suggested Riasantzeff.

Though Yourii thought Riasantzeff was little better than
a brute himself, he was glad to hear the latter abuse Sanine
to Sina when she defended him. However, as she noticed
Yourii's look of annoyance, she said no more. Secretly, she
was much pleased by Sanine's strength and pluck, and was
quite unwilling to accept Riasantzeff's denouncement of
duelling as just. Like Yourii, she did not consider that he
was qualified to lay down the law like that.

"Wonderfully civilized, certainly," sneered Ivanoff, "to

shoot a man's nose off, or run him through the body."

"Is a blow in the face any better?"

"I certainly think that it is. What harm can a fist do? A bruise is soon healed. You won't find that a blow with the fist ever hurt anybody much."

"That's not the point."

"Then, what is, pray?" said Ivanoff, his thin lips curled with scorn.

"I don't believe in fighting at all, myself, but, if it must be, then one ought to draw the line at severe bodily injuries. That's quite clear."

"He almost knocked the other's eye out. I suppose you don't call that severe bodily injury?" retorted Riasantzeff sarcastically.

"Well, of course, to lose an eye is a bad job, but it's not the same as getting a bullet through your body. The loss of an eye is not a fatal injury."

"But Sarudine is dead." .

"Ah! that's because he wished to die."

Yourii nervously plucked at his moustache.

"I must frankly confess," he said, quite pleased at his own sincerity, "that personally, I have not made up my mind as regards this question. I cannot say how I should have behaved in Sanine's place. Of course, duelling's stupid, and to fight with fists is not much better."

"But what is a man to do if he's compelled to fight?" said Sina.

Yourii shrugged his shoulders.

"It's for Soloveitchik that we ought to be sorry," said Riasantzeff, after a pause. The words contrasted strangely

with his cheerful countenance. Then all at once, they remembered that not one of them had asked about Soloveitchik.

"Where did he hang himself? Do you know?"

"In the shed next to the dog's kennel. He let the dog
loose, and then hanged himself."

Sina and Yourii simultaneously seemed to hear a shrill
voice exclaim:

"Lie down, Sultan!"

"Yes, and he left a note behind," continued Riasantzeff,
unable to conceal the merry twinkle in his eyes. "I made a
copy of it. In a way, it's really a human document." Taking
out his pocket-book he read as follows:

"Why should I live, since I do not know how I ought to
live? Men such as I cannot make their fellow-creatures
happy."

He stopped suddenly, as if somewhat embarrassed. Dead
silence ensued. A sad spirit seemed to pass noiselessly
through the room. Tears rose to Sina's eyes, and Lialia's
face grew red with emotion. Yourii smiled mournfully as
he turned towards the window.

"That's all," said Riasantzeff meditatively.

"What more would you have?" asked Sina with quivering
lips.

Ivanoff rose and reached across for the matches that were
on the table.

"It's nothing more than tomfoolery," he muttered.

"For shame!" was Sina's indignant protest.

Yourii glanced in disgust at Ivanoff's long, smooth hair
and turned away.

"To take the case of Soloveitchik," resumed Riasantzeff, and again his eyes twinkled. "I always thought him a nincompoop—a silly Jew boy. And now, see what he has shown himself to be! There is no love more sublime than the love which bids one sacrifice one's life for humanity."

"But he didn't sacrifice his life for humanity," replied Ivanoff, as he looked askance at Riasantzeff's portly face and figure, and observed how tightly his waistcoat fitted.

"Yes, but it's the same thing, for if . . ."

"It's not the same thing at all," was Ivanoff's stubborn retort, and his eyes flashed angrily. "It's the act of an idiot, that's what it is!"

His strange hatred of Soloveitchik made a most unpleasant impression upon the others.

Sina Karsavina, as she got up to go, whispered to Yourii, "I am going. He is simply detestable."

Yourii nodded. "Utterly brutal," he murmured.

Immediately after Sina's departure, Lialia and Riasantzeff went out. Ivanoff sat pensively smoking his cigarette for a while, as he stared sulkily at a corner of the room. Then he also departed.

In the street as he walked along, swinging his arms in the usual way, he thought to himself, in his wrath:

"These fools imagine that I am not capable of understanding what *they* understand! I like that! I know exactly what they think and feel, better than they do themselves. I also know that there is no love more sublime than the love which bids a man lay down his life for others. But for a man to go and hang himself simply because he is of no good to anybody—that's absolute nonsense!"

CHAPTER XXXIV

WHEN to the sound of martial music Sarudine's remains were borne to the churchyard, Yourii from his window watched the sad, imposing procession. He saw the horses draped in black, and the deceased officer's cap that lay on the coffin-lid. There were flowers in profusion, and many female mourners. Yourii was deeply grieved at the sight.

That evening he walked for a long while with Sina Karsavina; yet her beautiful eyes and gentle caressing manner did not enable him to shake off his depression.

"How awful it is to think," he said, his eyes fixed on the ground, "to think that Sarudine no longer exists. A handsome, merry, careless young officer like that! One would have thought that he would live for ever, and that the horrible things of life, such as pain and doubt and suffering, were unknown to him, would never touch him. Yet one fine day this very man is swept away like dust, after passing through a terrible ordeal known to none but himself. Now he's gone, and will never, never return. All that's left of him is the cap on the coffin-lid."

Yourii was silent, and he still gazed at the ground. Swaying slightly as she walked beside him, Sina listened attentively, while with her pretty, dimpled hands she kept twisting the lace of her parasol. She was not thinking about Sarudine. It was a keen pleasure for her to be near Yourii, yet unconsciously she shared his melancholy mood, and her face assumed a mournful expression. "Yes! wasn't it sad? That music, too!"

"I don't blame Sanine," said Yourii with emphasis. "He could not have acted otherwise. The horrible part of it all is that the paths of these two men crossed, so that one or the other was obliged to give way. It is also horrible that the victor does not realize his triumph is an appalling one. He calmly sweeps a man off the face of the earth, and yet is in the right."

"Yes, he's in the right, and——" exclaimed Sina, who had not heard all that Yourii had said. Her bosom heaved with excitement.

"But I call it horrible!" cried Yourii, hastily interrupting her, as he glanced at her shapely form and eager face.

"Why is it so?" asked Sina in a timid voice. She blushed suddenly, and her eyes lost their brightness.

"Anyone else would have felt remorse, or have suffered some kind of spiritual anguish," said Yourii. "But he showed not the slightest sign of it. 'I'm very sorry,' says he, 'but it's not my fault.' Fault, indeed! As if the question were one of fault or of blame!"

"Then of what is it?" asked Sina. Her voice faltered, and she looked downwards, fearing to offend her companion.

"That I don't know; but a man has no right to behave like a brute," was the indignant rejoinder.

For some time they walked along without speaking. Sina was grieved at what seemed their momentary estrangement, at this breaking of their spiritual bond which to her was so sweet, while Yourii felt that he had not expressed himself clearly, and this wounded his self-respect.

Soon afterwards they parted, she being sad and somewhat
hurt. Yourii noticed her dejection, and was morbidly pleased
thereat, as if he had revenged himself on some one he loved
for a gross personal insult.

At home his ill-humour was increased. During dinner
Lialia repeated what Riasantzeff had told her about Soloveitchik. As the men were removing the corpse, several ur-
chins had called out:

"Ikey's hanged himself! Ikey's hanged himself!"

Nicolai Yegorovitch laughed loudly, and made her say:
"Ikey's hanged himself," over and over again.

Yourii shut himself up in his room, and, while correcting
his pupil's exercises, he thought:

"How much of the brute there is in every man! For such
dull-witted beasts is it worth while to suffer and to die?"

Then, ashamed of his intolerance, he said to himself:

"They are not to blame. They don't know what they are
doing. Well, whether they know or not, they're brutes, and
nothing else!"

His thoughts reverted to Soloveitchik.

"How lonely is each of us in this world! There was poor
Soloveitchik, great of heart, living in our midst ready to
make any sacrifice, and to suffer for others. Yet nobody, any
more than I did, noticed him or appreciated him. In fact, we
despised him. That was because he could not express himself, and his anxiety to please only had an irritating effect,
though in reality he was striving to get into closer touch with
all of us, and to be helpful and kind. He was a saint, and we
looked upon him as a fool!"

So keen was his sense of remorse that he left his work, and restlessly paced the room. At last he sat down at the table, and, opening the Bible, read as follows:

"As the cloud is consumed and vanisheth away, so he that goeth down to the grave shall come up no more.

"He shall return no more to his house, neither shall his place know him any more."

"How true that is! How terrible and inevitable!" he thought.

"Here I sit, alive, thirsting for life and joy, and read my death-warrant. Yet I cannot even protest against it!"

As in a frenzy of despair, he clasped his forehead and with ineffectual fury appealed to some Power invisible and supreme.

"What has man done to thee that thou shouldst mock him thus? If thou dost exist, why dost thou hide thyself from him? Why hast thou made me thus, that even though I would believe in thee I yet have no belief in my own faith? And, if thou shouldst answer me, how can I tell if it is thou or I myself that makes reply? If I am right in wishing to live, why dost thou rob me of this right which thou thyself gavest to me? If thou hast need of our sufferings, well, these let us bear for love of thee. Yet we know not even if a tree be not of greater worth than a man.

"For a tree there is always hope. Even when felled it can put forth fresh shoots, and regain new verdure and new life. But man dies, and vanishes for ever. I lie down never to rise again. If I knew for certain that after milliards of years I should come to life again, patient and uncomplaining I would wait through all those centuries in outer darkness."

Once more he read from the book:

"What profit hath a man of all his labour which he taketh under the sun?

"One generation passeth away and another generation cometh, but the earth abideth for ever.

"The sun also ariseth, and the sun goeth down and hasteth to his place where he arose.

"The wind goeth toward the south and turneth about unto the north: it whirleth about continually; and the wind returneth again according to his circuits.

"The thing that hath been, it is that which shall be; there is no new thing under the sun.

"There is no remembrance of former things; neither shall there be any remembrance of things that are to come with those that shall come after.

"I, the Preacher, was King over Israel in Jerusalem."

"I, the Preacher, was King!" He shouted out these last words, as in vehement anger and despair, and then looked round in alarm, fearing lest some one should have heard him. Then he took a sheet of paper and began to write.

"I here begin this document which will end with my decease."

"Bah! how absurd it sounds!" he exclaimed as he pushed the paper from him with such violence that it fell to the floor.

"But that miserable little fellow, Soloveitchik, didn't think it absurd that he could not understand the meaning of life!"

Yourii failed to perceive that he was taking as his model a man whom he had described as a miserable little fellow.

"Anyhow, sooner or later, my end will be like that. There is no other way out. Why is there not? Because . . ."

Yourii paused. He believed that he had got an exact reply to this question, yet the words he wanted could not be found. His brain was over-wrought, and his thoughts confused.

"It's rubbish, all rubbish!" he exclaimed bitterly.

The lamp burned low, and its faint light illumined Yourii's bowed head, as he leant across the table.

"Why didn't I die when I was a boy and had inflammation of the lungs? I should now be happy, and at rest."

He shivered at the thought.

"In that case I should not have seen or known all that now I know. That would have been just as dreadful."

Yourii tossed back his head, and rose.

"It's enough to drive one mad!"

He went to the window and tried to open it, but the shutters were firmly fastened from the outside. By using a pencil, Yourii was able at last to unhook them, and with a creaking sound they swung back, admitting the cool, pure night air. Yourii looked up at the heavens and saw the roseate light of the dawn.

The morning was bright and clear. The seven stars of the Great Bear shone faintly, while large and lustrous in the crimson east flamed the morning star. A fresh breeze stirred the leaves, and dispersed the grey mists that floated above the lawn and veiled the smooth surface of the stream beside whose margin water-lilies and myosotis and white clover grew in abundance. The sky was flecked with little pink clouds, while here and there a last star trembled in the blue. All was so beautiful, so calm, as if the awestruck earth awaited the splendid approach of dawn.

Yourii at last went back to bed, but the garish daylight prevented him from getting sleep, as he lay there with aching brow and jaded eyes.

CHAPTER XXXV

EARLY that morning, soon after sunrise, Ivanoff and Sanine walked forth from the town. The dew sparkled in the sunlight, and the damp grass seen in shadow appeared grey. Along the side of the road banked by gnarled willows, pilgrims were slowly wending their way to the monastery. The red and white kerchiefs covering their heads, and their bright-hued coats and shirts, gave colour and picturesqueness to the scene. The monastery bells rang out in the cool morning air, and the sound floated across the steppe, away to the dreaming woods in the dim blue distance. A *troika* came jingling along the highroad, and the rough voices of the pilgrims as they talked could be distinctly heard.

"We've come out a little too early," said Ivanoff.

Sanine looked round about him, contented and happy.

"Well, let us wait a while," he replied.

They sat down on the sand, close to the hedge, and lit their cigarettes.

Peasants walking along behind their carts turned to look at them, and market-women and girls as they rattled past in rickety traps pointed at the wayfarers amid bursts of merry, mocking laughter. Ivanoff took not the slightest notice of them, but Sanine smiled and nodded in response.

At last there appeared on the steps of a little white house with a bright green roof the proprietor of the "Crown" tavern, a tall man in his shirt-sleeves who noisily unlocked the door, while yawning incessantly. A woman wearing a red kerchief on her head slipped in after him.

"The very thing!" cried Ivanoff. "Let's go there."

So they went to the little inn and bought vodka and fresh gherkins from the woman with the red kerchief.

"Aha! you seem to be pretty flush of money, my friend," said Ivanoff, as Sanine produced his purse.

"I've had an advance," replied the latter, smiling. "Much to my mother's annoyance, I have accepted the secretaryship of an assurance agency. In this way I was able to get a little cash as well as maternal contempt."

When they regained the high-road, Ivanoff exclaimed:

"Oh! I feel ever so much better now!"

"So do I. Suppose we take off our boots?"

"All right."

Having taken off their boots and socks, they walked bare-foot through the warm, moist sand, which was a delightful experience after trudging along in heavy boots.

"Jolly, isn't it?" said Sanine, as he drew a deep breath.

The sun's rays had now become far hotter. The town lay well in their rear as the two wayfarers plodded bravely on towards the blue, nebulous horizon. Swallows sat in rows on the telegraph-wires. A passenger-train with its blue, yellow and green carriages rolled past on the adjacent line, and the faces of drowsy travellers could be seen at the windows.

Two saucy-looking girls in white hats stood on the platform at the end of the train and watched the two bare-footed men with astonishment. Sanine laughed at them, and executed a wild impromptu dance.

Before them lay a meadow where walking barefoot in the
long lush grass was an agreeable relief.

"How delightful!" cried Ivanoff.

"Life's worth living to-day," rejoined his companion.
Ivanoff glanced at Sanine; he thought those words must
surely remind him of Sarudine and the recent tragedy. Yet
seemingly it was far from Sanine's thoughts, which surprised Ivanoff somewhat, yet did not displease him.

After crossing the meadow, they again got on to the main
road which was thronged as before with peasants in their
carts, and giggling girls. Then they came to trees, and reeds,
and glittering water, while above them, at no great distance
on the hill-side, stood the monastery, topped by a cross that
shone like some golden star.

Painted rowing-boats lined the shore, where peasants in
bright-coloured shirts and vests lounged. After much hag-
gling and good-humoured banter, Sanine hired one of the
little boats. Ivanoff was a deft and powerful oarsman, and
the boat shot forward across the water like a living thing.
Sometimes the oars touched reeds or low-hanging branches
which for a long while after such contact trembled above the
deep, dark stream. Sanine steered with so much erratic
energy that the water foamed and gurgled round the rudder.
They reached a narrow backwater where it was shady and
cool. So transparent was the stream that one could see the
bottom covered with yellow pebbles, where shoals of little
pink fish darted backwards and forwards.

"Here's a good place to land," said Ivanoff, and his voice
sounded cheery beneath the dark branches of the overhang-
ing trees. As the boat with a grating sound touched the

bank, he sprang lightly ashore. Sanine, laughing, did likewise.

"You won't find a better," he cried, plunging knee-deep through the long grasses.

"Anywhere's good in the sun, I say," replied Ivanoff, as from the boat he fetched the vodka, the bread, the cucumbers, and a little packet of *hors d'œuvres*. All these he placed on a mossy slope in the shade of the trees, and here he lay down at full length.

"Lucullus dines with Lucullus," he said.

"Lucky man!" replied Sanine.

"Not entirely," added Ivanoff, with a droll expression of discontent, "for he's forgotten the glasses."

"Never mind! We can manage, somehow."

Full of the sheer joy of living in this warm sunlight and green shade, Sanine climbed up a tree and began cutting off a bough with his knife, while Ivanoff watched him as the little white chips kept falling on to the turf below. At last the bough fell, too, when Sanine climbed down, and began to scoop it out, leaving the bark intact.

In a short time he had made a pretty little drinking-cup.

"Let's have a dip afterwards, shall we?" said Ivanoff, who was watching Sanine's craftsmanship with interest.

"Not a bad idea," replied Sanine, as he tossed the newly-made cup into the air and caught it.

Then they sat down on the grass and did ample justice to their appetizing little meal.

"I can't wait any longer. I'm going to bathe."

So saying, Ivanoff hastily stripped, and, as he could not swim, he plunged into shallow water where the even sandy bottom was clearly visible.

"It's lovely!" he cried, jumping about, and splashing wildly.

Sanine watched him and then in leisurely fashion he also undressed, and took a header into the deeper part of the stream.

"You'll be drowned," cried Ivanoff.

"No fear!" was the laughing rejoinder, when Sanine, gasping, had risen to the surface.

The sound of their merry voices rang out across the river and the green pasture-land. After a time they left the cool water, and lying down naked in the grass, rolled over and over in it.

"Jolly, isn't it?" said Ivanoff, as he turned to the sun his broad back on which little drops of water glistened.

"Here let us build tabernacles!"

"Deuce take your tabernacles," cried Sanine merrily. "No tabernacles for me!"

"Hurrah!" shouted Ivanoff, as he began dancing a wild, barbaric dance. Sanine burst out laughing, and leaped about in the same way. Their nude bodies gleamed in the sun, every muscle showing beneath the tense skin.

"Ouf!" gasped Ivanoff.

Sanine went on dancing by himself, and finished up by turning a somersault, head foremost.

"Come along, or I shall drink up all the vodka," cried his companion.

Having dressed, they ate the remainder of their provisions, while Ivanoff sighed ruefully for a draught of ice-cold beer.

"Let's go, shall we?" he said.

"Right!"

They raced at full speed to the river-bank, jumped into their boat, and pushed off.

"Doesn't the sun sting!" said Sanine, who was lying at full length in the bottom of the boat.

"That means rain," replied Ivanoff. "Get up and steer, for God's sake!"

"You can manage quite well by yourself," was the reply.

Ivanoff struck the water with his oars, so that Sanine got thoroughly splashed.

"Thank you," said the latter, coolly.

As they passed a green spot they heard laughter and the sound of merry girlish voices. It being a holiday, townsfolk had come thither to enjoy themselves.

"Girls bathing," said Ivanoff.

"Let's go and look at them," suggested Sanine.

"They would see us."

"No, they wouldn't. We could land here, and go through the reeds."

"Leave them alone," said Ivanoff, blushing slightly.

"Come on."

"No, I don't like to . . ."

"Don't like to?"

"Well, but . . . they're girls . . . young ladies . . . I don't think it's quite proper."

"You're a silly fool!" laughed Sanine. "Do you mean to say that you wouldn't like to see them?"

"Perhaps I should, but . . ."

"Very well, then, let's go. No mock modesty! What man

wouldn't do the same, if he had the chance?"

"Yes, but if you reason like that, you ought to watch them openly. Why hide yourself?"

"Because it's so much more exciting," said Sanine gaily.

"I dare say, but I advise you not to——"

"For chastity's sake, I suppose?"

"If you like."

"But chastity is the very thing that we don't possess!"

"If thine eye offend thee, pluck it out!" said Ivanoff.

"Oh! please don't talk nonsense, like Yourii Svarogitsch! God didn't give us eyes that we might pluck them out."

Ivanoff smiled, and shrugged his shoulders.

"Look here, my boy," said Sanine, steering towards the bank, "if the sight of girls bathing were to rouse in you no carnal desire, then you would have a right to be called chaste. Indeed, though I should be the last to imitate it, such chastity on your part would win my admiration. But, having these natural desires, if you attempt to suppress them, then I say that your so-called chastity is all humbug."

"That's right enough, but, if no check were placed upon desires, great harm might result."

"What harm, pray? Sensuality, I grant you, sometimes has evil results, but it's not the fault of sensuality."

"Perhaps not, but . . ."

"Very well, then, are you coming?"

"Yes, but I'm——"

"A fool, that's what you are! Gently! Don't make such a noise," said Sanine, as they crept along through the fragrant grass and rustling reeds.

"Look there!" whispered Ivanoff, excitedly.

From the smart frocks, hats and petticoats lying on the grass, it was evident that the party of bathers had come out from the town. Some were merrily splashing about in the water which dripped in silver beads from their round, soft limbs. One stood on the bank, erect and lithe, and the sunlight enhanced the plastic beauty of her form that quivered as she laughed.

"Oh! I say!" exclaimed Sanine, fascinated by the sight. Ivanoff started backwards as in alarm.

"What's the matter?"

"Hush! It's Sina Karsavina!"

"So it is!" said Sanine aloud. "I didn't recognize her. How charming she looks!"

"Yes, doesn't she?" said the other, chuckling.

At that moment laughter and loud cries told them that they had been overheard. Karsavina, startled, leaped into the clear water from which alone her rosy face and shining eyes emerged. Sanine and Ivanoff fled precipitately, stumbling back through the tall rushes to their boat.

"Oh! how good it is to be alive!" said Sanine, stretching himself.

> Down the river, floating onward,
> Ever onward, to the sea.

So he sang in his clear, resonant voice, while behind the trees the sound of girlish laughter could still be heard. Ivanoff looked at the sky.

"It's going to rain," he said.

The trees had become darker, and a deep shadow passed swiftly across the meadow.

"We shall have to run for it!"

"Where? There's no escape, now," cried Sanine cheerfully.

Overhead a leaden-hued cloud floated nearer and nearer. There was no wind; the stillness and gloom had increased.

"We shall get soaked to the skin," said Ivanoff, "so do give me a cigarette, to console me."

Faintly the little yellow flame of the match flickered in the gloom. A sudden gust of wind swept it away. One big drop of rain splashed the boat, and another fell on to Sanine's brow. Then came the downpour. Pattering on the leaves, the rain hissed as it touched the surface of the water. All in a moment from the dark heaven it fell in torrents, and only the rush and the splash of it could be heard.

' "Nice, isn't it?" said Sanine, moving his shoulders to which his wet shirt was sticking.

"Not so bad," replied Ivanoff, who had crouched at the bottom of the boat.

Very soon the rain ceased, though the clouds had not dispersed, but were massed behind the woods where flashes of lightning could be seen at intervals.

"We ought to be getting back," said Ivanoff.

"All right. I'm ready."

They rowed out into the current. Black, heavy clouds hung overhead, and the flashes of lightning became incessant; white scimitars that smote the sullen sky. Though now it did not rain, a feeling of thunder was in the air. Birds with wet and ruffled plumage skimmed the surface of the river, while the trees loomed darkly against the blue-grey heavens.

"Ho! ho!" cried Ivanoff.

When they had landed and were plodding through the wet sand, the gloom became more intense.

"We're in for it now."

Nearer, ever nearer to earth the huge cloud approached, like some dreadful grey-bellied monster. There was a sudden gust of wind, and leaves and dust were whirled round and round. Then, a deafening crash, as if the heavens were cleft asunder, when the lightning blazed and the thunder broke.

"Oho—ho—ho!" shouted Sanine, trying to outvie the clamour of the storm. But his voice, even to himself, was inaudible.

When they reached the fields, it was quite dark. Their pathway was lit by vivid flashes, and the thunder never ceased.

"Oh! Ha! Ho!" shouted Sanine.

"What's that?" cried Ivanoff.

At that moment a vivid flash revealed to him Sanine's radiant face, the only answer to his question. Then, a second flash showed Sanine, with arms outstretched, gleefully apostrophizing the tempest.

CHAPTER XXXVI

'THE sun shone as brightly as in spring, yet in the calm, clear air the touch of autumn could be felt. Here and there the trees showed brown and yellow leaves in which the wistful voice of a bird occasionally broke the silence, while large insects buzzed lazily above their ruined kingdom of faded grasses and withered flowers where luxuriant weeds now waxed apace.

Yourii sauntered through the garden. Lost in his thoughts he gazed at the sky, at the green and yellow leaves, and the shining water, as if he were looking on them all for the last time, and must fix them in his memory so as never to forget them. He felt vague sorrow at his heart, for it seemed as though with every moment something precious was passing away from him that could never be recalled; his youth that had brought him no joy; his place as an active sharer in the great and useful work upon which all his energies had once been concentrated. Yet why he should have thus lost ground he could not tell. He was firmly convinced that he possessed latent powers that should revolutionize the world, and a mind far broader in its outlook than that of anyone else; but he could not explain why he had this conviction, and he would have been ashamed to admit the fact even to his most intimate friend.

"Ah! well," he thought, gazing at the red and yellow reflections of the foliage in the stream, "perhaps what I do is the wisest and the best. Death ends it all, however one may have lived or tried to live. Oh! there comes Lialia," he murmured, as he saw his sister approaching. "Happy Lialia! She lives like a butterfly, from day to day, wanting nothing, and troubled by nothing. Oh! if I could live as she does."

Yet this was only just a passing thought, for in reality he would on no account have wished to exchange his own spiritual tortures for the feather-brain existence of a Lialia.

"Yourii! Yourii!" she exclaimed in a shrill voice, though she was not more than three paces distant from him. Laughing roguishly, she handed him a little rose-coloured missive.

Yourii suspected something.

"From whom?" he asked sharply.

"From Sinotschka Karsavina," said Lialia, shaking her finger at him, significantly.

Yourii blushed deeply. To receive through his sister a little pink, scented letter like this seemed utterly silly; in fact ridiculous. It positively annoyed him. Lialia, as she walked beside him, prattled in sentimental fashion about his attachment to Sina, just as sisters will, who are intensely interested in their brothers' love-affairs. She said how fond she was of Sina, and how delighted she would be if they made a match of it, and got married.

At the luckless word "married," Yourii's face grew redder still, and in his eyes there was a malevolent look. He saw before him an entire romance of the usual provincial type; rose-pink *billets-doux,* sisters as confidantes, orthodox matrimony, with its inevitable commonplace sequel, home, wife, and babies—the one thing on earth that he dreaded most.

"Oh! Enough of all that twaddle, please!" he said in so
sharp a tone that Lialia was amazed.

"Don't make such a fuss!" she exclaimed, pettishly. "If
you *are* in love, what does it matter? I can't think why you
always pose as such an extraordinary hero."

This last sentence had a touch of feminine spite in it, and
the shaft struck home. Then, with a graceful movement of
her dress which disclosed her dainty open-work stockings,
she turned abruptly on her heel like some petulant princess,
and went indoors.

Yourii watched her, with anger in his dark eyes, as he tore
open the envelope.

"Yourii Nicolaijevitch:
    "If you have time, and the wish to do so, will you come to the
monastery to-day? I shall be there with my aunt. She is preparing
for the Communion, and will be in church the whole time. It will
be dreadfully dull for me, and I want to talk to you about lots
of things. Do come. Perhaps I ought not to have written to you,
but, anyhow, I shall expect you."

In a moment all that had occupied his thoughts vanished,
as with a thrill of pleasure almost physical he read and re-
read the letter. This pure, charming girl in one short phrase
had thus in naïve, trusting fashion revealed to him the secret
of her love. It was as though she had come to him, helpless
and pained, unable to resist the love that made her give herself up to him, yet not knowing what might befall. So near
to him now seemed the goal, that Yourii trembled at the
thought of possession. He strove to smile ironically, but the
effort failed. His whole being was filled with joy, and such

was his exhilaration that, like a bird, he felt ready to soar above the tree-tops, away, afar, into the blue, sunlit air.

Towards evening he hired a *droschky* and drove towards the monastery, smiling on the world timidly, almost in confusion. On reaching the landing-stage he took a boat, and was rowed by a stalwart peasant to the hill.

It was not until the boat got clear of the reeds into the broad, open stream that he became conscious that his happiness was entirely due to the little rose-coloured letter.

"After all, it's simple enough," he said to himself, by way of explanation. "She has always lived in that sort of world. It's just a provinical romance. Well, what if it is?"

The water rippled gently on each side of the boat that brought him nearer and nearer to the green hill. On reaching the shore, Yourii in his excitement gave the boatman half a rouble and began to climb the slopes. Signs of approaching dusk were already perceptible. Long shadows lay at the foot of the hill, and heavy mists rose from the earth, hiding the yellow tint of the foliage, so that the forest looked as green and dense as in summer. The courtyard of the monastery was silent and solemn as the interior of a church. The grave, tall poplars looked as if they were praying, and like shadows the dark forms of monks moved hither and thither. At the church-porch lamps glimmered, and in the air there was a faint odour either of incense or of faded poplar-leaves.

"Hullo, Svarogitsch!" shouted some one behind him.

Yourii turned round, and saw Schafroff, Sanine, Ivanoff and Peter Ilitsch, who came across the courtyard, talking loudly and merrily. The monks glanced apprehensively in their direction and even the poplars seemed to lose something of their devotional calm.

"We've all come here, too," said Schafroff, approaching Yourii, whom he revered.

"So I see," muttered Yourii irritably.

"You'll join our party, won't you?" asked Schafroff as he came nearer.

"No, thank you, I am engaged," said Yourii, with some impatience.

"Oh! that's all right! You'll come along with us, I know," exclaimed Ivanoff, as he good-humouredly caught hold of his arm. Yourii endeavoured to free himself, and for a while a droll struggle took place.

"No, no, damn it all, I can't!" cried Yourii, almost angry now. "Perhaps I'll join you later." Such rough pleasantry on Ivanoff's part was not at all to his liking.

"All right," said Ivanoff, as he released him, not noticing his irritation. "We will wait for you, so mind you come."

"Very well."

Thus, laughing and gesticulating, they departed. The courtyard became silent and solemn as before. Yourii took off his cap, and in a mood half mocking, half shy, he entered the church. He at once perceived Sina, close to one of the dark pillars. In her grey jacket and round straw hat she looked like a schoolgirl. His heart beat faster. She seemed so sweet, so charming, with her black hair in a neat coil at the back of her pretty white neck. It was this *air de pensionnaire* while being a tall, well-grown, shapely young woman, that to him was so intensely alluring. Conscious of his gaze, she looked round, and in her dark eyes there was an expression of shy pleasure.

"How do you do?" said Yourii, speaking in a low voice that yet was not low enough. He was not sure if he ought to shake hands in a church. Several members of the congregation looked round, and their swart, parchment-like faces made him feel more uncomfortable. He actually blushed, but Sina, seeing his confusion, smiled at him, as a mother might, with love in her eyes, and Yourii stood there, blissful and obedient.

Sina gave no further glances, but kept crossing herself with great zeal. Yet Yourii knew that she was only thinking of him, and it was this consciousness that established a secret bond between them. The blood throbbed in his veins, and all seemed full of mystery and wonder. The dark interior of the church, the chanting, the dim lights, the sighs of worshippers, the echoing of feet of those who entered or went out—of all this Yourii took careful note, as in such solemn silence he could plainly hear the beating of his heart. He stood there, motionless, his eyes fixed on Sina's white neck and graceful figure, feeling a joy that bordered on emotion. He wanted to show everyone that, although faith he had none in prayers, or chants, or lights, he yet was not opposed to them. This led him to contrast his present happy frame of mind with the distressful thoughts of the morning.

"So that one really can be happy, eh?" he asked himself, answering the question at once. "Of course one can. All my thoughts regarding death and the aimlessness of life are correct and logical, yet in spite of it all, a man can sometimes be happy. If I am happy, it is all due to this beautiful creature that only a short time ago I had never seen."

Suddenly the droll thought came to him that, long ago, as

little children, perhaps they had met and parted, never
dreaming that some day they would fall violently in love
with each other, and that she would give herself to him in
all her ripe, radiant nudity. It was this last thought that
brought a flush to his cheeks and for a while he felt afraid
to look at her. Meanwhile she whom his wanton fancy had
thus unclothed stood there in front of him, pure and sweet,
in her little grey jacket and round hat, praying silently that
his love for her might be as tender and deep as her own. In
some way her virginal modesty must have influenced Yourii, for the lustful thoughts vanished, and tears of emotion
filled his eyes. Looking upwards, he saw the gleaming gold
above the altar, and the sacred cross round which the yellow
tapers shone, and with a fervour long since forgotten he
mentally ejaculated:

"O God, if thou dost exist, let this maiden love me, and
let my love for her be always as great as at this moment."

He felt slightly ashamed at his own emotion, and sought to
dismiss it with a smile.

"It's all nonsense, after all," he thought.

"Come," said Sina in a whisper that sounded like a sigh.

Solemnly, as if in their souls they bore away with them
all the chanting, and the prayers, the sighs and mystic lights,
they went out across the courtyard, side by side, and passed
through the little door leading to the mountain-slope. Here
there was no living soul. The high white wall and time-worn
turrets seemed to shut them out from the world of men.
At their feet lay the oak forest; far below shone the river
like a mirror of silver, while in the distance fields and meadows were merged in the dim horizon-line.

In silence they advanced to the edge of the slope, aware that they ought to do something, to say something, yet feeling all the while that they had not sufficient courage. Then Sina raised her head, and unexpectedly, yet quite simply and naturally, her lips met Yourii's. She trembled and grew pale as he gently embraced her, and for the first time felt her warm, supple body in his arms. A bell chimed in that silence. To Yourii it seemed to celebrate the moment in which each had found the other. Sina, laughing, broke away from him and ran back.

"Auntie will wonder what has become of me! Wait here, and I'll be back soon."

Afterwards Yourii could never remember if she had said this to him in a loud, clear voice that echoed through the woodland, or if the words had floated to him like a soft whisper on the evening breeze. He sat down on the grass and smoothed his hair with his hand.

"How silly, and yet how delightful it all is!" he thought, smiling. In the distance he heard Sina's voice.

"I'm coming, auntie, I'm coming."

CHAPTER XXXVII

FIRST the horizon grew dark; then the river vanished in a mist, and from the pasture-lands a sound came up of neighing horses, while, here and there, faint lights flickered. As he sat there waiting, Yourii began to count these.

"One, two, three—oh, there's another, right on the edge of the horizon, just like a tiny star. Peasants are seated round it, keeping their night-watch, cooking potatoes and chatting. The fire yonder is blazing up and crackling merrily, while the horses stand, snorting, beside it. But at this distance it's only a little spark that at any moment might vanish."

He found it hard to think about anything at all. This sense of supreme happiness utterly absorbed him. As if in alarm. he murmured at intervals:

"She will come back again, directly."

Thus he waited there, on the height, listening to horses whinnying in the distance, to the cries of wild duck beyond the river, and to a thousand other elusive, indefinite sounds from the woods at evening which floated mysteriously through the air. Then as behind him he heard steps rapidly approaching, and the rustling of a dress, he knew, without looking round, that it was she, and in an ecstasy of passionate desire he trembled at the thought of the coming crisis. Sina stood still beside him, breathing hard. Delighted at his own audacity, Yourii caught her in his strong arms, and carried her down to the grassy slope beneath. In doing this, he nearly slipped, and she murmured: "We shall fall!"—feeling bashful, and yet full of joy.

As Yourii pressed her limbs closer to his, it appeared to him that she had at once the sumptuous proportions of a woman and the soft, slight figure of a child.

Down below, under the trees, it was dark, and here Yourii placed the girl, seating himself next to her. As the ground was sloping, they seemed to be lying side by side. In the dim light Yourii's lips fastened on hers with wild passionate longing. She did not struggle, but only trembled violently.

"Do you love me?" she murmured, breathlessly. Her voice sounded like some mysterious whisper from the woods.

Then in amazement, Yourii asked himself:

"What am I doing?"

The thought was like ice to his burning brain. In a moment everything seemed grey and void as a day in winter, lacking force and life. Her eyelids half-closed, she turned to him with a questioning look. Then, suddenly she saw his face, and overwhelmed with shame, shrank from his embrace. Yourii was beset by countless conflicting sensations. He felt that to stop now would be ridiculous. In a feeble, awkward way he again commenced to caress her, while she as feebly and awkwardly resisted him. To Yourii the situation now seemed so absolutely absurd, that he released Sina, who was panting like some hunted wild animal.

There was a painful silence, suddenly, he said:

"Forgive me . . . I must be mad."

Her breath came quicker, and he felt that he should not have spoken thus, as it must have hurt her. Involuntarily he stammered out all sorts of excuses which he knew were false, his one wish being to get away from her, as the situation had become intolerable.

She must have perceived this, too, for she murmured:

"I ought . . . to go."

They got up, without looking at each other, and Yourii made a final effort to revive his previous ardour by embracing her feebly. Then, in her a motherly feeling was roused. As if she felt stronger than he, she nestled closer, and looking into his eyes, smiled tenderly, consolingly.

"Good-bye! Come and see me tomorrow!" So saying she kissed him with such passion that Yourii felt dazed. At that moment he almost revered her.

When she had gone, he listened for a long while to the sound of her retreating footsteps, and then picked up his cap, from which he shook dead leaves and mould before thrusting it on his head, and going down the hill to the hospice. He made a long detour so as to avoid meeting Sina.

"Ah!" thought he, as he descended the slope, "must I needs bring so pure and innocent a girl to shame? Had it all to end in my doing what any other average man would have done? God bless her! It would have been too vile . . . I am glad that I wasn't as bad as all that. How utterly revolting . . . all in a moment . . . without a word . . . like some animal!" Thus he thought with disgust of what a little while before had made him glad and strong. Yet he felt secretly ashamed and dissatisfied. Even his arms and legs seemed to dangle in senseless fashion, and his cap to fit him as might a fool's.

"After all, am I really capable of living?" he asked himself, in despair.

CHAPTER XXXVIII

In the large corridor of the hospice there was an odour of samovars, and bread, and incense. A strong, active monk was hurrying along, carrying a huge tea-urn.

"Father," exclaimed Yourii, confused somewhat at addressing him thus, and imagining that the monk would be equally embarrassed.

"What is it, pray?" asked the other politely, through clouds of steam from the samovar.

"Is there not a party of visitors here, from the town?"

"Yes, in number seven," replied the monk promptly, as if he had anticipated such a question. "This way, please, on the balcony."

Yourii opened the door. The spacious room was darkened by dense clouds of tobacco-smoke. Near the balcony there was more light, and one could hear the jingling of bottles and glasses above the noisy talk and laughter.

"Life is an incurable malady." It was Schafroff who spoke.

"And you are an incurable fool!" shouted Ivanoff, in reply. "Can't you stop your eternal phrase-making?"

On entering, Yourii received a boisterous welcome. Schafroff jumped up, nearly dragging the cloth off the table as he seized Yourii's hand, and murmured effusively:

"How awfully good of you to come! I am so glad! Really, it's most kind of you! Thank you ever so much!"

334

Yourii, as he took a seat between Sanine and Peter Ilitsch, proceeded to look about him. The balcony was brightly lighted by two lamps and a lantern, and outside this circle of light there seemed to be a black, impenetrable wall. Yet Yourii could still perceive the greenish lights in the sky, the silhouette of the mountain, the tops of the nearest trees, and, far below, the glimmering surface of the river. From the wood moths and chafers flew to the lamp, and, fluttering round it, fell on to the table, slowly dying there a fiery death. Yourii, as he pitied their fate, thought to himself:

"We, too, like insects, rush to the flame, and flutter round every luminous idea only to perish miserably at the last. We imagine that the idea is the expression of the world's will, whereas it is nothing but the consuming fire within our brain."

"Now then, drink up!" said Sanine, as in friendly fashion he passed the bottle to Yourii.

"With pleasure," replied the latter, dejectedly, and it immediately occurred to him that this was about the best thing, in fact the only thing that remained to be done.

So they all drank and touched glasses. To Yourii vodka tasted horrible. It was burning and bitter as poison. He helped himself to the *hors d'œuvres,* but these, too, had a disagreeable flavour, and he could not swallow them.

"No!" he thought. "It doesn't matter if it's death, or Siberia, but get away from here I must! Yet, where shall I go? Everywhere it's the same thing, and there's no escaping from one's self. When once a man sets himself above life, then life in any form can never satisfy him, whether he lives in a hole like this, or in St. Petersburg."

"As I take it," cried Schafroff, "man, individually, is a mere nothing."

Yourii looked at the speaker's dull, unintelligent countenance, with its tired little eyes behind their glasses, and thought that such a man as that was in truth nothing.

"The individual is a cipher. It is only they who emerge from the masses, yet are never out of touch with them, and who do not oppose the crowd, as *bourgeois* heroes usually do —it is only they who have real strength."

"And in what does such strength consist, pray?" asked Ivanoff aggressively, as he leant across the table. "Is it in fighting against the actual government? Very likely. But in their struggle for personal happiness, how can the masses help them?"

"Ah! there you go! You're a super-man, and want happiness of a special kind to suit yourself. But, we men of the masses, we think that in fighting for the welfare of others our own happiness lies. The triumph of the idea—that is happiness!"

"Yet, suppose the idea is a false one?"

"That doesn't matter. Belief's the thing!" Schafroff tossed his head stubbornly.

"Bah!" said Ivanoff in a contemptuous tone, "every man believes that his own occupation is the most important and most indisputable thing in the whole world. Even a ladies' tailor thinks so. You know that perfectly well, but apparently you have forgotten it; therefore, as a friend, I am bound to remind you of the fact."

With involuntary hatred Yourii regarded Ivanoff's flabby, perspiring face, and grey, lustreless eyes.

"And, in your opinion, what constitutes happiness, pray?" he asked, as his lips curled in contempt.

"Well, most assuredly not in perpetual sighing and groaning, or incessant questionings such as, 'I sneezed just now. Was that the right thing to do? Will it not cause harm to some one? Have I, in sneezing, fulfilled my destiny?'"

Yourii could read hatred in the speaker's cold eyes, and it infuriated him to think that Ivanoff considered himself his superior intellectually, and was laughing at him.

"We'll soon see," he thought.

"That's not a programme," he retorted, striving to let his face express intense disdain, as well as reluctance to pursue the discussion.

"Do you really need one? If I desire, and am able, to do something, I do it. That's my programme!"

"A fine one indeed!" exclaimed Schafroff hotly. Yourii merely shrugged his shoulders and made no reply.

For a while they all went on drinking in silence. Then Yourii turned to Sanine and proceeded to expound his views concerning the Supreme God. He intended Ivanoff to hear what he said, though he did not look at him. Schafroff listened with reverence and enthusiasm, while Ivanoff, who had partly turned his back to Yourii, received each new statement with a mocking "We've heard all that before!"

At last Sanine languidly interposed.

"Oh! do stop all this," he said. "Don't you find it terribly boring? Every man is entitled to his own opinion, surely?"

He slowly lit a cigarette and went out into the courtyard. To his heated body the calm, blue night was deliciously soothing. Behind the wood the moon rose upward, like a globe of gold, shedding soft, strange light over the dark world. At the back of the orchard with its odour of apples and plums the other white-walled hospice could be dimly seen, and one of the lighted windows seemed to peer down at Sanine through its fence of tender leaves. Suddenly a sound was heard of naked feet pattering on the grass, and Sanine saw the figure of a boy emerge from the gloom.

"What do you want?" he asked.

"I want to see Mademoiselle Karsavina, the school-teacher," replied the bare-footed urchin, in a shrill voice.

"Why?"

To Sanine the name instantly recalled a vision of Sina, standing at the water's edge in all her nude, sunlit loveliness.

"I have got a letter for her," said the boy.

"Aha! She must be at the hospice over the way, as she is not here. You had better go there."

The lad crept away, barefoot, like some little animal, disappearing so quickly in the darkness that it seemed as if he had hidden himself behind a bush.

Sanine slowly followed, breathing to the full the soft, honey-sweet air of the garden.

He went close up to the other hospice, so that the light from the window as he stood under it fell full upon his calm, pensive face, and illuminated large, heavy pears hanging on the dark orchard trees. By standing on tiptoe Sanine was able to pluck one, and, just as he did so he caught sight of Sina at the window.

He saw her in profile, clad in her night-dress. The light on her soft, round shoulders gave them a lustre as of satin. She was lost in her thoughts, that seemingly made her joyous yet ashamed, for her eyelids quivered, and on her lips there was a smile. To Sanine it was like the ecstatic smile of a maiden ripe and ready for a long entrancing kiss. Riveted to the spot, he stood there and gazed.

She was musing on all that had just happened, and her experiences, if they had caused delight, had yet provoked shame. "Good heavens!" thought she, "am I really so depraved?" Then for the hundredth time she blissfully recalled the rapture that was hers as she first lay in Yourii's arms. "My darling! My darling!" she murmured, and again Sanine watched her eyelids tremble, and her smiling lips. Of the subsequent scene, distressful in its unbridled passion, she preferred not to think, instinctively aware that the memory of it would only bring disenchantment.

There was a knock at the door.

"Who is there?" asked Sina, looking up. Sanine plainly saw her white, soft neck.

"Here's a letter for you," cried the boy outside.

Sina rose and opened the door. Splashed with wet mud to the knees, the boy entered, and snatching his cap from his head, said:

"The young lady sent me."

"Sinotschka," wrote Dubova, "if possible, do come back to town this evening. The Inspector of Schools has arrived, and will visit our school to-morrow morning. It won't look well if you are not there."

"What is it?" asked Sina's old aunt.

"Olga has sent for me. The school-inspector has come," replied Sina, pensively.

The boy rubbed one foot against another.

"She wished me to tell you to come back without fail," he said.

"Are you going?" asked her aunt.

"How can I? Alone, in the dark?"

"The moon is up," said the boy. "It's quite light out-cf-doors."

"I shall have to go," said Sina, still hesitating.

"Yes, yes, go, my child. Otherwise there might be trouble."

"Very well, then, I'll go," said Sina, nodding her head resolutely.

She dressed quickly, put on her hat and took leave of her aunt.

"Good-bye, auntie."

"Good-bye, my dear. God be with you."

Sina turned to the boy. "Are you coming with me?" The urchin looked shy and confused, as, again rubbing his feet together, he muttered, "I came to be with mother. She does washing here, for the monks."

"But how am I to go alone, Grischka?"

"All right! Let's go," replied the lad, in a tone of vigorous assent.

They went out into the dark-blue, fragrant night.

"What a delightful scent!" she exclaimed, immediately uttering a startled cry, for in the darkness she had stumbled against some one.

"It is I," said Sanine, laughing.

Sina held out her trembling hand.

"It's so dark that one can't see," she said, by way of excuse.

"Where are you going?"

"Back to town. They've sent for me."

"What, alone?"

"No, the little boy's going with me. He's my cavalier."

"Cavalier! Ha! Ha!" repeated Grischka merrily, stamping his bare feet.

"And what are *you* doing here?" she asked.

"Oh, we're just having a drink together."

"You said 'we'?"

"Yes—Schafroff, Svarogitsch, Ivanoff . . ."

"Oh! Yourii Nicolaijevitch is with you, is he?" asked Sina, and she blushed. To utter the name of him she loved sent a thrill through her as though she were looking down into some precipice.

"Why do you ask?"

"Because—er—I met him," she answered, blushing deeper.

"Well, good-bye."

Sanine gently held her proffered hand in his.

"If you like, I will row you across to the other side. Why should you go all that way round?"

"Oh! no, please don't trouble," said Sina, feeling strangely shy.

"Yes, let him row you across," said little Grischka, persuasively, "for there's such a lot of mud on the bank."

"Very well, then. You can go back to your mother."

"Aren't you afraid to cross the fields alone?" asked the boy.

"I will accompany you as far as the town," said Sanine.

"But what will your friends say?"

"Oh! that doesn't matter. They'll stop there till dawn. Besides, they've bored me enough as it is."

"Well, it is very kind of you, I am sure. Grischka, you can

go."

"Good-night, miss," said the boy, as he noiselessly disappeared. Sina and Sanine were left there alone.

"Take my arm," he suggested, "or else you may fall."

Sina placed her arm in his, feeling a strange emotion as she touched his muscles that were hard as steel. Thus they went on in the darkness, through the woods to the river. In the wood it was pitch dark, as if all the trees had been fused and melted in a warm, impenetrable mist.

"Oh! how dark it is!"

"That doesn't matter," whispered Sanine in her ear. His voice trembled slightly. "I like woods best at night time. It is then that man strips off his everyday mask and becomes bolder, more mysterious, more interesting."

As the sandy soil slipped beneath their feet, Sina found it difficult to save herself from falling. It was this darkness and this physical contact with a supple, masterful male to whom she had always been drawn, that now caused her most exquisite agitation. Her face glowed, her soft arm shared its warmth with that of Sanine's, and her laughter was forced and incessant.

At the foot of the hill it was less dark. Moonlight lay on the river, and a cool breeze from its broad surface fanned their cheeks. Mysteriously the wood receded in the gloom, as though it had given them into the river's charge.

"Where is your boat?"

"There it is."

The boat lay sharply defined against the bright, smooth surface of the stream. While Sanine got the oars into position, Sina, balancing herself with outstretched arms, took her place in the stern. All at once the moonlight and the luminous reflections from the water gave a fantastic radiance to her form. Pushing off the boat from land, Sanine sprang into it. With a slight grating sound the keel slid over the sand and cut the water, as the boat swam into the moonlight, leaving broad ripples in its wake.

"Let me row," said Sina, suddenly endued with strange, overmastering strength. "I love rowing."

"Very well, sit here then," said Sanine, standing in the middle of the boat.

Again her supple form brushed lightly past him and as, with her finger-tips she touched his proffered hand, he could glance downward at her shapely bosom. . . .

Thus they floated down the stream. The moonlight, shining upon her pale face with its dark eyebrows and gleaming eyes, gave a certain lustre to her simple white dress. To Sanine it seemed as if they were entering a land of faerie, far removed from all men, outside the pale of human law and reason.

"What a lovely night!" exclaimed Sina.

"Lovely, isn't it?" replied Sanine in an undertone.

All at once, she burst out laughing.

"I don't know why, but I feel as if I should like to throw my hat into the water, and let down my hair," she said, yielding to a sudden impulse.

"Then do it, by all means," murmured Sanine.

But she grew ill at ease and was silent.

Under the stimulating influence of the calm, sultry, unfathomable night, her thoughts again reverted to her recent experiences. It seemed to her impossible that Sanine should

not know of these, and it was just this which made her joy
the more intense. Unconsciously she longed to make him
aware that she was not always so gentle and modest, but that
she could also be something vastly different when she threw
off the mask. It was this secret longing that made her flushed
and elated.

"You have known Yourii Nicolaijevitch for a long while,
haven't you?" she asked in a faltering voice, irresistibly impelled to hover above the abyss.

"No," replied Sanine. "Why do you ask?"

"Oh! I merely asked. He's a clever fellow, don't you
think?"

Her tone was one of childish timidity, as if she sought to
obtain something from a person far older than herself, who
had the right to caress or to punish her.

Sanine smiled at her, as he said:

"Ye ... es!"

From his voice Sina knew that he was smiling, and she
blushed deeply.

"No ... but, really he is. .... Well, he seems to be very
unhappy." Her lip quivered.

"Most likely. Unhappy he certainly is. Are you sorry for
him?"

"Of course I am," said Sina with feigned *naïveté*.

"It's only natural," said Sanine, "but 'unhappy' means to
you something different from what it really is. You think
that a man spiritually discontented, who is for ever analysing
his moods and his actions counts, not as a deplorably unhappy
person, but as one of extraordinary individuality and power.
Such perpetual self-analysis appears to you a fine trait which

entitles that man to think himself better than all others, and deserving not merely of compassion, but of love and esteem."

"Well, what else is it, if not that?" asked Sina ingenuously.

She had never talked so much to Sanine before. That he was an original, she knew by heresay; and she now felt agreeably perturbed at encountering so novel and interesting a personality.

Sanine laughed.

"There was a time when man lived the narrow life of a brute, not holding himself responsible for his actions nor his feelings. This was followed by the period of conscious life, and at its outset man was wont to overestimate his own sentiments and needs and desires. Here, at this stage, stands Svarogitsch. He is the last of the Mohicans, the final representative of an epoch of human evolution which has disappeared for evermore. He has absorbed, as it were, all the essences of that epoch, which have poisoned his very soul. He does not really live his life; each act, each thought is questioned. 'Have I done right?' 'Have I done wrong?' In his case this becomes almost absurd. In politics he is not sure whether it is not beneath his dignity to rank himself with others, yet, if he retires from politics, he wonders if it is not humiliating to stand aloof. There are many such persons. If Yourii Svarogitsch forms an exception, it is solely on account of his superior intelligence."

"I do not quite understand you," began Sina timidly. "You speak of Yourii Nicolaijevitch as if he himself were to blame for not being other than what he is. If life fails to satisfy a man, then that man stands above life."

"Man cannot be above life," replied Sanine, "for he himself is but a fraction of it. He may be dissatisfied, but the cause for such discontent lies in himself. He either cannot or dare not take from life's treasures enough for his actual needs. There are people who spend their lives in a prison. Others are afraid to escape from it, like some captive bird that fears to fly away when set free. . . . The body and spirit of man form one complete harmonious whole, disturbed only by the dread approach of death. But it is we ourselves who disturb such harmony by our own distorted conception of life. We have branded as bestial our physical desires; we have become ashamed of them; we have shrouded them in degrading forms and trammels. Those of us who by nature are weak, do not notice this, but drag on through life in chains, while those who are crippled by a false conception of life, it is they who are the martyrs. The pent-up forces crave an outlet; the body pines for joy, and suffers torment through its own impotence. Their life is one of perpetual discord and uncertainty, and they catch at any straw that might help them to a newer theory of morals, till at last so melancholy do they become that they are afraid to live, afraid to feel."

"Yes, yes," was Sina's vigorous assent.

A host of new thoughts invaded her mind. As with shining eyes she glanced round, the splendour of the night, the beauty of the calm river and of the dreaming woods in moonlight seemed to penetrate her whole being. Again she was possessed by that vague longing for sheer dominant strength that should yield her delight.

"My dream is always of some golden age," continued Sanine, "when nothing shall stand between man and his happiness, and when, fearless and free, he can give himself up to all attainable enjoyments."

"Yes, but how is he to do that? By a return to barbarism?"

"No. The epoch when man lived like a brute was a miserable, barbarous one, and our own epoch, in which the body, dominated by the mind, is kept under and set in the background, lacks sense and vigour. But humanity has not lived in vain. It has created new conditions of life which give no scope either for grossness or asceticism."

"Yes, but what of love? Does not that impose obligations upon us?" asked Sina hurriedly.

"No. If love imposes grievous obligations, it is through jealousy, and jealousy is the outcome of slavery. In any form slavery causes harm. Men should enjoy what love can give them fearlessly and without restrictions. If this were so, love would be infinitely richer and more varied in all its forms, and more influenced by chance and opportunity."

"I hadn't the least fear just now," was Sina's proud reflection. She suddenly looked at Sanine, feeling as if this were her first sight of him. There he sat, facing her, in the stern, a fine figure of a man; dark-eyed, broad-shouldered, intensely virile.

"What a handsome fellow!" she thought. A whole world of unknown forces and emotions lay before her. Should she enter that world? She smiled at her new curiosity, trembling all over. Sanine must have guessed what was passing in her mind. His breath came quicker, almost in gasps.

In passing through a narrow part of the stream, the oars caught in the trailing foliage and slipped from Sina's hands.

"I can't get along here, it's so narrow," she said timidly. Her voice sounded gentle and musical as the rippling of the stream.

Sanine stood up, and moved towards her.

"What is it?" she asked in alarm.

"It's all right, I am only going to ..."

Sina rose in her turn, and attempted to get to the rudder.

The boat rocked so violently that she well-nigh lost her balance, and involuntarily she caught hold of Sanine, after falling almost into his arms. At that moment, almost unconsciously, and never believing it possible, she gently prolonged their contact. It was this touch of her that in a moment fired his blood, while she, sensible of his ardour, irresistibly responded thereto.

"Ah!" exclaimed Sanine, in surprise and delight.

He embraced her passionately, forcing her backwards, so that her hat fell off.

The boat rocked with greater violence, as invisible wavelets dashed against the shore.

"What are you doing?" she cried, in a faint voice. "Let me go! For heaven's sake! ... What are you doing? ..."

She struggled to free herself from those arms of steel, but Sanine crushed her firm bosom closer, closer to his own, till such barriers as there had been between them ceased to exist.

Around them, only darkness; the moist odour of the river and the reeds; an atmosphere now hot, now cold; profound silence. Suddenly, unaccountably, she lost all power of volition and of thought; her limbs relaxed, and she surrendered to another's will.

CHAPTER XXXIX

RECOVERING herself at last, she perceived the bright image of the moon in the dark water, and Sanine's face bending over her with glittering eyes. She felt that his arms were wound tightly around her, and that one of the oars was chafing her knee.

Then she began to weep gently, persistently, without freeing herself from Sanine's embrace.

Her tears were for that which was irretrievable. Fear and pity for herself, and fondness for him made her weep. Sanine lifted her up and sat her on his knee. She meekly submitted like some sorrowful child. As in a dream she could hear him gently comforting her in a tender, grateful voice.

"I shall drown myself." The thought seemed an answer to a third person's stern question, "What have you done, and what will you do now?"

"What shall I do now?" she asked aloud.

"We will see," replied Sanine.

She tried to slip off his knees, but he held her fast, so she remained there, thinking it strange that she could feel for him neither hatred nor disgust.

"It doesn't matter what happens, now," she said to herself, yet a secret physical curiosity prompted her to wonder what this strong man, a stranger, and yet so close a friend, would do with her.

349

After a while, he took the oars, and she reclined beside him, her eyes half-closed, and trembling every time that his hand in rowing moved close to her bosom. As the boat with a grating sound touched the shore, Sina opened her eyes. She saw fields, and water, and white mist, and the moon like a pale phantom ready to flee at dawn. It was now daybreak and a cool breeze was blowing.

"Shall I go with you?" asked Sanine gently.

"No. I'd rather go alone," she replied.

Sanine lifted her out of the boat. It was a joy to him to do this, for he felt that he loved her, and was grateful to her. As he put her down on the shore after embracing her fondly, she stumbled.

"Oh! you beauty!" exclaimed Sanine, in a voice of passion and tenderness and pity.

She smiled in unconscious pride. Sanine took hold of her hands, and drew her to him.

"Kiss me!"

"It doesn't matter; nothing matters now," she thought, as she gave him a long, passionate kiss on his lips.

"Good-bye," she murmured, scarcely knowing what she said.

"Don't be angry with me, darling," pleaded Sanine.

As she crossed the dike, staggering as she went, and tripping over her dress, Sanine watched her with sorrowful eyes. It grieved him to think of all the needless suffering that was in store for her and which, as he foresaw, she had not the strength to set aside.

Slowly her figure moved forward to meet the dawn, and it soon vanished in the white mist.

When he could no longer see her, Sanine leapt into the boat, and by a few powerful strokes lashed the water to foam. In mid-stream, as the dense morning mists rose round him, Sanine dropped the oars, stood erect in the boat and uttered a great shout of joy. And the woods and the mists, as if alive, responded to his cry.

CHAPTER XL

As though stunned by a blow, Sina at once fell asleep, but woke early, feeling utterly broken, and cold as a corpse. Her despair had never slumbered, and for no single moment could she forget that which had been done. In mute dejection she scrutinized every detail of her room, as if to discover what since yesterday had suffered change. Yet, from its corner, touched by morning light, the *ikon* looked down at her in friendly wise. The windows, the floor, the furniture were unaltered, and on the pillows of the adjoining bed lay the fair head of Dubova, who was still fast asleep. All was exactly the same as usual; only the crumpled dress flung carelessly across a chair told its tale. The flush on her face at waking soon gave place to an ashen pallor that was heightened by her coal-black eyebrows. With the awful clearness of an over-wrought brain she rehearsed her experiences of the last few hours. She saw herself walking through silent streets at sunrise and hostile windows seemed watching her while the few persons she met turned round to look at her. On she went in the dawn-light, hampered by her long skirts, and holding a little green plush bag, much as some criminal might stagger homewards. The past night was to her a night of delirium. Something mad and strange and over-whelming had happened, yet how or why she knew not. To have flung all shame aside, to have forgotten her love for

352

another man, it was this that to her appeared incomprehensible.

Jaded and sick at heart, she rose, and noiselessly began to dress, fearful lest Dubova should awake. Then she sat at the window, gazing anxiously at the green and yellow foliage in the garden. Thoughts whirled in her brain, thoughts hazy and confused as smoke driven by the wind. Suddenly Dubova awoke.

"What? Up already? How extraordinary!" she exclaimed.

When Sina returned in the early morning, her friend had only drowsily asked, "How did you get in such a mess?" and then had fallen asleep again. Now that she noticed that something was wrong, she hurried across to Sina, barefooted, and in her night-dress.

"What's the matter? Are you ill?" she asked sympathetically, as might an elder sister.

Sina winced, as beneath a blow, yet, with a smile on her rosy lips, she replied in a tone of forced gaiety:

"Oh! dear no! Only, I hardly slept at all last night."

Thus was the first lie spoken that converted all her frank, proud maidenhood to a memory. In its place there was now something false and sullied. While Dubova was dressing herself, Sina glanced furtively at her from time to time. Her friend seemed to her bright and pure, and she herself as repulsive as a crushed reptile. So powerful was this impression, that even the very part of the room where Dubova stood appeared full of sunshine, while her own corner was steeped in gloom. Sina remembered how she had always thought herself purer and more beautiful than her friend, and the change that had come caused her intense anguish.

Yet all this lay hidden deep in her heart, and outwardly she was perfectly calm; indeed, almost gay. She put on a pretty dark-blue dress, and, taking her hat and sunshade, walked to school in her usual buoyant way, where she remained until noon, and then returned home.

In the street she met Lida Sanina. They both stood there in the sunlight, graceful, young, and pretty, as with smiles on their lips they talked of trifling things. Lida felt morbidly hostile towards Sina, happy and free from care as she imagined her to be, while the latter envied Lida her liberty and her pleasant, easy life. Each believed herself to be the victim of cruel injustice.

"I am surely better than she is. Why is she so happy, and why must I suffer?" In both their minds this thought was uppermost.

After lunch, Sina took a book and sat near the window, listlessly gazing at the garden that was still touched with the splendour of the dying summer. The emotional crisis had passed, and now her mood was one of apathy and indifference.

"Ah! Well, it's all over with me now," she kept repeating. "I'd better die."

Sina saw Sanine before he noticed her. Tall and calm, he crossed the garden, thrusting aside the branches as if to greet them by his touch. Leaning back in her chair, and pressing the book against her bosom, she watched him, wild-eyed, as he slowly approached the window.

"Good day," he said, holding out his hand.

Before she could rise or recover from her amazement he repeated in a gentle, caressing tone:

"Good morning to you."

Sina felt utterly powerless. She only murmured:

"Good morning."

Sanine leant on the window-sill and said:

"Do come out into the garden for a little while and have a talk."

Sina got up, swayed by a strange force that robbed her of her will.

"I'll wait for you there," added Sanine.

She merely nodded.

As he strolled back to the garden Sina was afraid to look at him. For seconds she remained motionless, with her hands clasped, and then suddenly went out, holding up her dress so as to walk more easily.

Sunlight touched the bright-hued autumn foliage; and the garden seemed steeped in a golden haze. As Sina hastened towards him, Sanine was standing at some distance in the middle of the path. His smile troubled her. He took her hand, and, sitting on the trunk of a tree, gently drew her on to his lap.

"I am not sure," he began, "that I ought to have come here to see you, for you may think that I have treated you very badly. But I could not stay away. I wanted to explain things, so that you might not utterly hate and loathe me. After all . . . what else could I do? How was I to resist? There came a moment when I felt that the last barrier between us had fallen, and that, if I missed this moment of my life, it would never again be mine. You're so beautiful, so young . . . "

Sina was mute. Her soft, transparent ear, half-hidden by

her hair, became rosy, and her long eyelashes quivered.

"You're miserable, now, and yesterday, how beautiful it all was," he said. "Sorrows only exist because man has set a price upon his own happiness. If our way of living were different, last night would remain in our memory as one of life's most beautiful and precious experiences."

"Yes, if . . ." she said mechanically. Then, all at once, much to her own surprise, she smiled. And as sunrise, and the song of birds, and the sound of whispering reeds, so this smile seemed to cheer her spirit. Yet it was but for a moment.

All at once she saw her whole future life before her, a broken life of sorrow and shame. The prospect was so horrible that it roused hatred.

"Go away! Leave me!" she said sharply. Her teeth were clenched and her face wore a hard, vindictive expression as she rose to her feet.

Sanine pitied her. For a moment he was moved to offer her his name and his protection, yet something held him back. He felt that such amends would be too mean.

"Ah! well," he thought, "life must just take its course."

"I know that you are in love with Yourii Svarogitsch," he began. "Perhaps it is that which grieves you most?"

"I am in love with no one," murmured Sina, clasping her hands convulsively.

"Don't bear me any ill-will," pleaded Sanine. "You're just as beautiful as ever you were, and the same happiness that you gave to me, you will give to him you love—far more, indeed, far more. I wish you from my heart all possible joy, and I shall always picture you to myself as I saw you last

night. Good-bye . . . and, if ever you need me, send for me.
If I could . . . I would give my life for you."

Sina looked at him, and was silent, stirred by strange pity.

"It may all come right, who knows?" she thought, and for
a moment matters did not seem so dreadful. They gazed into
each other's eyes steadfastly, knowing that in their hearts
they held a secret which no one would ever discover, and the
memory of which would always be bright.

"Well, good-bye," said Sina, in a gentle, girlish voice.

Sanine looked radiant with pleasure. She held out her
hand, and they kissed, simply, affectionately, like brother and
sister.

Sina accompanied Sanine as far as the garden-gate and sorrowfully watched him go. Then she went back to the garden, and lay down on the scented grass that waved and rustled
round her. She shut her eyes, thinking of all that had happened, and wondering whether she ought to tell Yourii or
not.

"No, no," she said to herself, "I won't think any more
about it. Some things are best forgotten."

CHAPTER XLI

NEXT morning Yourii rose late, feeling indisposed. His head ached, and he had a bad taste in his mouth. At first he could only recollect shouts, jingling glasses, and the waning light of lamps at dawn. Then he remembered how, stumbling and grunting, Schafroff and Peter Ilitsch had retired, while he and Ivanoff—the latter pale with drink, but firm on his feet—stood talking on the balcony. They had no eyes for the radiant morning sky, pale green at the horizon, and changing overhead to blue; they did not see the fair meadows and fields, nor the shining river that lay below.

They still went on arguing. Ivanoff triumphantly proved to Yourii that people of his sort were worthless, since they feared to take from life that which life offered them. They were far better dead and forgotten. It was with malicious pleasure that he quoted Peter Ilitsch's remark, "I should certainly never call such persons men," as he laughed wildly, imagining that he had demolished Yourii by such a phrase. Yet, strange to say, Yourii was not annoyed by it, dealing only with Ivanoff's assertion that his life was a miserable one. That, he said, was because "people of his sort" were more sensitive, more highly-strung; and he agreed that they were far better out of the world. Then, becoming intensely depressed, he almost wept. He now recollected with shame how he had been on the point of telling Ivanoff of his love-

358

episode with Sina, and had almost flung the honour of that pure, lovely girl at the feet of this truculent sot. When at last Ivanoff, growling, had gone out into the courtyard, the room to Yourii seemed horribly dreary and deserted.

There was a mist over everything; only the dirty table-cloth, with its green radish-stalks, empty beer-glasses and cigarette-ends, danced before his eyes, as he sat there, hud-dled-up and forlorn.

Afterwards, he remembered, Ivanoff came back, and with him was Sanine. The latter seemed gay, talkative and per-fectly sober. He looked at Yourii in a strange manner, half-friendly and half-derisive. Then his thoughts turned to the scene in the wood with Sina. "It would have been base of me if I had taken advantage of her weakness," he said to himself. "Yet what shall I do now? Possess her, and then cast her off? No, I could never do that; I'm too kind-hearted. Well, what then? Marry her?"

Marriage! To Yourii the very word sounded appallingly commonplace. How could anyone of his complex tempera-ment endure the idea of a philistine *ménage?* It was impos-sible. "And yet I love her," he thought. "Why should I put her from me, and go? Why should I destroy my own hap-piness? It's monstrous! It's absurd!"

On reaching home, in order to take his thoughts off the one engrossing subject, he sat down at the table and pro-ceeded to read over certain sententious passages written by him recently.

"In this world there is neither good nor bad."

"Some say: What is natural is good, and man is right in his desires."

"But that is false, for all is natural. In darkness and void nothing is born; all has the same origin."

"Yet others say: All is good which comes from God. Yet that likewise is false; for, if God exists, then all things come from Him, even blasphemy."

"Again, there are those who say: Goodness lies in doing good to others."

"How can that be? What is good for one, is bad for another."

"The slave desires his liberty, while his master wants him to remain a slave. The wealthy man wants to keep his wealth, and the poor man, to destroy the rich; he who is oppressed, to be free; the victor to remain unvanquished; the loveless to be loved; the living not to die. Man desires the destruction of beasts, just as beasts wish to destroy man. Thus it was in the beginning, and thus it ever shall be; nor has any man a special right to get good that is good for him alone."

"Men are wont to say that loving-kindness is better than hatred. Yet that is false, for if there be a reward, then certainly it is better to be kind and unselfish, but if not, then it is better for a man to take his share of happiness beneath the sun."

Yourii read on, thinking that these written meditations of his were amazingly profound.

"It's all so true!" he said to himself, and in his melancholy there was a touch of pride.

He went to the window and looked out into the garden where the paths were strewn with yellow leaves. The sickly hue of death confronted him at every point—dying leaves and dying insects whose lives depend on warmth and light.

Yourii could not comprehend this calm. The pageant of dying summer filled his soul with wrath unutterable.

"Autumn already; and then winter, and the snow. Then spring, and summer, and autumn again! The eternal monotony of it all! And what shall I be doing all the while? Exactly what I'm doing now. At best, I shall become dull-witted, caring for nothing. Then old age, and death."

The same thoughts that had so often harassed him now rushed through his brain. Life, so he said, had passed by him; after all, there was no such thing as an exceptional existence; even a hero's life is full of tedium, grievous at the outset, and joyless at the close.

"An achievement! A victory of some sort!" Yourii wrung his hands in despair. "To blaze up, and then to expire, without fear, without pain. That is the only real life!"

A thousand exploits, one more heroic than the other, presented themselves to his mind, each like some grinning death's head. Closing his eyes, Yourii could clearly behold a grey Petersburg morning, damp brick walls and a gibbet faintly outlined against the leaden sky. He pictured the barrel of a revolver pressed to his brow; he imagined that he could hear the whiz of *nagaikas* as they struck his defenseless face and naked back.

"That's what's in store for one! To that one must come!" he exclaimed.

The deeds of heroism vanished, and in their place, his own helplessness grinned at him like a mocking mask. He felt that all his dreams of victory and valour were only childish fancies.

"Why should I sacrifice my own life or submit to insult

and death in order that the working classes in the thirty-second century may not suffer through want of food or of sexual satisfaction? The devil take all workers and non-workers in this world!"

"I wish somebody would shoot me," he thought. "Kill me, right out, with a shot aimed from behind, so that I should feel nothing. What nonsense, isn't it? Why must somebody else do it? and not I myself? Am I really such a coward that I cannot pluck up courage to end this life which I know to be nothing but misery? Sooner or later, one must die, so that ..."

He approached the drawer in which he kept his revolver, and furtively took it out.

"Suppose I were to try? Not really because I ... just for fun!"

He slipped the weapon into his pocket and went out on to the veranda leading to the garden. On the steps lay yellow, withered leaves. He kicked them in all directions as he whistled a melancholy tune.

"What's that you're whistling?" asked Lialia, gaily, as she came across the garden. "It's like a dirge for your departed youth."

"Don't talk nonsense!" replied Yourii irritably; and from that moment he felt the approach of something that it was beyond his power to prevent. Like an animal that knows death is near, he wandered restlessly hither and thither, to look for some quiet spot. The courtyard only irritated him, so he walked down to the river where yellow leaves were floating, and threw a dry twig into the stream. For a long time he watched the eddying circles on the water as the floating leaves danced. He turned back and went towards the house, stopping to look at the ruined flower-beds where the last red blossoms yet lingered. Then he returned to the garden.

There, amid the brown and yellow foliage one oak-tree stood whose leaves were green. On the bench beneath it a yellow cat lay sunning itself. Yourii gently stroked its soft furry back, as tears rose to his eyes.

"This is the end! This is the end!" he kept repeating to himself. Senseless though the words seemed to him, they struck him like an arrow in the heart.

"No, no! What nonsense! My whole life lies before me. I'm only twenty-four years old! It's not that. Then, what is it?"

He suddenly thought of Sina, and how impossible it would be to meet her after that outrageous scene in the wood. Yet how could he possibly help meeting her? The shame of it overwhelmed him. It would be better to die.

The cat arched its back and purred with pleasure, the sound was like a bubbling samovar. Yourii watched it attentively, and then began to walk up and down.

"My life's so wearisome, so horribly dreary. . . . Besides, I can't say if . . . No, no, I'd rather die than see her again!"

Sina had gone out of his life for ever. The future, cold, grey, void, lay before him, a long chain of loveless, hopeless days.

"No, I'd rather die!"

Just then, with heavy tread, the coachman passed, carrying a pail of water, and in it there floated leaves, dead, yellow leaves. The maid-servant appeared in the doorway, and called out to Yourii. For a long while he could not understand what she said.

"Yes, yes, all right!" he replied when at last he realized that she was telling him lunch was ready.

"Lunch?" he said to himself in horror. "To go in to lunch! Everything just as before; to go on living and worrying as to what I ought to do about Sina, about my own life, and my own acts? So I'd better be quick, or else, if I go to lunch, there won't be time afterwards."

A strange desire to make haste dominated him, and he trembled violently in every limb. He felt conscious that nothing was going to happen, and yet he had a clear presentiment of approaching death; there was a buzzing in his ears from sheer terror.

With hands tucked under her white apron, the maid-servant still stood motionless on the veranda, enjoying the soft autumn air.

Like a thief, Yourii crept behind the oak-tree, so that no one should see him from the veranda, and with startling suddenness shot himself in the chest.

"Missed fire!" he thought with delight, longing to live, and dreading death. But above him he saw the topmost branches of the oak-tree against the azure sky, and the yellow cat leapt away in alarm.

Uttering a shriek, the maid-servant rushed indoors. Immediately afterwards it seemed to Yourii as if he were surrounded by a huge crowd of people. Some one poured cold water on his head, and a yellow leaf stuck to his brow, much to his discomfort. He heard excited voices on all sides, and some one sobbing, and crying out: "Youra, Youra! Oh! why, why?"

"That's Lialia!" thought Yourii. Opening his eyes wide, he began to struggle violently, as in a frenzy he screamed:

"Send for the doctor—quick!"

But to his horror he felt that all was over—that now nothing could save him. The dead leaves sticking to his brow felt heavier and heavier, crushing his brain. He stretched out his neck in a vain effort to see more clearly, but the leaves grew and grew, till they had covered everything; and what then happened to him Yourii never knew.

CHAPTER XLII

THOSE who knew Yourii Svarogitsch, and those who did not, those who liked, as those who despised him, even those who had never thought about him, were sorry now that he was dead.

Nobody could understand why he had done it; though they all imagined that they knew, and that in their inmost souls they held of his thoughts a share. There seemed something so beautiful about suicide, of which tears, flowers, and noble words were the sequel. Of his own relatives not one attended the funeral. His father had had a paralytic stroke, and Lialia could not leave him for a moment. Riasantzeff alone represented the family, and had charge of all the burial-arrangements. It was this solitariness that to spectators appeared particularly sad, and gave a certain mournful grandeur to the personality of the deceased.

Many flowers, beautiful, scentless, autumn flowers, were brought and placed on the bier; in the midst of their red and white magnificence the face of Yourii lay calm and peaceful, showing no trace of conflict or of suffering.

When the coffin was borne past Sina's house she and her friend Dubova joined the funeral-procession. Sina looked utterly dejected and unnerved, as if she were being led out to shameful execution. Although she felt convinced that Yourii had heard nothing of her disgrace, there was yet, as it seemed to her, a certain connection between that and his death which would always remain a mystery. The burden of unspeakable shame was hers to bear alone. She deemed herself utterly miserable and depraved.

Throughout the night she had wept, as in fancy she fondly kissed the face of her dead lover. When morning came her heart was full of hopeless love for Yourii, and of bitter hatred for Sanine. Her accidental *liaison* with the last-named resembled a hideous dream. All that Sanine had told her, and which at the moment she had believed, was now revolting to her. She had fallen over a precipice; and rescue there was none. When Sanine approached her she stared at him in horror and disgust before turning abruptly away.

As her cold fingers slightly touched his hand held out in hearty greeting, Sanine at once knew all that she thought and felt. Henceforth they could only be as strangers to each other. He bit his lip, and joined Ivanoff, who followed at some distance, shaking his smooth fair hair.

"Hark at Peter Ilitsch!" said Sanine, "how he's forcing his voice!"

A long way ahead, immediately behind the coffin, they were chanting a dirge, and Peter Ilitsch's long-drawn, quavering notes filled the air.

"Funny thing, eh?" began Ivanoff. "A feeble sort of chap, and yet he goes and shoots himself all in a moment, like that!"

"It's my belief," replied Sanine, "that three seconds before the pistol went off he was uncertain whether to shoot himself or not. As he lived, so he died."

"Ah! well," said the other, "at any rate, he's found a place for himself."

This, to Ivanoff, as he tossed back his yellow hair, appeared
to be the last word in explanation of the tragic occurrence.
Personally, it soothed him much.

In the graveyard the scene was even more autumnal, where
the trees seemed splashed with dull red gold, while here and
there the grass showed green through the heaps of withered
leaves. The tombstones and crosses looked whiter in this
dull setting.

So the black earth received Yourii.

Just at that awful moment when the coffin disappeared
from view and the earth became a barrier for ever between
the quick and the dead, Sina uttered a piercing shriek. Her
sobs echoed through the quiet burial-ground, painfully affecting the little group of silent mourners. She no longer
cared to hide her secret from the others who now all guessed
it, horrified that death should have separated this handsome
young woman from her lover to whom she had longed to
give all her youth and beauty, and who now lay dead in the
grave.

They led her away and the sound of her weeping gradually
subsided. The grave was hastily filled in, a mound of earth
being raised above it on which little green fir-trees were
planted.

Schafroff grew restless.

"I say, somebody ought to make a speech. Gentlemen,
this won't do! There ought to be a speech," he said, hurriedly
accosting the bystanders in turn.

"Ask Sanine," was Ivanoff's malicious suggestion. Schafroff stared in amazement at the speaker, whose face wore an

inscrutable expression.

"Sanine? Sanine? Where's Sanine?" he exclaimed. "Ah! Vladimir Petrovitch, will you say a few words? We can't go away without a speech."

"Make one yourself, then," replied Sanine morosely. He was listening to Sina, sobbing in the distance.

"If I could do so I would. He really was a very re . . . mark . . . able man, wasn't he? Do, please, say a word or two!"

Sanine looked hard at him, and replied almost angrily. "What is there to say? One fool less in the world. That's all!"

The bitter words fell with startling clearness on the ears of those present. Such was their amazement that they were at a loss for a reply, but Dubova, in a shrill voice, cried:

"How disgraceful!"

"Why?" asked Sanine, shrugging his shoulders.

Dubova sought to shout at him, threatening him with her fists, but was restrained by several girls who surrounded her. The company broke up in disorder. Vehement sounds of protest were heard on every side, and like a group of withered leaves scattered by the wind, the crowd dispersed. Schafroff at first ran on in front, but soon afterwards came back again. Riasantzeff stood with others aside, and gesticulated violently.

Lost in his thoughts, Sanine gazed at the angry face of a person wearing spectacles, and then turned round to join Ivanoff, who appeared perplexed. When referring Schafroff to Sanine he had foreseen a *contretemps* of some sort, but not one of so serious a nature. While it amused him, he yet felt sorry that it had occurred. Not knowing what to say, he looked away, beyond the grave-stones and crosses, to the distant fields.

A young student stood near him, engaged in heated talk. Ivanoff froze him with a glance.

"I suppose you think yourself ornamental?" he said.

The lad blushed.

"That's not in the least funny," he replied.

"Funny be d——d! You clear off!"

There was such a wicked look in Ivanoff's eyes that the disconcerted youth soon went away.

Sanine watched this little scene and smiled.

"What fools they are!" he exclaimed.

Instantly Ivanoff felt ashamed that even for a moment he should have wavered.

"Come on!" he said. "Deuce take the lot of them!"

"All right! Let's go!"

They walked past Riasantzeff who scowled at them as they went towards the gate. At some distance Sanine noticed another group of young men whom he did not know and who stood, like a flock of sheep, with their heads close together. In their midst stood Schafroff, talking and gesticulating, but he became silent on seeing Sanine. The others all turned to look at the last-named. Their faces expressed honest indignation and a certain shy curiosity.

"They're plotting against you," said Ivanoff, somewhat amazed to see the baleful look in Sanine's eyes. Red as a lobster, Schafroff came forward, blinking his eyelids, and approached Sanine, who turned round sharply on his heel, as though he were ready to knock the first man down.

Schafroff probably perceived this, for he turned pale, and stopped at a respectful distance. The students and girls followed close at his heels like a flock of sheep behind a bell-wether.

"What else do you want?" asked Sanine, without raising his voice.

"We want nothing," replied Schafroff in confusion, "but all my fellow-comrades wish me to express their displeasure at——"

"Much I care about your displeasure!" hissed Sanine through his clenched teeth. "You asked me to say something about the deceased, and after I had said what I thought, you come and express to me your displeasure! Very good of you, I'm sure! If you weren't a pack of silly, sentimental boys, I would show you that I was right, and that Svarogitsch's life was an absolutely foolish one, for he worried himself about all sorts of useless things and died a fool's death; but you—well, you're all of you too dense and too narrow-minded for words! To the deuce with the lot of you! Be off, I say!"

So saying, he walked straight on, forcing the crowd to make way for him.

"Don't push, please!" croaked Schafroff, feebly protesting.

"Well, of all the insolent . . ." cried some one, but he did not finish his phrase.

"How is it you frighten people like that?" asked Ivanoff, as they walked down the street. "You're a perfect terror!"

"If such young fellows with their mad ideas about liberty were always to come bothering you," replied Sanine, "I expect that you would treat them in a much rougher way. Let them all go to hell!"

"Cheer up, my friend!" said Ivanoff, half in jest and half in earnest. "Do you know what we'll do? Buy some beer and drink to the memory of Yourii Svarogitsch. Shall we?"

"If you like," replied Sanine, carelessly.

"By the time we get back all the others will have gone," continued Ivanoff, "and we'll drink at the side of the grave, giving honour to the dead and to ourselves enjoyment."

"Very well."

When they returned, not a living soul was to be seen. The tomb-stones and crosses, erect and rigid, stood there as in mute expectation. From a heap of dry leaves a hideous black snake suddenly darted across the path.

"Reptile!" cried Ivanoff, shuddering.

Then, on to the grass beside the newly-made grave that smelt of humid mould and green fir-trees they flung their empty beer-bottles.

CHAPTER XLIII

"Look here," said Sanine, as they walked down the street in the dusk.

"Well, what is it?"

"Come to the railway-station with me. I'm going away."

Ivanoff stood still.

"Why?"

"Because this place bores me."

"Something has scared you, eh?"

"Scared me? I'm going because I wish to go."

"Yes, but the reason?"

"My good fellow, don't ask silly questions. I want to go, and that's enough. As long as one hasn't found people out, there is always a chance that they may prove interesting. Take some of the folk here, for instance. Sina Karsavina, or Semenoff, or Lida even, who might have avoided becoming commonplace. But oh! they bore me now. I'm tired of them. I've put up with it all as long as I could; I can't stand it any longer."

Ivanoff looked at him for a good while.

"Come, come!" he said. "You'll surely say good-bye to your people?"

"Not I! It's just they who bore me most."

"But what about luggage?"

"I haven't got much. If you'll stop in the garden, I'll go

373

into my room and hand you my valise through the window. Otherwise they'll see me, and overwhelm me with questions as to why and wherefore. Besides, what is there to say?"

"Oh! I see!" drawled Ivanoff, as with a gesture he seemed to bid the other adieu. "I'm very sorry that you're going, my friend, but . . . what can I do?"

"Come with me."

"Where?"

"It doesn't matter where. We can see about that, later."

"But I've no money?"

Sanine laughed.

"Neither have I."

"No, no, you'd better go by yourself. School begins in a fortnight, and I shall get back into the old groove."

Each looked straight into the other's eyes, and Ivanoff turned away in confusion, as if he had seen a distorted reflection of his own face in a mirror.

Crossing the yard, Sanine went indoors while Ivanoff waited in the dark garden, with its sombre shadows and its odour of decay. The leaves rustled under his feet as he approached Sanine's bedroom window. When Sanine passed through the drawing-room he heard voices on the veranda, and he stopped to listen.

"But what do you want of me?" he could hear Lida saying. Her peevish, languid tone surprised him.

"I want nothing," replied Novikoff irritably, "only it seems strange that you should think you are sacrificing yourself for me, whereas——"

"Yes, yes, I know," said Lida, struggling with her tears. "It is not I, but it is you that are sacrificing yourself. Yes, it's you! What more would you have?"

Novikoff was annoyed.

"How little you understand my meaning!" he said. "I love you, and thus it's no sacrifice. But if you think that our union implies a sacrifice either on your part or on mine, how on earth are we going to live together? Do try and understand me. We can only live together on one condition, and that is, if neither of us imagines that there is any sacrifice about it. Either we love each other, and our union is a reasonable and natural one, or we don't love each other, and then——"

Lida suddenly began to cry.

"What's the matter?" exclaimed Novikoff, surprised and irritated. "I can't make you out. I haven't said anything that could offend you. Don't cry like that! Really, one can't say a single word!"

"I . . . don't know," sobbed Lida, "but . . ."

Sanine frowned, and went into his room.

"So that's as far as Lida has got!" he thought. "Perhaps if she had drowned herself, it would have been better, after all."

Underneath the window, Ivanoff could hear Sanine hastily packing his things. There was a rustling of paper, and the sound of something that had fallen on the floor.

"Aren't you coming?" he asked impatiently.

"In a minute," replied Sanine, as his pale face appeared at the window.

"Catch hold!"

The valise was promptly handed out to Ivanoff and Sanine leapt after it.

"Come along!"

They went swiftly through the garden, that lay dim and desolate in the dusk. The fires of sunset had paled beyond the glimmering stream.

At the railway-station all the signal-lamps had been lighted. A locomotive was snorting and puffing. Men were running about, banging doors and shouting at each other. A group of peasants who carried large bundles filled one part of the platform.

At the refreshment-room Sanine and Ivanoff had a farewell drink.

"Here's luck, and a pleasant journey!" said Ivanoff.

Sanine smiled.

"My journeys are always the same," he said. "I don't expect anything from life, and I don't ask for anything either. As for luck, there's not much of that at the finish. Old age and death; that's about all."

They went out on to the platform, seeking a quiet place for their leave-taking.

"Well, good-bye!"

"Good-bye!"

Hardly knowing why, they kissed each other.

There was a long whistle, and the train began to move.

"Ah! my boy. I had grown so fond of you," exclaimed Ivanoff suddenly. "You're the only real man that I have ever met."

"And you're the only one that ever cared for me," said Sanine as, laughing, he leapt on to the foot-board of a carriage as it rolled past.

"Off we go!" he cried. "Good-bye!"

The carriages hurried past Ivanoff as if, like Sanine, they had suddenly resolved to get away. The red light appeared in the gloom, and then seemed to become stationary. Ivanoff mournfully watched its disappearance, and then sauntered homewards through the ill-lighted streets.

"Shall I drown my sorrow?" he thought; and, as he entered the tavern, the image of his own grey, tedious life like a ghost went in with him also.

CHAPTER XLIV

The lamps burned dimly in the suffocating atmosphere of the crowded railway-carriage, shedding their fitful light on grimy, ragged passengers wedged tightly together, and wreathed in smoke. Sanine sat next to three peasants. As he got in, they were engaged in talk, and one half-hidden by the gloom said:

"Things are bad, you say?"

"Couldn't be worse," replied Sanine's neighbour, an old grey-haired moujik, in a high, feeble voice. "They only think of themselves; they don't trouble about us. You may say what you like, but when it comes to fighting for your skin, the stronger always gets the best of it."

"Then, why make a fuss?" asked Sanine, who had guessed what was the subject of their grumbling.

The old man turned to him with a questioning wave of the hand.

"What else can we do?"

Sanine got up and changed his seat. He knew these peasants only too well, who lived like beasts, unable either to cope with their oppression or to destroy their oppressors. Vaguely hoping that some miracle might occur, in waiting for which millions and millions of their fellow-slaves had perished, they continued to lead their brutish existence.

Night had come. All were asleep except a little tradesman sitting opposite to Sanine, who was bullying his wife. She said nothing, but looked about her with fear in her eyes.

"Wait a bit, you cow, I'll soon show you!" he hissed.

Sanine had fallen asleep when a cry from the woman awoke him. The fellow quickly removed his hand, but not before Sanine could see that he had been maltreating his wife.

"What a brute you are!" exclaimed Sanine, angrily.

The man started backwards in alarm, as he blinked his small, wicked eyes and grinned.

Sanine in disgust went out on to the platform at the rear of the train. As he passed through the corridor-carriages he saw crowds of passengers lying prostrate across each other. It was daybreak and their weary faces looked livid in the grey dawn-light which gave them a helpless, pained expression.

Standing on the platform Sanine drank in draughts of the cool morning air.

"What a vile thing man is!" he thought. To get away, if only for a short while, from all his fellow-men, from the train, with its foul air, and smoke, and din—it was for that he longed.

Eastward the dawn flamed red. Night's last pale, sickly shadows were merged and lost in the grey-blue horizon-line beyond the steppe. Sanine did not waste time in reflection, but, leaving his valise behind him, jumped off the foot-board.

With a noise like thunder the train rushed past him as he fell on to the soft, wet sand of the embankment. The red lamp on the last carriage was a long way off when he rose, laughing.

Sanine uttered a cry of joy. "That's good!" he exclaimed.

All around him was so free, so vast. Broad, level fields of grass lay on either side, stretching away to the misty horizon. Sanine drew a deep breath, as with bright eyes he surveyed the spacious landscape. Then he strode forward, facing the jocund, lustrous dawn; and, as the plain, awaking, assumed magic tints of blue and green beneath the wide dome of heaven; as the first eastern beams broke on his dazzled sight, it seemed to Sanine that he was moving onward; onward to meet the sun.

THE END